THE HAVANA SYNDROME

JEFFREY JAMES HIGGINS

Copyright © 2025 by Jeffrey James Higgins.

All rights reserved.

No part of this book may be reproduced in any form or by any electronic or mechanical means, including information storage and retrieval systems, without written permission from the author, except for the use of brief quotations in a book review.

Severn River Publishing
www.SevernRiverBooks.com

This is a work of fiction. Names, characters, businesses, places, events and incidents are either the products of the author's imagination or used in a fictitious manner. Any resemblance to actual persons, living or dead, or actual events is purely coincidental.

ISBN: 978-1-64875-623-8 (Paperback)

ALSO BY JEFFREY JAMES HIGGINS

The Nathan Burke Thrillers

The Havana Syndrome

The Khorasan Retribution

Never miss a new release! Sign up to receive exclusive updates from author Jeffrey James Higgins.

severnriverbooks.com

I write all my books for my wife, Cynthia Farahat Higgins.

I also dedicate this book to my good friends, Douglas Cregar and Edward O'Shaughnessy. You both died far too young.

1

FBI Special Agent Nathan Burke stared into the eyes of a dead man. His confidential informant, Mohammad Gul, was still alive but unlikely to stay that way. Negotiating a deal between the Chinese Triad and radical Islamists was an easy way to get murdered. Danger electrified the air.

Mohammad slouched in the front passenger seat, hiding behind the tinted windows of Nathan's FBI-issued Suburban, known as a B-car. Eddie O'Shaughnessy, Nathan's partner in the FBI's Afghanistan-Pakistan counterterrorism unit, sat in back and watched a scattering of pedestrians wander down F Street NW in the heart of Washington, DC's Chinatown. Few people braved the frigid March weather at eleven o'clock at night.

"You're sure this guy's okay?" Mohammad asked. "I don't like meeting new people."

"Kei has as much to lose as you," Nathan said. "You certain you want to take this risk?"

"The time for this question has passed," Mohammad said. "I'm too deep inside the cave to see light."

Wind howled through the branches of a barren tree, and frost tinged the windshield. Nathan glanced in his review mirror, just in case, then focused on Mohammad. Never trust a snitch.

"I want you to introduce Kei to your cell leader," Nathan said, "but don't vouch for him. Tell Ghulam that Kei is Triad and promise him Kei can create official DMV licenses or whatever other documents they need. If they check on him, and I assume they will, they'll confirm he's a member of the Golden Dragons."

"I've never dealt with Chinese organized crime," Eddie said from the back seat. "I'm playing catch up."

"Triads have existed for hundreds of years. They spread to Hong Kong, Taiwan, Singapore, and Malaysia, and they exert influence in Chinese American communities on our coasts. The Golden Dragons are the newest incarnation inside the District."

"Great. Another fucking gang."

"A gang backed by the Shui Fong Triad in Hong Kong." Nathan squinted through the windshield. The red ember from a cigarette flared in the alley. "That's him."

Clicking emanated from the back seat, and Nathan stared into the dark behind him. Eddie played with a fidget toy, a metal contraption that clicked and clacked as he manipulated it. Eddie had some sort of anxiety disorder and claimed the distraction helped.

"I told you to keep that thing out of your gun hand," Nathan said.

"Sorry, I forgot," Eddie said. "Grabbed it without thinking."

"Then *think* next time. I don't want to get killed because you can't draw your Glock."

Eddie leaned forward between the seats. "How'd you turn Kei?"

Nathan avoided discussing one informant in front of another, but he'd worked with Mohammad for years, and Mohammad would need to work in concert with Kei if the operation was to succeed.

"MPD buddy of mine popped Kei with a handgun," Nathan said, "and Kei started talking. When Kei mentioned Triad, my buddy called me. Kei's looking at a five-year minimum mandatory for weapons possession. He's not a made guy with the Triad yet, so he bartered information for a get-out-of-jail-free card. He's connected with the Chinese government too."

"I don't know shit about Chinese OC," Eddie said, "but if the Triad learns Kei's double-crossing them, he'll get whacked faster than these Islamists will behead Mohammad."

Nathan grimaced. Getting Mohammad to inform on an Islamist recruitment cell operating in Northern Virginia had been hard enough, but convincing him to introduce Kei had taken every tool of persuasion Nathan possessed. But Mohammad looked no more worried than before. Identifying members of criminal organizations and then flipping them to work for the FBI often created moral dilemmas. Involving Mohammad could get him killed, but if things went well, the operation would hinder terror recruitment in the nation's capital and save untold lives.

Kei emerged from the alley. He stomped his feet and pulled a Vietnam-era green army jacket around him to ward off the bitter cold. His breath floated in the air like steam from a locomotive. The only other person on the block was an obese homeless man wrapped in blankets and asleep on a bench.

"You guys wait here," Nathan said. He confirmed the dome light was off and then cracked open his door and slipped into the night. He moved onto the sidewalk where Kei could see him and flashed three fingers with his left hand—the Triad's secret sign.

Kei hurried over. "Hilarious, man," Kei said. "When you join Golden Dragons?"

"I'm freezing my balls off. Sit in back with Eddie."

"Who is Eddie?"

"My new partner and the guy who's gonna help me pull your ass out of the fire if this goes sideways. Think of him as your fairy godmother."

Nathan patted Kei down as discreetly as possible.

"Really?" Kei asked.

"Trust but verify."

They climbed into the car, and Nathan leaned into the back seat. "Eddie, this is Kei. We're gonna call him 'Jason' during these meetings."

"Jason?" Kei asked.

"Jason and the Argonauts. The dragon slayer."

"You crazy," Kei said.

"Codenames have saved my sources more than once," Nathan said. "We need these Islamists to perceive you as Chinese Triad, the man who can provide forged documents."

"They'll be suspicious," Mohammad said.

"Greed overcomes all," Nathan said. "Mohammad, meet Jason."

"No codename for me?" Mohammad asked.

"Kei could have assumed it was a codename until you said that. Don't worry about it. There are about a million men named Mohammad, including half of ISIS. I'll save your last name for my diary."

"You're Triad, right?" Mohammad asked Kei.

"He's a Blue Lantern," Nathan said.

"A what?" Eddie asked.

"Uninitiated member of the Triad. He's been orbiting the forty-nines. The Triad uses codes to describe their roles, and forty-nines are regular members. The guys Kei associates with create fraudulent passports, driver licenses, and other fake identification. Kei provided them with the hardware to alter IDs."

"They Black Society," Kei said.

"They're black?" Eddie asked.

Nathan held up a hand to silence him. "He's not talking about race. Black Society is the entrenched and structured part of the Triad, as opposed to Dark Forces, who are less organized."

"What he say is true," Kei said. "They connected to government in Hong Kong. Have much *shílì*."

"Shitty?" Eddie looked perplexed.

"*Shílì*," Nathan said. "Power or influence. Gold Dragons's tentacles reach deep into Hong Kong's government, and they're almost a shadow government in some neighborhoods. Police protection allows them to shake down businesses."

"If they know I am twenty-five, they will kill me." Kei ran his finger across his throat.

"Twenty-five?"

"Informant," Nathan said.

Kei smacked his lips, seeming uncomfortable, then he leaned forward and looked hard at Mohammad. "You know these men we meet?"

"They're the real deal," Mohammad said. "Hardcore jihadists."

"What you do for them?" Kei asked.

"We ain't getting engaged," Mohammad said. "Stick to business."

"Mohammad's been assisting radical Islamists with recruitment efforts," Nathan said. "We suspect they have terrorist ties beyond their criminality, which is the point of this operation. Since Mohammad lives in Virginia, they asked him to find fake driver licenses, and he agreed to introduce someone."

"How did you tell them we meet?" Kei asked.

"I didn't tell them shit," Mohammad said.

"Mohammad will produce you, an active member of the Triad who can provide authentic DC and Virginia driver licenses," Nathan said. "How you guys met or what you did in the past is irrelevant. If anyone asks questions, tell them to fuck off. They don't need your biography."

Kei's face tightened into a fist.

"These guys could be affiliated with ISIS or al-Qaeda," Nathan said, "so it's too risky to put a Kel on you."

"Kel?" Kei asked.

"A transmitter," Eddie chimed in. "We're giving you this instead." He handed an iPhone to Kei.

"What's the plan?" Kei asked. "They start cutting my head off and I say, 'Excuse please, I must make call.'"

"It's a transmitter and an actual phone," Eddie said. "The password is six ones, but don't mess with it. I'll activate it and keep an open connection to my phone, but it'll look like it's off. We'll listen, and if anything goes wrong, we'll save you."

"Nothing will happen," Nathan said, "but if you think they're gonna hurt you, say 'egg roll.' We hear that and we're coming in, so don't say it unless your life is in imminent danger. If you feel something's wrong, schedule another meeting and leave. We'll run countersurveillance to ensure you don't have a tail. But we hear 'egg roll,' and we're barging in with guns out and the entire operation will be blown. That'll end your undercover role, and Mohammad will need to go into hiding. We clear?"

"Egg roll?" Kei asked. "You can't find a more racist signal?"

"We could change it to, 'Save me, I'm a huge pussy,'" Eddie said.

Kei's face turned to stone. The good humor gone.

"He's kidding," Nathan said. "You want to change it?"

"Egg roll is fine."

"Mohammad, you see anything bad, I'm counting on you to get Kei out."

"Don't worry, man," Mohammad told Kei. "I got you."

"Kei knows what to do," Nathan said. "Stick to your roles and everything will be fine." He nodded at Eddie. "Give him the device."

Eddie turned it on and handed it to Kei, who slipped it into his coat pocket.

"Mohammad," Nathan said, "after the meeting, you stay with the Islamists and get a read on what they thought about Kei. I'll debrief you tomorrow." He craned around in his seat. "Kei, when you're done, head down Seventh Street to the Navy Memorial Metro Station. Take the escalator down, and then use the elevator to return to street level. Walk up Indiana past the courthouse, and I'll contact you.

"If they follow?"

"I'll call with instructions. As a backup, if you see me take my hat off, you know there's a problem. Go to the Verizon Center and wait for me in the Thai restaurant. Got it?"

"I'm hungry," Kei said. "I want egg roll."

2

Both informants walked up Sixth Street NW and out of Nathan's view as they headed into Chinatown, a tiny enclave inside DC's Penn Quarter neighborhood. Ghulam's people had set the meeting in a studio apartment over a Chinese restaurant on I Street NW.

Nathan started the car but left it in park. "Let's give them time to reach the building. They won't acquire evidence other than a recording, so there's no need to stay too close."

"Why are Islamists operating in Chinatown?" Eddie asked. "They rent the place to be close to the Dragons?"

"Doubt it," Nathan said. "Why set up in someone else's backyard? I'm worried they chose the apartment because it's about halfway between the Capitol and the White House."

Eddie frowned. "How do we play it?"

Nathan flashed him a side-eye. Eddie had a law degree but little operational experience, a fact Nathan needed to remember as they learned how to work with each other.

"We stay within striking distance," Nathan said, "and you monitor that phone as if someone's life depended on it, which it does. We'll document the meeting and transcribe the audio later. For now, it's enough to show that we searched both CIs, gave Kei a recorder, and watched them arrive."

Eddie fidgeted. He'd graduated from the academy less than a year ago and had only dealt with white-collar crime. His reassignment to the Afghanistan-Pakistan Counterterrorism Unit had resulted from restructuring after a sexual harassment scandal rocked the FBI's Washington Field Office. How many source meetings had Eddie covered? No sense asking and making him more nervous.

Nathan had nine more years on the job than Eddie and another five years on the street as a sheriff's deputy in Florida before joining the FBI. In those five years, he'd arrested more people and experienced more traumatic incidents than ninety-five percent of the agents in the FBI. Being a Fed was great, but multiyear investigations did not come close to the daily adrenaline rush he'd experienced as a cop.

"Let's roll up the block and catch them going in," Nathan said.

Nathan drove up Sixth, passing Gallery Place and the Capital One Arena. He stopped at a red light and glanced out the window. Mohammad and Kei ambled up the sidewalk. Mohammad walked so damn slowly he probably drove Kei crazy. The informants turned onto I Street NW.

The light flashed green, and Nathan continued north, slowly accelerating to the speed limit. He slowed at the light before banging a left. Twenty yards ahead, Mohammad led Kei into a doorway. Nathan had studied the location, checking DMV records, city licensing, credit history, and open-source reporting. The stairs led up to a studio apartment above the South China Sea Restaurant and Good Eats. An Islamist safe house.

Nathan continued past the building without slowing. Eddie turned to stare.

"Don't look," Nathan said. "This close to the meeting location, bad guys will field countersurveillance, even if we can't see it. Always look like you belong."

Nathan maintained speed and stopped at the light on Seventh Street. "Got 'em on the phone?" he asked.

Eddie adjusted the volume on his iPhone and slipped an earpiece in. "Yeah, they're climbing the steps."

Nathan turned onto Seventh and found an open space on G Street, one block from their target. He parallel parked and shut off the engine.

"Keep it on," Eddie said. "It'll get icy in here."

"Suck it up. It's below freezing, so our exhaust will be visible, and two white dudes sitting in the Suburban with tinted windows would stick out like turd in a bowl of wonton soup."

"Nice job keeping the Chinese theme."

Nathan smiled, then turned serious. "It's okay to tease Kei, but he's sharp as hell. And tough. It takes gigantic balls to cooperate with the police against the Triad. Bigger still when he's infiltrating a bunch of radical Islamists who are begging to meet Allah. These guys are dangerous, so stay on your toes."

Eddie's jacket sagged.

"Don't tell me," Nathan said. He tapped Eddie's chest with his knuckles. Soft. No vest.

"Hey—"

"Where the fuck is your ballistic vest?"

"It's just a meet."

"Are you fucking kidding me? You never know when perps will start shooting. Hell, this is DC, which means we could roll into the middle of an unrelated drug deal. Forget that it's FBI procedure, and forget that a lightweight vest could save your life. If you get shot and knocked out of the fight because you're not wearing it, you'll put me in danger."

Click, click, click. Eddie played with that damn fidget toy again. "Sorry. I—"

"What's happening with our CIs?"

Eddie cupped his ear holding the earpiece. "Mohammad's talking to somebody in Arabic."

"Is your phone recording?"

Eddie looked at the screen. "Shit. Hold on." He fiddled with an app. "Yeah, all good."

Fucking rookies. "Don't shut it off until we have Kei safe in hand. If anything happens, I want an audio record."

Nathan checked the rearview and side mirrors. He cracked his neck and stretched his back, staying loose. Just in case. He wore a Level IIIA ballistic vest underneath a black, subzero tactical jacket which concealed the .40 Glock 22. The semi-automatic polymer handgun held fifteen rounds in the magazine and one in the pipe. He carried two additional magazines in a leather ammo pouch attached to his belt and handcuffs at the small of his back. Between the seat and the center console, he'd jammed a handheld radio programmed with tactical and emergency channels for the FBI and Metropolitan Police Department. CI meetings were common, but he never let his guard down, especially when dealing with potential terrorists.

"How long will this take?" Eddie asked.

"Thirty, maybe forty minutes." Nathan checked his watch. "Shit."

"We've got plenty of time," Eddie said.

"It's not that. I've got a sitter. It's almost midnight already, and Amelia and I are flying to the Dominican Republic in the morning."

"Taking her to see Reagan?"

Nathan's stomach cramped at the mention of his estranged wife's name. "Yeah, Amelia's spending the week with her. Reagan decided to act like a mother this month."

Eddie nodded, looking uncomfortable. "Don't worry, you'll be home in a couple of hours."

"Yeah, what could go wrong with a CI meeting jihadists?"

"You worry too much."

"I'm taking care of a seven-year-old girl by myself. I have to worry . . . all the time."

Eddie touched his earpiece. "Kei's talking to Ghulam, who's using a mix of English and Arabic. Kei agreed to deliver a dozen Virginia driver licenses. Ghulam asked about passports and other ID."

"They got down to business fast. That's unusual in Arabic culture. Thank you, Ghulam."

Eddie sat up straight. "Kei's moving."

"Alone?"

"Think so."

"What's he doing?" Nathan asked. "Did they agree on a timetable and payment?"

"It's hard to hear, and Kei's English ain't great."

"It's better than your Mandarin." Nathan started the car but stayed put. If Kei followed the plan, he'd walk right past them.

Nathan's phone rang, and he picked up.

"It me," Kei said.

Nathan put him on speaker so Eddie could listen. "You okay?"

"Deal is done. I am walking to Metro."

"Why are you calling? We're still recording your transmission. I'll debrief you in person."

The line hissed with static.

"Kei?"

"Those guys bad news. Very dangerous."

"They threaten you?"

"Not exactly. But they want documents, and once they get them, I don't know what they do."

"Passports?"

"US passports in same names as licenses. He also want identification from a federal agency."

"Which agency."

"Don't know, but I say, 'Yes we can do.'"

Nathan should hang up and debrief him in person, but Kei sounded nervous, and if Kei's instincts had forced him out of the meeting, he could be in danger. "What worries you about these guys?"

"They wore black hoods. Two had AK-47s. They ISIS."

"We haven't found a link to Islamic State," Nathan said. "What makes you say that?"

"They tell me."

3

Reagan Burke stared at a Word document on her computer screen, but images of Vincenzo Cabrera's body grinding on top of her flashed behind her eyes, and her body tingled from the memory. Her cheeks flushed and she glanced around the fourth-floor office inside the US Embassy in Santo Domingo, Dominican Republic. Good thing her cubicle mates didn't know what she was thinking.

"What are you working on?" a voice asked behind her.

She spun around in her chair. Vince stood behind her. He was the FBI's legal attaché at the embassy. And her lover.

"You startled me."

"Can you break free for lunch? I was thinking about driving to La Parrilla. It's been a tough morning, and an oceanfront table is the cure I need."

"That's too far," she said. "The ambo needs my assessment of the DR's evolving relationship with China before the country team meeting tomorrow."

"He should be more concerned about transnational crime and the flow of drugs passing through here."

"China dumped billions in loans and investments into the DR after the Ministry of Foreign Affairs agreed not to recognize Taiwan's independence.

China's exerting real influence in the Caribbean. I'm trying to convince the ambo to prioritize fighting corruption."

Vince rubbed his chin. "What's the point of being stationed here if we can't eat on the beach?"

"Some beach. The city dumps sewage into the ocean and—"

"The ice in your daiquiri will be clean."

Reagan smiled. "Doubt it. Nathan's dropping Amelia off today, and I need to be here when they arrive."

"Then schedule some alone time for us tonight." Vince winked and walked out of the political section. His office was upstairs, near the ambassador, whose corner office was situated directly above her desk. Vince was forty-eight, seventeen years her senior, but his rock-hard body moved with the flexibility of a twenty-year-old athlete. Especially in bed.

Vince wanted her, and she wanted him, but they had to keep their relationship on the down-low until her husband agreed to a divorce. And Nathan would not let her go.

Reagan turned back to her cluttered desk and looked over the stained walnut frame of her cubicle. She locked eyes with Mallory Jenkins. The young Georgetown valedictorian was a rising star in the State Department, and she'd landed an overseas diplomatic post five years quicker than Reagan. Mallory stood outside the break room sipping coffee with a group of frumpy women sporting abrupt hairdos and scowls. They discussed politics, and their voices seethed with rage, indignation, and unearned superiority. Mallory poised on edge like a cat—waiting, needing to hear something offensive so she could attack. A soldier in an army of the feeble-minded who couldn't separate emotion from reason. Mallory was her competition and someone to avoid, but Reagan didn't hate her. She pitied her.

Reagan glanced out the window. The Caribbean sun beat down on the city on yet another cloudless, eighty-degree March afternoon. She'd been lucky to get a window as a new employee. That must have made Mallory crazy jealous.

Reagan returned to the document on her screen. "One hour. Get going."

She opened her calendar to confirm the time of the country team meeting and noted the date. "Shit." She frowned. Thursday marked the one-year anniversary of her assignment to the embassy's political section, a move that had changed her life. For good and bad.

Mostly good.

She scratched a dry patch on her elbow, a habit she had acquired since she left Nathan and their then six-year-old daughter, Amelia, to work in Santo Domingo. They'd intended it to be a temporary separation, just until Nathan could get the FBI to assign him to the embassy. Why hadn't Vince agreed to help with Nathan's transfer? It had been his decision, in part.

Then her weekend trips home had gone from twice a month to once every other month, as Nathan's anger toward her grew and her own guilt and longing tore an emotional hole in her life.

Vince filled that vacuum.

Reagan pivoted to her classified terminal and stuck her Personal Identity Verification card into the chip reader to log into the restricted system. She opened a CIA file containing reports on Chinese negotiations with the Dominican deputy minister of Foreign Affairs, a corrupt son-of-a-bitch who accepted bribes from China. Reagan read the report's abstract with interest. She needed to hurry, because once Nathan dropped off Amelia, she'd have little time for work.

The next file didn't open. She clicked it again. Nothing. The hourglass icon rotated on her screen, then her monitor flickered.

Pain flashed through her sinuses.

Reagan jammed her eyes shut. Stinging darts pulsed between her temples. She bit her lip. A caffeine headache?

She rubbed her forehead as nausea swelled inside her stomach, threatening to eject her coffee and yogurt breakfast.

Bathroom. Now.

Reagan stood, and the room tilted. She grabbed the chair for support, and it swiveled, sending her crashing into the cubicle wall. She clung to it for balance as her legs fatigued. She wobbled. A wave of vertigo washed over her.

"You okay?" a woman asked, her garbled voice echoing in Reagan's mind.

Reagan looked up at her through blurred vision. A high-pitched whine filled her ears. She shook her head to clear it, but it grew louder, piercing her brain until she could think of nothing else.

Reagan reached for her chair and stumbled. Someone held her arm, but it wasn't enough. She collapsed onto the floor. Concerned shouts from her colleagues droned behind an incessant tone in her ears.

"I... I can't see," Reagan said. "The noise..."

"Get the nurse," a man said. "She's having a stroke."

"Someone call an ambulance," the woman said.

Reagan lay on the ground with her head in her hands. Her chair's roller ball pressed into her side. Everything faded in and out of focus, and she blinked.

Mallory stood in the entrance to Reagan's cubicle with a group of concerned diplomats. She glanced around then caught Reagan's eye and flashed a cruel smile.

4

Nathan shifted in a plastic chair and scanned the faces of people passing through the lobby of the US Embassy in Santo Domingo. He watched for furtive movements, physical signs of imminent violence, or other hints of evil intent. He did this out of habit. Being aware of his surroundings had been ground into him at the FBI Academy in Quantico, Virginia, and then reinforced during a decade in counterterrorism.

Amelia slumped in the chair beside him, holding *Charlotte's Web*. The book had been his childhood favorite, and he had given her his worn copy. Amelia's love of reading forecast a positive future.

"Daddy, is Bruno okay at home?"

"Read your book, honey."

"I left his chew toys out, but I'm worried about him."

A blonde woman wearing a pencil skirt and a gray jacket entered through a door marked "Staff Only" and scanned the lobby.

"He's a hundred-twenty-pound Rottweiler," Nathan said. "He's tough, and Betty promised she'd take care of him." Having Betty Cook around, a retired neighbor with time on her hands, was convenient. It almost made up for her constant monitoring of the block as if she were the town constable.

"I miss him," Amelia said.

"I'm flying home in the morning."

"But is he—"

"Mr. Burke?" the blonde woman asked.

"And Amelia." Nathan stood.

"I'm Ellen, the consular officer. I'll take you upstairs to Ms. Burke's office."

"It's Mrs. Burke."

"Excuse me?"

"Reagan Burke is my wife."

The woman's forehead wrinkled as if she had trouble processing the information. "Please come with me."

Nathan took Amelia's hand and followed. They stopped at a booth protected by bulletproof glass, and Nathan handed their passports to a sergeant in the Marine Security Guard. The sergeant handed back "Escort Only" passes, and Nathan led Amelia up the steps behind the consular officer.

"I'm afraid the elevator's out again," Ellen said. "It's hard to get reliable service."

"I always take the stairs," Nathan said. "Brief spurts of exercise add up."

She smiled. "You staying long?"

"I'm at the Juragua tonight, then back to DC in the morning. I'm just dropping Amelia off to spend the week with her mother. She—"

Footsteps pounded up the stairs behind him, and Nathan turned as a Marine raced past. Two paramedics in white uniforms carried a stretcher up the stairs, and a third medic trailed behind, huffing and puffing under the weight of a medical bag.

Nathan pulled Amelia to the side as they tramped up the steps.

"Daddy, what happened?"

"I don't know, sweetie. Give them room." He looked up at Ellen. "What's going on?"

"No idea."

They followed the men to the fourth floor then down the hall toward the Political Section, an office Nathan had visited three times during his and Reagan's year-long separation. His chest tightened with dread, as it had the time he'd come home to find an ambulance in front of his house after Amelia's last asthma attack.

Nathan quickened his pace and glanced at Ellen as he passed. She seemed worried.

"Why are we running?" Amelia asked.

"Something happened. I want to help."

Nathan stopped and peered into the Political Section. A dozen staff huddled around a cubicle against the far window, everyone staring at something on the ground.

No, no, no. A lump tightened in his throat. His body chilled.

"What is it, Daddy?"

"Someone's sick. Stay here."

"But, Daddy—"

Nathan raised his index finger and heat rose in his face. "Amelia, wait here." He pivoted and raced into the room.

"Mr. Burke," Ellen called after him.

He didn't stop. His pulse thumped in his temples as he caught up with the paramedics. The crowd parted, and there was his wife, lying on the floor.

"Reagan!"

A woman wearing a short skirt and ruffled top looked at him with concern. He recognized her—an Economic officer of some kind. Nathan had met few people during his in-and-out trips to drop off Amelia. He followed the paramedics through the crowd. One of them dropped a medical bag beside Reagan and ripped it open.

Nathan leaned over the man. "Reagan, are you okay?"

Her eyes fluttered, and she scrunched up her face into a ball of confusion. She rubbed her temples and grimaced. She was conscious. A good sign.

A paramedic held her head to stabilize her C-spine, a maneuver Nathan had executed many times as a cop. Every fall carried the possibility of cervical injury. At least the medics seemed competent.

"What happen?" the head paramedic asked Reagan in a thick Spanish accent.

Her eyes rolled to him. She opened her mouth then closed it without speaking.

"Let me through," Nathan said. He sidestepped around the men.

The paramedic speaking with Reagan looked up and gestured for Nathan to stop. "*Señor*, give me space. *Por favor.*"

Nathan was in their way, but he couldn't drag himself away. He needed to do something. Anything.

Reagan groaned then coughed.

"*Enrollarla*," the medic said. The man with the bag tilted Reagan onto her side while the first paramedic held her head and rotated with the movement. Reagan gagged and vomited on the floor.

"Oooh," a woman exclaimed.

"Mommy, what's wrong?" Amelia screamed.

Shit. "Baby, it's okay. Stay there," Nathan said. He wormed through the crowd toward her.

Reagan coughed and spotted her. "Amelia? Patootie? I'm okay." Reagan leaned up on an elbow. She gritted her teeth and closed her eyes. She vomited again.

Nathan reached Amelia. Her eyes widened in terror, and she held her arms stiff against her sides. "Everything's okay. Your mom has an upset tummy. That's all."

Amelia's eyes filled with tears.

He scooped her into his arms. "It's okay, baby. I've got you."

Nathan turned away so Amelia would not see the paramedics roll Reagan onto the stretcher. It took several minutes for them to strap her in and gather their gear. Two medics hefted the stretcher while the head medic shined a light in her pupils as he asked her questions.

Nathan followed, wanting answers.

"You're Mr. Burke, right?" a woman said, tugging on his elbow.

Nathan glanced at her but kept going. He had to stick with the paramedics.

"I'm Denise Williams, the embassy nurse. I'm good friends with your ex, uh . . . with Reagan.

"What happened?"

"She was lucid when I arrived. She told me she had a sudden pain in her head and dizziness, but her symptoms have deteriorated. She—"

"Meaning?" Nathan asked

"A stroke would . . . well, it could be many things. It's too early to speculate."

"She's too young to have a stroke."

"What's a stroke, Daddy?"

He squeezed Amelia's hand.

"We don't know what caused this," Denise said. "I'm sure they'll initiate stroke protocol and administer a CAT scan to rule that out first if—"

"Whose they?" Nathan asked. "Where are they taking her?"

"CEDIMAT downtown. The embassy uses them because they're TriCare approved. They're quite good."

"I need to be with her. *We* need to be with her."

"I'll drive."

5

Reagan opened her eyes, and the glare from the overhead lights sent lightning bolts through her skull. She groaned. She raised her hand to cover her eyes, and something tore at her skin. Reagan looked down at IV tubing protruding from her forearm.

"Where the hell am I?" Her voice sounded hoarse, and her throat ached.

"Reagan!" Vince said from across the room. He approached and flashed a white smile. "You gave us quite a scare."

"How . . . what happened?"

"They don't know yet. They ran a battery of tests, but they won't tell me anything."

"Why?"

He frowned. "I'm not your husband."

"Who?"

What was he talking about? Tests? Husband? She blinked to clear her brain fog. An image of a man in a white medical uniform leaning over her flashed behind her eyes. And there were others. People watching. She'd been on the floor.

"Oh my God."

"Calm down," Vince said. "It'll be okay. I flashed my FBI badge at the nurse, and she confirmed you didn't have a stroke. They don't understand what caused your symptoms, but she said your brain looks normal. Did you eat a bad piece of fish?"

"Just coffee. How long have I been here?" Her mouth felt thick and pasty, and her sinuses throbbed. She wiggled her nose, and a nasal cannula popped free.

"Overwork? Stress?"

"What the hell are you saying? I didn't—"

"An allergy? They'll keep you here tonight and run more tests."

"How long was I out?"

"I think they sedated you."

Images flooded back—falling to the floor, the crowd surrounding her, the awkward trip down the stairs on a stretcher—and wait, had Amelia been there?

"My baby girl? I saw her . . . I think."

"You did. Nathan brought her into the section after you collapsed. She—"

"Where is she?"

"Your ex took her to his hotel. They came to the hospital with you, but Amelia needed to sleep."

Nathan was not her ex-husband. At least not yet. But why open that can of worms? She gazed out the window at an inky sky.

"What time is it?"

Vince rotated the Rolex on his wrist. "Three fifteen in the morning."

"I'm so sorry. You've been here all night?"

"I, uh, I arrived about an hour ago. I had to brief the deputy chief, and then I had a conference call with HQ."

"A conference call at night?"

"The DCM told me you were stable and undergoing tests. The hospital wouldn't have let me see you anyhow, so I—"

"You knew I was in the hospital, and you didn't come?"

"I couldn't do anything then, but I'm here now."

She stared at him. Everything felt muddled, out of kilter. She shut her eyes and lay back.

"You're right," he said. "I should have been here. I'm sorry."

Her forehead ached as if someone had jammed a hot poker into it. She exhaled and opened her eyes. "When can I get out of here?"

"Tomorrow."

She nodded, and the pain intensified.

Vince placed his hand over hers. "I love you."

A butterfly took flight in her stomach. She'd heard the words many times over the past six months of their affair, but they still warmed her. That had to be a good sign. She tried to smile, and her stomach turned.

"What's wrong?" he asked.

"Just stay with me. I love you too."

6

The drone of the civilian medevac's engines filled the cabin as the jet climbed above the Dominican Republic en route to Dulles International Airport outside Washington, DC. Nathan rubbed his eyes and expelled a long breath. He leaned into the aisle of the air ambulance and glanced at Reagan, who reclined on a stretcher near the tail. A nurse wearing a white uniform sat in the jump seat beside her and monitored her condition.

Across the aisle, that asshole, Vince Cabrera, reclined in his seat and sipped a sparkling water. He stared back with a smug expression wavering between dislike and contempt.

Nathan settled in and smiled at Amelia who slept in the seat beside him. A two-day trip to drop her off with Reagan had turned into four emotional days in Santo Domingo. A traumatic experience for Amelia. And for him.

Seeing Reagan sick in a hospital bed was stressful enough, but not knowing the cause amplified everything. There had been similar incidents at the US Embassy in Havana. Was Reagan's condition related? The embassy had arranged the flight, but they hadn't identified what sickened her. The consular officer had mentioned stress, and when the deputy chief of mission had called to offer his support, he suggested Reagan had an underlying condition. Reagan may have taken a job overseas and fallen in love with another man, but she was not a hypochondriac. What was wrong with the State Department?

Nathan grabbed the airphone out of the headrest and dialed Eddie. The poor kid was in way over his head trying to manage Mohammad and Kei during Nathan's absence.

"Agent O'Shaughnessy," Eddie answered.

"I'm on the plane. I'll be in the office the day after tomorrow."

"About time . . . I mean, I know you're not on vacation, but I'm swamped and, uh, it's been—"

"I know what you mean," Nathan said. "Any word from Jason?"

"He's standing by and waiting for instructions on when to get the licenses from the Gold Dragons—"

"Don't use names over the phone." No one intercepted his calls, but avoiding sensitive information on an insecure line was good tradecraft.

"Sorry. The product, I mean. Mo called again this morning asking how long it'll take. His people are anxious. If the product looks good, he said they'll want more."

The clicking of Eddie's fidget toy came over the line.

"We have time," Nathan said. "Let's keep them on the hook until we confirm they're working for that foreign organization. I wonder . . . what's their rush? If they're card-carrying members, they could be planning something. Make sure Mo records his conversations with them."

"I still think we should have hit that apartment as soon as Jason told us ISIS was in there with AK-47s."

"Like I told you before," Nathan said, "it's just a meeting house, and they'd have been long gone. We would have blown Jason and Mo for nothing."

"Copy that. How's Reagan?

Nathan peered down the aisle again. Reagan appeared to be sleeping. "Not great. Her symptoms are worse. She's suffering from dizziness, fatigue, and nausea. She has trouble focusing, and she's getting killer migraines. The virus, or whatever is responsible, damaged her hearing too."

"Do the docs have any idea what's causing it?"

"The embassy nurse thought it was a stroke, but when I spoke to her this morning, she parroted the embassy line and said it could be stress. I've heard about similar cases in Cuba."

"Oh yeah," Eddie said. "They're calling it Havana Syndrome. Bunch of spies and diplomats got sick. You and Amelia feeling all right?"

"We're fine."

"You'll swing by the office tomorrow?"

"Give me a break, Eddie. Let the dust settle. I've got to make sure Reagan is okay."

"She staying with you?"

Nathan glanced back at Reagan then over at Vince. A pain stabbed his chest.

"No."

7

The rollers on Nathan's suitcase thumped over the red-brick sidewalk leading from Sixth Street NE to his condo in the tower of a renovated church. He carried Amelia, who'd slept during the hour-long cab ride from Dulles and showed no sign of waking.

The city had designated the former home of the Eastern Presbyterian Church as a historic landmark. It was situated across the street from Stanton Park, only six blocks east of the Capitol. Once frequented by worshippers, the 1875 building now held six condominiums. Nathan admired the striking combination of bluestone and limestone constructed in Romanesque Revival.

He dug out his keys and opened the exterior door to their private elevator. He shook Amelia awake and set her down.

"We're home, baby."

"Okay." She rubbed sleep out of her eyes.

The elevator car hummed as they rode up to their two-bedroom unit, the place Reagan had called home just a year ago. Strange to think of her as gone.

The elevator opened into a vestibule opposite their unit's door. Nathan slid his key into the lock. Bruno barked, and his nails clicked across the foyer tile. Nathan opened the door, and the alarm system beeped. Their Rottweiler burst across the threshold.

"Bruno," Amelia screamed with delight.

Bruno's body shook, and he bounced as if dancing on hot coals, acting as happy as the day they'd rescued him from the pound. Bruno slammed his paws into Nathan's chest. Nathan rubbed his ears as Bruno licked his face.

"You don't do well being left alone, do you, boy?"

Bruno dropped to the floor and rubbed against Amelia's leg, careful not to knock her down. A gentle giant. She petted him, and he licked her face.

"Ew, that's gross."

"He loves you."

"Can't he show it with less slobber?"

Nathan ushered Amelia into their living room, a clutter-free space with oak floors and high ceilings—just the way he liked it. The condo had two bedrooms on the second floor and an office in the 130-foot turret, which offered views of the Capitol and the Washington Monument.

The tempo of the security system's audio increased, indicating thirty seconds left to deactivate it. Nathan entered his code into the touchpad, and the beeping stopped.

He strolled into their contemporary kitchen, a canvass of stainless steel and black marble. His elderly neighbor, Betty, had stuck a note to the refrigerator door. It welcomed them home and said Bruno had been out three times starting at five o'clock in the morning. Elderly people got up so damn early.

Nathan dropped his bag and followed Amelia up the curving staircase to her bedroom. He helped her out of her coat and stashed her suitcase in the corner as she prepared for bed. He stretched his aching back and headed downstairs.

Worrying about Reagan had worn him down. A sleepless night, a waking dream, a flash of panic. He hung by a thread, his last reserves fading and leaving nothing left to fight his sense of impending doom.

In the living room, he poured himself an Oban, his favorite twelve-year-old scotch, and dropped a single ice cube into the crystal glass. Adding ice would make a connoisseur cringe, but chilled water brought out the flavor and mellowed the drink. Nathan took an ample sip, and the oily highlander tingled his throat and filled his sinuses with a floral, smoky scent before its oaky finish.

Normally, having a scotch would alleviate his tension, but not this time.

At least being home always comforted him, whether that was a forward operating base in Afghanistan, a five-star hotel in Brussels, or the renovated church he'd called home for five years—the longest he'd lived anywhere. Being on the road five months a year conducting counterterrorism investigations felt like a nomadic existence, but a home base provided security, a safe space that contained everything he owned and loved.

Well, almost everything.

He climbed the dark mahogany steps up the spiral staircase into the turret. Eight clerestory windows ringed the circular room. The faint aroma of wood, brick, and abandonment hung in the air.

Nathan reached for a switch to turn on the chandelier that hung from a cedar beam twenty feet above, then he hesitated. A full moon dominated the crisp March night and illuminated the city. He took another long pull of Oban and leaned against the brick. The Capitol's dome glowed before him as did the white-marble monument behind it.

"What the hell is Havana Syndrome?"

He took out his iPhone and entered the term into a search engine. He scrolled through dozens of articles about Havana Syndrome, which speculated about the mysterious symptoms afflicting hundreds of US and Canadian employees around the world. The illness, or whatever it was, first struck in 2016—and many times since at dozens of embassies. Experts opined about the cause, with some suggesting a virus or allergy was responsible, while others posited the source was exposure to pesticides or cleaning agents. Conspiracy theories abounded. The most concerning thesis blamed an intentional attack by an adversary using microwaves or other forms of directed energy. A potential attack meant law enforcement and intelligence agencies would be investigating.

And the FBI was both.

Nathan opened his contacts and called the National Counterterrorism Center, known as the CTC. The fusion center integrated all counterterrorism intelligence for analysis and distribution to the intelligence community. Nathan dealt with them frequently as his team hunted ISIS and al-Qaeda operatives around the country.

He identified himself, and the operator patched him through to Doug Cregar's cell phone. Doug was an FBI supervisory special agent assigned to the CTC's Directorate of Operations Support, and Nathan had relied on him for years.

"Cregar," Doug answered.

"What's Havana Syndrome?"

"Nathan?"

"State just medevaced my wife out of Santo Domingo."

"Jesus. Sorry to hear that. How bad is it?"

Nathan took another pull of scotch. "Not great. Nothing life threatening, but she has a dozen symptoms. What can you tell me?"

"It's not my area, unless it turns out al-Qaeda's behind it, but CTC has a team working the problem."

"Who's handling it for us?" Nathan asked.

"Group 346 at the WFO," he said, referring to the FBI's Washington Field Office.

"Who's in the group?"

"Looks like they're located at HQ. I'm scrolling through the office roster. Let's see, Johnson . . . Garcia . . . Davis . . . Chan—"

"Hold on. What's Chan's first name?"

"Meili."

"Perfect." Nathan smiled. Special Agent Meili Chan had been his classmate in the FBI Basic Agent Academy in Quantico, Virginia. The rigorous training program created lifelong bonds between recruits. Meili may have the answers he needed.

Nathan thanked Doug and hung up. He finished his scotch and headed for the stairs. Moonlight radiated through the window and glinted off the six-inch chess pieces on a marble chessboard atop his antique writing desk. He'd purchased the set in a Delhi bazaar on one of many trips to the subcontinent to debrief sources. The pieces depicted the crusaders against Saladin's forces, a reminder that man was always at war, struggling between power and independence, slavery, and freedom—an unending battle.

Was Havana Syndrome another attack on the West?

8

Reagan swayed, dizzy and disoriented, as Vince led her into his house in Falls Church, Virginia. The two-story colonial nestled in a wooded neighborhood, a thirty-minute drive from downtown DC.

"Maybe I should get a hotel room," Reagan said.

"Don't be ridiculous."

"We haven't talked about moving in together. It's a big step—"

Vince stopped and leaned in. "We love each other. You're leaving your husband for me. That's the big step. We were going to live together, anyway, after your tour ended. We just haven't discussed it yet."

"I could stay at my house. My stuff is there."

"With Nathan? Are you crazy?"

"Don't call me crazy."

"Forget about how I feel about you and Nathan back under the same roof. Wouldn't it confuse your daughter?"

Amelia. "I haven't had *the talk* with her yet. We only told her Nathan and I were taking a break because of my job."

"You haven't discussed me? It's been six months."

"It's just . . . it's hard." Fatigue weighed her down. "I need to lie down."

"Let's get you upstairs, then I'll bring the suitcases in."

"I don't have anything appropriate to wear. Most of my clothes are still in embassy housing, and they're all for warm weather. My winter clothes are still at my house . . . I mean Nathan's—"

The room tilted, and she clutched his arm.

"Go slow. I'll pick up whatever you need tomorrow."

"Nathan won't like that."

"Let me worry about Nathan."

He carried her upstairs to the bedroom, then he left to get luggage from the medical transport van the State Department had provided. She'd met Vince in Santo Domingo, so she'd never been to his home, but it had clearly been decorated by a bachelor. Divorcee, to be more accurate. Vince's wife had left him three years ago, and he'd purchased this 3,000-square-foot home and lived alone since then.

A blue-and-gray quilt covered the queen-sized bed opposite a fifty-inch television mounted on the wall. Contemporary lamps with black plastic shades illuminated both nightstands. The room was awash in gunmetal gray, a starkness only a man would desire. Concrete floors would not have surprised her, but at least Vince had covered them with lilac Berber carpeting. The place was immaculate. Soulless.

"God, what am I doing?"

Everything felt strange. She'd never meant for the affair to happen. She'd been content with Nathan and Amelia. Seven years of marriage and a beautiful daughter—she'd loved her life. Well, not *loved*.

She'd paused her career for Nathan, yet he had little time for her. Their sex life had cooled too. When Amelia entered first grade, it had made sense to push for a promotion at the State Department. Reagan had been as shocked as Nathan when State offered her a foreign posting in Santo Domingo. Nathan couldn't wrangle a transfer right away, so she'd gone alone. He'd planned to join her when an FBI position opened. She hadn't meant to fall in love with Vince.

But life happened.

Reagan entered the master bathroom, an undecorated, sterile vacuum of black and white tiles. She was sloppy, bordering on hoarding, and she took comfort in seeing her possessions around her, not this anal-retentive level of organization. But at least it was clean. She turned on the shower then stripped off her clothes and left them in a heap on the floor. She'd traveled directly from the hospital to the airport and hadn't showered in four days.

Reagan gawked at herself in the mirror. Deep bruising blotted her arm where the IV had ripped a vein, and her tangled hair glistened with grease. Dark circles swelled beneath her eyes, and her skin looked paler than usual. At least she'd lost weight, about ten pounds based on her visible ribs and flat abs. Her petite body had not needed to shrink, but she'd finally shed the tummy bulge she'd carried since giving birth to Amelia.

She'd never been satisfied with her body.

"God, you're beautiful," Vince said.

A jolt passed through her, and she turned. Vince stood in the doorway staring at her body.

"You startled me."

"I'd like to do more than that." He stepped into the bathroom and moved behind her. He placed his powerful hands on her hips and caressed her skin.

Her body tingled from his touch. She looked at him in the steamy mirror. He had a square jaw and broad shoulders, masculine qualities that aroused her. Nathan had them too.

He slipped his hand between her legs and sent a flood of warmth through her. Her balance wavered, and she held the sink to steady her equilibrium. She grabbed his hand and stopped him.

"I'm sorry. I can't. Not yet."

He frowned and withdrew his hand, then he nodded. He kissed her neck. "I'll be downstairs opening the house. I haven't been here for months. Holler if you need help getting dressed."

A headache and queasiness rushed into her like a storm. She lunged for the toilet and vomited.

9

"It's fucking good to have you back," Eddie said. He lumbered out of his cubicle and shook Nathan's hand.

"Thanks for not screwing up our case while I was gone."

A dozen muted conversations hummed through their office. The J. Edgar Hoover Building was only a few blocks away, but the FBI's unit specializing in counterterrorism in Southwest Asia occupied an office suite above a bowling alley in Gallery Place. Nathan still hadn't acclimated to walking past shoppers and diners on the way to investigate radical Islamic terrorism.

"I didn't do dick," Eddie said. "I caught up with paperwork, duplicated recordings, and entered them into evidence."

"Any problems with Mohammad or Kei?" Nathan asked.

"They want you back more than I do. Dude, this is all new to me."

Nathan slapped him on the back. "You'll get it."

"Hope so. I know the law, and I've memorized our handbook and procedures, but there's a divide between theory and practice. I'm just glad you came home. Captain, you have the conn."

Nathan bit his lip. "Yeah, uh, about that—"

"Uh oh."

"No, it's nothing bad. I just need a couple days to look into Havana Syndrome."

"What do you mean by *look into?*"

"Reagan and I may be separated, but we're still married, and it's my job to protect her."

"Isn't that the other guy's problem? Sorry, I meant—"

"She's my wife, not his, and if someone targeted her, I swear I'll find them."

Eddie leaned against the worn fabric covering the cubicle wall. "Targeted? I thought Havana Syndrome was a virus."

"That's the problem. Nobody knows what's causing it, but I've read enough open-source material to believe it could be an intentional act."

Eddie scratched his scalp.

"What?" Nathan asked.

"I'm not married, and I understand why you need to do something..."

"But?"

"If the US government with all its medical researchers, criminal investigators, and intelligence resources can't figure out what's causing Havana Syndrome, what makes you think you can?"

"Because I love her. I'll do whatever's necessary."

"We've got our hands full dealing with ISIS and the Triad," Eddie said.

"Radicals are all over DC, and someone's always making threats, but most don't turn into anything. I'm taking this seriously, but if it's real, we'll need more evidence before we can take action, so keep running the sources. Give me two days to ask around and get the inside scoop on Havana Syndrome. Once I understand it better, I'll make smarter decisions."

"Two days?"

"More or less."

Eddie stuffed his hands in his pockets. "Shit."

Supervisory Special Agent Rahimya Nawaz exited her office, scanned the cubicle farm, and made a beeline toward them. She was all bones and sharp angles, and her clothes hung off her like wet laundry on a rack. As a Muslim who had immigrated from Pakistan to the United States as a teenager, Rahimya's understanding of the region and culture had been invaluable in guiding their cases.

Rahimya shook Nathan's hand. "Welcome back. Your ex-wife okay?"

"*She's not my ex.*" *Why do I have to keep telling people that?* "She's still symptomatic. but the doctors say she's not in immediate danger. I'd feel more comfortable if I knew what caused it."

"Very good," Rahimya said. "Now that you're here, I want you and Eddie to go full steam on this case. Identify Ghulam and see if we can find a link to Islamic State to corroborate your source's intel. If they're ISIS, we need to stop whatever they're planning. I'll put the whole team on it if they're the real deal."

So much for touchy-feely time. "They want driver licenses, passports, and ID cards from a federal agency. They could be equipping operatives for an attack."

"Or bringing more people into the country," she said.

"Or both. Ghulam will provide Mohammad with aliases and photos, then we can use their pictures to identify them. Eddie will get with tech and copy the fraudulent documents before Kei delivers them."

Rahimya shook her head. "We can't assist a terror group by arming jihadists with fake IDs. If that got out, we'd be finished."

"The Golden Dragons are providing them, not us."

"Don't get cute," she said. "We're facilitating it."

"We'll run a sting," Nathan said, "and document everything. We deliver the IDs, then conduct surveillance when they distribute them to their people. We follow them until they do something serious enough that we can make an arrest stick."

"It's too much risk for the FBI."

"Tactically or politically?"

"Both, but we're getting ahead of ourselves. We don't know who they are or that they're affiliated with Islamic State. One step at a time. Get to work."

"About that," Nathan said. "I need time to work on my wife's situation."

"I thought she was stable."

"I want to understand what caused this, and—"

"Havana Syndrome," Eddie interrupted.

Shit.

Rahimya cocked her head. "You want to look into Havana Syndrome?"

"I, uh, I want a better understanding of this phenomenon, so I know what to expect."

"You don't have time for that. Take a few hours of sick leave if your wife needs help, but this ISIS case is too urgent to allow you to indulge in wild goose chases. Get back to your investigation."

Rahimya returned to her office, and Nathan stared at Eddie.

"What?" Eddie asked.

"If I wanted her to know I was researching Havana Syndrome, I would have said that."

"Sorry, dude."

Nathan settled behind his computer and scrolled through the Washington Field Office's telephone directory. He highlighted a number and dialed.

"Agent Chan," Meili answered.

"Meili the magnificent," Nathan said, using her academy nickname.

"Who is—"

"Nathan Burke. How the hell are you?"

"Naughty Nate. It's been years. You still in the AF-PAK group?"

"I'm right up the street from you. Got time for lunch?"

She paused before answering. "This work or social? You're still married, right?"

"That's why I'm calling. You heard about my wife in Santo Domingo?"

"Oh, shit. Reagan Burke. Of course. We get notified anytime there's an anomalous health incident, but I didn't connect her with you."

"Anomalous?"

"That's how we're instructed to refer to Havana Syndrome—as health incidents with unknown causes. Lumping the illnesses together made the bosses nervous, even though I think they're all related."

"I need a briefing."

"You're involved with the case?"

"This is unofficial. I need to know what's happening to Reagan and why."

The line was quiet for a few seconds. "You know what you're asking?"

"Forget professional courtesy. I need a favor from an old friend."

Meili sighed. "Come by my office this afternoon."

"I'll stop in after I check on Reagan. You're the best. Thank you."

"Don't thank me yet," she said. "I don't have many answers. And bring coffee. You're buying."

10

Reagan did a double take as Nathan approached her on the K Street sidewalk outside her psychiatrist's office. This was her first meeting with Dr. Erik Gunnarsen, so how did Nathan know the State Department had asked her to seek counseling?

"Nathan? Is Amelia okay?"

"She's fine."

Reagan expelled a long breath and tried to slow her heart rate.

"Other than losing her mother," Nathan finished.

Reagan's relief morphed into anger. "What are you doing here? How did you track me down?"

"Don't yell. I didn't come to fight."

"You're off to a poor start, and I'm not yelling. It's my hearing. Everything's muted since the attack."

"We need to talk without Vince staring holes through me."

"He's parking the car. How did you know—"

"Your doctor's office called to confirm the insurance information. They have my number associated with the account. Sorry, I know that sounds stalky."

"I'm late for my appointment."

Nathan's eyes widened. "Please, just a minute."

"Vince will be here any second."

"I deserve an explanation."

"We've talked about this."

"Not enough. I love you. Amelia loves you. Come back to us. I forgive you for—"

"Forgive me? I didn't mean for this to happen."

"You left us," he said. "You chose work over family."

"And you haven't been doing that since I met you? You could have taken a leave of absence and come with me. I put my career on hold to have Amelia, but where were you when it was my turn?"

"I tried. I called in favors, but your asshole boyfriend wouldn't give me an embassy spot. He—"

The pressure between her temples increased. "He wasn't my boyfriend then. I only met him once for ten minutes before I accepted the assignment."

"I guess you made an impression. What did you do in those ten minutes?"

Anger warmed her cheeks, and she rested her hands on her hips. "What's *that* supposed to mean?"

"It seems odd. The guy in charge of the FBI in the Dominican Republic refuses my transfer, then he steals you from me."

"I'm not your property. You don't own me and neither does Vince."

A lightning bolt shot through her forehead, and she leaned against the building for balance. She clung to the hard, cool granite, afraid to let go.

Nathan reached for her. "What's wrong?"

"I don't have time to list everything that hurts. I'm going to my appointment."

11

Case Officer Bashir Gemayel straightened his tie and smiled at the baby-faced receptionist in the anteroom outside the office of the Central Intelligence Agency's deputy chief of technology. As a case officer specializing in Russian counterintelligence, Bashir had little reason to interact with the technology section. This was only the second time he'd been in this wing of CIA headquarters at Langley and the first time he'd met with a senior executive.

A light flashed on the administrative assistant's desk, and she touched her earpiece. Her eyes darted to him. "Mr. Hamilton will see you now."

Bashir had done his homework. Trent Hamilton. Twenty-two years at the agency, all in technology and research. A Princeton grad with a science background, he had been a natural fit to study surveillance equipment, countermeasures, and weaponry. But he was not a scientist. That was worrisome. A manager who had supervised others but never done the work himself was someone to be wary around. Hamilton was a bureaucrat's bureaucrat who'd risen to a position of power, which meant people should fear him. Non-appointed bureaucrats who rose through the system into protected and influential positions were the most untouchable and dangerous.

They wielded real power.

Bashir opened the door and entered a spacious office with thin, rectangular windows overlooking the interior courtyard. Sunlight flowed through tinted film on the glass. Bashir had sat on benches in the courtyard and wondered who had used these offices. Now he knew.

"Thanks for coming," Hamilton said.

"Nice to meet you, sir."

Hamilton towered over Bashir, but at only five-foot-six inches in height, most people did. Hamilton pointed to a seat in front of his desk then reclined in a worn leather chair. Bashir settled in opposite him and waited.

"How are you adjusting to domestic life after your Moscow tour?"

"Fine." Of course, it wasn't fine. After ten years studying the Russians, learning their language, and excelling at his tradecraft, he'd landed a premier assignment in Moscow. Now he was back. Having his tour curtailed had been a severe disappointment. What had he done wrong?

"You're familiar, of course, with Havana Syndrome." A statement, not a question.

"We had seven confirmed cases at the embassy," Bashir said. "And another suspected attack, all with the same symptoms, rapid onset, and unexplained causes."

"I'm familiar with how it presents," Hamilton said. His tone had chilled. "It's why you're here. FBI Group 346 is coordinating the law enforcement response to these incidents. If it's a foreign attack, we need to defend ourselves. Then we need to respond."

"If it's state-sponsored," Bashir said, "it's an act of war, and if a terrorist group is behind it, they're as technologically advanced as any nation state and therefore, an existential threat."

"Precisely so. That kind of analysis is why I picked you. There are a lot of crazy theories floating around, from alien technology to animal attacks. We have—"

"I wouldn't call an animal source *crazy*," Bashir said. "I've read interesting causation theories dealing with crickets, allergens, and bacteria carried by animals."

"All bullshit," Hamilton said. "The Russians did this. There's no doubt in my mind. They've been studying microwave weapons since the seventies. They've used them before."

"If it's the Russians, I understand why I'm here." The tension ebbed in Bashir's shoulders. Maybe this reassignment wasn't a punishment, and they needed him focused on a Russian threat.

"We're assigning you as a liaison to the FBI. They've been passing RFIs through the usual channels," Hamilton said, referring to Requests for Information. "Tell them you're there to expedite the process. Convince them the CIA takes this seriously and we want to support their efforts. We're not falling into the pre-9/11 trap of stove-piping information. Tell them that."

"That's not the real reason?"

Hamilton stared out the window into the courtyard. He turned back to Bashir with steely eyes. "Keep tabs on them. Make sure their investigation stays on track. I don't want them wasting precious time and resources diving down ludicrous rabbit holes. I—"

"How do we avoid the prohibition on domestic operations if I'm running an operation to collect on—"

"This isn't an operation. You're there to assist them when they require information we possess, but I also want you to monitor their investigation. Sharing information and nudging them in a certain direction is not an operation. What they decide to do with their investigation is up to them."

"If we want them to focus on certain avenues of investigation, I suppose you'll want me to be careful with what I share."

Hamilton smiled. "Give them what they want, but just enough to answer their questions. And of course, there'll be things you're not allowed to divulge, like anything that compromises our sources or methods. Or intelligence that muddy the waters. You're smart. That's why I asked for you. Take their requests, analyze them, and figure out the best way to respond. Their questions will tell us which direction they're leaning. I don't want it to look like we're stonewalling, but I also don't want to throw gasoline on fires that will distract them from the truth."

"The truth as we see it," Bashir said.

"Is there any other kind?"

12

Reagan reclined in the soft leather chair in Dr. Gunnarsen's office. Her head pounded and her blood pressure rose until she wanted to clench her fists and scream. Nathan had a way of doing that to people. She gripped the arms of the chair and tried to smile.

"Gunnarsen sounds Norse," she said. "You Norwegian?"

"Danish, actually. But my grandparents immigrated from Aalborg, Denmark, so you're not far off."

People who used "actually" in conversation drove her crazy because it was unnecessary and pretentious. Gunnarsen's hands looked soft, and a roll of fat pushed against his sweater vest—a typical academic. Damn Nathan for making her irritable before her first visit with a psychiatrist.

"I'm here because I work for the State Department, and they insisted I consult a psychiatrist after my incident in the Dominican Republic. They wanted me to see a staff psychiatrist, but I told them I'm more comfortable with an independent doctor, and I don't want your session notes in my official record. Their health section recommended you."

"I received the medical records you asked them to forward. How are you feeling now?"

"Every symptom's still present. Migraines come and go. Dizziness, nausea, dulled sense of hearing, fatigue, a high-pitched tone that never goes away. When I wake up, my vision is blurry, and I need time to regain my balance. It sucks."

"That sounds unpleasant, but I meant are you feeling better now that you're home and away from all the stress at the embassy?"

"I'm not home. I'm staying with my . . . with a man I'm seeing. My husband and I separated."

"Ah, I see." Gunnarsen steepled his hands under his chin.

"And what did you mean by *stress at the embassy*?"

"Santo Domingo was your first posting, right?"

"Yes, but—"

"Foreign postings often increase anxiety," Gunnarsen said. "You're required to acclimate to a fresh set of duties, an unfamiliar work environment, and new colleagues. Expectations are unclear, as is your path to success. The weather is different, the food is unusual, and you must adjust to an alien language and culture. Many of my State Department patients have stomach issues for the entire first year they're overseas, and—"

"How's that germane to my attack?"

"Interesting you use that word. What makes you think this was an *attack*?"

"One minute I'm fine," Reagan said, "and the next thing I know, I'm on the ground."

"Acute onset for sure. Did that embarrass you?"

Heat rose in her neck again. Had Nathan made her short tempered? "I was too busy trying not to die to be embarrassed."

"But having your new colleagues watch you vomit must have been stressful."

"Yes but—"

"You're a smart woman. I'm sure you see my point. They buried you under levels of tension. The new job, the separation from your husband, a health emergency in front of people you're trying to impress."

"But anxiety from the incident came after. It didn't cause it."

Gunnarsen sat still in his chair and watched her. She fought the urge to fill the silence.

"Tell me about your separation," he said.

"How's that relevant?"

"We won't know until we explore it. A holistic approach will—"

"I'm here because State requires it as part of their post-incident response. I don't need a psychiatrist. I don't mean to insult you, but I don't see how talking about Nathan can help."

"Humor me."

13

On the third floor of the Hoover Building, Nathan read through the case file that had been awaiting him on Meili's desk. She sat beside him, typing on her computer. Folder after folder was stuffed with FD-302 investigative reports detailing interviews after anomalous health incidents involving American personnel. More reports filled a Moser safe behind a row of cubicles. Nathan had been reading for hours. He set the file down and rubbed his eyes.

"It'll take you a month to read everything," Meili said. "Much of it is repetitive."

"I guess that's the point," Nathan said. "The symptoms are similar, or at least within the same spectrum of neurological problems. It's pretty clear most of these people suffer from the same illness. Or injury."

"And that about sums up seven years of research. The first case hit in Havana in 2016, and everyone's immediate thought was medical. Then US personnel in other embassies exhibited similar symptoms, all with sudden onset. Most patients were spies or diplomats, and alarm bells went off. This had to be an attack, right? Then doubt crept in. Alternate theories. I've investigated Havana Syndrome more than anyone, and to be honest, we're no closer to cracking this than the day after the first episode."

"I've been reading incident reports, witness statements, victim accounts, and investigative summaries. Tell me what I'm not seeing here. I need a rundown of every reasonable theory. On second thought, give me every thesis. Least likely scenarios rarely receive sufficient attention or resources, which means they stand little chance of being proven, even if they're true. I'm coming at this with fresh eyes, so share everything."

"I'll do better than that," Meili said. "Let me introduce you to Huckleberry. He's an analyst and the closest thing we have to a scientific expert. He's been our group's unofficial liaison to the tech and medical communities for the past eight months."

"Huckleberry?"

"His name is Thomas Sawyer. He said his father was a Mark Twain fan. His parents must've had a sense of humor. He got tired of our ribbing and asked us to call him something else."

"So you came up with Huckleberry?"

"The surest way to incite harassment is to admit a joke bothers you."

Meili led Nathan down the hall to another office. She walked ahead of him, and his eyes dropped to her body. She was petite with slender legs and silky black hair that reached the center of her back. He hadn't seen her since the academy, but she looked fitter and sexier now. Experience on the job had given her confidence, and she'd become a force.

They entered an office suite, twice the size of the space used by Meili's group. The air hummed with clacking keyboards and murmured conversations, punctuated by an occasional laugh. The odor of old carpet tingled his nose. The cubicle ghetto resembled a rodent maze in a laboratory.

"This is where we keep our task force officers, experts, and anyone attached to us from other agencies," Meili said.

She stopped at a cubicle where an overweight man with a pocket protector and thick glasses poured over data.

"Huckleberry, meet Nate. He's with the WFO."

Huckleberry looked up and nodded but didn't offer his hand.

"Nice to meet you, Thomas."

Huckleberry smiled at the use of his real name. "You on this now?"

"I'm—"

"Nate works counterterrorism, and he's trying to get a lay of the land," Meili said. "Can you give him a sixty-second brief on causation theories?"

Huckleberry swiveled in his seat, appearing more comfortable heading into an analytic dissertation than with social interaction. "The syndrome has afflicted over two hundred American diplomats, agents, and spies around the world. The primary question is, are these anomalous health incidents, natural illness, environmental contamination, psychological phenomenon, or intentional attacks by a foreign power?"

"That's what I'm here to find out," Nathan said.

"We've been analyzing data to determine the source," Huckleberry said. "Everyone's been working on it from DOD advisors, to DOJ, to medical and scientific researchers, but we have more questions now than when we started."

"Like what?"

"Like everything. We don't know what's causing it, who's doing it, or why. What if a hostile power wants to do more than make people sick? What if they make their targets more docile? Or what if they're trying to remove specific diplomats or stop operations? Are these incidents a prelude for a broader attack?"

The hypothetical causes seemed endless. "You tell me."

"Microwaves could be designed to inhibit our listening devices or a signal to activate planted eavesdropping equipment. Our enemies could use high frequency radio waves to intercept conversations . . . or something worse."

"What are the leading theories?" Nathan asked.

"In my humble opinion, evidence and common sense indicates an attack, but there's almost as much justification for other explanations."

"Which are?"

"Directed energy weapons using lasers or microwaves, and more recently, using the microwave audio effect. Laser beams or sonic cannons, take your pick. Some suggested irradiation. Others suspect unintentional causes like exposure to allergens, pesticides, or other chemicals. Proximity to wind turbines or the odd sounds made by crickets have drawn traction. Right now, the government's leaning toward psychological triggers like mass hallucination or social contagion."

Nathan's muscles tightened. "They think the victims are delusional?"

"Mass panic and physical ailments can occur in times of intense stress. They've documented incidents before."

"You think that's what's happening?"

"My money's on death rays, but I've been hoping to find them since I read my first Buck Rogers comic book."

"I've read opinions from scientists that claim the symptoms mirror neurological damage from microwaves."

"That's true. Mind you, several experts have told us microwave weapons that could inflict brain damage would be too bulky to transport for operations. DOD won't even confirm we've developed microwave weapons, but we know they've been researching them for decades."

"We don't know that," Meili said. "We deduced it. I'm hoping to confirm it today when I interview Dr. Mandel."

"Who's he?" Nathan asked.

"A retired government researcher I tracked down." She looked at her watch. "I need to wrap this up and get going. Let's head back to my desk. I'll give you Huckleberry's email if you need anything else."

"Thanks for your help, Thomas."

"Anytime." Huckleberry swiveled back to his papers.

Nathan followed Meili back the way they'd come. The door to the hallway swung open as she reached for it. A diminutive, olive-skinned man with thick chestnut hair and an aquiline nose stopped in the threshold. "Excuse me."

"Nate, this is Bashir Gemayel, our liaison to the alphabet agencies," Meili said, meaning the intelligence community. "Bashir, meet Nathan Burke from the WFO."

Bashir flashed a bright smile and shook Nathan's hand with the firm grip of an athlete. "You joining the team?" He spoke with a slight accent that was hard to pinpoint.

"I'm—"

"Nate's with our AF-PAK group," Meili interjected.

Bashir cocked his head. "You found a terror link?"

"I'm, uh, looking into it."

Bashir rubbed his chin. "Seems like an odd set of targets for radical Islamists."

"I don't see a pattern, except they're all American."

"And Canadian," Bashir said. "And who knows how many other countries? We can't expect everyone to tell us about their employees' illnesses."

Nathan bit his lip. That was interesting. Which other countries could be involved? "I've read about incidents at US embassies in Havana, Guangzhou, Moscow—"

"Communist countries," Bashir said, locking Nathan with his rich, coffee-brown eyes.

"Not all," Meili said. "An administration official experienced acute symptom near the White House. Other attacks have happened in Europe and Africa."

"Still easy access for the SVR," Bashir said, referring to the Foreign Intelligence Service of the Russian Federation, the modern version of the KGB."

"You think the Russians are behind this?" Nathan asked.

"Da." Bashir smiled. "They seem like the most likely culprit. Intel has spotted GRU vehicles, that's Russian military intelligence, near the scenes of attacks. A truck or van could carry a microwave weapon."

Meili took Nathan's arm. "Anyway, we're getting a coffee, then Nate has to get back to the WFO."

"Keep your eye on the Reds," Bashir said.

"I'd like to hear more about—" Nathan said.

"We're going," Meili said. She led him out into the hallway then headed toward the exit.

"What's the rush?" Nathan asked.

"You're not here officially. I only agreed to give you an inside briefing and let you peek at our reporting. I need to interview a scientist about microwave weapons this afternoon, and you're not part of the investigation."

Nathan frowned. "I didn't want to be involved, but Havana Syndrome chose me when it attacked my wife."

Meili's face softened. "Let's grab a quick cup."

They walked to a kiosk on the first floor, and Nathan purchased coffees. It was his fourth of the morning, but it didn't touch his fatigue from the travel and trauma of the past few days.

"I don't want to be insensitive," Meili said. "I know how scary this must be for you and your wife, but I need to be careful. I've worked hard to become a supervisor. I don't have permission to share anything with you, and if—"

"I have a Top Secret-SCI clearance. There's nothing—"

"You aren't cleared for this investigation."

"Reagan's extremely sick. It's been hard enough since she abandoned Amelia and me. I've been trying to get her back, but she met someone."

"Oh, I'm sorry."

"And if the effects from this syndrome are permanent, or if she ... well, I don't know what I'll do."

Meili placed her hand on his forearm. "I'm sorry you're going through this. I really am."

He nodded.

"I don't mean to pry, but what happened? Why'd she leave?"

Nathan took a sip and sat on a bench. "Reagan works for State. She sort of put her career on the back burner to raise Amelia, then last year, they offered her a posting to Santo Domingo. I requested a hardship transfer, but the LEGAT, an asshole named Vince Cabrera, wouldn't accommodate me. Reagan decided to go, and I planned to follow with Amelia once a position opened. We did the long-weekend trip thing for about six months until she started fucking Cabrera."

"Oh, shit. That sucks." Meili squeezed his arm.

"She says she's in love." He sighed. "I should have gone with her."

"Couldn't you have taken time off or transferred to State?"

"I could've taken a leave of absence, but I'm working serious counterterrorism cases."

Meili's raised her eyebrows and tilted her head. "You didn't go because of your cases?"

Nathan shook his head. "It would have damaged my career, and who knows where they would have assigned me when I came back."

"She put her career on hold for you."

"Reagan abandoned us. She chose work over family."

"But you could have gone with her," Meili said. "Didn't you choose work over family too?"

Nathan ground his teeth and breathed through his nose. "That's what she said."

"Did she forgive you for not moving down there?"

"She's the one who left. What's there to forgive? I stayed with our daughter in our house while she absconded to the beach and slept with another man."

Meili nodded. "I won't condone cheating, but I understand her taking the job. It's hard to get ahead in these agencies, especially for a woman, and turning down a job can kill a career before it begins."

"It sounds like you've been talking to her."

"It's time to forgive her, for Amelia's sake."

Nathan's pulse thumped in his ears as his brain and heart fought for dominance. "The best way for me to help Reagan is to identify who attacked her."

"Is she still mad at you?"

"I don't know. It doesn't matter. She cheated on me. I hate her . . . and I love her."

"If she's serious about this guy, you need to move on."

"What I *need* to do is protect her. She's still my wife and Amelia's mother. Amelia would be crushed if . . ."

Meili lowered her voice. "Investigating Havana Syndrome won't make her come home. You think you can ride in like a white knight and win her back?"

Nathan stood and clenched his fists. "My job is to protect us. I swore an oath. Someone has attacked my country. And my family."

"I could get into trouble for letting you inside."

"Please, Meili. I need to find out what's causing this. Let me come with you to interview Dr. Mandel. Even if you think I can't contribute, do it for me. Help an old friend."

Meili shook her head. "I'm going to regret this." Her eyes sparkled. "Welcome aboard."

14

Nathan occupied the passenger seat of Meili's B-car, a silver Chevrolet Malibu, as she drove west on the George Washington Memorial Parkway away from the city. He flipped through the CIA briefing documents Bashir had given them. Foreign governments had been developing chemical, biological, nuclear, and other technological weapons for a long time. Microwaves were just one possibility in a long list of technologies used to inflict harm.

"Scary stuff," he said.

"I've talked to scientists who swear the symptoms are caused by microwaves," Meili said. "Others are just as certain radio waves are responsible. It could be particle beams or any directed-energy weapon. Or something new. It's complicated, and the technospeak is impenetrable."

"Great."

"We need to answer four questions. First, are we looking at intentional acts? If so, which type of weapon? And then, who's behind it and what's motivating them?"

"Solving any of those questions should lead to answering the others," Nathan said.

Meili glanced at him. "We think alike, which is why I want you to meet Dr. Mandel. His name popped up on my radar about a year ago. He was deeply involved in microwave research in the seventies and eighties. Out of dozens of scientific reports I've read, his seemed to be the only ones written in plain English, as if he actually wanted to impart knowledge."

"Why hasn't anyone from the FBI interviewed him before?"

"He retired in 1995 and kept a low profile, but I tracked him down."

"But still—"

"Our agents researching the more technical aspects of standoff weapons aren't interested in someone who dealt with technology during the last century."

"And you are?"

"He may have insight into who's behind this. Much of his research came during the Cold War. He'll have a perspective younger scientists may not."

Meili exited the parkway and took Route 123 into Langley. They drove past warning signs outside the entrance to the CIA and turned down Kurtz Road.

Nathan flipped through a file and found Dr. Mandel's name. He skimmed the report. "I see he worked on American research programs in the seventies for NewTech?"

Meili smirked. "He was CIA, a government scientist working on countering Soviet microwave technology. He was there at the start of the high-energy arms race."

"I guess that explains why he lives so close to CIA headquarters. Short commute."

She stopped in front of a two-story colonial house, a few blocks from downtown McLean. "Remember, you're not officially here. You can ask questions, but don't cause problems."

"I'm searching for answers. I'm not here to cause problems."

"I know." She touched his arm. "I'm just nervous about involving you without permission."

"You could ask if—"

"My supervisor would never grant you access. Not without evidence of a terror connection."

"You're taking a risk," he said.

"Better to ask for forgiveness than permission. Isn't that what you used to say in the academy?"

"That wasn't as serious as—"

"I know how government works," she said, "and I'm sympathetic to your situation. I'll take the heat."

"Who knows, maybe I'll figure this thing out."

Nathan followed her up a flagstone walkway to the house, which needed a coat of paint. Meili reached for the doorbell as Jakob Mandel opened the door. He must have been waiting for them. Mandel was bald on top, with a ring of unruly gray hair growing over his ears like weeds. He wore a tattered cardigan sweater with a shawl collar that he'd probably owned since his government service ended in the nineties.

"Ah, the FBI," Mandel said. "And you must be Agent Chang."

"Meili Chang, and this is Special Agent Nathan Burke."

"Come in."

They followed him into a living room, which was clean but cluttered. Vivaldi's *The Four Seasons* drifted out of speakers buried in the bookshelves.

"As I explained on the phone," Meili said, "I'm supervising the FBI's Havana Syndrome investigation. I've read many of your reports, but I want to hear your thoughts in person. It's my experience that much gets left unsaid in official documents.

"My work before seventy-two has passed the fifty-year mark, so they can declassify it, but they haven't, so there's much I'm not allowed to disclose."

"We're both federal agents," Meili said.

"I heard you the first time. I'm old, not senile."

Meili held up her hands in surrender. "I meant we both have SCI clearances."

"I doubt you possess the clearance tickets for some of these specialized areas. The CIA has a long reach, and they don't forget. I've survived this long, and I'd hate to incur their wrath at this stage of my life."

"We're not trying to cause trouble, and we don't want you to divulge anything beyond our clearances."

"And I won't."

"I appreciate your willingness to speak with us, Dr. Mandel." Meili said. "You managed the leading scientists on high-energy weapons for twenty years. Can you give us a summary of the history and ideas behind microwave weapons? We're interested how they could relate to Havana

Syndrome. We're still trying to determine if someone intentionally caused these incidents."

"Call me Jakob. *Dr. Mandel* makes me feel like my father. It confirms they've put me out to pasture."

Nathan watched him. Jakob's wrinkled skin matched his seventy-seven years, but his eyes retained the curiosity and fire of a younger man.

Meili laughed. "No offense, Jakob. You seem sharper than half the agents in my office, which is why I'm here."

"And you've brought a friend." He looked at Nathan.

Nathan shook Jakob's hand. "Thanks for agreeing to talk to us. I'm new to the investigations, and I—"

"He's looking for connections to terrorism," Meili said.

"You won't find the people responsible for this in Kabul or Tehran," Jakob said.

"You sound certain," Nathan said.

"The Russians are at it again."

"Again?" Nathan asked.

"The Soviets hammered our embassy in Moscow for a quarter century," Jakob said.

"You're referring to the Moscow Signal?" Meili asked.

"Those bastards aimed a four-gigahertz signal at our embassy for twenty-three years. They only backed down after we discovered it in seventy-six. They stopped that operation, but they never slowed their research."

"I'm late to the party," Nathan said. "Why did they do that?"

"That's an open question. Probably to jam our equipment. The beamed it from an apartment building a hundred yards across the street. They'd been doing it for decades. Some believe the Soviets were trying to modify behavior."

"The intelligence community knew about it in 1953," Meili said, "but they never warned the State officials who worked there."

"Was anyone hurt?" Nathan asked.

"The official answer is complicated," Jakob said. "A 1976 State Department study found no ill effects, but I disagree. The microwaves were 100 times the acceptable exposure rate. Employees must have been affected. A

Spanish study in 2019 showed negative long-term health outcomes, including higher cancer rates for embassy staff. The ambassador stationed there in the seventies died from leukemia."

"From his exposure?" Nathan asked.

"It's impossible to infer causation, but he started bleeding from his eyes. When I see a smoking gun, I know someone pulled the trigger."

"Could Russia be using a portable microwave weapon against our people?" Nathan asked.

"Havana Syndrome symptoms are different and far more acute, but I'd expect increased severity after fifty years of weapons development. The high-pitched sound victims hear is caused by microwaves striking their acoustic nerves. I'm certain the Russians are responsible."

"You worked on our weapons program for most of your career," Meili stated.

"Everyone wanted to develop a portable high-energy weapon with the capability to launch high-energy attacks on individual targets. The ability to take out a spy, traitor, or foreign leader without leaving fingerprints tempted us all. For decades, we engaged in a high-tech arms race."

Nathan scanned the room. An object that looked like a telescope sat on a table beside the window. "What's that?"

"That's a copy of one of the Russians' earlier models," Jakob said. "A radio transmitter from 1978."

"For communication?"

"For killing Americans. It's an antique. Well, not technically. That model is generations behind what the Soviets created before my retirement. It should be in a museum, but I wanted a reminder. I spent most of my life trying to beat the Russians at their game."

"Why haven't I heard about this?" Nathan asked.

"You're too young, and the nuclear arms race got all the headlines. A two-kiloton warhead detonating in Washington, DC, would kill millions. Radio-wave attacks target individuals or small groups. They don't get the same media splash, and we hid our research behind the highest classifications. Only a handful of people had access."

"How about after that?" Nathan asked. "Were you still researching in the eighties and nineties?"

"We never stopped. When I left in ninety-five, we were deep into Operations Hello, Goodbye, Goodnight."

"What—"

"All three operations experimented with triggering biological changes with standoff microwave weapons. Operation Hello aimed to make targets hear voices and to produce psychological impairment. We designed Goodbye to make people sick and disperse crowds."

"And Operation Goodnight?"

"It killed people. An assassination tool."

"How effective were these weapons?" Meili asked.

"I wish I could say my years of research resulted in success, but we didn't perfect it during my time there. The prototypes we designed were too impractical for the field."

"We heard they'd be too big to smuggle into cities and use against embassies," Nathan said.

"That wasn't the only problem. Achieving the required power to send a wave across long distances was an insurmountable obstacle for years . . . until we solved it using thermoelastic pressure waves."

"Thermo—"

"We heated waves to increase their potency and reduce the size of the weapon. A larger issue was keeping the cone of the wave narrow as it traveled through space. If it expanded, we'd hit large numbers of people. But that wasn't the biggest problem."

"What hung you up?" Meili asked.

"Keeping the power consistent through changing variables, like distance, weather, walls, and other interference. Too weak and the effort and risk to launch an operation would be wasted."

"And too strong?" Nathan asked.

"We'd murder everyone."

"So you abandoned the research?" Meili asked.

"Enthusiasm waned. The more impractical the weapon, the less excitement and funding it generated. We also had issues with human testing back in sixty-nine, an ethical dilemma that never concerned the Russians and Chinese."

"But the Russians kept trying?" Meili asked.

Jakob smiled. "Countries have experimented on new weapons since men started throwing rocks at each other. I'm older than dirt, and everyone was developing microwave and other standoff weapons in the seventies. God knows what leaps they've made with mind-altering weaponry."

"Mind control?" Nathan asked. "Are we still developing those types of weapons?"

"That was the purpose of the Pandora Project, to use electromagnetic radiation to alter the way cells communicate inside a brain. That was fifty years ago, so who knows what they're achieving now."

"But you know the research trajectory," Nathan said. "Hell, it was your research. Are we still experimenting?"

Jakob smiled and looked from Nathan to Meili. "DARPA has been testing ways to influence electromagnetic waves in the brain, but I'm afraid I'd need approval to delve any deeper into that topic."

"I understand," Meili said. "If you're uncomfortable with—"

"But," Nathan interrupted, "do you think Russia could have stolen microwave or electromagnetic technology from us? Could they be using your old research against American diplomats?"

"That's a mystery you'll have to solve for yourself."

15

At the entrance to the West Wing of the White House, Bashir collected his keys and cell phone from the bucket beside the metal detector.

"Ready?" Trent Hamilton asked.

"All set," Bashir said with as much confidence as he could muster. His stomach fluttered like a flag in the wind. In ten years as a CIA case officer, he'd never briefed a cabinet-level official and never been inside the White House. Not once.

"Mr. Hamilton?" a young man asked. He wore a lanyard with a half dozen IDs dangling from it and a suit that hung off him like his father's overcoat.

"Yes," Hamilton said. "This is Mr. Gemayel."

"Please come with me."

They followed him up a staircase and down a long hall past White House staff who scurried around like their jobs depended on it, which they probably did. Democratic incumbent president, David Winslow, was in a dead heat for the presidency with the election only seven months away. It was no secret White House aides frantically sought an edge. Failures in foreign diplomacy had hurt Winslow's presidency as much as the faltering economy had. The tension in the air seemed palpable.

"Please wait here," their escort said before he disappeared through a heavy cherrywood door.

Two women passed down the hall and gave Bashir long looks. Bashir was about to meet National Security Advisor Frederick Richardson, a senior presidential aid and old friend to President Winslow. Despite the president's affection for Richardson, if the news reports were accurate, Richardson's head was on the chopping block unless the administration scored a foreign-policy win.

"I still don't know why I'm here," Bashir said. "I've only been attached to the FBI for a few days. What can I tell him that he doesn't already know?"

"Havana Syndrome has all the warning signs of another foreign-policy fuckup. The last thing Richardson wants is another failure that makes the US look weak. He—"

"But doesn't he get regular briefings from the director?"

"The FBI briefs him daily, but he won't let the fate of this administration and his own career hang on politically sanitized briefings. Richardson wants to know what they're doing before they edit their briefing down to what they believe he needs to hear. Be careful to—"

The office door opened, and the young man waved them in. They followed him into an office too cramped for a man in such an influential position. An American flag hung behind the desk, and Bashir's heart stirred. He'd been a citizen since he was seventeen, but the patriotism that filled him in the presence of the stars and stripes never wavered. He loved his new country and had sworn an oath to protect it.

Richardson came around the desk and greeted them with a two-handed handshake common among politicians. He was short, round, and bald, with eyes too tiny for his head. He could have been a small-town mayor.

"Good to see you, Trent," Richardson said. "I'm meeting with the SecDef in eight minutes, so I'll get right to it. Where's the FBI with this investigation?" He nodded at Bashir. "This your guy inside?"

"I've—" Bashir began then stopped when Hamilton held up his hand.

"We're taking this as seriously as you are," Hamilton said. "Bashir Gemayel's one of our best case officers. He's been working with the FBI and keeping close tabs on their day-to-day operations."

Richardson looked at Bashir. "What's the FBI's theory on Havana Syndrome? Tell me what the line agents think?"

"They don't know," Bashir said. "The FBI's looking at everything. They're interviewing victims, witnesses, scientists, virologists, psychologists, weaponry experts, and every conspiracy nut who claims to have information. But they can't determine what's causing it."

Richardson smirked. "That may be the most honest briefing I've heard about the FBI's progress, or lack of progress, in the past three and a half years. Every time that damn director sits in my office, he smothers me with manpower hours, numbers of interviews, and other inputs. If I didn't know better, I'd come out of his briefings believing they were on the verge of cracking this thing. I wondered if they were telling the truth."

"I haven't been there long or met the entire team," Bashir said, "but they don't appear to be close to finding an answer."

"I told you Gemayel would give you an honest assessment," Hamilton said.

Richardson drummed his fingers against his leg. "The fucking Russians are going to stick it to us again. They meddled in our election and have intruded into our spheres of influence from Eastern Europe to the Middle East. Now they're attacking our diplomats and intelligence officers. That SOB, Putin, wants to make this administration look weak. If nations lose faith in the United States's ability to project power or in this president's fortitude, they'll be forced to welcome the Russians with open arms. We need proof they're behind this and fast before they rebuild the Soviet Union. We don't need another goddamn Russki imperial power."

"I haven't seen direct evidence of Russian involvement," Bashir said.

Hamilton scowled and shook his head, almost imperceptibly. Message received.

"You just got back from Moscow, right?" Richardson asked.

He knew Bashir's background. He'd done his homework.

"Yes, sir." He regretted calling Richardson "sir." While he had no problem acting deferential to a cabinet appointee, calling people from the Ivy League *sir* gave them unearned authority, as if Bashir acknowledged his inferiority. It wasn't like that in Lebanon, but here, elites, whether academics, celebrities, or politicians, were quick to jump on class distinctions.

"Then you understand what those bastards can do."

"I do."

"We went from fighting the communist menace to dealing with an aggressive oligarchy. In the end, it doesn't matter what we label them. They're a totalitarian regime that wants to beat us on the world stage. I won't let that happen."

"Frederick," Hamilton said, "Gemayel's our man, and he'll ensure the FBI heads in the right direction."

"I don't want details," Richardson said. "Just get me results."

16

Reagan lay in Vince's bed—at least that's how she thought of it—and stared at the ceiling. She may be in love, but this wasn't her home. Nothing here belonged to her, except a suitcase of clothes. Vince had offered her several drawers, but she hadn't unpacked. The church condo she had shared with Nathan was no longer her home either. Nathan wanted her back, but she was with Vince now. Homeless. Adrift. Maybe if she decorated Vince's home and added her personal touch.

That damn incident had rushed everything. She'd spent almost every night with Vince in the Dominican Republic, either in her embassy housing or his. They'd always been careful not to be seen because she was still technically married, and people would talk. Although, infidelity seemed like a team sport on the Caribbean island. State Department employees screwed like college freshman, as if being overseas suspended the rules and absolved them of personal responsibility and morality. Had that culture affected her too?

She removed earbuds connected to her laptop. For years, she'd watched mindless sitcoms to block out her stress, but everything changed after Santo Domingo. The embassy incident remained vivid in her mind, no matter what she did. What had happened to her brain?

"Reagan?" Vince called from downstairs. "You awake?"

"Getting up now."

"I'm heading into DC for a meeting. I stocked the refrigerator last night. Call if you need anything."

"See you tonight."

A wave of guilt crashed through her. Vince was meeting with State Department officials while she lay in bed like a lazy teenager. But she *had* been injured at work, so her insecurity wasn't justified. Would Workers' Compensation cover her medical bills?

She slid to the edge of the bed and lost her equilibrium. She jammed her eyes shut and squeezed the mattress until the world stopped spinning. Vertigo was the absolute worst. She opened one eye and found her bottle of meclizine in the nightstand. The drug fatigued her, but it reduced her dizziness and stopped her from throwing up. Not vomiting was her new goal. Wonderful. Losing her health had realigned her priorities. She downed the medicine with two Tylenol and waited for relief.

Her cell phone glowed, and she picked it up. Another email from Amelia.

Mommy, I hope you feel better. When are you coming home? Are you mad at me?

Reagan's chest ached with remorse. She'd told Amelia she and Nathan had taken a break because of her new job, but they'd avoided discussions about the future. The separation, Vince . . . everything so new. Nathan had brought Amelia to the Dominican Republic to visit, and Reagan had managed a couple of trips back to DC, but it was time to figure out how this would work. They must have *the talk* with Amelia.

"God, I miss her."

The phone rang in Reagan's hand, triggering another migraine. She grimaced and answered.

"Reagan Burke?" a man asked.

"Yes?"

"My name's Paul Johnson. I'm a foreign service officer in Moscow, or at least I was until recently. Is this a bad time?"

Pain undulated through her forehead, and she rubbed her eyes. "How can I help you?"

"I heard about your medevac from the DR. I've been on medical leave since February, and I try to keep track of other victims."

"Victims?"

"Of Havana Syndrome."

Reagan sat up straight. "Wait, who is this?"

"Paul Johnson. I'm with State too. I was stationed in Moscow until February eighth, when I collapsed in the cafeteria. I left—"

Everything became fuzzy, like peering through a foggy window. "Sorry, what do you want?"

"I've been following other victims who've been attacked."

"But I wasn't attacked. I got sick."

"That's State Department's theory, but we think it's an attack by a foreign power."

Reagan blinked and rubbed her temples. "What is?"

"Havana Syndrome. It's a deliberate act."

"Rumors spread around the embassy," Reagan said, "but I haven't followed the story. There've been others?"

"By my count, you're the one-hundred eightieth official to succumb to this weapon."

"Weapon?"

"Either a microwave or high-energy pulse device."

Reagan stared at the phone. Was this guy nuts?

"You there?" he asked.

Too tired to hold the phone to her ear, she put the call on speaker. "I'm exhausted. Uh, this isn't a good time."

"I understand . . . more than anybody. You've got my number now. Save it and call me when you have the energy. Just don't wait too long."

"What's the rush?"

"The government's trying to sweep this under the rug. Blame the victims. They're implying it's in our heads."

"That's crazy—"

"Their theory's gaining traction. Next, they'll ask you to see a psychiatrist. They want a medical opinion to back them up."

"How?"

"By saying it's all in your head. They'll claim stress caused your symptoms."

Oh shit.

17

Nathan followed Meili out of Dr. Mandel's house to her car. He checked his phone, which showed three missed calls from Eddie and a voicemail from his boss.

"Give me a second," Nathan said.

Meili leaned against her door. Nathan hit play and put the phone to his ear.

"Just checking in, Nathan," the message from Rahimya Nawaz said. "I didn't receive a completed leave slip, and I want to know when you're coming back to work. Your partner needs . . . oh, uh, how is your ex-wife doing? I assume State's providing the healthcare she needs. We need you back here. Call me."

Rahimya sounded impatient. Eddie must be struggling with the ISIS case. Nathan raised his finger for Meili to wait, and she rolled her eyes and made a show of looking at her watch.

Nathan dialed Eddie. "What's up, partner?"

"I know you're off, but Mohammad called and Ghulam—"

"No names, Eddie."

Click, click, click.

"Right, I mean Mo's people want to know when Jason will deliver the product."

"Have Mo tell them he'll get a timeline," Nathan said, "and reassure them Jason will deliver. Make sure Mo records the calls and notes the dates, times, and participants. And don't let him meet with Ghulam's people in person unless you're there to cover it."

"What if they pop up at his place or insist on meeting?"

"They don't have his address, but if they insist on a face-to-face, grab Murphy or Three Balls and surveil it as best you can."

"Three Balls?"

"I'm surprised you haven't heard that story yet," Nathan said. "Ron Winslow has gone to every Nationals home game for the past decade. He always brings a glove hoping to catch a foul ball. But he never got one. Not even close. Last season, he took Murphy and me to an inter-league game against the Boston Red Sox. In the fourth inning, a Red Sox batter slapped a curve ball foul, and the ball sizzled down the third-base line and into the stands, right at us. Ron yells, 'I got it,' and jumps in the air. The problem was the ball had English on it and sank at the last minute."

"He catch it?" Eddie asked.

"Oh, he caught it. Right in the groin. Thus, the name, *Three Balls.*"

Eddie snorted. "If Mo has a problem, I'll reach out."

Meili cleared her throat and opened her door. "We're gonna be late for our next interview."

"Gotta run," Nathan said. "I'll talk to you—"

"Hey, man. I know you're dealing with a lot of shit right now, but I could use your help."

"You're doing everything we can at this point. Identify cell members from the phone numbers Mo gave us. They're probably all burner phones, but subpoena them anyway, and ask the phone companies to preserve their data. We need photos of them too. They're planning something."

"I'll get the Special Surveillance Group to—"

"Don't use SSG, if we can avoid it. They don't know the players or investigation like we do, and they're not invested in the outcome. They've burned my surveillances twice. You never know who they'll assign, and they've got some inexperienced rookies."

"I'm kind of a rookie too."

"That's my point."

Meili started her engine. She wouldn't drive off without him, would she? Nathan edged toward the passenger door.

"Funny," Eddie said. "I could head to Chinatown and—"

"Don't go alone," Nathan said. "Three Balls is good with video. Check out the van and get footage of these guys. And ask tech to install a pole camera. There are plenty of public utilities on the street. I want a camera focused on the main entrance to that building. Transmit the feed to our office and record it. There's no expectation of privacy on the sidewalk but get a warrant anyhow so we don't lose the evidence. We need to act fast in case they're planning an attack."

"Got it," Eddie said. It sounded like he was taking notes. "Hold on."

The murmur of Eddie's muffled voice talking to someone came over the line.

"Eddie? You there? I've gotta go."

"Agent Burke," Rahimya said.

Nathan straightened at the sound of her voice. "Hey, boss."

"Can I expect you back today?"

"I'm not quite ready," Eddie said. "I need a few days."

Meili honked the horn.

"You took two days off without approval while you were traveling and—"

"You know why I couldn't leave Santo Domingo."

"It's forgiven," Rahimya said. "But you're back now, and other than popping into the office to check in, you've been AWOL."

Meili laid on the horn.

"I left a leave slip in your inbox."

"It doesn't have the dates filled in, so it's not valid. When are you returning?"

"I need more time."

Meili revved her engine.

"Give me a date," Rahimya said.

"A week from today."

"Too long. I'll have to reassign your investigation to—"

"Five days."

"Three days," Rahimya said. "If you're not in the office by then, I'm giving your case to Three Ball—er, Agent Wilson."

Meili pulled away from the curb.

"Okay, three days," Nathan said. He hung up and dashed to the car.

18

Bashir scrunched behind the wheel of his government-issued car as Meili rolled down the street, leaving Nathan gawking on the sidewalk.

"What the heck is she doing?" Bashir mumbled.

He smiled as Nathan chased after the car and banged on the window. Meili stopped, and Nathan jumped in. Bashir stayed low in his seat and waited for them to turn at the stop sign, then he threw his car into gear and followed.

Conducting surveillance on American citizens in the United States was illegal for the CIA—and following FBI agents made it exponentially worse. And more dangerous. One-car surveillances were challenging, and both Meili and Nathan had trained in countersurveillance, which made remaining undetected challenging. Assuming they paid attention.

To make his job easier, he'd checked out a Honda CR-V, the most commonly owned automobile in Virginia. He'd requested it in dark blue, because the color blended with the sky during the day and appeared black at night. Black would have been harder to see, but people made subconscious associations between black-colored cars and danger. The combination of an unremarkable make, model, and color gave Bashir a slight advantage. Why didn't every case officer incorporate behavioral economics and social psychology into operational planning?

Bashir paused at a stop sign as Meili and Nathan turned right at the next block. They were probably heading back to the office after meeting that old guy. Why was Nathan with her? Had they met a source who had terrorism information? Meili would have told the team about a terror connection, but she hadn't mentioned the meeting. Bashir would pass the address to Hamilton.

Traffic sucked, as always around DC, but this time, it benefited him. He stayed about eight cars back, close enough to see Meili head back the way they'd come. He'd close the gap on the Parkway.

Meili took the ramp at the Francis Scott Key Bridge instead of continuing east to the Fourteenth Street Bridge, which would have delivered them to the FBI building. Getting off in Georgetown would take longer, especially with the lunch crowd on the streets. Meili would know midday traffic was worse than rush hour.

He followed them across the Potomac onto the Whitehurst Freeway that paralleled the river. Bashir closed the gap to three cars in the stop-and-go traffic. If Meili made it through a light and left him stuck at an intersection, he'd lose them.

They continued east on K Street NW, and Meili slowed as if looking for a parking spot. Bashir double-parked. Meili continued east, and he drummed his fingers on the steering wheel to release his tension. Had he misjudged her intentions?

Meili stopped and parallel parked near the corner of Nineteenth Street, five blocks from the White House. Bashir waited for them to disembark to make sure they weren't heading his way. They walked east, and he tossed his official plaque on the dashboard. He'd get a ticket anyway, but it might dissuade the parking Nazis from towing him.

Bashir hurried after them, passing a homeless old man with soiled skin and dirt under his fingernails. He crossed the street, four lanes of traffic plus two access lanes, and followed from the opposite side. Cops only tailed from directly behind in the movies. Meili and Nathan stopped and looked around. Bashir bent to tie his shoe.

He counted to five then straightened. Meili and Nathan jogged across the street. Where to hide? Bashir moved to an ATM. He reached for his wallet and snuck a glance up the street.

Nathan held the door to a business for Meili, and they disappeared inside. Bashir walked past and noted the address of the building, some kind of office space. He ducked out of sight and pulled out his phone. A quick check of Google showed a variety of businesses in the building. If they hadn't known him, he would have gone inside. He'd identify whoever they were meeting later.

What was Meili doing, and why bring Nathan instead of an agent from the group? Was she concerned about leaks or was it related to one of Nathan's cases? Bashir would acquire a list of Nathan's recent investigations. Or maybe it was something else. The shimmer in Meili's eyes had been unmistakable.

She had feelings for Nathan.

19

Dr. Camilla Reyes inspected Meili's and Nathan's credentials then led them into her office at Aura Research Associates on K Street NW. She worked in a chaotic wilderness, where books, reports, and graphs covered every surface like insulation. The only object not buried in paper was a desktop computer with extra monitors attached like wings.

"As I explained over the telephone," Meili said, "we're investigating the possibility a high-energy weapon was responsible for the anomalous health incidents affecting our diplomats overseas."

"I've been warning about this since 2016," Reyes said, "but nobody's listening."

"We are," Meili said. "I read your article in *Scientific Researcher*, which is why we're here."

Nathan glanced at Meili. Her thoroughness as an investigator had turned up several experts and witnesses that everyone else had overlooked.

"I'm late for a meeting," Reyes said. "Is this urgent?"

"We only need ten minutes," Meili said.

Reyes checked the clock and sighed. "Five minutes." She remained standing.

"Your article laid out a convincing argument that man-made weapons are behind the incidents at our embassies," Meili said.

"I have to ask," Reyes said, "why are you coming here now? Nobody in government has taken my thesis seriously."

"I'm sure that's not true. We—"

"DOD even blocked my peer-reviewed article about the history of mind control."

"We're here," Meili said, "and we're interested."

"I feel like I'm spinning my wheels talking to the government. Honestly, it's—"

Nathan stepped forward. "Please share your theory with us. They attacked my wife in the Dominican Republic earlier this week. I'm desperate."

Reyes cocked her head and tapped her tongue against her front teeth. She looked at her phone again then dug through a pile of papers. She handed a document to Nathan. "You can read the details of my theory in this unpublished draft, but please don't share it until it's been peer-reviewed."

"I just joined the investigation," he said, "and I'd appreciate the CliffsNotes."

"I believe there've been tremendous advances in directed-energy weapons in recent years," Reyes said. "The complexity and refinement of the technology terrifies me. I sounded the alarm, but nobody in government seems worried. That'll change soon."

"A weapon causes Havana Syndrome?" Nathan asked.

"The symptoms we're witnessing are what we'd expect to encounter with a directed-energy weapon."

"How about a microwave?" Meili asked.

"It's possible, but my money's on high-energy radio waves. The Soviets claimed they ceased microwave weapon research after a diplomatic kerfuffle in the seventies, but I'm skeptical. Russia's still developing neurological weapons. China too.

"Why?" Meili asked.

"To attack the enemy without triggering a nuclear exchange. To kill without accountability. A massive lead in this technology could be a game changer. Analyzing military strategy is outside my expertise, but whatever the motives, we've seen a resurgence of interest in energy weapons research. The world is racing to find the deadliest weapon. Even us."

"I thought the US government shelved their research," Meili said.

"That's what they claimed back in the nineties, but then they developed MEDUSA."

"MEDUSA?" Nathan asked.

Reyes sighed, like a professor tutoring a slow student. "Mob Excess Deterrent Using Silent Audio. Leave it to the military to create that acronym."

"I don't know MEDUSA either," Meili said.

"We're groping around in the dark," Nathan said.

"You're not working in the field, but since you're FBI and these attacks are targeting our people, you'd think the military would brief you."

"We've had briefings from the intel community and a liaison assigned," Meili said, "but nobody mentioned MEDUSA."

Reyes walked around her desk and dropped into a chair with an exoskeleton design. "MEDUSA was a 2004 prototype weapon designed to incapacitate personnel. It used microwave auditory effect to render targets ineffective."

"To kill? Nathan asked.

"Disable. Low-energy pulses disorient personnel and are designed as less-than-lethal. Theoretically, law enforcement could use it to disperse violent crowds."

"Has it been used?" Meili asked.

"Contact DOD for that answer. I only mention it because the project's existence is publicly available and not classified. My point is the government built prototypes for portable devices using sound waves years after they claimed they'd suspended research."

"How do you know this?" Nathan asked.

"Besides my access to classified programs? The scientific community is collaborative, despite nation-state antagonisms. Sometimes, I can deduce more about what laboratories are researching by the questions scientists don't ask. Everyone's refining microwave technology to facilitate better mobility. It's the ultimate covert weapon."

"What makes it special?"

"Invisible attacks from a distance leave no residual evidence."

"Other than a trail of damaged victims," Meili said. She glanced at Nathan. "Sorry."

"Don't apologize. You're right."

"How's your wife's condition?" Reyes asked.

"Not great. The usual symptoms."

Reyes nodded and chewed on the end of her pen, lost in thought. "The question you should ask is why was she targeted? This is a sophisticated weapon and a most highly guarded secret of whichever nation is behind it. For them to risk exposure to attack your wife, they must have determined whatever they gained from removing her from the playing field was worth the risk."

Why hadn't he thought of that? Nathan had been so focused on viewing the group of victims as a whole that he hadn't considered what made Reagan a target, other than her diplomatic status. He needed to know what she'd been working on. And fast.

Reyes stood up. "I need to go."

"Please, just a few more minutes," Meili said.

"I've been through all this with you people already," Reyes said.

"Excuse me?" Meili asked.

"I told the FBI everything I know about wave weaponry a few weeks ago. I shouldn't have agreed to cooperate considering the Feds blocked my latest article in *Scientific Researcher*."

"Which article?" Nathan asked.

"About my thesis that a foreign government is behind the attacks. I—"

"Hold on," Meili said. "Who did you speak with at FBI?"

Reyes rolled her eyes up in thought. "Agents Smith and Jones. I remember thinking how silly those names were, how perfect for federal agents from a soulless bureaucracy. Sorry, that was rude."

"When did they interview you?" Meili asked.

Reyes picked her phone off the desk and scrolled through it. "March third. They called and then came over."

"Which number did they call from?" Meili asked.

Reyes scrolled through her phone. "The number came up as private."

"Please give me the exact time of the call," Meili said.

"Two forty-six. Is there a problem?"

"I supervise the FBI team investigating Havana Syndrome, and we never contacted you."

"But—"

"And we have no agents named Smith and Jones."

20

Nathan held the lobby door open, and Meili walked out of Dr. Reyes's building onto the sidewalk. The sweet odor of carbon monoxide hung on the crisp air as traffic inched down the street.

Meili stopped and scowled. "Who were those agents who interviewed her?"

"If they were agents."

"Who else would want to interview a think-tank researcher about sonic weapons?"

Nathan rubbed his chin. "Could be anyone. Russians?"

"Why would Russian agents risk posing as FBI agents?"

"Why would they attack our embassy personnel?"

She tapped her foot and frowned.

"You don't look happy," Nathan said. "But contacting Dr. Reyes was smart. We're onto something."

"I'm glad we spoke to her, it's just that . . ."

"What?"

"We need to be objective. People toss conspiracy theories around without a thought to consequences, but we're the FBI, and we're supposed to be driven by evidence."

"Dr. Reyes just gave a witness statement about two people claiming to be FBI. That's evidence."

"They could have been agents from another division, or from our Fly Teams, or from the DOJ. I'll check when we get back, but we can't jump to conclusions."

"There's a chasm between jumping to conclusions and being blind to reality," Nathan said. "Someone interviewed Dr. Reyes, and I want to learn why. What if her theories came too close to the truth?"

Meili ran her fingers through her hair. "That's not the only thing bothering me. I'm not convinced these anomalous incidents aren't psychological."

"You're kidding. What about—"

"There's a long history of mass psychosis and psychogenic illness."

Nathan rested his hands on his hips. "An intelligence panel found external source theories to be plausible, and high-energy weapons would cause the effects we're seeing."

"They're guessing, just like us."

Nathan's spine tingled. He scanned the area. Something wasn't right.

"Problem?" Meili asked.

"I thought I saw something."

"What?"

"I don't know. A face in the crowd, maybe. I had a moment of déjà vu or subconscious recognition."

"What are you talking about?" Meili asked.

"Instinct. Something I saw tickled my consciousness, but I was focused on you and not aware of our surroundings."

"What did you see?"

Nathan scanned the crowd. A woman pushing a stroller, two businesspeople fast-walking, a student sipping a coffee, a homeless man in a Hawaiian shirt. "I don't know, but I've learned to pay attention to my gut and not ignore my feelings."

Meili laid her hand on his arm. "Are you okay?"

He turned back to her. "I'm fine. Continue."

"I'm saying, we've spoken to two scientists today, and one thinks sonic waves are responsible and the other blames microwaves."

"But both agree high-energy weapons are responsible."

"Everyone has a theory," Meili said. "The CIA has a massive team on this, and their consensus is psychogenic causes."

"Their report admitted they couldn't eliminate pulsed electromagnetic energy."

"And we shouldn't eliminate that as a possibility, but I'm afraid you're married to your theory, which will skew how you interpret evidence. Right now, the intel community is leaning toward a psychological cause."

"My wife's not a lunatic."

"I'm not saying that. I—"

Meili's phone rang, cutting her off. She answered, and her eyes widened. "Oh my God... yes, I understand... I'll get my team to Dover. We can make that flight and be in Tallinn by tomorrow."

Nathan raised his eyebrows, and she shook her head.

She listened for a moment. "Will do." She hung up.

"What happened?"

"Another anomalous health incident," Meili said. "A bad one."

"Where?"

"Estonia. At the embassy in Tallinn. Word's coming in now, and it may be the worst incident yet."

"Worst how?"

"Highest casualties," she said. "Six DEA agents, two FBI, and at least four from the State Department. They were in a conference room meeting about a transnational criminal group. I assume one of those State officials was CIA. They'd want to be involved."

"Shit," Nathan said. "When did this happen?"

"Details are sketchy. The deputy chief of mission just reported it to HQ, and they contacted Mark Dalton, my ASAC. He wants my team on the ground immediately."

"I've flown into Eastern Europe a few times, and it's a pain in the ass getting anywhere east of Germany. You'll go through Frankfurt or de Gaulle and then catch something smaller into Tallinn. Last time I visited Estonia, we flew to Finland and took a ferry across the gulf.

"I don't think you understand the importance of this case right now. The SAC—"

"I don't understand? Are you kidding me?"

"I didn't mean that," Meili said. "There's significant political heat on my chain of command. The White House has been pressuring the director to get evidence of Russian involvement. They've loosened the purse strings and given us carte blanche."

"About time," Nathan said. "Maybe now we'll get some answers."

"They've got a private jet landing at Dover Air Force Base. They leased it for an extradition from Portugal, but this takes priority. I'll add those agents to the list of people pissed at me. I'm supposed to get my team there by this evening. It's a Gulfstream, so we'll fly direct to Tallinn."

"Get me on that jet," Nathan said.

"You're not assigned to this case. It's one thing to let you jump in my B-ride and another to fly you outside the country on a government charter."

"I'm familiar with the process," Nathan said. "We've done it with ISIS suspects. You'll hand the charter company a stack of passports and will climb onto the plane with our gear. No one will question the name of one of the FBI agents."

"And when we get to Tallinn?"

"The cops over there are good guys. I'll call my contact in their counterterrorism department if customs gives me a hard time."

Meili's eyes shimmered, as though she suppressed a smile. "I'd love to have you with us, but we'll both get screwed if the Estonians make a scene."

"We make a good team," Nathan said, "and I can help over there. I know how to talk to cops."

"Tell me you suspect a terror connection."

"I can't rule it out."

Meili shook her head. "You're a bad influence. Pack for at least three days and meet me outside my office. I've got to scramble my team."

Three days? Rahimya expected him back in three days. Fuck it. He wouldn't lose this chance.

"Thanks, Meili. You won't regret it."

"I already do."

21

Reagan lay in bed and stared out the window at thin branches on a leafless tree in Vince's backyard. The suburbs made her claustrophobic. The neighbor's houses lingered just out of view, all probably vacant in the middle of a workday, like Vince's house should be. But there she was. In her boyfriend's house.

Boyfriend.

God, she was too old to call someone that. She had been married with a child and—no, she was still married, and Amelia needed her. Why hadn't Nathan followed her to Santo Domingo? Vince seemed far more interested in her career. Of course, he wasn't there now either, having returned to the Caribbean to handle a crisis. She'd promised him she'd be fine staying alone, but her damn symptoms made everything difficult.

She removed her earbuds and glanced at the laptop. What had she been listening to last night to help her sleep? Her mind was foggy, and her memory, shot. Whatever she'd been playing, it hadn't stopped her nightmares. An image of her colleagues staring at her on the floor flashed in her mind. She shivered and shook it away.

Her phone dinged, and she snatched it off the nightstand.

A text from Nathan. *I'm checking in. Any better?*

She answered. *Still shitty.*

I need to talk to you.

Reagan sighed. Another relationship conversation was the last thing she wanted. Why couldn't Nathan accept the situation and move on?

She answered. *Not up for it.*

He responded immediately. *It's about the investigation.*

She sighed. *Fine.*

I'm out front. See you in a minute.

Just like Nathan to text from her driveway. No warning. She sat up, and the world oscillated around her. She slid out of bed. The house tilted, threatening to capsize like a ship, then it righted itself. She pulled her terry-cloth bathrobe off a hook on the closet door and wrapped it around her. The gift from Vince warmed her like his embrace.

She plodded downstairs, holding the banister for support, and opened the door. Nathan trudged up the path. He saw her, and empathy hung on his face like a mask. She must look awful.

"How you feeling?" he asked.

"Crappy. I've had bad vertigo for days, not that there's a good version of it, and my headache won't go away."

"Any improvement?"

"My doctor classified this as a traumatic brain injury."

"Crap. I'm sorry. At least they know the treatment protocol."

"I scheduled rehab."

"How's Vince?"

She pursed her lips. "You really want to know?"

"I'm making an effort here."

Her eyes softened. Hard to be angry when he was trying. She stepped aside. "Come in."

She escorted him into the living room. A dozen pillows covered the couch, a weird, almost feminine design choice Vince had made. "I appreciate you checking on me. Vince's been working long hours, and I'm alone most of the time."

"What time will he be home?" Nathan asked.

"Not for two days. He flew to the DR to put out a fire and—"

"You're here alone?"

Reagan brushed the pillows aside and curled up on the couch. The motion rocked her stomach. "A State Department nurse comes every two days, and I have my doctor's number. Puttering around by myself is the problem. If I wasn't crazy before, I am now."

Nathan settled beside her. "Listen to me. You're not crazy."

"I know that. It's just . . . I keep replaying what happened on a continuous loop."

"You experienced serious trauma. It's natural to have anxiety."

"PTSD?"

"Someone attacked you, and you're experiencing a normal stress response, not a psychological disorder."

Reagan bit her lip. "Who's to say? Maybe I imagined the whole thing. My brain's so foggy since the incident, and my short-term memory is terrible. I—" Her breath caught, and she suppressed a cry.

Nathan touched her knee. She looked at it and pulled her leg away.

He withdrew his hand. "You didn't imagine what happened to you. It's real. That's why I'm here."

"You found something?" Reagan snatched a tissue out of a box on the coffee table and dabbed her eyes. Sitting close to him felt familiar. She'd hardly seen him in six months, and his proximity flooded her with emotion. He wanted her, but he might also want to strangle her.

Nathan stood and paced. "I believe an adversary attacked you with either a sonic or microwave weapon. Russians are the most likely suspects, either SVR or GRU."

Reagan straightened. "Why me?"

"You're new to the embassy, so it's unlikely they targeted you because you're effective."

She scowled. "Excuse me?"

"I meant you haven't been there long enough to become a superstar and draw their attention. Am I wrong?"

She pressed her lips together then looked away. "I see what you're saying."

"Were you doing anything in Santo Domingo that would motivate Russians to knock you out of the game? How would they benefit from sidelining you?"

She fondled the gold locket dangling from her neck—jewelry Nathan had given her. "I was working on a report about China's growing influence in the Dominican Republic."

"That doesn't mesh with my Russian theory."

"The Chinese are expanding their footprint across the Caribbean and Central America. Their fingers are in every economic pie."

"What about the Russians?"

"They're a regional threat. Their foothold in Cuba has been a challenge since they ousted Bautista in fifty-nine. The communists took over in sixty-five as an outgrowth of the Cuban socialist movement. The Soviet's Comintern, Communist International, was command and control back then, and the Soviets dug in after the revolution."

"Is China working with the Russians in Santo Domingo?"

"They're both communist countries with many decades of cooperation, but only on certain issues. Even ideologically, Stalinism and Maoism are different."

"Russia hasn't been communist since the Soviet Union collapsed," Nathan said.

Reagan smiled. Nathan was out of his depth dealing with Russians. He seemed innocent. Cute. "Russia's an autocracy, another form of totalitarianism. Autocrats rule the country like the Politburo did, and Putin wants to restore the former Soviet empire. They're all collectivists."

"Is Russia helping China increase their influence in the DR?"

"I've seen no evidence of that. And my report didn't even mention Russia. They're both our competitors, but China's making the deepest inroads in the Caribbean."

"Adversaries," Nathan said.

Reagan raised her eyebrows. "Excuse me?"

"Russia and China are enemies, not competitors."

Reagan grinned. "Many people at State disagree with you."

"State never recognizes threats until it's too late." Nathan rubbed his face.

"You look exhausted," she said.

"The FBI's been investigating Havana Syndrome for years. What makes me think I can solve the riddle?"

"It's not your responsibility."

Nathan scowled. "I don't see it like that. I don't know, maybe it's hubris. Or desperation."

She hadn't solicited his help, but his protection provided a sense of security. Was she leading him on? His involvement was fine as long as he didn't get any romantic ideas. Maybe she should keep him at arm's length.

"I can take care of myself."

"You'll need to for a few days. I'll be out of town. I arranged for a sitter to watch Amelia."

Guilt stabbed her chest. She should care for Amelia while Nathan was gone, but her health wouldn't allow it. "An official trip?"

"There's been another attack. I'm tagging along with the response team. I just hope there's time to stop whatever the hell is happening."

22

Nathan slung his rucksack over his shoulder and climbed down the portable stairway pressed against the Gulfstream's fuselage. Aluminum steps creaked under the weight of the seven FBI agents and their gear. Chest-high snowbanks enclosed Lennart Meri Tallinn airport like castle walls, and a fresh dusting covered the tarmac. The temperature hovered below freezing, as an icy wind blew off the Gulf of Finland and pelted him with crystals. The air smelled wet and fresh, like a snow cone.

He followed Meili as she plodded across the tarmac to a waiting line of SUVs. She looked burned out. He did too. The long trip and the time difference tortured his body. The jet had traveled slower than commercial aircraft, but at least they'd had a direct flight. Cold seeped into his knee, flaring memories of his brutal fight to the death with a Haqqani Network operative in Jalalabad.

Nathan slid into the back seat beside Meili in the first SUV, drawing a scowl from Tyrone, the team's senior agent. Tyrone tossed his pack inside and squeezed into the third row.

"Welcome, Agent Chan," the driver said with a toothy grin. "To the hotel?"

"Please take us to the US Embassy," Meili said.

"Embassy?" Tyrone asked. "Let's drop our bags at the hotel and grab quick showers."

"We're already coming into this late," Meili said. "We need to hit the ground running."

Tyrone sighed. "Then let's interview victims at the hospital."

"We'll start at the embassy," Meili said.

The driver dropped the vehicle into gear, and they roared down the airport access road onto Tartu Maantee, the highway leading into the city.

"The attack happened almost two days ago," Tyrone said. "The only evidence will come from victim interviews."

"Doctors are treating them," Meili said, "and even if we can steal a few minutes, the patients will be disoriented. We can talk to them tomorrow, give them time to recover."

"Any evidence at the embassy will still be there tomorrow," Tyrone said.

"I agree with Meili," Nathan said, drawing a scowl from Tyrone. "A sonic or microwave attack would mean the weapon had to be close. We should search the surrounding buildings."

Meili rolled her eyes. "You're supposed to sit back and observe."

"You brought me to help."

"I've responded to a dozen of these attacks, and I know what I'm doing. I'll assign two people to interview uninjured witnesses, have someone copy and review the security footage to look for trucks or vans parked nearby during the attack, and have the rest of the team search buildings in proximity to the embassy."

"Sounds good, boss," Nathan said.

The driver glanced at Meili

"US Embassy," she said.

Tyrone leaned back in his seat and crossed his arms over his chest.

They wormed through city streets, then parked near the embassy on Kentmanni, inside the highway that circled the modern downtown section. The old city, known as Vanalinn, lay to the north and abutted Tallinn Bay. The Estonians had blocked the area around the embassy to vehicular traffic, so the team disembarked and hoofed it down the snowy street. A brisk wind chilled Nathan's skin.

The five-story, gray-brick embassy blended into the surrounding vintage residential and office buildings, except for its modern glass entrance that jutted out like a glass box. Two uniformed officers from the Police and Border Guard stood near the entrance beside a heavyset man in plainclothes—probably a detective from the Central Criminal Police, a unit Nathan had worked with on a terrorism case.

"Getting everyone through security will take forever," Meili said. "Wait here, and I'll touch base with the LEGAT."

Meili and Tyrone went inside while Nathan stood in the cold with five other FBI agents. One of the Estonian police officers nodded at him, and Nathan waved.

Ten minutes later, about the time stomping his feet no longer warmed them, Meili and Tyrone exited the embassy. Meili spoke to the plainclothes detective then joined them. She ordered the agents to head inside to start witness interviews, then she turned to Nathan.

"You and Tyrone shadow the police while they canvass the neighborhood, but only observe and report."

"Got it, boss," Nathan said. He turned to go.

"I'm not your boss," Meili said. "And Nathan?"

He stopped and looked at her.

"Don't get into trouble."

23

Nathan and Tyrone introduced themselves to Estonian Police Lieutenant Marcus Tamm, a detective from the Organized Crime Bureau, and two patrol officers detailed to assist with the search.

"This is, how you say, wasted the time?" Tamm said.

Tyrone nodded. "We haven't found evidence at a single anomalous health incident scene. Not one."

Nathan cleared his throat. "Intel identified a van belonging to the GRU outside the Moscow Embassy before the attack."

Tyrone brows knitted together. "No proven connection."

"GRU, SVD, they all KGB to me," Tamm said. "Once KGB, always KGB."

"The KGB hasn't existed as an agency for over thirty years," Tyrone said.

"Changing name does not give you new heart," Tamm said. "A black heart is forever."

The imagery Estonians used in their language could have come from Russian literature. Did Tamm realize that? But he was right. The agency names changed, as did the propaganda, but the same people staffed them. Russia had accepted a level of capitalism, but the lack of individual rights and the collective willingness of the people to submit to authority had led to oligarchy, and leaders exerted the same control the Communist Party had exercised for generations. Freedom only existed for the elite.

"Looking for evidence isn't a waste of time," Nathan said. "Even if we come up empty, finding nothing tells us something too."

"Ha," Tamm laughed. "There is famous American optimism. You should live here. Estonian winter kills hope."

Nathan surveyed the street. The employees affected with acute symptoms had occupied the executive conference room at the back of the embassy. "We'll have to search every building, but our highest probability of finding something will be opposite the Northwestern rear wall.

"Like it matters," Tyrone grumbled.

"Let's get starting, eh?" Tamm said. "My balls make ice cube."

"Where's that Estonian winter toughness?" Nathan asked.

Tamm threw a playful punch into Nathan's shoulder. "I like you, my American friend. Tonight, you buy lager."

Despite the bone-chilling wind, jet lag, and urgency, Nathan smiled. Cops were the best people. Well, in most places. Officers who faced human depravity were under no illusions about the good and evil that resided in all men. They saw reality.

"It would be my pleasure," Nathan said. "Let's begin before I make ice cubes too."

"Ha," Tamm laughed and slapped Nathan on the back.

They walked past a long row of connected buildings to the embassy's rear wall. Large shrubs, outbuildings, and cement walls surrounded the courtyard. Nearby structures looked like apartment buildings.

"We start there," Tamm said and pointed at the closest building.

"Let's get this shit over with," Tyrone said. He followed Tamm and the two uniformed officers toward the entrance.

Nathan regarded the embassy. The conference room was on the fourth floor, which meant a high-energy sonic blast needed to penetrate the courtyard wall unless someone positioned it high in a nearby building. He scanned the surrounding neighborhood. Three buildings behind the embassy afforded a view over the courtyard walls.

"Hold up a minute," Nathan said. He waited for Tamm and the others to stop then walked around the courtyard and surveyed the buildings again. A laser weapon above the second floor in any of those buildings could angle up and have an unobstructed view of the conference room windows. "Let's try this one first. It makes the most sense."

"Don't matter," Tyrone said.

"Yes, good," Tamm said. "Now we do Yankee policing. We don't use psychics in Tallinn."

"Funny," Nathan said. "Remember, I'm the guy buying your beer."

"Come," Tamm said. "We go." He hurried to the building and yanked open a wooden door on the ground floor. They entered a narrow, poorly lit hallway. Tamm pointed down the hallway and yelled orders to the officers in Estonian. Tamm's accent had notes of Võro, a language spoken in southeastern Estonia. A police captain Nathan had worked with years ago on an al-Qaeda investigation had the same accent. The officers walked toward the last door.

"We divide and make faster, yes?" Tamm asked.

Separating would accomplish the mission faster, for sure, but not being present to see every apartment with his own eyes created pressure in his temples. Did he have control issues or a lack of trust in the Estonians? They were as competent as American police departments, but relying on others came hard.

Nathan nodded.

Tyrone joined the officers in the hallway, and Nathan accompanied Tamm to the door opposite them. Tamm banged on a wooden door, and a moment later, an ancient, hobbit-sized woman swung it open. She wore a fabric dress with colorful patterns that looked homemade.

"*Jah?*" she asked.

Tamm questioned her in incomprehensible Estonian, then he turned to Nathan and shrugged his shoulders. "No visitors. Nothing unusual. No strangers in the building or trucks parked outside."

"Can we look inside?" Nathan asked.

Tamm rolled his eyes, then he spoke to the woman again. She frowned but swung open the door and stepped aside. Tamm bowed and gestured inside.

"Thanks, Lieutenant," Nathan said and entered. The apartment was tiny but uncluttered. Photographs of family members, probably dating back generations, littered every wooden surface. Nathan hurried across the room, feeling like an intruder, which of course he was, and poked his head into a doorway. The bedroom was small enough to be a closet, and its windows looked as if they hadn't been opened in years. Nathan walked past the old lady's icy stare and out into the hallway.

Tamm joined him a moment later. "Perhaps she KGB." He smirked.

"Maybe you're SVD."

Tamm narrowed his eyes and muttered something in Estonian. He stormed down the hallway then looked back over his shoulder. "Come."

Nathan followed him up a rickety staircase to the second floor. They checked the apartments there and repeated the scene twice on the third floor and once again on the fourth. Tyrone looked increasingly annoyed as the fruitless interviews continued. But it had to be done.

Nathan followed Tamm to the last apartment. After this, they had two more buildings to inspect, then they would conduct a cursory check of another half dozen structures farther away. Nathan grimaced as his calves cramped from the interminable days of travel.

"No fun, Yankee policeman?" Tamm asked. "You tell me when it time for lager."

"Hey, he's not in charge," Tyrone said as he followed the other officers down the fourth-floor hallway.

"No?" Tamm asked with gleaming eyes. He banged on the door and waited. Nothing. He banged again. No answer. "That's it for this building."

"Can you ask the super to let us in?" Nathan asked.

"Super?"

"Superintendent. The owner. Someone with a key."

"This building private," Tamm said. "They own. No manager. We need judge to give access."

"Shit," Nathan said.

"Come," Tamm said. He walked down the hallway toward the stairs.

The faster they finished, the sooner they'd start drinking beer, which sounded better and better as fatigue set in. But being thorough was simply good police work. They could leave a business card or ask the neighbors if they knew how to reach the owner. Or—

What was that smell?

Nathan sniffed his shirt. He stank from the long trip, but that wasn't the scent he smelled. The odor was sweet, familiar.

Tamm paused halfway down the hall and shot him a quizzical expression. Nathan held up a finger for him to wait, then he leaned close to the door and inhaled.

The odor came from the apartment. Rich and organic. And something else. An acrid sent. Metallic.

Blood.

24

The odor of death filled Nathan's sinuses. He locked eyes with Tamm and shook his head.

Tamm saw his expression and tromped back down the corridor. "What is it? The joviality had gone from his voice. All business.

"Smell," Nathan said.

Tamm's forehead wrinkled, and he put his nose close to the doorjamb. His nostrils flared. His face hardened to stone as he turned to Nathan. "A body."

Nathan nodded. "Can you call that judge now?"

Tamm snorted. He stepped back and kicked the door with the heel of his shoe, just above the knob. The wood frame shattered, and the heavy oak door swung in. Copper pieces of the locking mechanism clanged against the floor.

Tamm peered inside then reached inside his jacket and pulled out a Tokarev, a cheap Russian-made handgun.

Nathan peeked around the threshold too. The reason for the gun was obvious. A lake of blood covered the living room floor and spread out between the bodies of a middle-aged man and woman.

Tamm darted into the room with his gun extended. He swept the corners with his barrel as he moved toward the back corridor. Nathan followed. Why had the FBI not obtained permission for them to carry firearms?

Tamm swept through an empty bedroom and then moved to the last room. He entered and a gasp escaped his lips. Nathan sidestepped to see around him. His heart skipped a beat.

The bodies of two children lay on the bed, their throats slit from ear to ear. They remained tucked under the covers, wearing pajamas. If not for the blood-darkened blankets and the smell, it would have been possible to believe they were asleep.

Tamm stomped into the sitting room. He paused at the front door and hunched over. Was he going to throw up? No judgments. When kids were involved, everyone became human.

Tamm recovered and glowered at Nathan.

"Bad stuff," Nathan said. There was nothing else to say.

Tamm stuck his head out the doorway and shouted for the other officers. Boots thudded down the hallway.

Nathan looked back at the crime scene. The couple on the floor wore nightclothes too. Whoever did this had come the previous night. Had the man's employers missed him at work? Had anyone noted the children's absence from school?

Nathan stepped around the bodies, careful not to disturb the scene. He shouldn't be in there at all, but he had one chance for a firsthand look before Estonian homicide detectives arrived. He leaned in close and inspected the corpses.

Both lay on their backs, and each had a single bullet hole in their forehead. The back of the woman's skull was missing where fragments had taken out a large section of bone. The man had no visible exit wound, which meant the bullet had bounced around inside, turning his brain into oatmeal. A small-caliber bullet.

So much blood.

"Come out," Tamm called from the door. Tyrone and the other police officers peered around him.

"One minute," Nathan said.

Nathan squatted and studied the man. Blood caked the front of his shirt, even though it didn't touch the floor. There were two small tears in the fabric above his left nipple. They had shot him three times, which might make him the second victim. He had watched as his wife was killed, then he'd fought back. Two to the chest, one to the head. A standard special forces grouping.

"This is not your business," Tamm said. "Out, please."

"Okay." Nathan stood and stretched his back.

Were these murders related to the Havana Syndrome? What were the chances of mass murder within sight of the embassy at the same time US personnel were stricken with illness? These deaths must be part of it.

"Don't fuck evidence," Tamm said from the doorway. Tyrone peeked over his shoulder.

Nathan's eyes dropped to the floor. He froze.

Two long scratch marks, about six feet apart, had gouged the wooden flooring close to the window. Nathan inspected the glass.

"Yankee, stop. Come now."

Nathan ignored him. The window was unlatched, unlike the others, and someone had removed the screen. Something heavy had been positioned in front of the window.

But what?

25

Bashir followed Trent Hamilton into the national security advisor's White House office and closed the door behind them.

"What the hell's the FBI doing?" Frederick Richardson asked from behind his desk. He made no move to rise.

"Bashir's been with them every step of the way," Hamilton said. "After Tallinn, most line agents think it was an attack."

"*Think?*" Richardson said. He didn't yell, but the tone of his voice sent a chill up Bashir's spine. "They've been investigating this for years, and you are reporting agents' intuition?" He turned to Bashir. "Can't you talk?"

"I wasn't asked to travel to Estonia with Agent Chan," Bashir said. "She was skeptical of the laser theory when she left, but now she's leaning toward it."

"What else do they fucking need?" Richardson said. "The Russians might as well be shooting spies on the embassy steps. Get me the fucking evidence I need."

"Since Agent Burke involved himself, he's been pushing them toward Russian suspects. He seems convinced. He's a bit of a wild card, but he's making progress."

"The FBI needs to get on board with the Russia theory, but once they are, push back a little. Sow doubt. Keep Chan off balance by insinuating people are floating disinformation. I want them moving in the right direction, but I can't have the FBI forcing our hand."

Bashir cleared his throat. "There's still plenty of doubt about Russian involvement with—."

"What does that mean?"

"They've interviewed every victim, surveyed the neighborhood, tasked every source, and they haven't found a link. Nothing tangible."

"We've had evidence Russia's been planning this for decades. What the fuck are you talking about?"

"They've had the technology," Bashir said, "and yes, they've used it before, but there's no direct evidence tying them to these attacks. They're the most obvious suspect, but unsubstantiated theory and credible evidence are different things. Especially when the consequences could be World War III."

26

While Meili met with Estonian homicide detectives, Nathan holed up inside the Tallinn Embassy and found a Secure Telephone Unit to call the States. He checked his notes and dialed Dr. Jakob Mandel.

"Hello?" Jakob's voice sounded rough, full of unfinished dreams.

"Dr. Mandel, Nathan Burke calling."

Scratches and hisses popped over the line while Nathan waited. He glanced at a clock—6:22 a.m. in Washington, DC.

"Sorry to wake you," Nathan said. "Are you there, Doctor?"

"What?"

"You've heard about the anomalous health incident in Estonia?"

"More Russian savagery," Jakob said. "Their boldest move yet."

"I want to ask you—"

The line crackled.

"Where are you calling from?" Jakob inquired with a hint of alarm. "Are you in Tallinn now?"

"I'm calling from the embassy. It's a secure line."

"It's not secure on my end. What can I do for you?"

"We agree on who's behind this," Nathan said. "Civilians are dead. They—"

"What?"

"It won't make mainstream media in the US," Nathan said, "but someone killed a family nearby. I'm certain it's connected. They had two young children—"

"Dear God."

"It's bad. That's why I'm calling. You were involved with this technology for years. Can you provide any guidance? I need to find someone with access to Russian development or operations."

"Be careful what you say," Jakob said. "We shouldn't be talking over the phone."

"My time here's limited," Nathan said. "Estonia is a former Soviet republic. Can you think of anyone here who may help me."

Silence.

"Dr. Mandel?"

"There is someone."

Nathan's heart jumped. "Who?"

"I'm going to create a Gmail account right now," Jakob said. "Write this down. Jakob and Nathan talk at Gmail dot com. The password will be the first name of the agent with you when we met, plus the first three letters of my street. Understand?"

Interesting tradecraft for a weapons researcher.

"Yes."

"I'll start an email and write the name of a person who may agree to speak with you. I'll leave the email in the draft folder of this account. Log in and go into the drafts to read it, then delete the email. When I see that it's gone, I'll know you received it. Use this email and password until you return, then come see me and we'll establish a better process."

"That's clever for a scientist," Nathan said.

"Good luck, Nathan."

The dial tone came through the receiver, and Nathan hung up. How much time did he have before they ordered Meili's team to return? If Jakob's information was accurate, this might be the only chance to get insight into what the Russians planned. The image of the children's faces flashed behind his eyes, and an involuntary shudder passed through him. Geopolitics could be deadly, but killing children went too far, even for the SVD. He wanted a drink. Bad.

The Russians, Estonians, or some other intel service probably intercepted unscrambled calls coming out of the embassy, but were they monitored live? Even if they were, it would take time for a surveillance team to report the information to a case officer who would try to check the Gmail account. How long would it take them to discover Jakob's identity? Nathan had time. At least he hadn't called from the hotel. Host countries always bugged overseas hotels frequented by diplomatic staff.

America's adversaries did too.

Nathan slid behind an unclassified terminal. The FBI's legal attaché had been kind enough to create a temporary visitor account for Meili's team to access the internet. Nathan entered the user password, opened Gmail in a browser, and typed in the information Jakob had given him. The draft folder showed one entry. Jakob had worked fast. There was more to him than met the eye. Nathan opened the email and read Jakob's message.

My chief adversary for twenty years was Timor Balakin. He ran the KGB's high-energy weapons research group. For years, we only knew him as the Bear, but after the collapse of the Soviet Union, he retired from the KGB and lived in Germany. I won't tell you how I learned about him, but after I retired, I used a mutual friend to find him. Maybe it was ego or maybe I needed resolution after too many years of cold war. I met him in Frankfurt, and we had lunch. Two former adversaries of a cold war. We talked for hours, and I can tell you he cares about the science as much as I do. He was not a communist ideologue. Not even close.

I don't know if Timor is still alive or if he still lives in Germany, but if anyone from the other side would help you understand why the Russians murdered children and attacked our people, it's Timor. Delete this email and empty the trash can. If anyone asks, you did not get Timor's name from me. Good luck tracking him down. I hope you stick it to the Russkies.

Nathan stared at the screen. If he could locate the Bear, and if Timor would talk, Nathan might learn what the Russians hoped to achieve. He glanced around the office at State Department employees pecking away at their computers. Everyone seemed on edge after the incident, and no one paid attention to him.

"That crime scene was a mess," Meili said, coming up behind him. "I'll never scrub the faces of those children from my memory."

Nathan shut down the computer and swiveled to face her. "Are the Estonians taking it seriously?"

"Everyone's taking the slaughter of a family seriously."

"I mean, did they connect it to the embassy?"

Meili rolled her eyes. "There's nothing linking those deaths to our incident."

"But the scratches on the floor . . . they could have used a high-energy weapon. They—"

"The police pulled video surveillance footage from surrounding businesses, and Tyrone has copied the embassy security recordings. If there's evidence of a technological attack, we'll adjust, but right now, nothing ties this to Havana Syndrome."

Heat rose in Nathan's face, and he stood. "This was an act of war."

Meili's phone rang.

She answered and pursed her lips like she'd bitten into a lemon. "Yes, boss. I just—" She stared at her shoes. "Uh, huh. I understand, but—" She rubbed her face as she listened. "He's with me now. I know, but—" Meili paced as her supervisor's yelling bled out of the speaker. "Got it. Okay. I will. Yes, sir." She hung up.

"Good news?" Nathan asked.

"Funny. That was my ASAC. He caught your name on the updated manifest. He learned you've been shadowing me."

"How does he know? We just—"

"It doesn't matter how. He's pissed I allowed you inside. He told me to wrap up our interviews today and come back. I've been ordered to cease your involvement immediately."

"Are you in trouble?" Nathan asked.

"I'm not suspended, at least not yet, but this won't be great for my career. Mark was livid. Said he had enough pressure on this thing without me sharing our group's inner workings with an outsider. He made me sound disloyal, like I wasn't on his team."

"Shit. I'm sorry. I never wanted to get you in trouble, and I—"

"Don't worry about me. I'm a big girl. And a group supervisor. I decided to give you access, and I'll take the heat."

"How will we track down—"

"There's no *we*," Meili said. "You're not hearing me. I can't talk to you about our case anymore. You're out."

Nathan shook his head. "I can't accept that. I'm not giving up. Russians attacked our sovereign territory."

"Your assignment is Islamic terrorism in Southwest Asia."

"They injured my wife and ... huh."

Meili cocked her head. "What?"

"The DEA agents were TDY, not stationed here. They weren't threatening Russia, and neither was Reagan. Why risk operations to attack diplomats?"

"That's for my team to solve," Meili said. "Not you."

"I need to protect my wife."

"Let this go."

"I can't."

"You're not getting this. I'm lucky my ASAC didn't suspend me. You should have heard him. And you know what? He's right. I like you. I always have. But this is a sensitive case, and it doesn't involve Islamic terrorism. It's not your lane."

"The day Reagan collapsed, it became my lane."

"This is serious," Meili said. "I'll bet Mark will call your supervisor too. He didn't seem to want to—"

Nathan's phone rang. He pulled it out and looked at the caller ID. Rahimya Nawaz.

"Shit."

27

Nathan leaned against a double-parked CNN news truck and watched a cameraman adjust a tripod to frame the US Embassy in his shot. A reporter who looked familiar stood in the street and read something off a piece of paper, mouthing the words in rehearsal. The press had reported the incident, but they were oblivious to the Russian threat, and they didn't know about the dead children.

Nathan could change that.

Rahimya Nawaz had chewed him out and ordered him home. And Meili's team was packing their gear and heading to the airport within the hour. This was his chance to blow the whistle and warn the world the stakes had risen.

Time to act.

Nathan rubbed his arms to fight off the frigid air and clenched his jaw. He stepped off the curb and strode toward the reporter.

"What do you think you're doing?" Meili shouted.

Nathan stopped and turned.

Meili stomped into the street with her fists balled, either from the cold or rage. "You're not authorized to speak to the press. Hell, you're not part of this investigation."

"The Russians attacked us," Nathan said. "We should be at war."

"If you keep talking like that, you'll get one. Keep spouting hyperbolic rhetoric and you'll start World War III."

"If we don't stop this, our enemies will damage our diplomatic, law enforcement, and intelligence communities. They downgrade our ability to analyze threats and our ability to execute foreign policy will be in shambles."

"Nathan." She grabbed his hands.

He looked down at her. "What?"

"I can't watch you throw your career away like this. You're taking risks for nothing. You—"

"Protecting my wife isn't nothing."

"The damage has been done, and she's not in danger anymore."

"You don't know that."

"No one has been afflicted with this syndrome twice."

"You mean attacked," he said, "and an American family was hit overseas, and then again in Pennsylvania."

"That's still being investigated. It's possible they just experienced a recurrence of the initial trauma."

"That's bullshit, and you know it."

"Why would the Russians risk everything to disrupt our capabilities and—"

"They could be preparing for something bigger."

Meili lowered her voice. "Or it's a natural biological occurrence. Whatever's behind it, victims have been untouched after incidents. Wanting to help Reagan is noble, but you're not protecting her. You're out for revenge."

Nathan looked at the sky. "I'm defending our country too. And so what if I want revenge? Is that wrong? I'm doing this for my wife."

"She's not your wife. Not anymore. She's with another man."

Her words stabbed him like a dagger in the heart. "Reagan doesn't understand what she's doing. She's confused, angry with me for not moving with her. She just needs time. She'll come around."

"Reagan knows what she wants, and it's not you," Meili said. Her eyes widened, and she covered her mouth. "I'm sorry. That sounded harsh."

A weight pressed down on him, as if he carried the world on his shoulders. He'd slept little, and anxiety had taken a toll. He sighed. "She'll come back to me."

"That won't happen. I'm sure she's thought this through. Leaving her family was a big decision. Reagan's with someone else now."

"She was lonely. She made a mistake."

"Having a one-night stand is a mistake. Reagan's living with our legal attaché."

"She's just staying there until she recovers—"

Meili put her finger to his lips to silence him. "You're not listening. Reagan left you, and she's not coming back. She's made her choice. You must move on."

Nathan hung his head. Why couldn't he go back and make things right? How had his life disintegrated so fast?

Meili put her arm around him. "I get this is hard to hear, but you need to accept it. You lost your wife. Don't lose your career in a misguided attempt to win her back."

Nathan sighed. "Dammit."

"Come on. Tyrone will drive you to the airport."

28

Reagan inched up into a sitting position in bed, and the bedroom floor yawed like the deck of a ship. She placed her hands flat on the mattress then steeled herself and slid her feet out from under the covers. No sudden movements. She perched on the mattress and rocked forward until her feet touched the cold wood. She stood.

The room swayed, but less than before. She shuffled into the bathroom and examined herself in the mirror. Her eyes fell to the slight paunch around her midriff. Her weight loss after the initial incident had not lasted long, and her body had returned to normal.

She sighed.

She was thirty-one and feeling it. The lankiness of her youth had disappeared soon after her breasts had appeared and become the object of desire for every boy in high school, but she had maintained her tight waist and toned legs until Amelia arrived. Women didn't like her and often glared with envy, but Reagan didn't care. She hadn't been gifted with good genes—her fitness had come from rising early each morning to run. Then she had added yoga to her routine and improved her diet. Yet her tummy bulge still came.

"Aging is a bitch."

Her phone rang, and she stumbled back into the bedroom to answer it.

"Hey, gorgeous," Vince said.

"I can't wait to see you tonight. It's weird being in your house alone."

"Uh, yeah. About that." He cleared his throat. "The ambo wants me to stick around a little longer."

"How long?"

"Another week."

Reagan closed her eyes and moderated her breathing. "You promised you'd be back today, and I—"

"I told the ambo I needed to get home, but he insisted because of fallout from this latest attack."

An icy wind chilled her body. Her mouth went dry. "What attack?"

"Sorry, I assumed you'd heard. Isn't State keeping you in the loop?"

"Those bastards want me under psychiatric care. They're treating me like a mental patient. Where was the attack?"

"Our embassy in Tallinn."

Reagan put her hand to her mouth. "How many people?"

"A dozen, at least. FBI and DEA agents."

Reagan dropped onto the bed, and the world spun. She grabbed the mattress and gritted her teeth. Dizziness overrode everything, because when the earth moved, nothing else was possible.

She held her breath then let it stream out. She returned the phone to her ear.

"—worried about you. Reagan? Are you there?"

"Sorry. I'm not feeling well."

"Dammit. I wish I could be there with you."

"You said you'd take care of me, but I'm here alone and—"

"That's not fair."

"I left my husband and daughter to be with you, but we're not together. Should I go back home?"

Silence filled the line. She regretted saying that. Her anger, fear, and sorrow had bubbled up without a filter since the incident. What was wrong with her?

"Please don't threaten to leave." His tone had cooled. "I'm the LEGAT, and the ambo needs me to solidify our response protocols and activate our intelligence network to figure out what's happening."

"I'm sorry that sounded like an ultimatum. I realize your job is critical, but can't you do some of it from here?"

"I'm meeting with the DSS tomorrow," he said, referring to the Diplomatic Security Service. "The RSO's out of the country, but he returns soon." RSO stood for Regional Security Officer, the top State official responsible for security at the embassy.

Tears welled in her eyes. "I understand. It's just so hard..."

"I miss you."

"Me too."

"We're okay, then?" he asked.

"I'm fine. Do whatever's necessary to protect our people down there. The attacks are worsening."

"If they're attacks."

Her stomach turned to stone. "Excuse me?"

"There's been talk of mass hysteria and, uh, other causes."

"Mass hysteria?" she asked. "I hadn't given Havana Syndrome a second thought after my onboarding. It was the last thing on my mind."

"They're saying stress is an issue—"

"My stress is caused by people not believing me, or any of the victims."

His breathing came over the line. Cars honked in the background, as the sounds of Santo Domingo penetrated the embassy. "I believe you, kiddo. No one's saying your symptoms aren't real. It's just—"

"If you were here, you'd see they're real."

"I'll be home in a week. I promise."

"Come back as soon as—"

"Hey, I've got to run. The DCM just walked in. Talk soon."

"Okay, I'll—"

The call disconnected.

She sighed and looked around the bedroom. She scratched her elbow, and something wet her fingertips. Spots of blood stained her long-sleeved tee shirt. She pulled up the sleeve and inspected her elbow. The skin had become dry and cracked, and her incessant scratching had opened the wound again. She needed to control her nervous tics.

"Great. Just great."

29

Amelia pushed past Nathan the moment Reagan opened her front door. Nathan's body ached from jet lag and punishing hours in cramped seats.

"Mommy!" Amelia squealed. She wrapped her arms around Reagan.

"Hello, sweetheart," Reagan said. "I've missed you so much." Tear glistened in Reagan's eyes.

Nathan's set his jaw and refused to descend into the familiar haze of self-pity and heartbreak. He needed to conceal his pain from Amelia. His wife had abandoned him, but Amelia had lost her mother, and he'd never experienced that kind of loss.

"It's good to see you together," Nathan said.

Reagan narrowed her eyes with suspicion. He'd meant the comment to sound kind, but it dripped with passive-aggressive innuendo. Amelia didn't release her mother's waist.

Bruno ran inside with his nose to carpet, following invisible scent trails. He wagged his stubby tail, and his entire body shook. He didn't seem bothered to be in Vince's house. Where was his loyalty?

"I meant what I said," Nathan said. "You need more time with Amelia, even if . . . no matter where you're living."

Reagan's scorn seemed to melt away. A tear ran down her cheek, and she turned away.

Nathan shifted uncomfortably. Her mind remained a mystery to him. "Uh, you're sure you'll be okay taking care of Amelia for a few days? I mean, I feel better having someone with you, but if it's too much to handle—"

"We'll take care of each other."

"I need to be in my office when my boss arrives. I've got some explaining to do. Eddie needs help too. He sounded lost when we spoke last night. The sitter I used when I was in Estonia is busy today and tomorrow, and I've relied too much on my elderly neighbor."

"We'll be fine, Daddy," Amelia said. She released Reagan and hugged him.

"I'll miss you," he said. This time, he turned away.

"Come on, Daddy. Time to go to work." Amelia pulled him down the step.

Nathan looked over his shoulder at Reagan, and she gave a reassuring nod.

"Go help Eddie and be careful," Reagan said.

"Call if you don't feel well, or if you—"

"We're fine. It'll be good to spend time together, and it's reassuring to have someone else here. Vince doesn't come back until Mon—"

"Let's talk about that when I pick her up."

Reagan nodded.

Nathan kissed Amelia, then hurried to his car. He didn't want them to see him cry. Why was marriage so hard? Only family problems carried this kind of weight.

And trying to solve the mystery of Havana Syndrome before the attacks escalated into World War III.

30

Rahimya glared at Nathan from behind her desk. She pointed to a chair opposite her. "Shut the door and sit."

"Morning." Nathan's smile felt like a grimace.

He turned to close the door and steeled himself. Fighting for his wife and country was the moral choice, but he'd risked everything to pursue an invisible enemy.

He settled into a chair and waited for the storm.

She glowered at him as if he'd killed her dog. "When did you get back?"

"Early this morning." The trip had beaten him up like ten rounds in the ring.

"You thought jetting to Tallinn was a good idea?"

"I needed to—"

"You told me you were taking care of your wife."

"I've been helping her, sort of. She's, uh . . ." Admitting Reagan lived with another man would crush his ego, but he didn't want to lie. "I've been checking on her."

Rahimya's eyes bore through him. The only sound was air moving through her nose. "You weren't watching your wife from Estonia, and you never asked permission to travel."

"You would have said no."

"Of course I would have rejected that idea. What's worse, you were on sick leave when you attached yourself to that operation. It could've been a diplomatic nightmare."

Nathan raised his hands in surrender. "You're right, but I had to go. The government is ignoring obvious attacks on our personnel and—"

"Not your responsibility, Nathan."

"They hurt my wife, and I can't stand by and watch everyone pretend her injuries are psychological."

Rahimya leaned back, and her face softened for a fleeting moment, then she hardened again. "Traveling on Bureau business without permission is inexcusable. I won't tell you how livid the ASAC was when he called. He said—"

"I don't give a shit what he—"

"Don't speak. Listen. I sympathize with your situation, but I can't allow you to run wild. I won't start disciplinary action. Unfortunately, the ASAC may not be as lenient, and if he refers this to OPR, they'll give you days on the beach without pay."

"I need to know what happened."

"You *need* to get back to work. Help Eddie pursue your ISIS case. If that thing blows up because you're running an unauthorized investigation, you'll lose your job."

Nathan opened his mouth to speak, but Rahimya leaned forward and raised her finger. "I'm serious, Nathan. You may avoid punishment for Tallinn because everyone understands you're upset about your wife, but one more transgression, and I can't guarantee you'll keep your badge. Am I clear?"

"Yes, ma'am."

"Now, get back to your investigation. You've got lost time to make up. Don't let me down."

"I'll get us back on track."

"Bring Eddie in here at nine o'clock tomorrow morning and be ready to brief your plan."

Nathan nodded and left. He'd help Eddie go after those ISIS fucks, but he wouldn't abandon the Havana case. Reagan and his country needed him.

31

Nathan dropped the case file on the conference table and rubbed his eyes. Eddie's reporting on the suspected ISIS group was thin. After Mohammad had introduced Kei to the Islamists, there'd only been two phone calls between Kei and Ghulam, the cell leader. Thankfully, Eddie had recorded them, with Kei's consent.

Nathan grabbed the transcript and leafed through it. Tone was impossible to discern from a written transcript, but Ghulam seemed eager to receive the fake licenses.

"Finished?" Eddie asked as he entered the conference room carrying a stack of expandable folders.

"Is this everything?"

Eddie looked like a puppy caught chewing on sneakers. "I've tried to identify the cell's members, but it's tough. I staked out the apartment where they met for two days, but I didn't recognize anyone coming or going."

"Did you get the pole camera up?"

"They install it tonight, and they'll stream the video to tech. We can watch it live or review the recordings later."

"Good man." Nathan forced a smile. This case required proactive policing—investigative stings always did—and Eddie was green.

"You back to stay?" Eddie asked without making eye contact.

"Rahimya made it pretty clear I can't investigate Havana Syndrome anymore."

Eddie nodded then met Nathan's eyes. "That didn't answer my question."

Nathan smiled. This kid was sharper than he appeared. "I'm still helping to care for Reagan, and I have a couple other things on my plate, but yeah, I'll be around."

"Good to hear, partner. You know, if you need help with anything else you may be working on, I'm here for you."

Nathan glanced at the conference door to make sure they were alone. "I appreciate that, but you don't have enough time on the job to weather a storm. Better stay out of it."

"Don't get fired."

"How about phone tolls? Anything come back?"

"They're in these folders. I also dumped the address for all DMV registrations, utilities, and financial listings, like you suggested. I got a bunch of names, addresses, and vehicles but none of them fit the profile. The apartment where Mohammad met Ghulam is rented by the Med Five Corporation, which is based in Delaware. Their contact info comes back to a law firm."

"Run everything through CTC. Which telephone numbers did you identify?"

"Ghulam's number that he gave Kei, and six others Mohammad used to contact members of the group."

"And?" Nathan asked.

"Mohammad gave me first names to go with the phones, but he thinks they're aliases."

"Jihadi names," Nathan said. "If they're ISIS, they've assumed warrior names."

Eddie handed him a folder. "All the numbers are prepaid drop phones without subscribers."

Nathan flipped open the folder and inspected the toll records. "The company can tell us where the phones were purchased, and we'll check the stores, but they probably used cash. Unless a security camera recorded them buying the phones, we won't find much."

"The phones are a dead end?"

"Hell no," Nathan said. "These guys knew enough to buy drop phones, but they weren't smart enough to only use them once." He flipped through the pages of tolls. "They're calling more than Kei, and based on the other area codes in here, they're calling people outside their group."

Eddie face lit up. "Then these help?"

"You done good, Eddie. Come here, and I'll show you how to analyze these fast." Nathan perched on the edge of his chair and spread out the toll records for the prepaid cell Ghulam had used to call Kei.

Eddie sat beside him and leaned against the table. "Teach me, Yoda."

"Subpoena every number that was in contact with our suspects and ask for subscriber and toll information. We can build a link chart showing numbers they are calling. Run all the overseas numbers though the NSA's classified system. Once we build up enough probable cause, we can apply for wire intercepts. We not there yet, but if we can tie some of their calls into known bad guys and add it to our undercover calls, we should reach the legal threshold."

"Got it."

"And plug every incoming and outgoing number into PenLink. Run frequency reports, but I can tell most calls will be Ghulam's people contacting each other."

"They don't help?"

"They're useful. Look here." Nathan pointed to calls on Thursday morning then flipped back to Wednesday. "The calls were made before dawn, which means Ghulam was home. We have the incoming number, probably another prepaid, and the cell tower number. Check the phone company's service map and pinpoint which side of the tower he's hitting. That'll give us his general area."

"No shit?"

"And look at this," Nathan said. "See how he calls the same number late at night?"

"Yeah."

"Those are probably booty calls. I'll bet you lunch that number's registered to a young woman. Or a young man."

Nathan scrolled through the pages looking for patterns. He found it on page thirty-one. "This is a deal for something nefarious. Like drugs."

"How can you determine that from a call log?" Eddie asked.

"He calls this overseas number at ten thirty at night. That's Lebanon. Half an hour later, he gets an incoming call from the same number. That's probably his controller telling him where he can get whatever it is he wanted. Six minutes later, Ghulam dials a number in New York. That's the contact for drugs, weapons, or whatever. The guy calls back forty-two minutes later. He's telling him when to meet."

"Come on, really?"

Nathan turned the page to the next day's tolls. "See, the New York number's calling in the morning. That's the call to meet. Ghulam calls these other numbers, which I assume are his guys, then he calls New York again three hours later. That's confirmation they picked up the product."

"How could you know that?"

"A decade of experience, but it's not usable in court until we catch one of them and flip them. We need a cooperating witness to explain what happened, then we use the tolls to corroborate their testimony."

"Man, I thought these were useless," Eddie said.

"Wait until you get the other subscriber and toll info back and start charting. We'll uncover their associates fast."

"That's the plan?"

Nathan rubbed his eyes. They were far behind. Unraveling an organization could take months, but they might not have that long. "We need surveillance to bed them down at night. Once we have addresses, I'll feel more comfortable—"

"They haven't returned to the meet house in Chinatown."

"Then have Mohammad set up a face-to-face between Kei and Ghulam. We'll follow whoever shows."

"But we don't have the documents yet."

"Have Kei tell them there was a delay. He can give them a sample. Props will give him credibility. Besides, every time he and Mohammad have a recorded meeting, we improve our evidence." Nathan yawned and checked his watch. "Damn."

"Hot date?" Eddie asked.

"I left Amelia with Reagan."

"Reagan's back home?"

"She's staying with a friend." Nathan closed his eyes and inhaled through his nose. "I need to get Amelia home in time for bed. She has school in the morning, and . . . shit, I haven't taken Bruno out to pee since this morning."

"Bro, you make me glad I'm still single and playing the game. No family, no responsibility."

Nathan grunted. "You're having fun, but once you have a wife and child, you'll look back on these days as shallow and empty."

"I got two ladies lined up this week who'd disagree with you."

"You'll see."

Eddie looked skeptical. "I'll call Mohammad to arrange a meeting. Anything else?"

"This is a sting, right? We're using the lure of documents to identify ISIS cell members and wrap up some of the Red Dragons too. In my experience, the best plan is a simple one. We get a few recorded conversations, then we do a controlled delivery."

"They won't do much time for those charges," Eddie said.

"No, but we'll have something on them if we're forced to act. Maybe we turn somebody into a cooperator or get lucky and catch them armed. Carrying an AK-47 in DC carries a minimum five-year sentence. Worst case, we've identified them and disrupted whatever they're planning."

Eddie rotated his fidget toy between his thumb and forefinger. *Click, click.* "Couldn't we watch them longer?"

"We'll investigate as much as we can, but once we have serious charges, we'll jump. If we wait too long to act, they may execute whatever they're planning. I'd like to stay in the shadows longer, but at some point, it makes sense to take their pieces off the board. Let's identify them before we're forced to show ourselves."

Click, click, click. "I want these guys."

"Me too, but be careful what you wish for."

32

Moonlight illuminated Nathan's home office through the tower's windows as he reclined in his chair and sipped a twelve-year-old Oban. Bruno snored at his feet, and Amelia had gone to sleep hours ago, leaving him alone with his thoughts. Why had the Russians killed an Estonian family? Were the deaths of four people worth gaining a launching pad for a high-energy weapon? And what did they gain by sickening American agents?

His private iPhone glowed and vibrated on his desk. The screen showed a private number.

"Hello?"

"Nathan Burke?" a man asked in a thick Russian accent. "Special Agent Nathan Burke?"

Hair rose on Nathan's neck. "Yes?"

"A mutual friend passed word you wanted to talk to me."

Did he mean Timor Balakin? "Who is this?"

"I'd rather not say over the phone. An old acquaintance, once my enemy, said you had technical questions."

"I didn't give my personal number to anyone."

"I think you understand my reluctance to talk over your FBI phone. Can you meet tomorrow?"

"Where" Nathan asked.

"In front of your Lincoln Memorial, by the Reflecting Pool."

Your. Nathan looked out the window and scanned the street. A couple walked through the park, but the neighborhood remained quiet. Unoccupied vehicles lined the curb.

"You don't want to give me your name, but you're comfortable telling me where to meet?"

"The business has changed. No one's listening anymore. It's all done with algorithms searching for keywords. You are familiar with this, no?"

"What time?"

"I'm an old man. I'm afraid a lifetime of searching for monsters in the night has made me unable to sleep. Come at sunrise."

"How will I recognize you?"

"I'll be the only one not jogging in Spandex." He hung up.

Nathan stared at the phone. How had Timor contacted him? He scrolled to Jakob's number, then paused. Jakob had said he'd ask Timor. It had to be him.

He slipped his cell into his pocket.

33

Bashir turned up his coat collar and headed for Hamilton, who sat on a bench in the interior courtyard at Langley. Dark clouds blotted the sky, and the temperature hung around freezing, cold enough to snow. Having been tasked to the Developmental Section was odd enough, almost as concerning as running a domestic covert operation, but meeting a deputy chief outside was bizarre.

"Good morning," Bashir said.

"Don't sit," Hamilton said. "You don't have time."

"Time for what?"

"Your FBI friend, Agent Burke, is meeting the Russians."

"Excuse me?"

"Burke's been in contact with Timor Balakin, who managed Russia's mind-control experiments."

"That doesn't make sense," Bashir said. "How would Nathan, er, Agent Burke, even know about Balakin?"

Hamilton smirked. "He had help."

Bashir bit his lip and looked to the sky. A snowflake landed on his cheek and melted. "How did you learn about the meeting?"

"Knowing the players is my job."

"Are we eavesdropping on FBI communications?"

Hamilton transformed into an Easter Island statue, and the air chilled between them. Bashir didn't blink. If the CIA intercepted federal agents on American soil and someone outside the agency found out, things would get ugly.

Hamilton broke eye contact. "That would be illegal."

"And unpatriotic," Bashir said. "The FBI's on our side."

Hamilton snorted. "The FBI's been a political tool since their inception. They manufactured their own image of clean-cut G-man fighting crooks."

"I know these people," Bashir said. "They care about our country, and they follow the law."

"Agents do what they're told, but the people giving orders aren't as pure as the warriors beneath them. Administrations use the FBI for political purposes, whether or not agents realize it. It's all about perception."

"Then you *are* monitoring them."

"If you're asking me if I'm breaking the law, the answer is no, but you know better than to ask about methods. Agent Burke is meeting one of the most dangerous adversaries of the Cold War. Keep tabs on him."

Bashir rubbed his hands together to stem the chill. "We're straying farther into operational territory."

"I don't see it that way. Now, will you do what I asked, or do I need to make alternate plans?"

Bashir studied his shoes. Nothing about this felt right. But Hamilton would still have Nathan followed if Bashir refused.

"Well?" Hamilton asked.

"I'll cover the meeting."

34

Red streaks slashed across the early-morning sky, and the sun glowed behind the Washington Monument. Nathan exited his car at the Lincoln Memorial and transversed the stone steps as he scanned the Reflecting Pool. A young couple jogged past a woman walking her dog. A lone man nested on a bench.

Timor Balakin.

It was obvious why Jakob had called him the Bear. Timor was over six feet tall and three feet wide, with a broad chest, ample belly, and thick limbs. Scraggly chestnut hair covered his enormous head and hanging jowls.

Nathan headed for him. Timor watched from behind hooded eyes. Nathan stopped a few feet away, wary, as if the Bear may bite.

"Thank you for agreeing to speak with me," Nathan said.

"How could I decline, Mr. Burke? I've been away from this work for a decade. My employers left me alone to sip espresso and rethink my missed opportunities and mistakes over a long career—the fate of all warriors put out to pasture."

"You didn't have to come."

Timor nodded. "And despite my curiosity, I would never have met you except for who introduced us. Jakob and I were on opposite sides for most of our lives, but we shared one thing, a desire to see science used properly."

"Microwaves?"

"Ah, the American propensity for jumping right in. So much for our introspective time. All right, my American friend, what is it you want?"

"Why are the Russians attacking our embassies?"

Timor's eyes hardened. "Why ask an old man? I know nothing."

"You were a central figure in the Soviet Union's development of high-energy weapons for over twenty years. Why are they doing this now? Open attacks against American personnel don't make sense. I need to stop it."

"Because of your wife? The beautiful Reagan Burke?"

It was Nathan's turn to harden. "And how would a man ten years removed from intelligence work learn my wife's name?"

"Ha." Timor smacked his lips as if he had food in his teeth. He was a bear. "I may be out of the business, but I still know many people."

"Then help me understand."

"Do you know how hard it was to survive in a world of secrets and death?" Timor asked.

"That's my world too. Intelligence and law enforcement are similar. The only difference between us is intelligence writes history books, while law enforcement acts."

"A typical police officer's perspective. We took action too, only you didn't see it."

Gooseflesh rose on Nathan's arms. "Why risk World War III to sicken a few hundred diplomats?"

"Why do you think Russians are behind this?" Timor asked. "What proof do you have?"

"History," Nathan said. "History is the best predictor of future behavior. The Soviet Union did this in the seventies, and you were involved. You experimented with radio, sonic, and microwaves to alter brain chemistry and control behavior. You used it to kill."

"Ah, the old *my enemy is the devil* argument," Timor said. "A demon on the other side makes things black and white, no? But life is gray. Your country created lasers and experimented with assassination too."

"The United States isn't targeting Russian diplomats."

"Neither are the Russians. We—"

"Bullshit." Anger sizzled inside him. Reagan was almost bedridden, and this former spy made excuses for the animals who attacked her. "You targeted a national security advisor outside the White House. You attacked FBI, CIA, and State Department employees across the globe. The United States stopped human experiments in the nineties, but Russia never did. How far has your technology come?"

Timor braced his palms against his legs like a tripod. "My friend, this may have been a mistake. If you think I'd betray my country, you're mistaken. What kind of fool would divulge technological secrets to an FBI agent? If I was that type of man, they would have executed me decades ago."

"I'm not asking you to betray your country. I want your help to understand Russia's motivation. What gain could come from causing traumatic brain injury to low-level diplomats?"

"Like your wife?"

Nathan balled his fists. "Yes."

"My friend, I will give you some advice I learned over decades of dealing in science. When you cannot find evidence to support your thesis, and when your theory does not seem to make sense, it's time to question your assumptions."

"Which assumptions?"

"That Russia is responsible. The stakes are very high. I'm not revealing secrets by telling you I worked on these programs for a generation. Everyone in your government's counterintelligence knows who I am. When I ran my unit, I controlled many RF devices, weapons we could use at will. We possessed the technological capability to sicken people with microwaves thirty years ago."

"Then you admit the Russians—"

Timor struggled to his feet. He looked more intimidating at his full height. "You're not listening. If we had the capability three decades ago, why not attack then? You call it the Cold War. Wasn't the temperature freezing when I wore a uniform? Why wait and attack now?"

Cognitive dissonance made Nathan's pulse thump in his temples. He tried to hide his discomfort, but the wrinkling lines around Timor's eyes showed he noticed. Nathan stomped his feet in the cold, hoping to cover his physical tells.

"There are dozens of reasons SVD would want to disrupt US operations overseas," Nathan said. "Is Russia planning a large-scale attack?"

"If they were, they'd never tell me. You need to speak to an active participant in the mind-control arms race. Sergei Popov lies at the heart of the Russian program, but I doubt you will ever find him. He hides in the belly of the beast."

"He's SVD?" Nathan asked.

"I'm uncomfortable giving details about my countrymen. I've been gone too long, and since I started splitting my time between the US and Europe, my former employers have doubts about me. They're suspicious."

"Then why live here? Why not stay in Russia?"

Timor stretched and cracked his back. He towered over Nathan, and despite his age, he'd be tough to take down in physical confrontation. If it came to that.

"Why indeed? I love Mother Russia. My country is in my blood, like antibodies—"

"Or a virus."

"Not funny, my friend. You will never understand what it means to grow up Russian, to feel the sting of ice on your face or the warmth of vodka in your stomach."

"And yet you're here."

"Russia is your adversary, yes, but she is also a competitor, a trading partner, an ally against radical Islam. She fields a large military. She is many things, but her economy pales to the West. Our entire GDP is that of Florida."

"You came here for money?"

"I spent my life sacrificing for the motherland, and I'd do it again, but I deserve to live out my days in a comfort, no?"

"That's it? You expect me to believe Russia used these weapons before, but they're not guilty now?"

"Da."

"Why should I believe you?"

"Because if you don't, you'll never stop these attacks, and I have a feeling this is only the beginning."

35

Nathan clipped his badge to his jacket as he followed Bashir into the main lobby of CIA headquarters in Langley. This agency had driven foreign policy decisions, directed the deaths of foreign adversaries, and been fodder for movies and novels since its inception. Even so, it was just another gray government building infested with bureaucrats in the woods of northern Virginia. He snorted.

"Impressive site, right?" Bashir asked.

"Not what I was thinking."

Bashir stopped and faced him. "What's going on inside your head?"

"Why do citizens trust governments to control their lives? They argue people can't be allowed to make their own decisions, but why would politicians and bureaucrats do better? The people we empower to govern us are members of the same group we assume will makes poor decisions."

"These are experts," Bashir said.

"An appeal to authority. A logical fallacy. Nobody is better equipped to make decisions about their life than the affected person. They know their own priorities and the stakes."

Nathan followed Bashir across the lobby. On a marble wall, 137 nameless stars of fallen officers stared back at him. Those patriots had given everything for their country. Warriors on the pointy edge of the sword had pure motivations, but was their trust in leadership justified?

Bashir led him through security, down a series of halls, then up an elevator to the executive floor. They stopped outside the office for the Deputy Chief of Technology and waited in silence for several minutes before the secretary told them to go in.

They entered, and Trent Hamilton met them in the middle of the room. He shook Nathan's hand. "I understand you wanted to talk with me."

"Yes, sir," Nathan said. "The lack of response to Havana Syndrome has frustrated me. I asked Bashir to give me access to better understand why these events aren't being treated as acts of war. If—"

"I can assure you, Mr. Burke, we intend to solve this mystery," Hamilton said. "All our scientific, intelligence, military, and diplomatic assets have marshaled to address the problem."

"I originally asked for this meeting hoping to push you to target Russia," Nathan said, "but now I have doubts."

Hamilton licked his lips. "You're not alone. We're heading in another direction too."

"You're what?" Bashir asked. He narrowed his eyes.

"There's compelling data to suggest the majority of cases are psychological in nature."

Nathan blinked. "You think victims made up their symptoms?"

"Made up?" Hamilton asked. "Of course not. The symptoms are real, but the source is emotional."

Nathan shook his head. "I can't believe what I'm hearing."

"It's not farfetched," Hamilton said. "When our people are stationed in hostile environments and exposed to high levels of stress, they become susceptible to mass psychosis. We've seen examples throughout history. Even recently. Everyone became a hypochondriac during the Covid pandemic."

Nathan glanced at Bashir, who wore an odd expression but said nothing. Why hadn't Bashir mentioned this before? He returned his attention to Hamilton.

"My wife didn't imagine her symptoms."

"Your wife was in her first foreign posting, correct?"

"Yes."

"Personnel deployed for the first time are most at risk."

"We've had foreign service officers for hundreds of years," Nathan said, "but these anomalous health incidents didn't start until 2016."

"It only takes one person to exhibit symptoms, maybe from an allergic reaction, then another sniffling whiner thinks they have the same thing," Hamilton said. "Soon everyone's worried and employees fall like dominoes."

"But CIA has had more than a dozen case officers afflicted with the syndrome," Nathan said. "You're saying they're having psychogenic reactions too?"

"Stress causes the symptoms," Hamilton said, "and I can't think of a more stressful job than being a CIA officer."

Try arguing with a bureaucrat. Nathan sighed.

"This is the direction the White House wants to go," Hamilton said. "It's a legitimate theory, and one the CIA itself has suggested since 2022."

Nathan cracked his neck, but it didn't relieve his tension. "That's it? You're blaming victims and giving up the investigation?"

"Hardly," Hamilton said. "We're still seeking answers. Some incidents could have other causes. Allergens, chemicals, whatever."

"I have doubts the Russians are responsible," Nathan said, "but I'm certain these incidents were intentional attacks, and I'll find out who's behind them."

Hamilton placed his hand on Nathan's shoulder and led him to the door. "The FBI has failed to substantiate that theory after years of investigation. I wish you luck."

36

Bashir sat across from Hamilton. He had returned to the deputy director's office after ensuring Nathan had left Langley. Hamilton's comments to Nathan had blindsided Bashir, and stiffness settled into his jaw. He gave an exaggerated sigh.

"What the hell happened?" Bashir asked. "You tasked me with pushing the FBI to find a connection to Russia, and now we're floating psychogenic causes?"

"That's what the White House has decided."

"Since when does the White House dictate intelligence analysis. Isn't that backward?"

Hamilton smiled. "Don't be naïve. How long have you been with the agency?"

Bashir started to answer then stopped. Hamilton knew his hire date and had researched Bashir. Something was going on, and Bashir needed to be careful.

"If we've pivoted, should I wrap up my liaison work?" Bashir asked.

Hamilton tapped a pen against the desk. He swiveled and gazed out the window. Seconds ticked off the clock on the wall.

"Stay in place for now," Hamilton said, without turning around. "Pulling you out after this change in direction could raise flags. And maintain visibility on their internal machinations so we don't get surprised. I have a feeling Agent Burke won't go away quietly. Too many subordinates want to drive policy instead of shutting up and following orders."

Did Hamilton mean him? "You want me to observe and report?"

"Keep a close eye on Burke. Follow him when he's not at the office. See who he's meeting. This business with Balakin is troubling. Something may have to be done about agent Burke."

Bashir raised his eyebrows involuntarily. "Done?"

Hamilton stared hard. "You're in the major leagues now."

"Meaning?"

"Do you like your position?" Hamilton asked. "Is it everything you expected?"

Bashir's stomach fluttered. "Being a CIA case officer is nothing like I expected. Not like the spy novels, not the action movies, not the mythology. The biggest hurdle has been navigating bureaucracy."

Hamilton nodded. "You have a promising future here. Show me you can follow orders. Don't screw up what could be a long and successful career."

37

Nathan read the latest source debriefing of Mohammad, but his mind kept drifting back to Havana Syndrome. He hunched over the FBI conference table down the hall from his office and downed the last of his coffee. It was black and cold, and grounds stuck to his tongue. He spit them back into his mug and stared at Eddie who seemed immersed in the case file. The poor kid was lost.

"Keep it simple, Eddie," Nathan said.

Eddie looked up and rubbed his eyes. "There's nothing simple about developing a federal investigation against ISIS. Haven't you heard the expression, 'Don't make a federal case out of it?' I thought law school was hard, but this shit is complicated."

Nathan smiled. "It *can* become complex, which is why we need a straightforward strategy. Think about it. What are we trying to accomplish?"

"Stop whatever these jihadists have planned."

"That's a positive outcome we want, but our immediate goal is to obtain evidence for a charge that will stick, then lock them up. And even before we figured out the customers may be Islamic State, we wanted to develop evidence against the Golden Dragons. We—"

Eddie rolled his eyes. "That doesn't sound complicated at all."

"It's the reason I recruited Kei. He has connections with the Triads, the Chinese government, and criminals ranging from drug smugglers to human traffickers. I wanted to use him to dismantle Chinese organized crime in DC. Kei is the key, so to speak."

Eddie manipulated the spinner between his thumb and forefinger, and it clicked over and over. "Sure, piece of cake. The Triads have existed for a few thousand years. Let's wrap them up while we're stopping a bunch of radical jihadists from blowing up DC."

"We don't know why they ordered fake identification," Nathan said.

"Why can't Mo just ask them?"

"He's a local Muslim they met at the mosque, not a part of their cell. They think he's a criminal and a radical, but Mohammad just projected his Islamist image to infiltrate them. If he asks questions about their operations, they'll suspect he's an informant."

"Why's he risking his life by betraying Islamists and organized criminals?" Eddie asked.

Click, click, click. God, that was annoying.

"He's motivated by greenbacks, the best kind of snitch."

Eddie's forehead wrinkled. "Best? I'd prefer a source with purer motivations."

"Passions change and ideological motivations can be tricky, but money I understand. As long as we're offering to submit him for a reward, we'll control him. I like a source who has his cards on the table."

"I guess."

Eddie scratched his head then ran his fingers through his hair. Did he get what they were doing? Running sources and developing high-profile cases was part art and part science, and as smart as Eddie was, it took years to develop the skills to be a well-rounded agent.

"Kei's a great cooperator," Nathan said. "The last thing he wants is to spend five years in jail."

"With all his connections, why doesn't he flee to China?"

"Always a possibility, but if he flees and we ask China for extradition, they'll see our case and he's blown. Once he started working for us, he was all in. If he runs now, the CCP will know he cooperated. I think he'd rather take his chances with us."

Eddie rolled the fidget toy between his fingers. "Tell me, Yoda, how do we make the case simple without—"

Rahimya entered the conference room, looking angular and tense, as if her clothes were held up with wire hangers. "I have to be in the SAC's office in five minutes. Give me the short version. What's your plan?"

"We're setting up surveillance and running checks to identify these Islamists while we drag out the sting," Nathan said.

"Stings worry me," Rahimya said. "Explain."

"Kei will inform the Gold Dragons he's lined up a customer for fake identification, then we let them produce the bogus Virginia driver licenses and the passports. We flag the names and put silent lookouts on them, so we're notified if they arrive at the border or show up anywhere in the system. Then Kei delivers them to our jihadist friends—"

"We need close surveillance," Rahimya said, "because if they use those IDs for any crime, we're on the hook."

"Once Kei makes the controlled delivery, which we'll capture on audio and video, we'll have charges on both groups.

"Manufacturing and using fake driver licenses are misdemeanors, not federal charges."

"Mostly, but it's something. We need to start somewhere, and fraudulent passports are a federal offense. It's enough to arrest the ISIS players if we think the operation is going down and—"

"Have you confirmed they're ISIS?"

"We have an audio recording of Ghulam claiming membership when he met with Mohammad and Kei. Self-identification meets the legal threshold."

"It may not be enough to prosecute," Rahimya said.

"We've just started investigating and—"

"We?" Eddie asked.

Nathan shot him a hard look, and the smile slid off Eddie's face. Nathan returned his attention to Rahimya who glanced at her watch. Whatever the agenda was for her meeting with the SAC, she seemed more worried about it than Nathan's absence from the office.

"We'll build charges slowly," Nathan continued, "and develop evidence for a variety of crimes and charge the Triad with running a Continuing Criminal Enterprise or racketeering."

"And ISIS?" Rahimya asked.

"Best case, we learn what they're planning and charge them with terrorism. Worst case, we use lower charges to disrupt their plot and deport them."

Rahimya looked at her watch again. "I need to run. This sounds feasible, but I want a detailed surveillance plan before we deliver fake documents. I don't want this blowing up on us. And try to get up on their phones."

"They're burners but we're analyzing tolls. We'll have Mohammad push a little harder, and once Kei delivers the documents, the jihadists should trust him more. Asking for a federal agency ID worries me the most."

"Keep me posted and don't let them destroy the Capitol."

38

Nathan slogged up the steps to his condo wearing fatigue like a heavy overcoat. Amelia should have arrived home from school an hour ago, and he smiled in anticipation. She was the best part of his day. But she'd better be doing her homework.

He unlocked the exterior door and rode the elevator up to the second floor. He stepped into the vestibule with his keys in his hand and froze.

A manila envelope was taped to his door.

Nathan ripped it off and opened it. The envelope contained a single sheet of paper. He read the note.

The man you want to find has agreed to meet you.
He will signal when he is ready.
Look for a Dr. Pepper can stuck on the iron fence across the street.
Instructions will be in a container tied to a branch above it.
Tell no one about this meeting.

Was the note referring to Sergei Popov, the man Timor Balakin said was deep inside the Russian's high-energy weapons program? Nathan's spine tingled. Someone had broken in and been inside his vestibule.

Amelia!

The door appeared undamaged, but the exterior door had looked fine too. Whoever had burglarized his condo knew what they were doing. He fumbled with his key and the envelope as he unlocked the door and burst into the foyer.

Bruno jumped off the couch with a guilty expression and raced across the living room to him. Nathan brushed him away.

"Amelia. Where are you?"

No answer.

Her pink book bag rested on the counter and a bottle of Diet Coke lay on the floor beneath it.

"Oh, God. No."

Nathan's heart pounded as adrenaline flooded his system. He raced upstairs.

"Amelia!"

His breath came hard and fast as he ascended. He bolted down the hallway and pushed through her door with his chest full of dread.

Amelia lay on her bed reading a book. She looked up with alarm and yanked earbuds out of her ears. Taylor Swift's voice floated through the room.

"What the hell, Dad?"

Nathan's knees weakened with relief, and he leaned against the doorjamb to catch his breath. "You're okay?"

"You're supposed to knock. Remember?"

"Sorry."

"You scared me."

He plopped onto the mattress beside her and pulled her into a hug. "Sorry, baby. You didn't answer me."

"I didn't hear you."

"Did anybody come to the front door?"

"What?"

"Did we have visitors?"

"When?"

"Nothing. Sorry I startled you."

"Dad, you're getting weirder all the time."

He kissed her on the head, and the scent of raspberries tingled his nose.

"What's that?" She pointed to the envelope crumpled in his hand.

He hadn't realized he was still holding it. "I'm not sure. I think it's a clue."

39

Reagan rang the bell to her condo—no, it was Nathan's condo now. She'd lost the right to claim it the moment she allowed Vince into her bed. Her eyelids hung heavy, swollen from hours of crying. That would make her crow's feet worse.

She pressed the doorbell again and scratched her elbow. Panic threatened to burst out of her chest and seize control. She'd lost her health, her family, and probably her job, all in a few days.

How had everything gone so wrong?

The elevator opened, and Nathan's mouth dropped open. "Reagan? What's wrong?"

"Those fuckers are blaming us. My career's over. Everything's ruined."

Nathan looked around. "Is Vince with you? How did you get here? Tell me you didn't drive in your condition."

"I barely have the balance to walk, let alone drive. I took an Uber. I need to talk with someone who understands."

"You came to the right place."

They rode up in the elevator and she followed him into the kitchen. The midday sun sparkled through the windows, and the room glowed beneath its warmth. This place had been her home for years, but now it felt both familiar and foreign.

"Amelia?" she asked.

"At school."

She entered the living room and dragged her fingertips over the sofa's back. This place was immaculate. Was she the only slob? Photographs of Amelia, Nathan, and her covered the credenza beneath the windows. Why had Nathan kept her picture on display? If he had cheated on her, she would have sliced out his image with shears.

"What's happening?" he asked.

Reagan faced him. "The government's claiming all the victims are crazy."

"Nobody thinks you're crazy."

"State does. That's what *psychogenic symptoms* mean. They think we heard about Havana Syndrome, and our minds mimicked the illness. That would make us fucking crazy—"

"I know this is real."

Tears welled in her eyes. "You believe me but no one else does."

"That's not true."

"You should have seen the way my colleagues looked at me when I picked up my paperwork. Their eyes were filled with pity and, oh, I don't know... disgust."

"The government's looking at every angle. The NSC has launched a massive investigation. They're even looking for unreported historical cases that—"

"CIA said we're crazy. I read the intelligence report myself. I'd quote you passages, but my memory has been awful since the incident. CIA doesn't care about the truth."

"A few agency folks pushed this theory," he said, "but even their report claimed not every incident was psychogenic. Other agencies are investigating hard. CIA too. They've had officers injured, and they want to identify the source."

"That's crap, and you know it. Members of Congress from both parties have accused CIA of failing to take appropriate action. The Senate Intelligence Committee berated CIA for shoddy investigation and lack of urgency in providing medical care to their people. The agency didn't even form their task force until 2020, and it has been a total failure."

Nathan rubbed his face. "The director promised to make Havana Syndrome a top priority. Look, I've got a CIA case officer working with us. He thinks these incidents are attacks too."

"One man's opinion doesn't help. His agency has branded us as lunatics, and my career at State is fucked. Unless we identify who's doing this, there'll always be a cloud of doubt hanging over me. I'll be finished."

Nathan grabbed her shoulders and held her in his muscular hands. His touch made her worry dissipate.

"I'll find out who did this to you. I promise."

40

Nathan watched the street in the heart of Chinatown. Most policework involved waiting and reacting, even during a proactive sting. Eddie sat beside him in the Suburban's passenger seat rubbing his hands to burn off nervous energy.

Eddie sat up. "Here he comes."

A block away, Kei exited the Happy Family restaurant on H Street NW and walked to his car.

"Got him," Nathan said.

"All units, Oh-Nine," Eddie said into the microphone attached to the inside of his shirt collar. "Subject exited building."

"Oh-Nine, Oh-Three, good copy," Murphy's voice came through Nathan's earpiece. "You taking him?"

"Oh-Nine," Eddie said. "We've got the eye."

Three Balls and Murphy sat in a silver Chevrolet Malibu, two blocks to the east. Murphy carried a Remington 870 shotgun in case things went south. Four other agents from their group spread throughout the neighborhood, and Rahimya monitored their surveillance from the office, ready to launch a van carrying additional team members. It had seemed like overkill, but Mohammad and Kei were acting as go-betweens for two ruthless criminal elements.

Anything could happen.

Nathan checked the light at Seventh Street NW as it changed to green. He needed to time it correctly to cross before it turned red and separated him from Kei.

"Subject's in his vehicle," Eddie broadcast.

Kei pulled out and headed east. Nathan eased away from the curb and followed.

"He knows where we're meeting, right?" Eddie asked.

"Yeah, but he's holding the forged documents, and they're valuable. The Golden Dragons could be suspicious and follow him or ISIS could try to rip him off and save their cash. Hell, Ghulam may want to extinguish the only person who knows he ordered the documents and has seen his face. "

"Oh-Nine," Eddie transmitted, "right turn, south on six."

Eddie's transmission came though Nathan's earpiece a second later. Nathan scanned the street and sidewalks looking for anything unusual. He memorized cars and faces in case he saw them again, but Kei didn't appear to have a tail.

Nathan turned south on Sixth Street. "There he is."

Kei had stopped at a light. Nathan stopped three cars back and waited.

Kei had persuaded the Golden Dragons he had legitimate buyers—and not government agents—for the fraudulent documents. Kei said they'd been skeptical of the large order for eleven sets of US passports and Virginia licenses, for which they wanted $72,000. Mohammad had pressured Ghulam to up his offer from $50,000 and pay half up front—not an easy sell—but greed and the promise of a quick payday had won the day. The Golden Dragons produced the documents in two days.

The light changed, and Kei continued south. Nathan followed.

They'd monitored Kei's meeting with the Triad and recorded the conversation. The Metropolitan Police's Asian Liaison Unit and Intelligence Fusion Division knew most of the Golden Dragons, so matching names to surveillance photographs would not take long, especially with Kei's help.

Nathan checked his review mirrors. Three Balls and Murphy trailed a block behind—not a normal surveillance pattern, but they didn't care if Kei spotted them. They watched for Triad or ISIS countersurveillance.

"Oh-Two, Oh-Six, you look clear from back here," Three Balls transmitted.

"Oh-Six, Oh-Two, stay alert," Nathan responded. "They could have a tracker on his car or be monitoring his phone."

Or Kei or Mohammad could be working both sides.

"Thanks for the direction," Three Balls responded, his voice dripping with sarcasm.

Nathan wanted to tease him, but not with Rahimya monitoring their chatter. Nathan was in deep enough shit already.

He glanced at his watch. They only had thirty minutes before Ghulam expected Kei to deliver the documents. Ghulam would pay the remaining $36,000 upon receipt, which gave Nathan little time to meet Kei and photograph the documents. The FBI needed photographic evidence in case the documents weren't recovered. They also needed to record the personal data and enter it into the system to monitor the ISIS members.

For eight minutes, Kei weaved through DC streets along the preplanned route Nathan had given him, then he took Ohio Drive into East Potomac Park, which occupied a small man-made island in the Potomac River. The island contained tennis courts, a golf course, and other sports amenities.

Kei pulled into a parking area near a miniature golf course, and Nathan parked beside him.

"All units, subject arrived at staging location," Eddie transmitted.

"You're clear," Three Balls responded.

"Copy," Eddie transmitted. "Meeting now."

Nathan waved Kei over, and his source climbed into their back seat carrying a bag.

"We heard everything," Nathan said. "You okay?"

"Too easy, Mr. G-man."

"Don't get too comfortable," Nathan said. "Pay attention during this drop and follow my directions. You remember what to say if you're in danger?"

"Egg roll." Kei smiled. "Hard to forget that racist shit."

"Drive to the tip of the island," Nathan told Eddie. "If the Golden Dragons are tracking his car, we can't be sitting here when they show up."

"Nobody followed me," Kei said. "They accept me."

"We hope," Nathan said.

Kei frowned as Eddie drove south to Hains Point. Nathan stared over the dark water at the convergence of the Potomac River, Anacostia River, and Washington Channel.

Nathan looked at Kei. "Show me."

Kei opened his duffle bag and stacked the passports in two piles on the center console.

"We should fingerprint them," Eddie said.

"No time, and if we leave a trace of fingerprint power on them, Ghulam won't react well. Besides, we know most of the Dragons already. Take photographs, front and back to capture all identifying info."

Nathan started with the passports, holding them open until Eddie confirmed the pictures were in focus. The licenses took less manipulation and went quicker. When they finished, Kei secured the documents in his bag.

"Oh-Six, Oh-Two," Nathan broadcast.

"Oh-Six, go," Murphy responded.

"Any activity near the CI's car?"

"You're clear," Murphy said.

"Heading back," Nathan said.

They returned to the parking lot, and Nathan scanned a handful of the parked cars, all unoccupied.

"Mohammad is with Ghulam now," Kei said. "He say text when I ready, and he give me place to meet."

"Do it."

Kei typed a text into WhatsApp. Ghulam had insisted Mohammad use it for secrecy—a good sign. Law enforcement had learned how to defeat the application's encryption and intercept messages, but that news had not trickled down to its members. They wouldn't be nervous if they knew how long it took to obtain a wireless intercept order, get funding, and start intercepting.

A few seconds later, Mohammad responded with a text.

E Street SE / Henderson Street. 20 minutes.

Nathan read it, the entered the Southeast DC address into Google Earth on his phone. Shit. "It's at the entrance to the Congressional Cemetery.

They're going to have Mohammad lead you into the cemetery to make the exchange."

"Should I broadcast the address to our team?" Eddie asked.

"We're not doing it there," Nathan said.

Lines creased Kei's forehead. "What?"

"We need to switch the location," Nathan said. "We'll have trouble getting eyes on you once you're on foot in the cemetery, and it's remote, so they won't be worried about shooting you and taking your bag. The cemetery's huge, and it would be easy for them to escape."

"You kill deal," Kei said. "I'm not afraid to—"

"We always give an excuse to move the location. They've been preparing this for a while, so they'll have lookouts emplaced and their plan ready. We'll move it to a neutral location that's more public and easier to surveil, then we'll get there first and watch them arrive."

Nathan studied the map. "This is perfect. We'll use a parking lot at RFK Stadium. It's only five minutes away, but it's wide open, and it'll be easy to cover you. Even in the off-season there's enough traffic to conceal our team. Get two cars over there, Eddie."

"What if the bad guys won't move?" Eddie asked.

"We don't do they deal."

"Won't that destroy the sting?"

"It'll make us seem more authentic," Nathan said. "They won't expect cops to cancel a deal, but a nervous criminal might."

Eddie radioed the new location, and Murphy and Three Balls headed toward the stadium with the surveillance team.

"What do I tell them?" Kei asked.

Nathan zoomed in with Google Earth. "The spot they picked is right across the street from the Correction Treatment Facility. All Department of Corrections facilities have exterior cameras. It's a good excuse. Give me your phone."

Kei handed it to him, and Nathan typed a message.

Too close to jail. Meet at RFK. Lot Four. Fifteen minutes.

Mohammad didn't respond, which meant he was arguing with Ghulam. Could he convince Ghulam to move? Mohammad texted back.

Cemetery safe.

Nathan responded.

No good. Meet RFK Lot Four. Bring money.

"Shit," Eddie said. He tapped his foot with nervous energy.

They waited a full minute. Mohammad sent a text.

Coming.

Nathan smiled and keyed his mic. "Target agreed to new location. Get the van into position in case we need an extraction."

"Oh-Two, Oh-One," Rahimya responded. "Already sent them. They'll be in place in five."

"Copy. Leaving now. Set up for takeaway." Nathan turned to Kei. "We'll listen through the open line on your phone. The distress word is 'egg roll.' Raise your hands high over your head as a visual backup."

"No problem."

"Get going and drive slow."

"No problem, boss."

"Get your head in the game. If you get killed. I'll be doing paperwork all night."

Kei frowned. "Not funny man."

"Take their money and hand over the documents. When you're done, meet us at the rendezvous location. We'll follow you to make sure you're clean. Got it?"

"The Yotel on New Jersey Avenue, right?" Kei asked.

"Room four twenty-three. Someone will follow you up in the elevator."

Kei looked down at his shoes.

"What is it?" Nathan asked.

"You won't forget what I do for you when it is time to talk to judge about my case?"

Nathan grinned. "You're my guy. You're taking a chance for us, and I'll step up for you when the time comes. Just take care of yourself tonight. These guys are dangerous."

41

Nathan stopped outside the DC Armory, a stone's throw from RFK Stadium, and listened to surveillance units call out the action. He concentrated to hear over Eddie's fidget toy. Did Eddie even realize he was doing it?

The first two agents had set up a few minutes before Ghulam arrived in a Chevrolet Tahoe with limousine tint. Ghulam had passed through Lots One, Two, and Three, before entering Lot Four. He parked at the northern end, away from two unoccupied cars.

The lot was adjacent to the northwest side of the stadium, positioned between C Street and Twenty-Second Street NE. Nathan had instructed everyone to stay out of Lot Four, since they could observe it from anywhere west or north of the stadium. Two units had eyes on the Tahoe and the rest waited blocks away, prepared to follow Ghulam when he left.

The closest FBI vehicle was their white panel van, parked in Lot One, about forty yards across Twenty-Second Street.

Click, click, click.

"Take it easy, Eddie."

Eddie looked sheepish. "Sorry. Can't we get closer? I can't see."

"We followed Kei into the area and were last to arrive, so Ghulam's countersurveillance saw us trail him in. We only need one agent to call out the action. Everyone else stays ready to respond in case this thing goes sideways."

Nathan wanted to have eyes on too, but moving closer was tactically unsound, and curiosity foiled surveillances. The stakes were high, with more to lose than ruining the investigation. Both Triad and ISIS were deadly organizations that would not think twice about murdering Kei, Mohammad, or any responding police officer who stood between them and freedom. Nathan had been working radical Islamist cases for years, and one common mistake police made was to overlay a Western epistemology on jihadists. True believers welcomed death and martyrdom in pursuit of jihad because it guaranteed a place in heaven. Most Islamic terrorism he dealt with had been Sunni, but the Shiites scared him more, because the Twelver sect sought death and the return of the last Imam—sort of an Eastern version of waiting for the Rapture.

"Nothing over his phone?" Nathan asked.

"Not getting audio. Not sure what's wrong."

"All units, Oh-Two," Nathan transmitted. "We lost audio. Stay alert."

"Charlie's parking two spots south of target vehicle," Agent Mark Gallagher transmitted. Charlie was phonetic radio talk for C, which was short for CI, which were initials for Confidential Informant. Law enforcement loved acronyms.

"Copy," Nathan responded. He may not have the eye, but this was his case, well, his and Eddie's, and he needed to control the surveillance.

"Tahoe doors open," Mark transmitted.

Nathan remained silent and hoped the other agents would stay off the air too. Normally, transmissions would be acknowledged, but things happened fast at critical junctures, and protocol allowed only the agent with the eye to speak. Simultaneous transmissions canceled each other.

"Two suspects out of the Tahoe," Mark said. "Black Jacket and Long Hair." Referring to unidentified subjects by their description was an easy way to keep them separate and avoid the confusion numbering them caused when suspects started moving around. It had the added benefit of giving agents without the eye a memorable description of the bad guys.

"Charlie's out too. Standing behind his car. Out of view."

Shit. "Anybody have an eye on Charlie?" Nathan asked.

"Hold on," Mark said. "I got him. Charlie's talking to Long Hair. Third suspect's out of the SUV. Heavyset male. Chubby moving around the back of the van and joining Long Hair and Charlie."

Nothing came over the radio for at least ten seconds.

"What's happening?" Nathan asked.

"Still . . . yeah, still talking," Mark said. "Charlie's gesturing at the Tahoe. They may be arguing. Hold on, Charlie's got his hands up."

"That's the distress signal," Eddie said. "Let's go."

Nathan held up his hand to wait. "Mark, confirm hands over his head."

"Negative, hands out to his side."

Had Kei forgotten the signal? "All units hold."

"Chubby's patting Charlie down," Mark broadcast. "I don't see any weapons. Charlie looks calm."

He was the only one.

"All units, standby," Nathan said. "Let this play out."

"Chubby's done searching," Mark said. "Everything looks okay. Black Jacket's back at the Tahoe. He's coming out with a red knapsack. All three suspects are with Charlie now. Black Jacket's unzipping the bag. Charlie's looking inside. Nodding his head. He looks happy."

Whew. Thank God they hadn't raced in to rescue him.

Eddie stayed quiet, sheepish after his misread of the signal.

"Charlie's opening his trunk. He's got our black duffle bag. He's opening it and showing Long Hair."

This was it. If Ghulam and his ISIS thugs planned to rob Kei, they would do it once they had the documents in hand. Nathan wanted to tell his team to be ready to move, but they were professionals and all thinking the same thing. Commentary from him would put them on edge and risk walking over an important transmission.

"Long Hair and Black Jacket have the bag on the ground. Long Hair's pulling something out of the bag. He's looking at it."

"Inspecting the product," Nathan told Eddie.

"Still checking. Yeah, he's got some kind of papers. Leafing through them."

"Fuck," Eddie said. "Not seeing this is killing me."

"Be ready," Nathan said.

"Chubby's walking up behind Charlie," Mark broadcast.

"What's he doing?" Nathan mumbled.

Nathan cranked the ignition, and his car roared to life. He dropped it into gear and rolled toward East Capitol Street SE, which led to the stadium. He tapped his brakes and crawled forward, keeping out of sight.

"Okay," Mark said. "Long Hair zipped up the bag, and he's standing up. He's shaking Charlie's hand. Chubby's shaking Charlie's hand too."

Nathan expelled a long stream of air.

"Long Hair, Black Jacket, and Chubby heading back to the Tahoe. Charlie put the red knapsack in his trunk, and he's getting into his car."

"Confirm Long Hair has the black duffle bag with the documents," Nathan said.

"Affirmative," Mark said. "Hold on, okay, the Tahoe just peeled out of the parking lot, headed toward Independence Ave. Charlie's sitting there and ... okay, he's moving now. Headed for C Street."

"Oh-Two will take Charlie," Nathan said.

"Tahoe's heading out of view," Mark said.

"Oh-Nine, I have the Tahoe approaching Independence."

"All units, Oh-Two taking Charlie. Everyone else, on the van. But stay back. If you can put him down, great. If not let him go. Better to lose him then burn it. Mark, you stay put until everyone clears the area."

"Good copy," Mark said.

Nathan hurried down East Capitol Street to Twenty-Second Street NE and headed north.

"There he is," Eddie said and pointed to the intersection with C Street.

"Don't point," Nathan said. "If anyone's watching, you're telegraphing our intentions."

"Sorry."

Click, click, click.

Nathan fell in behind Kei as he turned onto C Street NE and headed downtown. A lightness filled him for the first time since the case began. They only had minor charges from the exchange, but they could arrest at least a dozen members of ISIS and the Golden Dragons if circumstances forced their hand.

"I'm pumped," Eddie said.

"You did good, but don't lose focus. We need to debrief Kei and recover the money. Hopefully, our guys will put Ghulam down at his residence."

They'd decided to follow Ghulam and not his other goons, because if any agent was burned, Ghulam would break off contact with Kei and maybe even Mohammad.

"Target Alpha headed north on Nineteenth," Unit Four broadcast to the chase team.

"Oh-Four, Oh-Eight's got the eye."

"Take it."

Nathan listened to the moving surveillance but focused on Kei.

Ten minutes later, Nathan parked on New Jersey Avenue NW, a few cars behind Kei. They followed him into the hotel. The street was deserted, as was the lobby, except for Special Agent Ed Watson, who fell in beside Kei. They all entered the elevator and rode up.

"Ghulam planning bad things," Kei said.

"Not here," Nathan said without looking at him. Elevators had cameras.

They got out on the fourth floor and walked down the hallway in silence. Nathan knocked on Room 423, and Rahimya opened the door. She stepped aside, and they entered. Nathan sat on the bed and directed Kei into one of the chairs Rahimya had positioned opposite it.

"Well?" Rahimya asked.

Nathan held his finger to his lips for her to stay quiet. "Recorder, please."

Kei handed it over. The recording light glowed red—a great sign. Nathan clicked it off and put it in his pocket.

Nathan grinned at Kei. "Nice job."

Kei nodded. "He inspect documents. He very happy."

Nathan held out his hand. "Bag please."

Kei gave it to him, and Nathan pulled out six equal-sized bundles wrapped with red rubber bands and a smaller pile of bills paper clipped together. "Eddie, count these while we're talking and make sure we have $36,000. We can photograph them and log the serial numbers when we get back to the office."

"I count," Kei said. "All there."

"And pat down our friend, then go search his car," Nathan said. "We need to swear in court that Kei gave us everything."

"On it," Eddie said. He looked embarrassed as he patted down Kei.

"We'll get the recording transcribed," Nathan said, "but I want every detail of the meeting. Did you have any problems?"

"They give money, and I hand over documents. Ghulam check, then Amir check too. They thorough. They planning something huge."

"Huge?" Rahimya asked.

Nathan scowled at her. She was in charge, but debriefings needed to be led by one person—the case agent—or else they turned into verbal scrums where everyone in the room bounced questions off the source.

"He need more documents," Kei said. "Must have soon."

"Did he say what they're planning?" Nathan asked, already knowing the answer.

"Ghulam calls it *amaliya*."

"Uh, oh," Rahimya said.

"What does *amaliya* mean?" Eddie asked.

Nathan swiveled around. "It's Arabic for *operation*."

"Big operation," Kei repeated.

Nathan's heart pounded in his chest. Something was about to happen, and they'd have to act sooner than he'd hoped. He leaned close to Kei. "You said Ghulam asked for more documents. Did he want more passports?"

"He want agency ID."

Rahimya moved beside Nathan "Which agency?"

"He say FAA."

"The Federal Aviation Administration?" Nathan asked.

"They want employee ID badges. Ghulam say he need six Personal Identity Verification cards that allow full access."

"What the fuck?" Eddie asked. "Why does he want access to FAA?"

"He doesn't want to infiltrate FAA," Nathan said. "He wants to get into restricted areas in airports. These bastards are using planes again."

42

Nathan sat in Dr. Camilla Reyes's office at Aura Research Associates and squinted to minimize the effect the fading sunlight had on his headache. His body tingled from fatigue and two pots of coffee.

Nathan and Eddie had worked long into the night organizing evidence. Then, with Rahimya's assistance, they'd spent the day reviewing the video and expediting facial recognition and voice analysis from the recordings. Identifying the involved ISIS members took on new urgency after Ghulam's statement about an operation. Luckily, nothing should happen without the FAA identification cards, and that let Nathan squeeze in a private meeting with Dr. Reyes. He needed answers about Havana Syndrome, and if investigated on his own time, who'd complain?

Yeah, right.

Reyes settled in behind her desk. She looked annoyed about talking to the FBI again, but at least she'd agreed to see him.

Nathan flashed a smile. "I appreciate your staying late to see me, so I'll make this quick. The government has doubled down on their cognitive psychogenic theory. The CIA's official stance is these anomalous incidents are mass psychosis. They—"

"Utter bullshit," Reyes said.

"How can you be certain?"

"Many reasons, but the CIA's conclusions are not even logical. They claim most incidents were generated in employee's minds, but that doesn't explain the other incidents. Even if they believed only ten percent of the attacks result from foreign microwaves, sound waves, or radio waves, which they don't, they're still admitting the Havana Syndrome is an attack. And if some attacks are intentional aggressions by a foreign power, why not most or all of them? If you're worried about a wolf eating your sheep and your investigations determine that ninety percent of your sheep died of natural causes, are you less concerned about the wolf? Ten percent were still killed by it, and that number will leap whenever the wolf gets hungry."

"But how do we know any percentage of incidents were acts of aggression? CIA concluded the majority of cases were not caused by a weapon."

"They confirmed nothing. The CIA's official response is guesswork, not a statement of fact. They haven't proven or disproven anything. They've only pushed in all their chips behind a single theory. And they know it's not true." Her passion bordered on anger. Either way, it was contagious.

"How do you know it's a lie?"

"Because of Fido."

Nathan scrunched up his face. "Huh?"

"I'm sure you're aware of the attacks in Washington, DC."

"April 2021. Outside the White House near the Ellipse."

"That's right. They hit a National Security Council official. The National Academy of Sciences determined the attack was likely the result of a directed-pulsed, radio-frequency, high-energy weapon, but the CIA ruled in favor of psychological phenomena. But that's beside the point. Do you know about the attack in Arlington?"

"In 2019?"

"They attacked a White House employee. She had all the symptoms—acute onset of headache, tingling, ringing in the ears. Except we're sure that one wasn't psychological."

"Why?"

"She was attacked while walking her dog, and the dog had a seizure at the same time. Unless you believe her dog was a hypochondriac, then the cross-species reaction is incontrovertible proof that physical phenomenon caused the symptoms. The CIA didn't address that, did they? And if that was an attack, why assume psychological factors in other incidents with the same symptoms?"

Nathan hadn't considered that. "You're right."

"Now you see why I'm annoyed they discredited my sonic-wave theory. They're trying to marginalize me, make me sound like a crackpot."

"I believe you," Nathan said, "and I'm convinced the Russians are to blame."

"Then why is the CIA running interference? Why won't they listen to me?"

That's a good question. "I wish I knew. They—"

Nathan's phone rang. Eddie.

"I've gotta take this," Nathan said. "Thanks for seeing me on such short notice. I appreciate your insights. You're one of the few objective voices in this debate."

He turned to leave, and she touched his sleeve. He stopped and faced her.

"Was there something else?" Nathan asked.

"It . . . I thought . . . well, you may not tell me."

"What?"

"I hope I don't sound crazy, especially after that lovely compliment you just gave me, but I have to ask."

Nathan waited.

"Have you . . . I don't mean you, but has the FBI been following me?"

Alarm bells rang in Nathan's mind. "Why do you ask?"

"I noticed a car tailing me. I mean, I think it was following me. I saw it here, then again on the street outside my sister's house. And last night, I could swear the same car drove by my home around ten o'clock. I've been feeling like someone's watching me, and when I looked out my window, I spotted it."

His stomach hardened. "Which kind of car?"

"A sedan. A black one. Chevrolet maybe. Talk about psychogenic symptoms. I'm getting paranoid. I—"

Nathan raised his finger to his lips and motioned for her to follow him. He stopped in the hallway and took out his phone. He powered it off then leaned close to her. "Do you have your cell phone on you?"

"You're scaring me."

"You're not crazy, and I don't think you imagined that car. I've done fieldwork for a decade, and one thing I know for certain is ignoring your instincts is a mistake. Listen to your subconscious. If you feel you're in danger, you're probably right."

Reyes covered her mouth with her hands.

"It's okay," Nathan said. "You were smart to tell me. I'll look into it."

"Who's doing this?" Her skin had gone pale.

"I'll find out. Until then, do you have somewhere you can stay for a couple of days? A friend? Family?"

"I have another sister in Baltimore. Why would anyone follow me?"

"You've been the most vocal advocate for the nation-state perpetrator theory. You've tried to publish your ideas, and you've been advising the FBI. I don't know who's following you, but someone may want to silence you."

"My, God. I can't be the only one who sees these are intention attacks."

Jakob!

Reyes wasn't the only scientist who could be in danger.

"Pretend like nothing's wrong and go home tonight as usual. Pack a bag and wait. Shut off your lights at your normal bedtime then wait a couple of hours. If anyone is watching your house, they'll assume you're down for the night. Head to your sister's house and call me when you arrive. If you see anyone following you, dial 911 and drive to the nearest police station. Be sure to hide your car in her garage."

"What will you do?"

"I'll find out what's going on, but first there's someone else I have to warn."

43

Nathan dialed Meili as he raced to his car on K Street. The sun had dipped below the skyline, and streetlamps glowed like stars. It was six o'clock and still rush hour, yet the streets seemed oddly empty. Only a handful of pedestrians shuffled past. A combination of pandemic and poor government policies had run many businesses into bankruptcy, and people had fled the city in a migration reminiscent of the 1970s. The city's vibrancy had evaporated.

"Hi, Nate," Meili answered with a lilt in her voice.

"Camilla Reyes thinks someone's following her."

"Why are you talking to her?" Meili asked. "You trying to get fired?"

"If she thinks she's being followed, it's probably true. Why else—"

"Or she's a crackpot."

"She didn't sound like one. She's rational, and her conclusions seem logical."

"She thinks the CIA is blocking her publication too."

"It's happened before. Speech is suppressed more now than at any time in recent history. If the CIA's discrediting her work, it's because it conflicts with their theory."

"Her claim of being followed sounds like a tinfoil-hat conspiracy," Meili said. "Be careful taking her seriously."

"I evaluate every conspiracy theory objectively, at least at first. It's the only way to spot authentic ones. The real question is, why would Russia waste a surveillance team on her?"

"If anyone *is* following her, which I doubt."

"Humor me," Nathan said. "Are the Russians afraid her theories about a sonic weapon will lead to them? If we catch them watching her, it'll almost confirm her theory."

Meili sighed. "Okay, I'll play your hypothetical game. Maybe they know they aren't using sonic weapons and think her bizarre accusations will hurt Russian-US relations."

"Huh." Nathan scratched his head. "No, that doesn't make sense. Her papers would only concern them if her work exposed their operations."

"I've got a briefing in five minutes. Let it go, Nate."

"Hold on," Nathan said. "If Russia's worried about Reyes's writing, what's the purpose of watching her? Are they trying to intercept her submissions to academic journals, and how would they do that by following her around?"

"They're not following her," Meili said. "Nobody is."

"But if they are, she's in danger. I instructed her to stay with family for a while. Can you assign a countersurveillance team?"

"You've got to be joking. If the press learned the FBI's following a scientist who claimed the government suppressed her speech, we'd get crucified."

"What if the Russians are trying to silence her? They—"

"Time's up, Nathan. Don't let that nutjob drag you down with her. If she's being harassed, tell her to call the police."

"If Russia's after her, wouldn't they go after anyone who's pushing a high-energy weapon theory? What about Jakob?"

"Do not talk to Dr. Mendel," Meili said. "Don't contact any of my experts. Go back to your cases, and I promise I'll call the second anything breaks in our investigation."

"I helped in Tallinn. You wouldn't have found those bodies without me."

"We don't know that's connected, but I appreciated your support, at least until my ASAC found out. I like spending time with you."

"But the murders—"

"I've got to run. Don't speak to Dr. Mandel. I'm serious."

Nathan stared at the phone after Meili hung up. He scrolled through his saved contacts and dialed.

"Dr. Mandel, it's Nathan Burke. I need to speak with you."

"Nathan? Oh, good. I was about to call you. I—"

"Call me?"

"I have something urgent to tell you."

Jakob sounded scared, and Nathan's stomach tightened. "What is it?"

"Not on the phone. Are you in DC?"

"I can be at your house in twenty minutes," Nathan said.

"Please hurry."

Nathan disconnected and raced to his car. He edged into traffic and headed west toward I-66. If he avoided accidents, he'd be in McLean in twenty minutes.

His chest fluttered with anticipation and dread. The attack in Tallinn had been the most destructive to date, and now Russia surveilled a scientist on American soil. Were they using sonic weapons to degrade American capabilities before some type of foreign aggression? Was Estonia in their crosshairs? It had been a Soviet republic, and like Ukraine, they might want it back.

But why attack other embassies?

Nathan fought through gridlock over the Potomac, past the US Marine Corps Memorial, and along the George Washington Memorial Parkway. His neck and shoulders tightened with each mile until a dull headache radiated through his skull.

He should move to a small town on Virginia's eastern shore, far from the Beltway, and find a job that didn't require life-and-death decisions. He could buy a sailboat and spend his weekends drifting on the Chesapeake. He smiled at the fantasy. And that's what it was—fantasy. More than a week in the country would drive him crazy. He needed excitement and to be part of something meaningful. His daughter needed him. His wife needed him. His country needed him. Nathan wanted to be the person they called on in a crisis. He demanded the ball when the game was on the line.

He turned onto Kurtz Road in McLean, and his headlights illuminated the quiet street. Lights glowed inside most houses as families settled in for dinner or plopped in front of their televisions. He slowed as he neared the residence. Jakob's Volvo was parked in the driveway, but the house was dark. Nathan's senses came alive, alert for trouble. He parked in front of a neighbor's house and slipped out of his car, careful not to slam his door.

He strode down the street keeping his eyes on the house. No movement. No sign of life. Nathan stopped and took out his phone. He pulled up his recent call log, found Jakob's number, and pressed send. It rang five times and went to voicemail. Nathan hung up.

Something was wrong.

44

Nathan climbed onto the mulch and edged his body between shrubs that ringed Dr. Mandel's house. A leafless twig from a winterberry bush dug into his thigh. Nathan cupped his hands and pressed his forehead against the living room window. He strained to see inside.

Nothing.

The sun had set, so why hadn't Jakob turned on his lights?

Nathan pushed through the shrubbery onto the lawn. He scanned the cars parked on the street. All appeared unoccupied.

Where the hell was he? Jakob knew Nathan was coming.

Nathan dug out his phone. No missed calls, no messages. Why would Jakob leave without telling him? Was this a setup?

Nathan glanced around to confirm he was alone then dialed Jakob again. The phone connected and rang once, twice—

He lowered the phone and climbed back onto the mulch. He leaned close to the glass. Vivaldi's *The Four Seasons* emanated from inside. Jakob loved that piece, and it had been playing when Meili and Nathan visited.

But wait. It hadn't been playing a moment ago.

Jakob's ringtone.

The music stopped. Nathan put his phone to his ear. The call had gone to voicemail. He hung up. Jakob's phone was inside, but he wasn't answering. Trouble.

Nathan darted away from the window and pressed his back against the wall. He unzipped his coat and grasped his Glock. He looked around, confirming he was alone, and drew his handgun. He held it against his leg.

Through the thick glass running along the frame of the front door, only shadows draped the hallway.

He hurried around the stoop and scanned the dining room windows as he passed. Moonlight illuminated the dark outline of a table and armoire.

Nathan continued into the side yard. Twenty yards separated Jakob's residence from his closest neighbor. A woman passed by a window inside a nearby house, but she didn't notice him.

He put both hands on his gun and kept it at the low ready. If a neighbor saw him and called the police, he'd welcome the help. Nathan moved along the side of the house and paused at the corner. He placed a hand on the cool siding and quick-peeked around the edge into the backyard.

High grass grew under a rusted swing set, and a barbecue sat atop a warped deck with peeling paint. Jakob didn't enjoy yard work. No light came through the sliding glass doors attached to the deck.

Nathan slipped into the yard and crept to the stairs. He climbed up the outer edge, where the wood would be strongest, but they still creaked under his weight. He looked over his Glock's front sight and scanned the windows.

No movement.

Nathan inhaled to slow his pulse. This was McLean, Virginia, not Afghanistan or any of the shitholes where he'd worked. Had Jakob fallen asleep? Old people did that.

Nathan reached the top of the deck and inched forward. His eyes fell to a crack between the sliding glass door and the doorjamb.

Bad news.

Someone had left it open. Nathan pivoted and concealed himself against the siding. The door's metal frame looked scratched and bent.

Pried open.

He could call 911. But if Jakob was asleep, or had gone out, or had changed his mind about talking to Nathan, there'd be hell to pay. Nathan wasn't supposed to be there, and outing Jakob as a former CIA program manager would not be good for anyone. But Jakob was detail-oriented, not the type of person to leave his door open, and unless he'd locked himself out, someone else had let themselves in.

Nathan tiptoed across the deck and dialed his phone.

"What's up?" Meili asked.

"I'm at Dr. Mandel's residence and—"

"You're where? You've got to be shitting me. When my ASAC—"

"Listen, something's wrong. Jakob wanted to talk. He had something urgent to tell me, and he sounded worried."

"Nathan, I explicitly told you not to—"

"I came right over after I spoke to him, but he's not coming to the door, and the lights are off. I called, and he's not answering his phone. I heard it inside."

"He's exercising more commonsense than you. He—"

"Someone jimmied the back door. Jakob's in trouble."

"Dammit," Meili said. "All right, stay where you are. I'm coming over."

"It'll take you thirty minutes. Call 911. If somebody hurt Jakob, they could still be inside."

"Don't do what I think you're planning to—"

"This just happened. Jakob could be injured. I'm going in."

"Nathan, don't—"

Nathan powered off his phone and dropped it into his pocket. He raised his Glock and moved forward. He slid open the door, keeping his gun pointed into the room. The door squeaked.

Nathan slipped inside and dodged left. He swept the dark corners as he pivoted in an arc. He covered the empty room and aimed down the hallway.

Why hadn't he brought his flashlight? He would never have made that kind of operational mistake investigating terrorism overseas. Being in Virginia had dulled his instincts.

He moved through the kitchen, and something registered in his peripheral vision. He stopped.

Icy fingers climbed his back.

A motionless shape lay on the floor beside the marble island.

Jakob.

Nathan watched the hallway as he sidestepped across the tile to him. A siren blared in the distance.

Good.

Nathan knelt beside Jakob, keeping his gun trained down the hall. He groped for Jakob's neck and felt for a pulse.

Nothing.

Nathan readjusted his fingers over the carotid artery.

No pulse.

Dammit. He had to perform CPR, but not before he cleared the house.

Nathan kept his gun up and used his offhand to roll Jakob onto his back.

Blood spilled out of a jagged hole in Jakob's forehead. His lifeless eyes stared back.

The siren grew louder.

45

Nathan brooded as he rode his condo elevator down to the street. Coincidences did not exist. Not like this. Someone murdered Jakob because of Havana Syndrome. He was dead because he'd helped Nathan. But who had killed him and why?

Finding Jakob's body had impacted Nathan more than any corpse he'd encountered during his time investigating terrorism, including agents and police officers he'd known who had died in the line of duty. Jakob's murder felt different. He'd been retired. Out of the game. If they were willing to kill Jakob, nobody was safe—not Reagan, not Amelia, not him.

He played for life-and-death stakes.

The ISIS case heated up too. Ghulam's paying for fake identification made the threat real, and his request for FAA identification had upped the stakes. Nathan dialed Eddie.

"What's up?" Eddie asked.

"We need to stay on top of our sources and step up surveillance. This is serious, and I don't want to get sloppy."

"We're monitoring the pole camera, but I'll double check the tapes."

"Let me know if—"

Nathan exited his house and stopped short. Someone had jammed a can of Dr. Pepper on the iron fence across from his front door. That was the sign that Timor Balakin had arranged a meeting with SVD Colonel Sergei Popov.

"You there?" Eddie asked.

"Gotta go. Call me if you need anything."

Nathan crossed the street and examined the tree beside the can. Nothing. He stepped closer and scrutinized the bare branches.

There.

Wire affixed a tiny plastic container, no larger than a pencil eraser, to a thin branch. It looked like a flower bud. He glanced around, then uncoiled the wire and opened the container. A tiny piece of rolled paper slid out. He unraveled it.

InterContinental Hotels, Kyiv Ukraine. Friday, 1500 hours.

46

Reagan sunk into a threadbare couch with red patches and waited for Nathan inside a coffee shop a mile from Vince's house. The decor tried hard to be chic, as did the hipster sporting a goatee and facial piercings. Anxiety built inside her like steam. When would she be herself again? She clasped her coffee mug in both hands and let the heat and the rich aroma comfort her.

Nathan pushed through the glass doors, spotted her, and waved. Warmth radiated through her. Despite his lack of attention during their marriage, he loved her. She knew that. But it was too late to turn back the clock. She was with Vince now, not physically since he had remained in Santo Domingo for an extra week, but emotionally. Sort of.

Nathan made his way through a phalanx of young people typing on MacBooks and sipping five-dollar coffees while probably posting about the evils of capitalism.

"May I?" He slid onto the cushion beside her.

"Is the sofa okay?" she asked.

"It's fine."

"We could move to a bistro table by the window if—"

He put his hand on top of hers. "You seem agitated."

He always saw right through her. "I guess I'm not as together as I'd hoped."

"You're in pain?"

"Constant. My headache's throbbing, but my lack of equilibrium bothers me most. It's not improving."

"You shouldn't leave the house alone."

She pulled her hand away. "I didn't ask you here to mother me."

He frowned then leaned back. "It's the middle of a workday."

She regretted her tone but didn't have the strength to apologize. Not for anything. "They attacked our embassy in Bangkok last night. I heard about it on a Facebook page for Havana Syndrome survivors. The frequency of attacks is increasing."

"Information's just coming in," he said. "One employee had symptoms on her lunch break. It could be an unrelated health incident."

"You sound like them."

"Who?"

"CIA, State . . . they're all the same. Nobody takes this seriously."

"That's not true. Politics may affect the investigation, but dozens of dedicated scientists and agents are trying to find the source. Is this why you asked to meet? To tell me to work harder?"

She wanted his help, but did she have a right to ask for it? She'd hurt him badly. Waves of pain pulsed in her head, and she rubbed her temples.

He softened. "Can I get you anything?"

"I had a thought, and I don't know if it's legitimate or some kind of paranoia brought on by brain trauma."

"No judgment," Nathan said.

"No judgment from you? You've done nothing but judge me since I accepted the position at the embassy."

"I . . . okay, that's fair. But I'm not criticizing you now. Not about this. I believe you, and I want you to get better. What's worrying you?"

"The total number of suspected Havana Syndrome cases is over 300, and likely much higher if we include unreported historic cases that agencies didn't bother to count. The government has categorized incidents based on acute onset of symptoms, but what if microwaves or whatever else they're using cause damage without visible symptoms?"

Nathan scowled. "That's an unpleasant scenario."

"What if huge numbers of our employees have brain damage and we don't know yet? What if radio waves or microwaves cause behavioral changes or cognitive impairment? The government hasn't been measuring that."

"You think we should give all our deployed personnel MRIs?"

"At a minimum."

He frowned and shook his head. "That would take forever and cost a fortune, not to mention disrupting operations."

"We should devise behavioral and medical questionnaires looking for changes in our personnel. These attacks could do permanent damage that won't become obvious for years. What if a significant number of our embassy personnel develop Alzheimer's or less noticeable cognitive issues as they move up the ladders in their various organizations? Russia or whoever could be destroying our entire diplomatic and intelligence core."

"Jesus." Nathan said.

"Am I paranoid?"

"There's no evidence to back your theory, but it's possible. Russia directed microwaves at our Moscow embassy in the seventies, and we didn't discover higher rates of cancer among embassy personnel until years later."

"They're doing it again," Her eyes burned. Would she develop cancer?

"If you're right, it would be a disaster for national security. We need to list every health symptom our employees experience."

Her stomach knotted. "Just hearing the word 'list' gives me cramps."

"I'll pass your thoughts up the chain. I've been working with the lead FBI team. Well, sort of. My contribution is unofficial."

"They'll think you're crazy too."

"Before 2016, I would have thought anyone who claimed they'd been attacked by Russian lasers was wacko. Not anymore. There's a movement in Europe to ban governments from using high-energy weapons."

"I can't let the government paint us as lunatics. I'll lose my career. I've decided to talk to the press."

Nathan's eyes widened. "Don't do that."

She glared at him. What gave him the right to dictate her actions? They'd damaged her brain, not his.

"CIA wants this to disappear," she said. "They're dismissing Havana Syndrome as the rantings of emotionally fragile people. It's not right."

"They leaned toward the Russia theory until recently."

"What changed?"

"Wish I knew."

She stood, and the world tilted for a moment before it stabilized. "I'm not waiting for them to flip-flop again. The public needs to know."

"It's dangerous. Someone was killed."

That took her breath away. "What?"

"Sit down, please."

Reagan lowered herself back on to the couch, slower this time. "Who?"

Nathan lowered his voice. "A scientist working with the intelligence community. He was involved with this type of research years ago."

"Who killed him?"

"Had to be the Russians."

"Where?"

"Northern Virginia. He provided me with information."

Her heart pounded in her chest. "Are you in danger? Am I?" She glanced around the room.

He touched her leg, and she shrank from his touch. She didn't need to be treated like a schoolgirl. She'd been injured, and she'd fight back.

"I don't think we're in immediate danger," he said, "but take precautions. Keep your eyes open and lock your doors. Don't go out alone."

An icy wind blew through her. "You're scaring me."

"A little fear is good. It'll keep you sharp. Understand why whistleblowing is perilous?"

"Yes."

Nathan smiled and got up. "I need to get back. Don't mention the murder to anyone. It hasn't been publicly linked to the FBI investigation. And please take care of yourself."

"Thanks for coming."

She watched him leave. He was right—this wasn't the best time to become a whistleblower.

It was the perfect time.

47

"Are you crazy?" Meili asked Nathan.

They stood outside a Starbucks in Penn Quarter, a block north of the Navy Memorial and halfway between their offices. Traffic whizzed past, and the odor of bacon from a nearby restaurant hung in the air.

"There's an active war in Ukraine," she said. "You want to meet a KGB spy in a former Soviet republic after you've seen what they did to our embassy staff? After what they did to Jakob?"

"Former KGB," Nathan said.

"What?"

"Sergei's SVD now."

"Sergei? You're best friends?"

"I don't know *who* my friends are," Nathan said.

Meili frowned.

"Except you."

Her eyes glistened for a moment, then her face tightened. "And travel to Kyiv? The Russians control vast swaths of the country, and they may have taken out half a dozen CIA officers and FBI agents in Tallinn."

"Whoever set up this meeting broke into my house. If they wanted to kill me, they'd have done it already."

Meili's mouth dropped open. "Your house? When?"

"Yesterday, while I was following ISIS operatives around DC."

"What did the police say? Did they get fingerprints?"

"I didn't report it."

"You must report it to—"

"And what? Tell them I'm meeting a Russian intelligence officer? Withhold the information about the note? No, I need to keep this quiet. Popov's giving me a glimpse behind the curtain."

"You're walking into a trap."

"He's the only person with the information I need."

She bit her lip. "Gee, I guess you should believe him, then. It's not as if the KGB ever assassinated anyone."

"Timor swears Russia's not involved. I need to—"

Meili put her hands on her hips. "You're not going. First, you're not working the case. Second, you can't meet a foreign spy without permission. You're not authorized to collect foreign intelligence on your own, and meeting a spy—"

"Former spy."

"... meeting a spy will jeopardize your security clearance. You'll have to disclose it on your next polygraph. Third, your boss will report you to OPR if she finds out. And you don't have operational coverage, which means you'll be on your own with no countersurveillance, no backup, no . . . dammit, Nathan. If you're trying to trash your career and get arrested, this is a great way to accomplish that."

"We're not getting anywhere with the investigation. It's been years, and we're no closer to finding an answer." Nathan stared at the sky and sighed. "And Reagan's not doing well. I can't turn my back on a chance to acquire evidence because I'm afraid."

"You can't run an intelligence operation alone."

"Then come with me."

"You know I can't. And you're not going. That's final."

"It's not up to you. The only way to protect Reagan is to stop the Russians."

"We talked about this in Tallinn. You're out for revenge."

Nathan sighed. "I get your point."

She cocked her head. "You're not just saying that to shut me up?"

He smiled.

Meili looked down and played with a button on her shirt. "You know I like you, right?"

"I like you too."

"I mean, I care about you. Always have. Traveling to Kyiv would be a one-way trip. I can't allow you risk it."

Would Meili report his intentions to her boss? To his? How far would she go to stop him? She cared about his safety, but the ferocity in her eyes indicated she wouldn't budge. If he pushed, she'd ruin the operation.

"Okay," he said. "You're right."

Her body deflated, and she smiled. "Thank, God. We'll figure this out. I promise. Let me go through official channels and see if your KGB buddy will meet Bashir and me."

Bashir. He could help.

"We'll arrange Popov's travel and do it in Washington," she said, "but officially, with safeguards. If he declines, he was setting you up."

Popov would never travel to the US, but Nathan nodded. "It's worth a shot."

Meili hugged him. "You had me worried."

Nathan smiled. Lying to her felt wrong, but he had to talk to Bashir. He needed a visa to Eastern Europe and a way into Ukraine.

48

"I want to arrest them now," Rahimya said. She settled behind her desk like a statue, her mind made up.

"We don't have evidence to charge a continuing criminal enterprise." Nathan said.

Eddie shifted in the seat beside him.

Rahimya pointed her bony finger at Nathan. "You talked me into delivering the fake passports to establish charges."

Nathan nodded. "We can indict for possession of fraudulent documents. The passports are a federal charge, but they won't get prison time, and a judge will release them on bail."

"At least we'll disrupt them," Rahimya said. "I believe that's how you phrased it."

Damn her for paying attention. "We would delay their operation only until they get new people in place. The problem is we don't understand what they're planning, and jihadists won't betray ISIS and their god to avoid a minor felony."

"They may."

"You know better than that. We need real charges to break the weak link and develop a cooperating witness."

"Then why do the delivery? What about what you said before?" The air moving through her nose became audible, and her features sharpened.

"That was a first step. It still gives us the arrest option as a last resort. We have photos of eleven operatives and the aliases we gave them on the documents, but only Ghulam and three of his cronies were involved in the purchase. We could never make charges stick on the other eight. Their attorneys will claim they didn't know their pictures were used to get fake identification."

"But they want FAA employee IDs. They're targeting airports or airlines. We can't risk it."

Eddie raised his hand like a child in class. "We could follow them and keep close track."

Rahimya stared at Eddie until he averted his eyes, then she returned her attention to Nathan.

He had to tread lightly here. If she pulled the plug and ordered arrests, they wouldn't send anyone to prison. Most of them would flee back to the Middle East and then return under different names. That's how it worked.

"Our surveillance team followed Ghulam to a location," Nathan said. "It could be his residence, but we don't know where the others are staying. Our most effective strategy is to let this play out."

"That's a dangerous game," Rahimya said.

"Terrorism's a dangerous business. I agree we can't let it go much longer, but if we're too conservative, we won't stop anything."

"Delaying operations has worked since 9/11."

"This one won't save lives because we don't know what they're plotting. It's catch and release. We need to uncover their plot, gather evidence, and arrest them before they execute it."

Rahimya leaned forward on her elbows and locked Nathan with her deep brown eyes. "How do you propose we do that?"

She was biting—a good sign. Now he had to reel her in. "We push Mohammad to get more involved, tell them he wants in."

"Isn't he more of a facilitator? Will they buy that?"

"He's a criminal, not a jihadi, but there's only one way to determine if they'll let him inside. Have him ask."

"They may kill him."

"Like you said, it's a dangerous game."

"I don't know—"

"Mohammad has agency. If he feels it worth the risk, he'll do it. If not, he's free to walk away."

"And we make it worthwhile, how?"

"We give him a solid payment for information and services now, then promise to submit him for a large reward. There are several government funds we can use."

"But no promises."

"Never."

Rahimya studied the ceiling tiles then lowered her gaze to Nathan, "Let's say I agree to this, and Mohammad is clever enough to talk himself inside. What's next?"

"We'll work out the details, but we'll gather evidence through surveillance, sources, and wiretaps. We might have enough to bug their apartment. They'll be careful on their phones, but I'll bet they speak freely when—"

"We don't have probable cause to monitor their apartment," Rahimya said. "One meeting doesn't show a pattern of criminal behavior, and we only have passport fraud as an underlying crime. No way a judge signs that paper."

She was right, of course. "Mohammad can give us more PC. Meanwhile, we'll identify their residences and get search warrants, then ask a grand jury for arrest warrants so we're ready to act. We'll create and deliver the FAA identification to them and intercept them doing whatever they're planning."

"Risky, risky, risky. I don't—"

"We'll call audibles as we go. We can take them down whenever we want."

Rahimya rocked back in her chair and rubbed her temples. "You'll be the death of me."

"I've been getting that a lot lately."

49

Bashir and Trent Hamilton stood before Frederick Richardson's desk in the West Wing. The national security advisor didn't look happy with them, as per their usual arrangement. The White House had experienced a malfunction with its climate control, and the office was sweltering. Richardson's face had turned beat red, either from the heat or lack of progress in the FBI's investigation.

"Gimme the latest," Richardson said.

"I traveled to Estonia after Agent Chan," Bashir said.

"And?"

"She's after the Russians."

"What changed her mind?"

"The bodies of children."

Richardson looked like he had received a shock. "Children?"

"Agent Burke found two children and their parents murdered in an apartment behind the embassy. It's in my report."

Richardson shot daggers at Hamilton.

"We just received it," Hamilton said. "I added it to today's report."

"It didn't make the briefing," Richardson said.

"If I may," Bashir said. Both men looked at him. "There's nothing tying the family's murder to the embassy incident. The Estonians don't see a connection."

Richardson rubbed his chin. "But you do?"

"It's a hell of a coincidence. I spoke to Nathan when he returned, and he's certain it's related."

"Does his team agree?"

"Chan's on board with the microwave weapon theory."

"Are they following up on the murders?" Richardson asked.

"The Estonian police sent reports from both the homicide and the embassy incident. Nothing tangible to connect them yet."

Hamilton puffed out his chest. "We're staying on top of it."

"Gimme regular updates," Richardson said. "Thanks for coming in."

Hamilton turned to leave, but Bashir stayed. He waited until Richardson looked up.

"Excuse me," Bashir said. "You were certain Russia was to blame, but then CIA issued a report blaming psychogenic causes. I'm confused. Do you want the FBI to find Russia responsible?"

"Let's not bother Mr. Richardson with this now," Hamilton said.

Richardson raised his hand. "No, it's a fair question. The FBI needs to get answers. I wanted evidence of Russian chicanery, but they've turned up nothing."

"They're looking hard at Russia now," Bashir said.

"Took long enough," Richardson said, "but these may be psychogenic. Either way, the FBI can't get ahead of us. Foreign policy comes from the White House, not the FBI. Political timing is critical."

"That should be easy. Burke's wavering on the Russian angle."

"How?"

"I followed him to a meeting with Timor Balakin."

"Who?" Richardson asked.

"The former Russian KGB officer who managed their sonic program. Couldn't get all the audio, but it sounded like Balakin denied Russia's involvement."

"How did you hear—never mind, I don't want details. My point is it's possible these are psychological in nature."

"That doesn't seem feasible," Bashir said.

Hamilton touched Bashir's arm. "I think that'll do."

Richardson's face darkened. "Our diplomatic staff is under incredible stress, 24/7. People crack, especially when colleagues succumb to an invisible predator."

"Personnel deployed in hostile nations are most at risk," Hamilton agreed.

"Havana Syndrome didn't appear until 2016," Bashir said.

"Let's not ignore the possibility and start a war with Russia for the wrong reasons. Good day, gentlemen."

50

Eddie slammed his office phone down. "Man, I'm getting nowhere with FAA security. It takes an act of God to have them print up employee identification cards with our targets' names."

"Not a surprise," Nathan said. "I've been running federal investigations for more than a decade, and my biggest obstacle has always been bureaucracy."

"But this is a terrorism case," Eddie said. "We're trying to stop a group of jihadis from perpetrating another 9/11—"

"We don't know what they're planning," Nathan said, "only that they want to penetrate someplace where FAA identification cards will grant access. They could target an airport, airplanes, or even an FAA facility. It's possible they aren't planning an attack at all. They could use their FAA credentials to access a restricted area at Dulles, DCA, or BWI to offload smuggled cargo, or people, or who knows what."

"Whatever they're doing, it's bad."

"Agreed. Where did you leave it with FAA?"

Eddie looked at his notes. "Since nine o'clock this morning, I've spoken to a dozen people and had every level of small-minded manager read me chapter and verse on FAA policy and US criminal code. It's as if they're looking for reasons to say no."

"They are," Nathan said. "It's the bureaucratic mindset. If they do something unorthodox, they take a chance, but they risk nothing if they don't deviate from the norm. It doesn't matter to them if you accomplish your mission or not. They want to protect their jobs, do as little as possible, and stay out of trouble. Most are there for a steady paycheck."

"Unbelievable. We're trying to protect their facilities and planes."

"If I can teach you one thing from my time working for the federal government, it's this—anything significant you accomplish, any leap forward in the FBI's mission, gets done despite the agency, not with its cooperation."

"You're saying we break the rules? Violate the law? I went to law school because I believe in rules."

"If you want to accomplish anything, bend them," Nathan said. "I don't mean engaging in criminal acts or violating people's constitutional rights. I mean coloring outside the policy lines to avoid roadblocks the administrative framework emplaced. Every time somebody crashes a government car or does something stupid, they form a new rule. It's all about covering the agency's ass, even if it makes our job harder. When an organization exists for long enough, the rules become incomprehensible and contradictory. Worse, administrative employees are unable to think outside the box. That's an inherent point of friction. Unprecedented situations crop up in counterterrorism more than in other areas of law enforcement. Rules are great, but when the stakes are high—like trying to stop an attack—standard protocols are too slow and ineffective."

"What happens when you break the rules?" Eddie asked.

"Whenever you violate a policy, you expose yourself to every form of administrative punishment, from verbal warnings to termination. Even prosecution. I've been careful not to violate the criminal code, because I believe in the rule of law. But administrative policies designed by bureaucrats trying to show they've accomplished something and approved by people who've never hunted terrorists are different. I'm willing to violate nonsensical rules if the stakes are high enough."

Eddie smirked. "You kind of dodged my question. If you've been bending rules for over a decade, people must've noticed. You never got reprimanded?"

"Oh, they noticed. I've taken calculated risks when following rules would've resulted in loss of life. I'd rather get fired than live with that." Nathan leaned forward. "But to answer your question, I've received nothing harsher than a verbal warning, and I've disobeyed orders, bent regulations, and run unapproved operations."

"I'm not saying I approve, but how'd you get away with it?"

"Since I'm imparting wisdom today, here's a good one. If you violate policy, you better be successful. If you break a rule and a case ends in disaster, I guarantee they'll hang you out to dry. They always need a fall guy. Think twice before you cross the line and violate procedure, but always do what's moral and ethical, not what some dumpy bureaucrat wearing a polyester suit thinks is right."

Eddie studied his nails then nodded. "Tell me, Yoda. FAA's stalling, so what can we do?"

"We could designate this as a significant operation and request permission from the attorney general to deviate from DOJ policy. Ask them to green-light FAA to print out the fake identification."

Eddie's face lit up, and he sat up straighter. "Great. Let's do it."

"Slow down, my friend. I said we *could* do that. The problem is, it'll take a week to get every level of FBI concurrence before it even makes it to Main Justice, then another week or more to get it on the attorney general's desk. At every stage of approval, there's a fifty-fifty chance the manager who is reading it will ask for more information or changes to our operational plan. If it ever makes it to the top, you won't recognize the plan. Worse, even if we rush it by calling in personal favors, too many people would be exposed to our plan, and operational security would be weakened."

"You're saying ISIS has moles at the Department of Justice?"

"Not ISIS per se," Nathan said. "But the Muslim Brotherhood does, and they control almost every radical Islamist group. The Brotherhood has infiltrated the highest levels of our government, and all it takes is for one person to catch wind of our operation, and it's over."

"Shit." Eddie slumped back in his chair, his enthusiasm gone.

"And when I say our case is over, I mean the brotherhood warns ISIS, and the eleven suspects we're investigating all disappear. But not before they kill Mohammad and Kei. The bureaucrats would breathe easier, relieved to avoid a risky and unorthodox plan, and they'd never be held accountable when ISIS launches another attack. And nobody will go looking for the Brotherhood spies in the upper echelons of our leadership. Without direct proof that a terror group compromised the case, agencies will circle the wagons to protect their own."

"We don't request an AG exemption?"

"If we got lucky enough to receive approval, it'll still take weeks—longer than Ghulam will stay patient. And if the AG says no, then we're screwed, because we won't be able to violate policy without getting indicted."

"Better to ask forgiveness than permission, right?" Eddie asked.

"Now you're getting it."

"I'm starting to understand how to be an agent. I'll need less hand-holding soon. So, what's next?"

"We don't need the FAA to issue fraudulent IDs."

"The Golden Dragons?"

Nathan smiled. "Exactly."

"But Kei said they just made fake passports and driver licenses. Will they be able to create passable FAA identification?"

"We can't answer that until Kei asks them to try."

51

Dark clouds hovered over Mykhailivska Square in Kyiv, Ukraine, and an icy wind chilled Nathan to his core. He entered the Kyiv funicular, a cable car on the rocky face of Volodymyrska Hill that connected Upper Town with the historic Lower Town neighborhoods. He found an empty seat and waited for the short three-minute descent down the steep embankment. The tram's doors whooshed shut, rocking the half-full carriage. Nathan stood and gave his seat to an old woman carrying a shopping bag. The tram lurched forward, and he grabbed a metal pole to maintain balance.

Nathan plastered a simple smile on his face to project the image of a harmless soul, then he scanned the passengers. A couple in their early twenties huddled in their seats, snuggling as if they were about to be separated forever. Young love. Nathan's forced smile turned genuine.

The tram moved down the concrete gully, and jagged rock rose on either side where engineers had gouged a deep scar into the earth. In the distance, the Dnieper River glistened a frosty bluish gray. The icy waterway was one of the longest rivers in Europe and split Kyiv in half. Three teenage boys struggled to maintain balance in the oscillating carriage as they watched the amorous couple with a mixture of curiosity, embarrassment, and lust. Two old ladies, with faces wrinkled like Sukkari dates, balanced giant fabric handbags in their laps.

That left three men as potential intelligence agents. A slender guy in a shiny suit read the *Kyiv Post* while he clung to a bar. The middle-aged man beside him wore a tattered woodsman's jacket and was missing three front teeth. And the last passenger, an older, dark-haired man wearing wool trousers and a sport jacket, sported an impressive belly that bulged over his belt buckle like a balloon.

None of the occupants paid attention to Nathan, but he committed their faces to memory.

The car shuddered to a stop at the bottom, and Nathan stood aside to allow everyone to exit. The simple maneuver made it more difficult for a surveillance agent to monitor him. Nathan followed the people out of the station and down the steps into Poshtova Square in the city's Podil section. The group dispersed onto streets lined with cafes and retail stores. Shiny Suit headed east. Woodsman greeted a plump woman and kissed her. Belly wandered into a store. Nathan waited for a moment, but none looked back.

Three blocks away, the Dnieper River flowed toward the Black Sea. Nathan headed for it. He approached a bookstore on the corner and peered through the windows. Another door exited onto the street on the far side. Nathan opened the door and glimpsed over his shoulder. Nobody behind him. He entered the bookstore and smiled at the proprietor as he strode down an aisle and out the other door. He stepped onto the intersecting street and picked up his pace. At the top of the block, he stopped and spun around.

Nobody followed.

Earlier, Nathan had executed similar maneuvers traveling to his hotel, and while Ukrainian and Russian intelligence had likely identified where he was staying, they didn't appear to be watching.

But his greatest danger waited for him.

Sergei Popov was a Russian asset, and if they wanted to hurt Nathan, they didn't have to stake out his hotel. Nathan was headed to meet them.

The Fairmont Grand Hotel Kyiv overlooked the river. Popov had set their meeting in the restaurant on the second floor, but Nathan was an hour early. Arriving first to a meeting was standard security protocol. Of course, debriefing a source alone was against protocol, as was not having backup or official permission to meet a Russian asset.

Nathan had broken too many rules to count.

He passed the hotel and crossed the street to the river. He lost himself in a group of people near a pedestrian bridge and removed a crumpled map from his pocket, a souvenir he'd snatched from the hotel. Nathan pretended to read as he stared over the map at the hotel entrance. Countersurveillance was almost pointless because he was at the mercy of the Russians in the Ukraine—but old habits died hard.

The slender man in the shiny suit from the tram rounded the corner of the hotel. Nathan smiled, surprised his countersurveillance tactics had worked. Shiny Suit paused outside the hotel then crossed the street in Nathan's direction.

Anxiety stirred inside his stomach, but Shiny Suit didn't look at him. He did what Nathan had done and established a vantage point across from the hotel. Was he Ukrainian intelligence, SVD, or someone else?

Shiny Suit pushed through the crowd and settled on a bench facing the river. He crossed his legs and opened his newspaper, keeping the hotel's entrance in his line of sight. Under normal circumstances Nathan would cancel a meeting once he detected countersurveillance, but Shiny Suit probably worked for the Russians. If Popov's and Nathan's roles had been reversed, and a foreign law enforcement officer—whom he'd spent a career avoiding—had contacted him, Nathan would want overwatch too. But was Shiny Suit there to protect Popov or arrest Nathan?

Or kill him.

The smart move would be to flee to the airport and get the hell out of Ukraine. Procedure dictated that, but every element of this operation involved risk, and Nathan wouldn't return home without getting the answers he sought. He must protect Reagan.

Nathan turned his back on Shiny Suit and maneuvered through the crowd until he was out of view, then he jogged across the street. He rounded the block and made his way to the rear of the hotel.

He slipped inside the Intercontinental and scanned the faces of staff and guests, but no one took notice. He always wore local clothing on overseas operations, and his European collar and a hand-knit Ukrainian sweater had done the job.

Spotting his watcher gave him a slight advantage, but how had Shiny

Suit picked him up on the tram? Nathan had made two heat runs after leaving the hotel and had observed no surveillance. And he'd left his cell phone in his hotel room to avoid electronic tracking, hiding it to make it more difficult for intelligence to locate and download its contents. Not spotting a tail sooner indicated aerial surveillance or a robust team of agents on the ground. That meant Ukrainian or Russian intelligence had committed assets. If the Ukrainians wanted to arrest him, slipping across the border would be difficult, and if the Russian wanted to kill him, he'd be dead.

One person possessed the answers—Sergei Popov.

Nathan hurried across the lobby and upstairs to the second floor. Only a handful of patrons occupied the restaurant. Tall windows overlooked the river and the crowd where Shiny Suit concealed himself. Meeting in the lull between lunch and dinner had ensured some measure of privacy, but it also made him stand out to surveillance. That Popov picked this time and place meant he was not concerned about being seen with Nathan.

Nathan scanned the room. A young couple dined near the window as they held hands and gazed into each other's eyes, ignoring everyone else. Two businessmen, both wearing gray suits, sat in the center of the room and chatted with serious expressions. Behind them, three women drank tea over the remains of a meal. At the far end of the room, a man sat alone at a table and watched Nathan.

The Russian spy.

52

Popov wore an expensive suit like other businessmen, but he looked lean and hard, and he stood out to those in the business of death. He sat in the far corner with his back against the wall, a habit law enforcement and intelligence shared. Popov's posture betrayed his underlying fitness and the danger he posed to anyone who found themselves in his crosshairs. This man feared nothing.

A lion among prey.

Popov's eyes roamed over the room, taking in everything, and he didn't try to conceal his interest. Nathan crossed the floor, ignoring the butterflies in his stomach. Leaders of men emitted arrogance, and even at a distance, the sparkle of amusement in Popov's eyes was evident. Was he excited to meet an adversary or because Nathan had fallen into his trap?

Nathan reached the table, and Popov pointed at the chair across from him. He didn't offer his hand. Another similarity between intelligence and law enforcement.

Nathan perched on the chair with his back to the door, and hair rose on his neck. He had been unable to face away from an entrance since graduating from Quantico, and Popov had intentionally put him in a position of discomfort. Each little trick of tradecraft seemed foolish, but together they created advantages for a field operative. Nathan was on his own, in a country infiltrated by his adversaries and facing his Cold War enemy. He was alone and unprotected.

He kept his discomfort off his expression.

"I did not think you come," Popov said. His accent was strong, like Boris from an episode of *Bullwinkle*.

Don't show weakness. "You have balls meeting me after what you did to my wife."

"We did not do this."

Nathan saw red. He balled his fists. "You're lying."

"After Tallinn, I make inquiry. Russia not behind attack."

"Don't bullshit me. First Putin invaded Ukraine, and now he's planning to drag Estonia back under his sphere of influence."

"That may be true, but he did not attack your embassy."

"He wants to weaken us by taking out diplomats with the experience necessary to respond to future incursions. Who the fuck else would interfere in Tallinn?"

"He has motive, yes," Popov said. "I cannot deny it. But he did not order aggression."

"Why should I believe denials? Russia has targeted us with disinformation and propaganda for a hundred years."

"America has done the same."

"When I uncover proof Putin is responsible, the US will turn Russia into a third-world country."

Popov snorted. "You hard man to like."

"I've got enough friends. You're lucky I don't kill you for what you did to Reagan."

Popov scowled and downed a shot of vodka. Russians always had vodka, no matter the time. He glared across the table. "Tough talk, for man alone in Kyiv."

"Did I make a mistake trusting you?" Nathan asked.

He smiled. "If you trust me, then yes, you make mistake. Never trust adversary."

"The Cold War is over."

"You better hope you are wrong. Nature abhors vacuum. When Cold War ends, Hot War follows."

"Is that why you're targeting us?"

Popov glowered, like a schoolmaster assessing a pupil. "Why would we do that?"

"Why invade Georgia or Ukraine? They—"

"Those are Russian lands. We defend oppressed Russian people."

"The Ukrainians didn't want your help.".

Popov smirked. "Ironic coming from American. Your tentacles spread around the world."

"There's a difference between defending democracies and conquering independent peoples, but I'm not here to discuss geopolitics. I want to stop this from escalating into a nuclear war."

"On that, we agree," Popov said. "This is why I meet you."

"Then why deny knowing anything?"

"I did not say I knew nothing."

"Evidence points to a GRU operation."

"Your theory makes no sense," Popov said. "When Mother Russia start laser weapon research, our goal was mind control. These attacks were blunt trauma from high-energy. We could do this fifty years ago. And if attacking diplomats is prelude to war, Tallinn is final step before world war. Last war for everyone."

"That's my theory."

"Not possible."

"Why?"

"Russian technology more advanced."

Nathan analyzed Popov's every movement "If it wasn't GRU, it could be SVD or another military unit."

"You misunderstand, my wide-eyed American friend. None of them do this. Russia does not condone these actions."

"Russia developed these weapons, and you expect me to believe someone else initiated the attacks?"

"Your own C-I-A," he dragged out the sound of each letter, as if they dripped with honey, "say this health problem."

"The CIA claimed most are likely psychogenic—not all of them. And that's bullshit. These were intentional acts of aggression."

Popov braced his hands on his knees and grunted as he pushed himself to his feet. "I try to give you information. Can you hide anger about wife and listen?"

Nathan rolled his head and cracked his neck trying to process what Timor said. "You're suggesting SVD or GRU did this on their own? A rogue commander taking foreign policy into his own hands?"

"Nobody hides from Putin."

"Then who?"

"The Communist Party of China."

"I'm supposed to believe you?"

Popov reached into his jacket and removed an envelope. He slid it across the table.

"What's that?"

"Open it later."

Nathan tapped the envelope on the table. "If China's the culprit, why tell me?"

"Some of us do not want seventy-five years of effort wasted. Or a reckless China committing acts of aggression and blaming Russia. Why you think they attack in Moscow?"

"Logistical ease," Nathan said.

"Incidents happen all over. Why Moscow? China wants to obfuscate their involvement and shift blame."

Obfuscate? Popov understood more English than he let on.

"You're telling me the Chinese used a high-energy weapon against Americans on Russian soil, without the consent of the Russian government?"

Popov spread his hands wide. "Da."

"China is Russia's strongest ally, a communist regime that—"

"Russia is no longer communist. We have free trade. Perhaps you heard, the Soviet Union is gone."

"Putin's oligarchy's the same as the Soviet regime. A handful of autocrats still control everything, but let's not argue political theory. My point is, China supports Russia around the world, and now you're accusing them."

"They pointed at us first. I give you intelligence to solve problem. Isn't this why you came?

"I don't believe it."

"But your CIA will, yes?"

"Are you acting on your own or on the Kremlin's orders?"

He snorted. "I give what you want. But you not happy."

"I don't intend to look like a fool. If the CCP's to blame, why throw them under the bus?"

Popov flashed a thin, cruel smile. He crossed his hands and laid them on his belly.

"Is this gift meant to ease economic sanctions?" Nathan asked.

Popov tapped his finger on the envelope. "This will help you find who responsible. What you do about it?"

Nathan looked at the envelope. Was he being used?

"We enemies for long time," Popov said, "but in this, our interests same. I wish you luck, my American friend." He rose from the table and stomped away.

Nathan watched him leave. Two thugs at a table near the door stood and fell in behind him. Bodyguards.

Nathan opened the envelop and removed a photo of an Asian man in his forties. He had a long scar that ran down his cheek. The photo was grainy, as if taken from a surveillance camera. Nathan flipped it over. On the back, Popov had written a telephone number with a 202 area code.

Washington, DC.

53

Nathan gave Popov time to clear the hotel, then he left under the waiter's glare. Nathan continued down an empty hallway to the stairwell that led to the lobby. He stopped at the landing, where a din of conversation rose from the ornate lobby. If Popov wanted to hurt him, he had the opportunity already, but maybe he wanted to hear what Nathan had to say first. And Ukrainian intelligence could be lying in wait, trying to determine why Nathan had met with a Russian spy.

Why take the chance?

Nathan turned and continued down the hall. He summoned the elevator and read the number on the photograph. He memorized it, then stuck it back in his pocket.

The elevator dinged, and the door slid open. Nathan stepped into the tiny car and rode it to the lower level beneath the lobby. He exited into a stark industrial hall, a world of sealed concrete and a glaring contrast to the opulence of the hotel guest spaces. Employees operated inside the building's skeleton, like servants in a nineteenth-century mansion. Nathan headed toward the rear of the hotel. A maid approached with a quizzical look, but Nathan hurried past.

At the back of the building, he took a stairwell up to the ground level and sidestepped two kitchen workers carrying boxes of fruit. One of them said something unintelligible in Ukrainian, but Nathan ignored him and pushed through a metal door into the alley behind the building. He entered a parking lot, boxed in on three sides by the back walls of other businesses. His shoes clip-clopped on the gray bricks as he shuffled between parked cars and headed down the alley leading to the street.

A man stood at the far end smoking a cigarette.

Nathan stopped. Friend or foe? The man's gray Cossack hat and upturned overcoat collar concealed his face in shadow. His hands were empty. Nathan glanced back at the empty lot behind the hotel.

The man took a drag from his cigarette then ground the stub under his toe.

No sense risking it. Nathan pivoted to return to the hotel.

"How was your meeting?" the man called out.

Nathan stopped and looked back at him.

Bashir sauntered down the alley and stopped in front of him.

"I guess I shouldn't be surprised to see you," Nathan said. "I appreciated your help fast-tracking a visa, but how'd you find me?"

Bashir smiled. "Who do you think set up the meeting?"

Nathan gawked, then shut his mouth. "You broke into my house."

"Just your elevator."

"Why?"

Bashir reached into his overcoat and came out with a pack of Capri cigarettes, a popular local brand. Only then did Nathan notice all of Bashir's clothes were Ukrainian. And used.

"Nice outfit," Nathan said.

Bashir looked him up and down, taking in Nathan's local clothing. "Good tradecraft for an FBI agent."

"Not my first rodeo," Nathan said. "You didn't answer my question."

Bashir lit his cigarette and inhaled the harsh smoke. "Let's just say recent events have made me question things too."

"You thought Popov had answers?"

"People will be interested in what he said."

"I doubt it."

"And?" Bashir asked.

"Popov claims Russia didn't do it."

"Of course."

Nathan scanned the lot. They were still alone. He looked at Bashir. "He blamed the Chinese."

"Huh." Bashir took a long drag and stared at the glowing ember.

"That's your analysis—*huh*?"

"It makes sense the Russians are responsible," Bashir said, "but the attacks in Africa don't jibe with that theory. What was Russia trying to accomplish there?"

"Meili asked CIA what they were doing at those embassies," Nathan said, "but she never received a straight answer. If CIA won't hint about their operations, we'll never crack this."

Bashir smirked. "The agency will never divulge their most closely held secrets."

"Why would the Russians risk a war to hit our embassies in countries with little geopolitical value?"

Bashir blew out a long stream of smoke. He never seemed ruffled. "To cause confusion and fear."

"Not worth the gamble."

"What are you thinking?" Bashir asked.

"Who else would benefit from disrupting American officials in Africa?"

Bashir took another puff. "The Chinese have pursued mineral rights across the continent."

"A couple of the attacks wouldn't benefit Russia."

"If they were attacks," Bashir said.

"Aren't we past that? Of the attacks we believe were real, two were counter-productive for Putin. Follow me for a minute. Assuming our enemies kept researching microwave, radio waves, and related weapons, what makes us certain the Russian's had the breakthrough with a man-portable unit? What about the Chinese?"

"The Russians were the closest and—"

"But who's to say China didn't surpass them? Russians are dangerous, but economically, they're a third-rate power. The Chinese are too, but they're the world's leader in intellectual property theft. Maybe they stole the technology from Russia. Or from us. Or Russia could have shared it with them. Russia, North Korea, Iran, and a host of other totalitarian countries have assisted each other whenever it hurts our interests. They could be working together."

"That's a lot of *ifs*." Bashir ground out his cigarette, his second in five minutes. Hadn't he received the memo that nicotine was bad for his health?

"The first Havana Syndrome case appeared when?" Nathan asked.

"Late 2016, in Cuba."

"A communist country, in a region where the Chinese have rapidly expanded their influence. We think of Cuba as a Russian ally, and there's no doubt it was a puppet of the Soviets, but which communist government is expanding the fastest in the Caribbean?"

"Interesting," Bashir said. He looked at the gray sky and clucked his tongue.

"And where was the next attack?"

"China."

"Bingo."

54

The growl of an engine reverberated off Vince's house, and Reagan bolted upright in bed. Vince was home! She checked her hair in the mirror then wobbled downstairs, clinging to the banister for support.

The door swung open as she reached the bottom, and Vince entered carrying a suitcase and a briefcase. He looked ready to start his day, with an unruffled suit and every hair in place. He showed no sign of the long trip. How did he do it?

She stepped into the foyer, brimming with excitement.

Vince's face brightened, and he lifted her into his arms. Vertigo swept through her, but she shook it away and melted into the safety of his grasp. God, she'd missed him.

"How are you, baby?" he asked without putting her down.

Her eyes filled with tears, but she couldn't keep from smiling. "You're home."

"Forgive me for leaving?"

"You're back now, and everything's right again. The world's in balance, even if I'm not."

He set her down but kept his arm around her. Being held by him made her feel invincible, like no one could hurt her and no disease could touch her.

She was falling for this guy. Hard.

"Symptoms any better?"

"I don't notice a daily difference, but when I think back to the hospital, it's obvious I'm trending in the right direction."

"Coffee," he said. A statement, not a question.

He entered the kitchen, and she shuffled after him, the exertion of her emotions had spent her energy. She slid onto a soft yellow cushion at the bistro table. The March sun streamed through the window and warmed her. Sharp pain flashed between her temples, and she grimaced.

Vince paused with the bag of coffee hovering about the machine. "What's wrong?"

"Light triggers my headaches."

He bounded across the kitchen and lowered the blinds then returned to the coffee machine. "Has State done anything to help?"

"Other than sending me to a psychiatrist?"

"I mean medical care, security, updates on the investigation?"

"Those bastards," Reagan said. "They're—"

"I didn't mean to upset you." He sat across from her as the coffee percolated and the rich odor of French roast spiced the air.

"They're paying lip service to my condition, but underneath is the unspoken accusation that I'm faking. Or crazy. They won't say that explicitly, but it's always behind their eyes."

"There's dissension between CIA and other agencies over causation."

"CIA's gaslighting everyone. Sudden crippling attacks are not how mass psychosis presents. I know what happened."

Vince didn't say anything. Did he doubt her mental state?

"What bothers me most," Reagan said, "is how mainstream media repeats whatever CIA publishes. What happened to investigative journalism? Where's their critical analysis of obvious disinformation?"

Vince rose and sauntered to the counter. He grabbed a mug and watched the coffeemaker, as if willing it to brew faster. "The press have become activists for whoever's in the Oval Office. Conservative outlets support Republican administrations and leftists support Democrats."

"American Pravda."

"Unfortunately."

"But I offered a first-hand account. I provided supporting documentation and the names of experts who—"

"They're not interested in truth. They want to validate preexisting narratives and fuel outrage to draw viewers."

Her head throbbed beneath a growing migraine, waves on an incoming tide. It promised to be a bad one.

He narrowed his eyes, sensing her distress. "You're overdoing it. Let me pour a cup, then I'll help you upstairs."

"Good idea." Asking for help made her feel crippled, but she needed assistance. "I'll lie down for a while, then I'm going to fight back."

Vince raised an eyebrow. "How?"

"I'm calling the press to blow the whistle."

"Blow the whistle on what?"

"The whole thing. What happened to me, State's response, CIA's bogus analysis. I'm not the only one suffering. The public needs to hear the truth. If they knew—"

"That's a career ender."

She shook her head, and pain shot between her temples. "If the fucking CIA brands me as a lunatic, my career's finished anyhow."

"You've wanted to work for State since you were a little girl. What happened to carrying on your father's legacy?"

The mention of her father stopped her cold. If her dad hadn't been killed in Eastern Europe, what would he counsel her to do?

"I've been passive and taking it, but no more. I have a voice. I won't be a victim."

Vince put a hand on her shoulder. "Take it easy. You're recovering from a serious incident, whatever the cause."

"Excuse me?"

"You experienced a traumatic incident. Don't make decisions with career implications until you weigh your options."

"Is that what they told you to say?"

"Who's *they*?"

"You tell me. Did the ambo order you to keep me quiet?"

Vince looked away for a moment—just a flicker, but enough to betray him. He *had* been told to handle her. "The ambassador feels responsible for what happened. You worked under him. He told me to help you however I could. He asked me to task all our sources with force protection."

Her father's face appeared behind her eyes. He'd been gone for most of her life as he tended to the business of State, and he'd never emotionally connected with her. Had he even been capable of that? But before a criminal's bullet took his life, he'd been a rock with a constitution as strong as his granite jaw. Her father would tell her to fight.

"I'm calling every newspaper, television station, and podcast that will listen."

55

Nathan shifted on a bench beside Eddie and Agent Sharif Khan as they watched a video monitor in the windowless cabin of a surveillance van parked on H Street NW. Mohammad's and Ghulam's faces filled the black-and-white screen as they talked in the front seat of the FBI's undercover BMW parked a block away. A pinhole camera and microphone concealed in the car's instrument panel transmitted their conversation, and the recording would be used to prosecute Ghulam and his ISIS associates.

Ghulam uttered something in Arabic, and Mohammad responded, also in Arabic. Nathan caught Sharif's eye.

"Ghulam asked why Mohammad wanted to meet him alone," Sharif interpreted. "Mohammad said he didn't want the other guys to hear."

Mohammad spoke again, and Ghulam watched him with pinched lips and narrowed eyes.

"Come on, Mohammad," Nathan said. "Convince him he needs your help."

Sharif looked up. "Mohammad's asking Ghulam to give him a bigger role in their jihad."

Mohammad and Ghulam spoke for thirty seconds, and Nathan strained to read their body language. "What's happening?"

"Ghulam says he has enough warriors. He said Mohammad's not vetted.

Mohammad is arguing he wants to wage jihad and do more than logistical support. He... hold on."

Ghulam had turned in his seat and faced Mohammad. He stayed silent for a moment. Then spoke.

"*Ayowah.*"

"Ghulam agreed," Sharif said.

"Yes," Nathan said. "That's what I'm talking about."

Mohammad started the undercover vehicle and pulled into traffic.

"He's moving westbound H Street," Eddie transmitted to the surveillance team.

Nathan studied Ghulam's face for any sign of deception as Mohammad drove to meet with Kei, but Ghulam only radiated intensity.

Five minutes later, Mohammad stopped beside a Chevrolet Tahoe, and Ghulam lowered his window and spoke to the driver. When he finished, Mohammed drove away, and the Tahoe fell in behind him.

They drove across the Fourteenth Street Bridge into Arlington, apparently unaware of the five-car surveillance team covering them. They entered Crystal City and parked a block from the Crystal City Marriott, where Kei waited in a hotel room. In an adjoining room filled with surveillance equipment, special agents prepared to swoop in and save Kei if Ghulam double-crossed him.

Nathan and Eddie jumped out of the van, leaving Sharif inside to guard it, and hustled into the hotel a few minutes behind Mohammad, Ghulam, and three ISIS goons. They took the stairs, and Nathan peeked into the hallway to avoid running into their suspects outside the undercover hotel room. Nathan and Eddie hurried into the adjoining room and entered using an extra key Eddie had acquired when he rented the rooms.

Five agents looked up with alarm, then recognized them and relaxed. Nathan closed the door quietly behind them and joined a circle of agents hovering around a video monitor. They had replaced the undercover room's lamps and clock with FBI electronics that wirelessly transmitted video and audio to the receiver in the adjoining room. A tech agent recorded everything.

On the monitor, Ghulam moved to the desk where Kei had laid out eleven sets of fraudulent FAA identification cards his Golden Dragons had illegally manufactured. More charges to add to the indictment, but letting ISIS walk with fake identification was a tremendous risk. At least Mohammad's deeper involvement would improve their chances of catching the jihadists in the act.

"You getting the audio?" Nathan whispered.

The tech agent—Ted, or Terry, or something like that—wore headphones so the sound wouldn't leak into the target room. He gave a thumbs-up and returned his attention to the screen.

"Ghulam's inspecting them," Three Balls said.

"Sh," Nathan said.

Three Balls raised his eyebrows and shrugged.

Nathan walked into the bathroom, grabbed a thick towel, and pressed it against the crack at the bottom of the dividing door between the rooms. All it would take to ruin the operation was for one of Ghulam's crew to overhear a snippet of conversation between FBI agents. People called baseball a game of inches, but federal investigations could also hinge on one sloppy agent following too closely or a slip of the tongue by an undercover. Tiny details, the things not written in manuals but learned through hard experience, were the difference between success and failure.

"What an anal fuck," Three Balls whispered.

Nathan ignored him. It wasn't Three Balls's case, and if things went south, only Nathan would be blamed. They wouldn't come down hard on Eddie, despite his being a co-case agent, because everyone knew Nathan mentored him. The win or loss would fall on Nathan's shoulders. He liked it that way. Why would anyone play in the game if they didn't want the ball?

"He's finished," the tech agent said.

Ghulam set down the last FAA badge and turned to Kei.

This was it. Would Ghulam deliver the promised $45,000 or steal the cards at gunpoint? If Ghulam had no further use for Kei, he might try to eliminate the link to his crew, unless the wrath of the Golden Dragons was a deterrent. Or Ghulam needed additional forgeries in the future.

Nathan tapped his Glock with his elbow to assure his holster had not slid on his belt. He moved closer to the door leading to the adjoining room and watched the monitor over his shoulder.

Ghulam shook Kei's hand and smiled. Kei smiled too. Ghulam muttered something and collected the IDs. The agent listening to the audio gave Nathan a thumbs-up.

Ghulam and his men exited the target room, and its door thunked shut. Their footsteps thudded into the hall. Nathan was so close to his quarry, with his hand on his gun. Ready. Ghulam's voice grew louder and then faded as his men passed the surveillance room and continued down the hallway.

Nathan removed his walkie-talkie from his bag and transmitted. "All units, Oh-Two. Targets departed and are headed for the elevator."

"Oh-Seven copies," the agent positioned in the lobby responded.

"Confirm when they're inside their vehicle and take them away. I want to know where they stick that red knapsack. Keep it tight."

"Copy," Murphy responded. "We got it from here."

God, Nathan wanted to join the mobile surveillance, but he needed to debrief Mohammad and Kei, both of whom waited in the hotel room next door. Giving up control of the jihadists was hard. Mohammad should be able to provide advance notice of the ISIS operation, but if the jihadists disappeared with the fraudulent identification and executed an attack, people would die.

So would Nathan's career.

56

Trent Hamilton's cheeks flushed, and he glared across his desk at Bashir. Was he angry at Bashir or the situation? Hamilton's deputy sat against the wall and waited with his back erect and his eyes sharp. He must sense the danger in Hamilton's mood. The deputy's presence unnerved Bashir. Did Hamilton need a loyal minion to witness their conversation? Hair rose on Bashir's neck.

Be careful.

"What I don't understand," Hamilton said, "is how Agent Burke contacted Sergei Popov and Timor Balakin. Where did he find Russian contacts?"

Bashir had to tread lightly. If he admitted his involvement, Hamilton would crucify him. "Agents Chan and Burke interviewed Dr. Jakob Mandel. It's likely Mandel introduced Balakin . . . before Mandel was murdered."

"Possible." Hamilton cracked his knuckles. "But how did Mandel meet Balakin? They wouldn't have interacted during Mandel's employment at the agency."

"Unknown," Bashir said.

"And why would Popov contact Burke? He's an unlikely messenger to choose to deliver a message to the CIA."

"Burke's been targeting the Russians since his wife was injured—the conspiracy narrative you ordered me to encourage."

Hamilton shot a sharp look, and Bashir almost regretted his barb, except Hamilton's pivot from Russian involvement to blaming cognitive issues had been abrupt. Unexplainable. Had the new causation theory come from Richardson? Was the White House behind it? If so, that proved politics drove intelligence analysis.

Hamilton ground his teeth. "I want to figure out how an FBI agent investigating Islamic terrorism became our go-between with a highly placed Russian intelligence officer in their energy weapons program."

Bashir stayed quiet. He'd deny connecting Nathan with Balakin and Popov, even though lying to a section chief was a fireable offense. Did Hamilton suspect him? Was this an interrogation?

Hamilton waited for an answer. He chewed on his lip. "You flew to Ukraine at the last minute. How'd you learn Burke set up the meeting?"

Avoid lying. "After Burke met Balakin, I knew he sought Russian contacts. I surveilled him to the airport, and when I saw his destination, I guessed he planned to meet a source. I was as surprised as you it was someone in the Russian's weapons program."

Hamilton nodded. "Still monitoring Burke's phone?"

Bashir glanced at the deputy. This was a sticky legal area. The law prohibited them from warrantless interception of US citizens on American soil, but the NSA had intercepted foreign calls to Nathan's number, and Bashir had listened to them. He'd never told NSA he already knew the masked identity of the American subscriber. He'd also reviewed toll records for Nathan's personal and work phones. FBI administrative subpoenas didn't require a judge's signature, so he'd forged Meili's signature and faxed it from her office.

"We're still getting content summaries," Bashir said.

"Audio?" the deputy asked. Lines creased his forehead.

"Only with overseas contacts," Bashir said. "NSA intercepts."

Hamilton pounded his desk. "What's Burke doing?" He swung his chair around and looked out the window.

Bashir glanced at the deputy. The man bit his lip and stayed still.

Hamilton swiveled back around with focused eyes. "Burke's a wild card.

He needs to be reined in. Meeting the Russians without our knowledge is unacceptable. Our analysis can't be driven by a rogue agent out for revenge."

"Our analysis?" Bashir asked.

"US policy."

"The national security advisor is already dictating our conclusions." Bashir regretted saying that as soon as it came out, but he couldn't keep it inside. Anger roiled his stomach like lava in a volcano. "The CIA is supposed to provide independent analysis to the White House and make decisions based on intelligence, not the other way around."

"This is the real world," Hamilton said.

Bashir waited, struggling to keep emotion off his face, like a poker player who'd gone all-in.

"Stop Burke in his tracks," Hamilton said. "No more meetings with foreign nationals. No more wild conspiracy theories. Send him back to his AF-PAK group."

"I'm a liaison. How do you expect me to stop Burke when his own supervisor can't control him?"

"He's violating FBI policy. Make FBI management aware of that. I don't care how you do it."

Bashir leaned back. Why were they concentrating on the FBI when Russia or China was attacking American diplomats? The molten rock boiled inside him. "What's happening with Dr. Mandel's murder investigation?"

"Fairfax County is handling that," the deputy said, drawing a glare from Hamilton.

"FBI's done nothing," Bashir said. "They're calling it local crime."

"It is," Hamilton said.

"But Mandel worked for the CIA," Bashir said, "and he assisted Chan and Burke investigate Russians. There's a national security component here. It could be a foreign assassination."

"Havana Syndrome may be an illness, and we've no hard evidence of Russian involvement. Even Burke's wavering on that. Besides, Mandel's murder could have been a burglary."

"Nothing was taken," Bashir said.

"He lived alone. Who knows what went missing from his residence?"

How did Hamilton know Mandel lived alone? He had more interest than he acknowledged. "It would be prudent to assume the worst—foreign intervention—and put our people on it. Or pressure FBI to open a case."

"Instead of chasing ghosts and drawing attention to a former CIA employee who worked on sensitive projects, let's focus on stopping a cowboy from starting World War III."

"But—"

Hamilton jabbed a finger at Bashir. "Burke's a national security threat. Drag him in for a polygraph. If he fails, I'll refer the matter to the US Attorney's Office for prosecution."

57

Nathan waited for Meili at the bar inside Oyamel, a trendy Mexican restaurant in Washington's Penn Quarter neighborhood. Where was she? He checked his watch, but Meili wasn't late, he was early—as always—a habit he'd developed trying to stay a step ahead of terrorists.

He examined the blurry image on the photograph Sergei Popov had given him. Nathan had run subscriber and database checks on the telephone number, which may or may not belong to the man in the picture, but either way, finding him was the key.

Meili entered the restaurant wearing black leggings under a fluffy white sweater, a casual outfit she'd never wear into the office. He'd forgotten it was Saturday, a day off for overworked agents.

He rose to greet her, and she smiled and hugged him. Her candy-apple lipstick shimmered as she settled in beside him.

"Let me guess," she said. "A working lunch and not a date?"

He hadn't dated in over a decade. What would that feel like? He shook away the thought. He was married. But she looked stunning. He could choose not to tell her about his trip and enjoy the afternoon with a beautiful and intelligent woman, but she'd find out what he'd done when she returned to the office on Monday.

"Bashir called this morning."

The smile slid off her face. "You shouldn't be talking to him. He's my group's OGA liaison, not your personal consultant. I assume you weren't discussing Islamic extremism?"

"We're making progress on our ISIS case. I can fill you in if you're interested. It—"

"What interests me is making sure you stay in your lane. My ASAC was clear about this. You can't be anywhere near our investigation."

Nathan took a calming breath. "CIA wants to polygraph me."

"What?"

"I met Sergei Popov in Kyiv."

Meili covered her face with her hands. When she looked up, her eyes flared with fury. "You agreed that was dangerous and a bad idea. You promised you wouldn't go."

"I agreed it was perilous, but I never said I wouldn't—"

Her nostrils flared beneath flinty eyes. "You led me to believe you'd decided against it."

"It's done, and I can't take it back."

Meili shoved her stool back and stood.

"Meili—"

"I'm going to the restroom. I need a moment."

She walked away, and guilt washed over him. They'd been close at the academy in Quantico, so many years before, but the pressures of passing academic, physical, and practical tests had prevented them from exploring anything more than a plutonic relationship. A decade later, he still cared for her and didn't want to deceive her. She deserved better.

Halfway through his bottle of Amstel, Meili returned. She leaned against the bar but didn't sit.

"What did he say?" she asked.

"Bashir?"

"Sergei Popov."

"He denied Russian involvement."

"What did you expect him to say? You risked everything to learn what you could have read in Pravda. Is Pravda still a thing?"

"Unfortunately."

"You gambled your life for nothing."

A wave of fatigue passed through him. "Popov made a convincing argument. He said Russia had this technology fifty years ago, so why wait to act? He insinuated their sonic weapons had advanced, so why attack our embassy in Moscow and finger themselves?"

"Because it was an easy target."

"Embassies have been attacked all over the world, so the tech's mobile. They didn't need to hit us in their backyard."

"Unless they chose Moscow to make that argument."

Layers upon layers of deception. Too many questions and not enough answers. Nathan leaned his elbows on the bar. If he closed his eyes, he'd be asleep in a minute.

"It's a chess game." He sipped his beer. "Popov blamed the Chinese."

Meili cocked her head. "Now, that's surprising. Reds usually stick together, but it's an interesting thought."

Should he give her the photo? Once he did, the investigation would be out of his hands. He finished his beer and stared at a glistening bottle of tequila.

"What?" Meili asked.

"Popov gave me something."

She rang her tongue on the inside of her cheek. Cute and sexy.

Nathan looked around. The bartender flirted with a young brunette twenty feet away, and a handful of patrons remained deep in conversation. He dug out the photo and placed it on the bar.

Meili didn't touch it. "Who is he?"

"That's what we need to know. Popov insinuated he's involved."

Meili scanned the room then picked up the photo. "The shot's grainy, with poor definition, but we can run it through facial recognition and see if anything pops."

"Run it by NSA. They can access some civilian security databases and widen the net. I'll bet DHS gets a hit at an airport."

"I've had mixed results from facial recognition," Meili said. "It's only as accurate as the data we input."

"Flip it over."

She did and looked at the number. "This his?"

"Comes back to Far East Imports, an antique jewelry company, here in the District."

"Can I take this?"

"It's yours. I kept a copy."

Meili slipped the photo into her purse. She stared at the ceiling and sipped her mojito. She leaned close. "You never told me what Bashir wanted. Did he have information about the photograph?"

"I didn't show him the picture."

Wrinkles formed in the corners of her eyes. "Why not?"

"I wasn't sure I could trust him, and I'm glad I didn't. He ratted me out to the CIA."

"Why do—"

"They're giving me a polygraph in the morning."

Meili tensed. "That's outrageous. What reason could they have—"

"National security."

"Every case you work has national security implications."

"I met Popov off the books. Bashir told me his boss, Trent Hamilton, is causing problems. Thinks I'm a loose cannon."

"You *are* a loose cannon, but they can't make you take a poly without FBI approval. What did your supervisor say?"

"I didn't tell her."

Meili's mouth hung open. "I don't know where to begin."

"Bashir said the CIA's worried I'm encroaching on their turf. If I ask Rahimya to run interference, this thing will become official. Hamilton could ask the DOJ to open a criminal investigation, and things could spiral out of control. I'll end up sitting at home, suspended, with no hope of investigating this—"

"You shouldn't be investigating. If you take the polygraph, they can ask you anything."

"It wouldn't be admissible in a criminal case, if it comes to that."

"They could yank your security clearance and get you fired."

"Only if I fail the exam."

"You don't know the questions. How do know you'll pass?"

Nathan smiled and ordered another beer.

58

Nathan squirmed in a hard plastic seat, in a windowless room, in an office park in Chantilly, Virginia. A polygraph machine rested on the table beside him, its tubes and wires dangling like tentacles. Thirty minutes ago, he'd arrived at Wilson and Wilson Associates, a CIA front used to administer polygraph examinations. A pleasant, redheaded receptionist had escorted him to the examination room.

He checked his watch. They made him wait on purpose, to increase his anxiety. If he was hiding something, he'd stew about it until it blossomed into an emotional trigger. The stakes were high—his job and his freedom. He pictured Amelia's face and remembered her giggle the last time he'd taken her to the park. He thought about anything except Russian spies.

A middle-aged balding man wearing Malcolm X-style glasses entered the room carrying a folder. "Good morning, I'm Mr. Smith. I'll be your examiner."

"Mr. Smith? Really?"

He smiled without humor. "I see you've taken polygraphs before."

"During the FBI's initial screening process and again when I was read-on to certain tickets for my SCI Top Secret clearance."

"Any failures or problems with any examination?"

"No."

"Since you've been through this before, I'll explain this quickly. I'll ask a series of questions, and you'll respond only with a *yes* or *no*. Remain still during the exam, which should last thirty minutes."

"Sounds good." Nathan smiled.

Polygraph machines measured physical changes in the body. Smith would determine a baseline then apply external stimuli in the form of questions to generate psychological responses. Anxiety caused increased pulse and blood pressure, perspiration, and rapid breathing, and the examiner's job was to detect these changes after specific questions. A physiological response revealed stress, which indicated deception.

Smith dragged a chair in front of Nathan and sat too close for comfort—another interrogator trick. "I'll read the questions now, so there are no surprises."

Nathan nodded. Smith wanted to create anxiety about the questions Nathan was worried about answering.

Smith lifted a notebook out of his briefcase and flipped through it. "*Hmmm, ummm de dum*," he hummed—an annoying habit and probably not an interrogation technique. Smith's ring finger was bare, with no tan line. Either he didn't believe in wearing jewelry or he was single. Not surprising he had poor self-awareness. Living alone did that. Or had his humming come first and kept him single? The chicken or the egg?

"I'll read these, and you stop me if a question needs clarification," Smith said. "Remember, only respond with a *yes* or *no* during the exam."

"Got it." Birds took flight in Nathan's belly, and he exhaled through his nose.

"Is your name Nathan Burke? Were you born in Maine? Are we sitting in Virginia right now? Are . . ." Smith droned on with simple questions designed to establish a baseline psychological response before the serious questions began.

"Do you work for the FBI? Are you assigned to the Southwest Asia Counterterrorism group? Do you . . ."

Nathan barely listened as he prepared himself. He had two primary strategies to deceive a polygraph. The first was to control his overall physical and mental state throughout the test by staying calm, minimizing his physiological reactions, and exuding confidence. The second was to display nervous reactions to benign questions, to keep his elevated physiological response to worrisome questions closer to the norm. Both strategies could be effective, but each had challenges. Maintaining a constant state was difficult, if not impossible for most people, and inducing anxiety during meaningless parts of the test could show erratic movement, which also suggested deception. Worse, these tactics were widely known, and if the examiner noticed them, he'd realize Nathan was lying.

"Did you meet Sergei Popov in Ukraine? Did you discuss Havana Syndrome?" Smith moved into relevant questions. "Did you receive official permission to travel to Ukraine? Did...?"

Nathan would implement both strategies. He'd meditated for years and could control his anxiety, blood pressure, and heart rate. Instead of trying to make his heart race, he'd stop meditating and return to normal, which would cause only minor increases and fluctuations during the baseline questions.

"Did Popov give you anything?"

Uh-oh. Nathan had withheld the photograph and number from the CIA because he didn't trust them. If he admitted that now, they'd be more suspicious of his meeting with Popov. He had to lie.

Nathan would also attempt to influence the examiner. The polygraph machine was hard to manipulate, but a human administering the test added an element of subjectivity. Nathan would make Smith believe him by not displaying deceptive body language and by being charismatic and respectful.

But Nathan had a secret weapon—his own special technique.

"Okay, that's everything I'll ask," Smith said. "Any concerns or questions?"

"Nope," Nathan said. He smiled again, trying to appear relaxed.

"Let's get started." He turned to the machine.

Nathan filled his lungs then released his breath while Smith wasn't looking. He dried his hands on his khakis, because increased sweat during the test could be a problem.

"Place your feet flat on the ground and sit up straight," Smith said. He slid a cuff over Nathan's arm, which would monitor Nathan's blood pressure.

Time to work the examiner.

"These things make me nervous," Nathan said, "no matter how many times I take them."

"Just relax and tell the truth." Smith wrapped pneumograph tubes around his chest and abdomen to measure the movement of Nathan's diaphragm.

"It's freaky to think this machine can tell what I'm thinking."

Smith looked at Nathan askance. "It just monitors your bodily reactions."

"Awesome technology."

Making Smith think Nathan believed he couldn't beat the polygraph would subconsciously lower Smith's suspicion. Pretending he misunderstood the technology would insinuate Nathan hadn't prepared countermeasures and wasn't very bright.

Assuming Smith believed him.

Smith clipped metal galvanometers to Nathan's fingers to detect changes in perspiration, then he checked the inputs to make sure it functioned. "All set here." He moved behind the machine. He laid his notebook flat and took out a red marker to make notes on the chart.

Nathan relaxed his facial muscles to appear unconcerned and focused on a tiny smudge on the wall opposite him. He concentrated like a master yogi, gazing deep into the discoloration until the world around him faded away.

"We're ready to begin," the examiner said in an other-worldly voice that barely penetrated Nathan's consciousness.

Nathan stared intently at the wall. An image of the ocean appeared behind his eyes, and he focused on the waves lapping against granular sand. His muscles relaxed.

"I'll start the questions now. Remember, *yes* or *no* answers only."

"Okay."

"Is your name Nathan Burke?"

"Yes."

"Were you born in Maine?"

Nathan shifted his focus off the wall, breaking his meditation to jog his pulse. Perfect relaxation would make later changes more significant. He needed ripples in his response.

"Are we in Virginia?"

Nathan refocused on the spot on the wall. The waves tickled the shore in his mind.

"Yes."

"Are you a father?"

"Yes."

The questioning continued through the baseline questions, into Nathan's employment, then through his involvement with Havana Syndrome. Nathan maintained a meditative state throughout, only diverting his focus during a few benign questions to vary his physiological response.

"Did you investigate your wife's incident in Havana?"

The saltwater foamed against the beach.

"Yes."

"Did you have permission from any government agency to investigate this?"

"Yes."

"Other than Supervisory Special Agent Meili Chan, did anyone give you permission to investigate Havana Syndrome?"

"No."

Smith droned on, probing Nathan's activities since Reagan's attack, then he asked a series of questions about Jakob Mandel and Timor Balakin. Smith transitioned into Nathan's meeting with Sergei Popov.

"Did you initiate contact with the Russians?"

The surf in his mind merged with the sand and dragged grains back toward the warm aqua-green water. Deep focus exhausted him, but the fatigue helped relax his body language, and Nathan had his secret weapon —a technique that never failed.

He didn't lie.

"Did Popov give you anything?"

Splash, splash, splash.

"No."

If Nathan believed what he was saying, his body wouldn't produce any extraordinary physiological response. All it took was justification. Popov had handed Nathan a paper, but if Nathan planned to give it back, then Popov hadn't given it to him—he'd lent it. The semantic game allowed Nathan to believe, deep in his heart, that his responses were true.

"Are you working with the Russians against the interests of the United States?"

"Never."

"Yes or no, please." Smith marked something on the polygraph machine. "Are you working with the Russians against the interests of the United States?"

"No."

The tide rolled in as the questions continued, and Smith's voice barely penetrated Nathan's meditative state.

"We're done."

The statement took a moment to register. It was over.

He looked at Smith. "That's it? Not as scary as the first one I took. I guess I trust the machine more."

"Let me examine the data and ensure I don't need to repeat anything."

Nathan blinked to shake off his deep concentration. The test had ended, but the examiner continued to evaluate him. Nathan had to impart innocence through his words, tone, and body language until he left the building.

Smith adjusted his glasses and read through the charts showing the data collected. "*Hum de dum dum.*"

Nathan looked away to avoid smiling and insulting him.

"I think I've got everything I need," Smith said. "Someone will be in touch once we analyze the results."

"Great." His fatigue remained, but a wave of giddiness welled inside him. He didn't need to wait for the results.

He'd beaten the box.

59

Nathan's agency phone vibrated on his nightstand and jerked him out of REM sleep. He rolled over and opened one eye. His alarm clock read 4:04 a.m., a time when every phone call brought bad news. He reached for his cell with the clumsy movement of a zombie and sent it clattering across the wooden floor.

"Dammit."

He rolled out of bed and banged his knee hard as he scooped up his phone. He blinked sleep out of his eyes and looked at the screen.

Mohammad.

He answered. "What's happening?"

"Bad things," Mohammed said.

"I'm listening."

"This shit may be going down tomorrow . . . I mean today."

A jolt of adrenaline snapped Nathan out of his grogginess, and he willed himself to be sharp. "Start at the beginning."

"Remember I asked Ghulam if I could join his jihad."

"And he agreed."

"Yeah, well, I didn't bring it up again. If I pressed him, he'd get suspicious—"

"He's already suspicious."

"—so I waited for him to make the next move."

"And?"

"He just called."

Nathan's pulse thumped in his neck. "You're killing me. What did he say?"

"Not much . . . not over the phone, but he said he'd send someone to pick me up in the morning. He said I wanted to help and now I'd have my chance."

"What else?"

"No details but he talked about Allah. He said we were about to do his bidding."

"Did you record it?"

"I, uh, no. I was sleeping, man."

"It's okay. Is this it? Is Ghulam talking about a terrorist attack?"

"I know guys like him. The way he spoke of Allah, the finality and excitement in his voice . . . yeah, we're doing this today."

Nathan stood and paced his bedroom floor. They had to be ready, and it was almost dawn."

"You there?" Mohammad asked.

"I'm thinking."

"What should I do?"

"Go with him. Be a witness, but don't do anything illegal. If—"

"You want me there?"

"You can't disappear now. If they come to get you in the morning, and you're gone, they'll be in the wind."

"But they're doing something bad."

"You'll be there as a safety. If we miss something or if things go south, you'll be our guy on the inside."

"I don't wanna get whacked . . . or arrested."

"Nobody will charge you because I'm instructing you to do this. If we move in to make an arrest, follow commands and show the agents your empty hands."

"What if those fuckers start shooting?"

"Stay out of the line of fire."

"I don't know—"

"You bail now, you blow our case, and they'll know you went to the police."

"This is bad."

"It's what you signed up to do."

"You'll be there?"

"We'll have people on you all day. Let me go. I gotta make calls."

Mohammad signed off, and Nathan dialed Eddie.

"It's on for today." Nathan said.

"Ghulam's op?" Eddie asked.

"They're picking up our guy. We need every swinging dick in the field. I'll brief Rahimya, and you call everyone in the group."

"What's the target?"

"The FAA IDs indicate they're targeting an airport. My money is on a local airfield. You look at the latest tolls?"

"Two calls from Ghulam's cell to DCA."

"That's it? Who'd he call at National?"

"Number came back to the baggage department, but I don't think he was looking for missing luggage."

"This is going down today."

"We'll take them down?"

Nathan took a deep breath to keep the excitement out of his voice. "No choice. We'll surveil Mohammad and the cell members we've bedded down. We'll cover all the airports from BWI to the private airfields. We see them taking any overt act, and we intercede."

"That's a lot of manpower."

"We need everybody. We'll monitor every airport, but you and I are going to DCA. Best guess, that's where Ghulam's headed."

"We'll finally get to arrest that prick."

"We'll end it . . . one way or another."

60

Nathan slipped between steel bollards outside Ronald Reagan Washington National Airport in Arlington, Virginia. Wind whipped off the Potomac River, chilling his bones, and flurries danced on air currents as the Mid-Atlantic experienced a late-March snowstorm. The temperature hovered above freezing, and the pavement only held a temporary dusting. The last storm of the season was gorgeous, but blowing snow obscured visibility for the surveillance team.

Nathan scanned the area outside the main terminal. Cars lined the sidewalk, dropping off passengers, and a group of old ladies dragged roller bags out of the garage and across the walkway toward the entrance.

Would Ghulam park in there?

Rahimya had decided to take down the cell as soon as Nathan briefed her on the active threat. The right call. Mohammad had not been privy to operational details, but Ghulam had invited Mohammad to join their jihad.

This was it. Probably.

"Looks like most of them are in the parking lot," Murphy's voice crackled in Nathan's earpiece.

Murphy and twenty-six agents on loan from three groups in the FBI's Washington Office had followed Ghulam and two of his cronies to a parking lot near the Pentagon City Mall. They waited as Ghulam assembled his team.

Nathan toggled the transmitter that hung through his sleeve and dangled into his palm. Two clicks meant he copied, without having to talk.

"I count Ghulam and eight men in the parking lot," Murphy said. "They're all wearing some kind of blue overalls under their jackets, except Ghulam. Looks like airport maintenance uniforms, maybe, or food services. I can't see what's written on them."

Rahimya had wanted to make arrests last night. Intercepting them before they launched their operation was the safe call, but they'd only located residences for Ghulam and two of his jihadists, which meant the rest roamed free. If they only scooped up three of them, the rest could execute the operation or flee and return to launch the attack later.

FBI agents watched all three airports in the DC region and copies of the fake FAA documents had been distributed to key members of FAA security at every airport in the country with instructions not to disseminate the information. Just in case.

"They've broken into two groups," Murphy said. "First group is Ghulam, Abbas Gul . . . and your Charlie. They're standing beside a metallic-green Ford Bronco."

According to Mohammad, Abbas Gul was Ghulam's deputy. Eddie had identified him through facial recognition. He was an Afghan national with family members in the Haqqani Network—a radical Islamic terror group that had murdered many Americans. Gul had entered the US under his real name with a visa he'd received in Egypt. Apparently, his connections to terrorism were not known until Eddie asked NSA to conduct a deep dive into his online communications.

"And the other group?" Rahimya asked over the channel. Her voice sounded high and tight.

"Wait one," Murphy said.

Nathan peered through the terminal's glass doors. People carried luggage and herded children through the main hall, everyone hurrying. The airport seemed busy for a Tuesday afternoon.

"Second group is one, two, three . . . seven bad guys. They're moving through the parking lot toward a white GMC van, Virginia license. F, B—

shit, I'll get the rest when they pull out. Driver's wearing a tan windbreaker and jeans. Everyone else is in uniforms."

"Oh-Two, Oh-One," Rahimya said. "Want to take them now?"

Nathan rubbed his chin. They had nine of the dozen ISIS members in sight, but not all of them. They could intercept them, but they'd miss the last two, and they still didn't know what Ghulam planned or the identity of his target, though Reagan National was their likely destination.

Tough call.

Nathan waited for a young couple to walk past him into the terminal, then he transmitted. "Oh-One, we're missing two suspects, and this could be a dry run. Let it play out a little longer. Arriving at the airport would be a strong overt act."

They still didn't have serious charges.

Nathan remained outside the entrance. If Ghulam's crew headed west toward Dulles, Nathan would race to Eddie's car and give chase. They had people in IAD too, but his gut told him Ghulam would strike Reagan.

"Seven suspects in the van," Murphy transmitted. "Two in the Bronco with Charlie. Want me to block the street?"

"Let them go," Rahimya responded. "All units, prepare to take them away, and keep your eyes peeled for the last two suspects."

"Copy," Murphy said. "They're leaving now."

Surveillance units chimed in as Murphy passed off the van and Bronco to them. Rahimya had ten two-man cars assigned to follow Ghulam and his men. Another nine agents covered DCA, IAD, and BWI. At Reagan National, one agent sat in the FAA security chief's office and the other two waited in the A and B terminals. For extra security, two vans containing members of the Washington Field Office's SWAT team waited in the area, ready to respond as needed. Rahimya had also put the FBI's Hostage Rescue Team on alert in case things went sideways.

Agents called out the surveillance as Ghulam's Bronco and the white van wormed through secondary streets in Crystal City. Ghulam must be watching for surveillance.

Be invisible.

"Both vehicles southbound on Route One," an agent transmitted.

Ghulam was close to Reagan National, but if he kept heading south, he'd enter Old Town Alexandria. What would be worth targeting there?

"Van and Bronco both exiting. Standby . . . traveling east on Airport Access Road."

Headed right for him.

The hum of a jet engine changed to a whine as it accelerated along the tarmac on the opposite side of the terminal. Nathan looked up as a Delta Airbus A320 rumbled above the airport and disappeared into the low-hanging clouds.

"Van's headed toward the departures terminal."

Reagan National's old terminal lay to the south, where an agent waited out front, but most passenger traffic came through the newer terminal—a long, thin building shaped like a J. The primary terminal had three stories, with baggage claim on the lower level, shops and departures on the first floor, and ticketing on an open-air balcony.

If any operative tried to pass through security on the main level, their bags would go through x-ray, and they'd be subject to metal detectors, pat downs, and swabbing for explosives detection. Ghulam's men would probably avoid those screening areas and gain access through an employee gate, but which one?

And what would happen once they were inside?

"Bronco's turning right away from the airport," a unit broadcast. "Looks like he's headed to the parkway. Can anyone take the eye if he jumps back on?"

"Ten's behind you. I can take him."

"Copy. Letting him go. I'll stick with the van."

"Got him. Ten has the Bronco. Northbound GW Parkway, lane one, thirty-five miles per hour."

Why was Ghulam leaving? Had he made the tail? Or did he want to escort his men to the airport before he did something else? Maybe he planned to meet the missing members of his team.

"White van stopping in front of B Terminal, just south of United Airlines."

"Oh-Two, Oh-One," Rahimya transmitted. "Any talk about explosives with your Charlie?"

Rahimya must be worried about a Vehicle Borne Explosive Device, but if that was Ghulam's plan, why order the FAA identification?

"Negative," Nathan responded. "They want to infiltrate the building's restricted areas."

I think.

"Van door's opening. Seven men disembarking, all carrying knapsacks."

What was in those bags? Guns? Bombs? Chemical agents? If this wasn't a practice mission and Ghulam's men carried weapons, Nathan could make serious charges stick.

"Surveillances units move in tight," Nathan broadcast. "We'll take them on the sidewalk. Don't let anyone access a restricted zone."

Nathan had covered the plan during his early-morning briefing, but he needed to remind everyone. He took a colossal risk letting the operatives get this close, and they had no room for error. He entered Terminal B and turned right. If his team didn't grab the operatives on the sidewalk, Nathan would intercept them outside passport control. He acted like a free safety.

"Unit Ten, Bronco's got his turn signal on. Yeah, right turn into Gravelly Point Park. Can anyone take?"

"Oh-Four will cover. I'm fifteen seconds behind. Let him go."

Gravelly Point Park was part of the Mount Vernon trail. It lay on a peninsula on the Potomac's western shore, sandwiched between Reagan National and the Fourteenth Street Bridge Complex that led into the District.

"Oh-Four. He pulled into a spot on the southern end of the park, opposite the airport. All three subjects still in the vehicle."

What the hell was Ghulam doing?

"Oh-Four, Oh-Two," Nathan said. "Stay tight on him and get another unit ready to take him away. All Bronco surveillance units switch to channel three to keep this channel free for airport surveillance."

"Break, break," a surveillance unit transmitted. "I've got seven suspects moving away from the van and approaching the southern entrance to terminal B. Looks like they're leaving the van unoccupied."

Nathan picked up his pace. "All units close in. Don't let them reach the checkpoints."

His heart raced. Making a plan and executing it were not the same thing. How ready were his agents? Nathan jogged through Terminal B. Beyond towering glass windows, snow-frosted planes parked at their gates. Shops lined the opposite wall, and above, people bustled along the balcony.

"Suspects entering beneath the United Airlines sign," a unit transmitted.

Nathan stopped and faced the entrance as the sliding doors opened with a sucking sound. Cool air rode in on a gust of March wind followed by seven men wearing blue food-service overalls and carrying identical knapsacks.

The arrest team hadn't arrived. If Nathan drew on the suspects now, it would be seven against one. What was taking his team so long?

Behind Nathan, a dozen passengers shuffled in line through zig-zagging blue tape outside the security screening area. Gates fifteen to twenty-two lay beyond the metal detectors. He positioned himself between the men and the gates.

Their suspects entering the airport gave Nathan enough evidence to show intent.

The men broke into two groups. Four turned left, toward gates C and D, and three continued toward Nathan. Two agents from another group entered the terminal, wide-eyed and rushed.

Three of Ghulam's men moved past Nathan and headed toward the hallway that led to Terminal A. The other four continued toward Terminal C.

Nathan turned his head and whispered into his radio, "Oh-Two to the agents who just entered B terminal, when you have the numbers, take the suspects moving north toward Terminal C. I'm following three toward Terminal A. I need backup to affect the arrest."

The agents fast-walked past him in pursuit. Beyond them, more agents entered the next entrance. They'd have the men surrounded in seconds.

Nathan marched after the three jihadists. He stayed fifteen feet behind and waited for help to arrive. The men slowed near the security entrance then headed for a steel door under an *Employees Only* sign.

"Police, hands up!" an agent yelled far down the hallway behind Nathan.

"Get down, get down!" another agent yelled.

The jihadists spun around and looked past Nathan into the terminal. Passengers shrieked and yelled, but Nathan focused on the men.

He wanted to wait for backup before making the arrest, but the FBI had revealed themselves. The jihadists huddled together, gesturing, and speaking with urgency. Two turned toward the restricted door, and the third strode down the long hallway leading to terminal A.

No time to wait.

Nathan brushed back his jacket and drew his Glock with a practiced motion. "Freeze! Police. Stop right there."

All three men stopped and faced him.

"Let me see your hands."

The men closest to the door raised their hands and glanced at each other. The third bolted down the hallway.

"Police, stop!" Nathan yelled.

The man kept going. One of the two ISIS operatives closer to him lowered his hands, perhaps sensing an opportunity.

"Get on the ground, now!" Nathan closed the distance, aiming his gun center mass.

The man raised his hands again, and both terrorists lowered themselves to the ground.

Nathan keyed his radio. "Oh-Two, I've got two suspects at gunpoint in front of Terminal B security. A third suspect wearing a gray jacket fled toward Terminal A. I need assistance."

Footsteps pounded the tile behind him. He risked a glance over his shoulder. Eddie and another agent raced in from the street and headed for him.

"What we got?" Eddie asked.

"Cuff them," Nathan said. "I'm going after the last guy."

61

Nathan dashed down the corridor without waiting for an answer. He ran with his Glock held high as he blew past gawking passengers. With his jacket open, his gold FBI badge was visible on his belt, but people only saw the gun. They screamed and ducked out of his way.

Ahead, Gray Jacket charged down the hallway past gates ten through fourteen. He disappeared around the bend.

Nathan pumped his arms, picking up speed. He followed the curve of the hall, ready to dive to the ground if the man stopped and fired. A woman saw his Glock and pulled her child against her.

"Police!" he shouted.

He skirted a luggage cart beside a kiosk and sprinted down the curving passageway. He scanned the thinning crowd.

There!

Gray Jacket stopped at a red steel door with a *Restricted* sign. He punched a number into the keypad and flung the door open. Where had he obtained an access code? He disappeared into a stairwell and the door clanked shut.

Nathan reached it and grabbed the handle.

Locked.

Beside the door and beneath a gray telephone, a keypad required a security code, which he didn't possess. No airport employees were in sight. He snatched the phone off the receiver.

"Operations," a breathless woman answered. The administrative offices must be in disarray.

"This is FBI Special Agent Nathan Burke. I'm at a restricted stairwell between A and B terminals. I'm in pursuit of a suspect, and I need the door unlocked."

"Who is this?"

His pulse pounded in his temples. "FBI Special Agent Burke. This is an emergency. Open the door."

"Sir, I can't open any door without proper verification of—"

Nathan slammed the phone down. Bureaucrats everywhere. He stepped back and torqued his body like a spring. He jumped and delivered a straight front kick just below the door's handle.

The frame shook, and the sound cascaded down the hallway—but the door stayed closed. Nathan reset and kicked again with all his strength.

The frame twisted, and the door cracked open as bolts of lightning burst from his heel into his femur. He grimaced and caught the door before it shut. Steps led down to a landing then zigzagged out of sight. A door slammed below, and the sound reverberated through the stairwell.

Nathan keyed his mic. "All units, Oh-Two. I've got a suspect fleeing toward A terminal. He took a restricted stairwell down to the ground floor. I think it leads to the tarmac. Suspect described as Middle Eastern male, twenties, short beard, blue overalls, gray jacket. I'm in pursuit."

Nathan touched his toe to the ground. His foot had gone numb, but it supported his weight. Great timing.

He lurched into the stairwell and used the handrail for support as he stumbled down the stairs. He reached the landing then aimed his handgun down the flight of stairs. Through thick safety glass on a door, the controlled chaos of the flight line flashed past.

"Oh-Two, Oh-One."

Nathan toggled his mic. "He's on the tarmac. I don't have eyes."

"Copy suspect on the tarmac between A and B terminals." Rahimya issued a series of orders to form a perimeter. Setting a cordon made sense, but if the suspect had a bomb in his knapsack, he could do a lot of damage before they caught him.

Nathan hurried down and burst through the door onto the tarmac. He scanned the flight line. An Airbus 130 parked at the closest gate. The pungent odor of jet fuel tingled his nostrils.

Twenty yards away, Gray Jacket dashed across the tarmac. Got him.

A luggage cart with a heavyset driver rumbled toward Nathan. He flagged the man down. "FBI. Take me to that guy running in overalls."

"What?"

"He's going to blow up a plane."

The driver's eyes widened, and his mouth hung open. He looked at the fleeing suspect then gawked Nathan.

Nathan jumped onto the cart. "Get moving."

"Fuck this," the driver said. He bailed out and scurried into the terminal.

At least he'd left the vehicle running. Nathan slid behind the wheel. He threw the cart into gear and gunned the engine. The vehicle lurched forward under the weight of the trailer then picked up momentum. Nathan holstered his firearm and grasped the wheel with both hands.

The jihadist ducked beneath an Airbus 320 parked at the second gate. The aircraft only carried 150 passengers, but from the tarmac, it resembled a massive steel beast.

Nathan reached it in seconds. He eased off the gas and gripped his Glock, ready to draw. He wrestled the steering wheel and angled away from the plane's tail. He paralleled the line of aircraft.

Where was Gray Jacket?

"Look out, man," someone shouted near the next aircraft.

Nathan pushed the pedal to the floor and careened down the line of planes. A crew of four ground workers unloaded suitcases from the hull of a smaller commuter plane. Two stared away from the building, and Nathan followed their gaze to his suspect.

Gray Jacket scurried beneath another Airbus and cocked his head up at its belly. What was he planning?

Nathan sped past the plane to put the trailer between them and use it for cover, but the suspect sprang from beneath the fuselage and rushed for the last aircraft. Was he searching for a way to get on board? The only access to these planes was through the jetway, twenty feet above.

The man emerged from behind the last jetliner. He stopped and surveyed the area. Nathan scrunched down, as if he could make himself invisible, but the man's eyes rolled over him without recognition. With just Nathan's head and shoulders above the cart's dashboard, he probably blended with the ground crew.

The man swung his backpack off his shoulders and knelt. Nathan lifted foot off the gas to slow.

Gray Jacket unzipped the backpack and dug into it. The plane's engine throttled up with a deafening roar.

Nathan drew his gun and centered the sight on the man's chest.

"Police, hands up," Nathan yelled.

Gray Jacket didn't look up. He probably couldn't hear over the whine of the jet's engines. Nathan closed within twenty yards. What was in the bag? He could shoot—a tough shot from a moving cart. And the man had not displayed a weapon.

Fifteen yards.

The jihadist removed a gray sweatshirt from the bag and laid it on the ground. Did Nathan have another option?

"Police!" Nathan yelled again.

Ten yards.

The man pulled some type of container out of his knapsack. It looked like PVC pipe.

A bomb.

Nathan rammed his Glock back into his holster, not bothering to snap it shut, and cut the wheel hard. The jihadist jerked his head up as Nathan barreled down on him.

But too late.

Everything moved in slow motion. The baggage cart's bumper struck Gray Jacket in the chest. The cart shuddered from the impact as his body thudded against the grill. He catapulted across the tarmac, and the device flew through the air.

Nathan slammed on the brakes. Tires squealed over the aircraft noise.

The man rolled to a stop and lay still. Nathan jammed the cart into park and leapt out, drawing his gun as he approached.

A siren came from somewhere behind him, growing louder. Nathan slowed, watching the man's hands. He didn't move. Nathan risked a glance at the device. It could be a pipe bomb but was probably something much worse.

Eddie and two FBI agents raced across the tarmac toward him. They arrived ahead of a Metropolitan Washington Airports Authority police car.

"What's happening?" Eddie asked, gasping.

"You guys cuff him," Nathan said. He pointed to the device on the ground. "And make sure nobody touches that fucking thing . . . whatever it is."

"We've got more of 'em inside. Cops are clearing the terminal," Eddie said. "Bomb squad's en route."

The other FBI agents rolled Gray Jacket onto his stomach, and he groaned. They handcuffed him, despite his semiconscious state, and patted him down.

"Jesus," the older agent said. "This guy is fucked up."

"What happened?" Eddie asked.

"I hit him with the baggage cart."

Eddie raised his eyebrows.

"I didn't have time to stop and shoot."

The man squirmed in pain. He was alive but not doing well. His ribs were probably broken, and he likely had internal damage. Nathan would have to write an interesting incident report to explain his use of force.

A plane roared down the runway, and the noise from its engines vibrated through him. Nathan examined the device. It resembled an IED, and it could contain anything, including a biological or chemical agent. What had Ghulam planned?

Nathan's radio cackled with calls between Rahimya and the team who had taken the men inside into custody. All without firing a shot.

Nathan switched to channel three to check on the surveillance team following Ghulam. He keyed his radio. "What's the status of the Ford Bronco?"

"Both suspects and your Charlie are still in the vehicle on the southern end of Gravelly Point Park. They're ... I don't know. The vehicle's just sitting there."

"We're ten-fifteen on all suspects here," Nathan said, indicating arrests. "And we seized some kind of explosive devices. I'm headed your way. Don't let Ghulam leave."

"Break, break," Three Balls came over the air. "All units, Oh-Nine. I've got a black Chevy Tahoe parking outside the lower level. I think it may be the same vehicle they used at RFK."

Oh shit.

62

What was the black Tahoe doing on the lower level? Every operative who'd entered the airport was in custody, and Ghulam waited in his Bronco at Gravelly Point Park. More operatives arriving was a bad sign.

"Gimme a twenty," Nathan transmitted, wanting to know their location.

"Near the baggage area, past the taxi stand," Three Balls responded. "Two occupants in the Tahoe. They're just sitting there."

"Get close," Nathan said. "Be ready to intercept."

"Copy."

Nathan turned to the FBI agents and police officers watching Gray Jacket. "You guys got this?"

"On it," a young agent said.

Eddie approached Nathan. "Think that's the same vehicle?"

"I'm not waiting to find out. We're spread too thin." Nathan slapped Eddie's arm. "Come on, let's get down there."

"What—"

Nathan jogged across the tarmac toward the terminal without waiting for Eddie to finish. His ankle howled, inflamed and raw.

He entered on the lower level and slowed as he scanned the baggage claim area. Bathrooms were located on each end and beside the escalator that disgorged disembarked passengers. Six baggage carousels lined the interior walls near the escalators, and passengers clustered around them waiting for their luggage. Weary travelers trudged down the hall opposite glass doors leading to the taxi stand. Everyone jabbered about the police activity upstairs.

The Tahoe belonging to ISIS, assuming it was the same vehicle, had parked on the far end. Nathan hoofed it down the corridor, dodging grouchy passengers. Eddie's footsteps pounded on the tile behind him.

"What we doing?" Eddie shouted.

"Follow me." Nathan exited through sliding doors onto the sidewalk. A frosty wind burned his cheeks. At least thirty people waited in line for taxis, and the sweet smell of carbon dioxide filled the air.

Nathan continued past the travelers and stopped. The black Tahoe remained parked outside the terminal. It looked like the same one. Three Balls had a good eye.

"In here," Nathan said. He darted into the next entrance. Eddie followed. Nathan watched the Tahoe through the tinted glass.

The vehicle's doors opened.

"We've got two occupants getting out of the Tahoe," Three Balls radioed to the team. "Black Jacket and Red Jacket, both carrying long duffle bags. Looks like the bags have some weight to them. Both moving toward baggage claim."

"Shit."

"What's wrong?" Eddie asked.

"Baggage is nonsterile area."

"Meaning?"

"It's landside. Anyone can enter from the street without screening. Or they could access weapons from checked luggage."

"Like Miami in 2017."

"Exactly," Nathan said. "Terminals have been targeted around the world."

"I thought our perps were going for planes."

"Could be both."

"If these guys are ISIS and not innocent passengers."

"Err on the side of caution and assume they're Ghulam's men. He may have launched them after we intercepted their comrades upstairs. Security focuses on passengers boarding planes with weapons, but killing passengers in the terminal is every bit as effective."

Eddie's brow furrowed, and he strained to see the Tahoe through the worsening visibility. "They could be picking up the guys who were supposed to sabotage the planes. Or someone else."

"No."

"How can you be sure," Eddie asked

"Why carry duffle bags into baggage claim?"

"Fuck."

"Let's take them."

Nathan raced toward the doors opposite the Tahoe, and his footsteps echoed off the walls. Eddie followed.

Thirty feet away, two olive-skinned men with black beards entered the baggage area carrying heavy canvas bags. They turned toward Nathan and Eddie.

Nathan slowed to buy time. A row of plastic chairs separated the baggage carousels from the hallway, which kept the bulk of the passengers off to his right, but a dozen people moved through the corridor near the suspects. Nathan angled close to the chairs, so when he confronted the men, the windows and street would be behind them, and he wouldn't be aiming down the hallway into a crowd.

"Wait till we're closer," Nathan said.

"We're making the arrest?"

"Watch your background," Nathan said. "If you have to shoot, don't miss."

"Fuck."

The men scanned the crowd. Their duffle bags were large enough to conceal rifles. Nathan closed the distance to twenty feet.

Both jihadists stopped and spoke to each other. They set their bags on the floor, then knelt and unzipped them.

"Now," Nathan said. He drew his Glock.

"You sure they're bad guys?"

Hope so.

"Police, hands in the air!" Nathan yelled. He moved toward them, walking heel-to-toe to maintain a stable shooting platform.

The men looked up wide-eyed, but their faces didn't show fear. They radiated anger. And hatred.

Eddie extended his Glock in Nathan's peripheral vision. A woman screamed, then others shouted and scrambled for safety.

Red Jacket narrowed his eyes then reached into his bag.

Nathan dropped his finger onto the trigger. He squeezed. His Glock discharged with a pop. He pulled the trigger a second time and fired another round at the man's chest. Nathan's hearing shut down and the edges of his vision blurred as he focused on his target.

The man grimaced, his face a mask of pain, then he toppled forward onto the duffle bag. Nathan shifted his aim to the second man. The jihadist's hands disappeared inside his duffle bag.

Nathan squeezed the trigger twice in rapid succession, aiming for his breastbone. The recoil from his Glock raised his sights. Nathan held his breath and fired a third round into the man's forehead. His head snapped back. A pink cloud filled the air, and the window cracked behind him.

The man collapsed backward with a thud.

Screams filled the terminal, barely audible to Nathan. The smell of gunpowder burned his nose. He sidestepped, swinging his muzzle between both men.

Neither moved. A pool of blood spread under the second man's head, and a trickle oozed out of the tiny hole in his forehead.

He was dead.

"Holy shit, holy shit, holy shit," Eddie said.

"Cover me." Nathan glanced at Eddie to make sure he'd heard.

"Are they bad guys?" Eddie asked. "I don't see a weapon."

"Eddie! Cover me."

Nathan's tone seemed to shake Eddie out of his panic. "Got you."

Nathan holstered and dropped to a knee beside the first man. He grabbed the man's wrist and elbow, controlling the arm inside the bag. Blood dripped from the man's fingers as Nathan bent the man's arm behind his back.

Nathan held his wrist in an escort hold to control it and used his free hand to wrench the suspect's other arm back. The man offered no resistance. Nathan yanked handcuffs off his belt and snapped them on with a practiced motion.

Grabbing the suspect's shoulders, he pulled him off the duffle bag and laid him on his back. Blood soaked the man's chest, but it rose and fell with breath. Still alive.

Nathan glanced at Eddie, who stared wide-eyed at the men. "Cuffs," Nathan said.

Eddie took his support hand off his firearm, unhooked his handcuffs from his belt and tossed them to Nathan.

Nathan moved to the second suspect. He hopped over the growing crimson lake and cuffed him. The man was dead, but procedures existed for a reason. More than once, a suspect presumed dead had risen to rejoin the fight.

Passengers cowered behind chairs and the carousels. Nathan stepped back and keyed his radio.

"Shots fired, lower level. Two suspects down. Request EMS code three."

"What's your status?" Rahimya came over the air.

"Twelve and Oh-Two are fine. We engaged the suspects who were in the Tahoe. One's still alive. Get the cops down here to cordon off the scene."

"EMS is en route. They're already on scene. I'm on my way."

"Copy."

Eddie holstered his gun. "Did we do the right thing?"

"Yes."

"I didn't see a gun. Did you?"

"Didn't need to see it," Nathan said. "And lower your voice." Comments like that could be heard by civilians and taken out of context. That had happened before.

Nathan crouched beside the first man's bag. He flopped it open, careful to avoid whatever pathogens the man carried. Inside was a Colt AR-15, covered in blood. The carbine had polymer foregrips and an MPS-B package. A dozen magazines loaded with 5.56 or .223 ammo filled the duffle.

"Holy shit," Eddie said.

Nathan moved to the second bag and opened it. It contained a black Mossberg, dozens of shells, and three Ruger semi-automatic handguns.

"You were right," Eddie said.

Nathan nodded. His heart pounded in his chest. Every instinct had warned him the men posed a deadly threat, but if he'd opened the bags and seen nothing but clothing, his life would have been over. Split-second, life-and-death decisions were part of law enforcement, but the public no longer allowed for error. Hesitate, and you were dead. Shoot too soon, and you went to prison. Those who carried badges and guns walked a tightrope—with life-altering consequences on either side.

Three police officers stomped down the stairs with weapons drawn. Nathan held his badge up as the officers covered the room.

"FBI," he called out. "Two suspects down. I think that's all of them."

"What ya need?" the older cop asked.

"Keep the passengers back, and don't let anyone leave. We need witness statements. And make room for EMS."

Nathan knelt beside the first man he'd shot. He ripped open a medical kit on the back of his belt and donned rubber gloves. He opened the suspect's shirt. Blood pumped out of two small bullet holes near the man's left nipple.

"Nice grouping," the officer said.

Cops loved black humor. Nathan nodded with a mixture of relief at being alive and worry about what would happen next. Shootings were not taken lightly by anyone.

Including him.

Nathan removed a dressing from his kit and applied pressure to the wounds. So much blood. Based on the location, one or both bullets had struck the man's heart. Nathan would try to save him, but the man would not live to reach the hospital.

A paramedic dropped his trauma bag at Nathan's feet, and Nathan slid to the side as he took over.

"You both okay?" Rahimya asked. She was breathing hard.

"The first guy reached for his AR-15, and I shot him. The second perp knew what I'd do, but he went for his shotgun anyway."

"Don't say anymore," Rahimya said. "Take a moment to think about what happened, but don't make a statement until you're ready. I'll get the shoot team out here."

An ambulance screeched to a halt outside the windows, and more EMTs and police filled the corridor.

"Let's move out of the way," Nathan said to Eddie, and they walked to an unoccupied area near the last carousel.

Click, click, click. Eddie worked his stress toy like his life depended on it.

"You okay?"

"Holy shit," Eddie said.

"We did what we had to do. They gave us no choice."

"I'm sorry I—"

"Nothing to be sorry about. You did a good job."

"I didn't shoot."

"You didn't see weapons. You did what you thought was right."

"But you shot," Eddie said.

"I saw furtive movement. That's enough."

"I want to be you when I grow up," Eddie said. "How'd you know?"

"Instinct."

"But how were you sure?

"Fifteen years of watching criminals, reading body language, and thinking like they do. I recognized the physical signs of pre-violence, but more than that, I saw hate in their eyes. It's a thousand micro movements that when taken together, forecast an attack."

"You were certain?"

"I went with my instinct. If I was wrong, I'd be indicted, but if I was right and didn't act, we'd be dead. I went with my gut, and it paid off."

"Even without complete information?"

"You gotta decide in seconds. Action beats reaction every time."

"I think I got it."

"No, you don't. It takes years of experience. Until you get there, use good tactics and be extra cautious. Complacency kills."

"Oh-Four, Oh-Two," Jimmy radioed.

Shit. Ghulam. "Go for Two."

"Target's out of the vehicle with Charlie. They're standing close together. Too close. Ghulam has something in his hand."

"Confirm a weapon?"

"Can't tell from here. I can't get out without burning it. Hold on . . .

Ghulam's deputy is out too. They're moving to the rear of the Bronco. Standby..."

"This is bad," Nathan said.

"Oh-Two, Oh-Four. They've got the Bronco's hatchback open, and they're fiddling with something inside."

"How many units at Gravelly Point?" Rahimya cut in.

"Oh-Four's alone in the lot."

"We need another team," Rahimya said.

"Oh-One, Oh-Two. Get more agents in there and arrest him. There's no reason to wait. Their op's blown."

"They're lowering the flatbed," Jimmy transmitted. "There's something big inside. You better hurry."

63

Nathan slapped Eddie's back. "You drive."

"We can't leave," Eddie said. "We're supposed to wait for the shoot team."

"Agents are spread over four chaotic crime scenes, and Jimmy needs backup. Ghulam must have seen the police activity. He knows his plan's compromised."

"Think he'll run?"

"I don't know what's doing, but he's not running. We need to get there."

Nathan led Eddie across the corridor. They stepped aside as two EMTs rolled a stretcher through the exit doors.

"Don't go anywhere," Rahimya called out.

Nathan pretended not to hear her and kept moving. Eddie hesitated, and Nathan dragged him through the sliding door.

"Nathan, Eddie!" Rahimya called after them.

"Remember," Nathan said, "forgiveness is better than permission."

They ran to Eddie's car and peeled out.

"Oh-Two, Oh-One," the car radio cackled.

Eddie reached for the mic.

Nathan smacked his hand. "We had the volume turned down and didn't hear her."

"She's gonna be pissed."

"Just drive."

Eddie looped around the airport and merged onto the George Washington Parkway. He stomped on the gas, and the revving engine vibrated through the car.

"Hit the blue light," Eddie said.

"We can't telegraph our approach. And take it easy when you pull into the lot."

"Four to One," Jimmy broadcast. "Target's sliding a large polymer Gorilla box onto the tailgate. He's unlocking it. What should I do?"

"Who can assist?" Rahimya broadcast.

"Oh-One, Oh-Two, we're thirty seconds out," Nathan responded.

"Oh-Two, I told you . . . dammit . . . keep me posted. I'm launching SWAT."

Eddie and Nathan pulled off the George Washington Memorial Parkway into Gravelly Point Park. A running trail bordered the river, and three teenagers threw a frisbee near an elderly couple sitting at a bench in Vance Field. The parking lot faced the airport, and a handful of people watched a plane fly low overhead as it landed at the airport.

"They've got the box open," Jimmy said. He sounded nervous.

"Stay left," Nathan instructed Eddie, "and keep that row of cars between us and Ghulam's vehicle."

"He's taking something out," Jimmy said.

Eddie slowed. "Where's the Bronco?"

"Oh shit," Jimmy said.

That transmission jolted Nathan. Agents rarely used profanity over the radio. He strained to see over the parked cars.

"Target's got some kind of shoulder-mounted weapon," Jimmy said. "Like a bazooka."

"Step on it, Eddie."

Their car fishtailed on loose gravel, and Eddie's acceleration pressed Nathan into his seat. They careened between the row of cars, drawing glares from a couple getting out of a Volvo.

"Stop," Nathan said.

Eddie slammed on the brakes, and the car skidded, sending a cloud of dust into the air. Nathan had the door open before they came to a complete stop.

"Stay behind cover," Nathan said,. He leapt from the vehicle and drew his handgun, counting the shots he'd already taken. Too late to switch magazines now.

He crouched and shuffled behind a parked Toyota Camry. He peeked over its engine.

Ghulam, Abbas, and Mo stood behind the Bronco with an open plastic box resting on the tailgate. Ghulam held a long, green tube by its pistol grip and supported a three-foot-long weapon with his other hand. Not a bazooka, but something worse.

A surface-to-air missile launcher.

Nathan gripped his Glock with both hands and aimed over the engine. He remained in a crouch, exposing only his head and upper torso. "Drop the weapon!"

The men gawked at him. Movement to Nathan's right drew his attention as Jimmy darted down the next row of cars with his gun aimed at Ghulam.

"Police, police, police," Eddie yelled.

Abbas grabbed Mohammad in a headlock and used him as a shield. He yanked him backward, off balance. A Ruger nine-millimeter appeared in Abbas's his hand, the same model the dead man in the airport had stashed in his duffel bag.

"Let him go!" Eddie yelled. "Drop it."

The whine of aircraft engines came from behind Nathan and drew Ghulam's attention. Nathan forced himself not to turn. Commercial aircraft followed the Potomac on final approach to Reagan National and would pass over their heads before touching down less than a hundred yards away.

Ghulam stepped back, putting Abbas and Mo into Nathan's line of fire. Ghulam fiddled with something above the trigger assembly.

"Fuck this."

Planes at Reagan carried hundreds of passengers. Nathan stood and sidestepped around the Toyota, searching for a shot.

He locked his elbows and dropped his index finger onto the trigger's grooves. He inhaled, held his breath, and laid the white dot on his front sight over Ghulam's sternum.

Ghulam tilted the tube up at a forty-five-degree angle.

No time.

Nathan squeezed the trigger, and the gun bucked in his hand. The crack of the shot echoed over the water, but nobody moved. Ghulam still aimed the anti-aircraft missile over Nathan's head.

Had Nathan missed?

He released the trigger until it reset with a click, then he fired three times in succession.

Ghulam spun like a ballerina executing a pirouette, with the weapon still mounted on his shoulder. His knees buckled, and he collapsed onto the gravel.

Another shot. Abbas had fired too.

Nathan pivoted and aimed at Abbas as Mo crumpled to the ground. Nathan centered his sights on Abbas's chest.

Eddie and Jimmy opened fire. Abbas's body jerked with the impact of bullets. He stumbled backward and pointed his gun at Eddie.

Nathan fired until his slide locked back empty.

The gun fell out of Abbas's hand, and he collapsed to the ground.

Nathan thumbed the magazine release and reached for a fresh one on his belt as the spent magazine clattered against the gravel. He inserted the magazine and hit the slide release, driving a fresh round into the chamber.

He looked over his sights and surveyed the scene.

The Bronco appeared to be empty. Ghulam, Abbas, and Mohammad all lay motionless on the ground. Eddie and Jimmy approached the bodies.

"Eddie, cover the suspects," Nathan said. "Jimmy, clear the Bronco."

Nathan fought his instincts to run to Mo. Instead, he turned away and scanned the other cars in the parking lot. Did Ghulam have backup?

The young couple who had glared at Eddie's driving, lay on the ground. The husband shielded his wife with his body. Half a dozen other people gaped as if watching a cop drama on television. Didn't they realize the danger?

Nathan swept the parking lot with his muzzle. The vehicles all appeared to be unoccupied.

He keyed his Mike. "Oh-One, Oh-Two."

"Go ahead, Oh-Two." Rahimya said, her voice on the verge of panic.

"Shots fired. Two suspects down. Charlie's down too. Better get up here."

"En route."

Blue revolving lights from three police cars caught Nathan's eye as they raced up the parkway.

"Bronco's clear," Jimmy called out.

Nathan jogged to the bodies.

Eddie shoved the surface-to-air missile launcher away from Ghulam with his toe.

"Careful," Nathan said. "That's gotta be armed and ready to rock'n'roll. The firing mechanism may be sensitive."

Eddie froze and stepped back. Nathan looked closer. *IGLA-S* was stamped into the metal.

"Ghulam's dead," Eddie said. "I don't have cuffs."

"Me neither."

Abbas lay in a puddle of blood, his handgun several feet from his still body. He stared up at the approaching aircraft with unseeing eyes.

"Jimmy, cuff these assholes," Nathan said.

Nathan bent to check Mohammad's pulse and stopped. The left side of his head was missing. Gray matter sprinkled the ground.

Nathan closed his eyes.

"I'm sorry," he whispered, too low for anyone to hear.

64

Reagan's health provided some good days, but today wasn't one of them. Nightmares and a throbbing headache had kept her from achieving deep sleep, and nausea twisted her stomach all morning. Nothing like waking up vomiting. The slightest movement disrupted her balance, and while meclizine took the edge off, sudden movement brought vertigo. She'd stayed in bed for hours, lacking the motivation to rejoin the world.

And now she had to deal with Vince.

He stood at the foot of her bed—or his bed, or maybe their bed—and glared at her. "That was the ambo on the phone," he said. "He caught your CNN interview."

"Did he call to see how I'm feeling?"

Vince's face reddened. "This isn't funny. He's fucking pissed. You work for him, and you don't have—"

"I worked for him until they made me an outcast."

"Yeah, he heard that line on television."

"Someone attacked me because I worked for the embassy, because I'm American."

Vince put his hands on his hips. "We don't know that."

"Are you kidding?" Reagan tried to sit up, but the room tilted. She leaned back and let the queasiness subside.

"You can't criticize State publicly like—"

"The ambo should defend me, not condemn me for speaking the truth."

"Everything you say reflects on him. When you're a State employee, you represent our government on the world stage."

"Thanks for the civics lesson."

"Dammit, Reagan."

"Keep your voice down. You'll wake Amelia."

"Sorry, I forgot she stayed overnight. When's Nathan picking her up?"

Amelia had spent the night, the third time in a week. Nathan had called at the last minute and asked Reagan to take her. Normally, she'd jump at the chance to make up for lost time, but introducing her into a new relationship with Vince was a big step.

"He didn't confirm," Reagan said. "You okay with her being here?"

"I love having her. She's yours, so she's always welcome." He looked at the floor.

"I feel a *but* coming."

"How will this work with my travel and your health issues?"

"It's only temporary," she said. "Nathan's in a bind over that thing at the airport."

Vince nodded, his anger somewhat mollified. "That was incredible. I read the Significant Activity Report, but it only listed the groups assigned to the operation, not individual agents. How involved was he?"

"He didn't say. He never talks about work with me—not in all our years together. Most of what he does is classified, or at least law enforcement sensitive, so it's easier for him to just avoid discussing it altogether. At least that was his reasoning."

Vince frowned, then seemed to catch himself doing it and put his hand over his mouth to clear his throat. Did talking about Nathan make him uncomfortable?

"I'll call him today," she said, "and discuss finding a backup babysitter —someone available on short notice."

"I'm not complaining. Amelia's a joy. I see so much of you in her."

Reagan warmed. How did Vince do that to her with even the tiniest of compliments? Was she that needy for a man's affirmation? Or was this genuine love? With Nathan, that romantic mixture of excitement and contentment had gone missing at some point during their marriage.

"I told the ambo you won't make any more statements to the press."

"You had no right to promise that."

Vince plunked down on the mattress and the musky scent of his cologne reached her. Who knew men still wore the stuff? Nathan had never used cologne. It felt so 1990s. Vince used something by Nautica, and an image of the blue liquid flashed in her mind.

Why couldn't she concentrate?

"I don't think you realize how serious this is," Vince said. "If you weren't ill—"

"Injured."

"Whatever. If you hadn't been . . . *compromised* at the embassy, I think he'd fire you."

Fired? A shock passed through her. She'd always excelled at her job, and now the ambassador considered terminating her? And for what, speaking her mind?

Anger focused her. "State can't touch me after my television appearance. They can't fire a victim."

"They can . . . and they might."

She glowered. "I won't stop telling the truth."

"You're risking everything. And for what? Half the government's investigating Havana Syndrome. You think spouting off in the media will speed up the investigation?"

"I'm fighting back. I need to—"

"Fighting back against whom?"

She sipped water from the glass on her nightstand to calm herself. How did Vince not understand this? "The CIA, for starters. State. Everyone blaming the victims. They're ruining our reputations."

Vince's eyes flared. "Your unauthorized interviews hurt my career too."

"Your career?"

He exhaled. "We're linked now. You gave State my address as your residence, and everyone knows about our affair. When you buck the system, they blame me."

"That's not fair," she said. "You don't control me. You can't—"

"Fair or not, the ambo's not playing around."

"Why doesn't he call me instead of sending you? He afraid I'll record our conversation and play it for the *New York Times*?"

"He did call you. Three times."

Oops.

"I turned my ringer off." She reached for her phone, and her stomach flipped. She closed her eyes then checked her cell. Three missed calls from unknown numbers. Yep, that had been the embassy.

"This whole thing has been difficult," Vince said. "All I'm asking is for you take a breath and think about the career ramifications."

"I'm more worried about my health."

He squeezed her leg. "Me too." He stood and stretched. "Promise me you won't do anything until we talk about it?"

She rolled onto her side away from him, wanting to escape the controversy. But this wouldn't solve itself. "I'm not planning to call anyone else."

He said nothing, but she didn't hear him leave either. He was probably scowling. At least she hadn't lied. She wouldn't stop standing up for herself, but she had no plans to call another media outlet.

Not today.

65

Nathan waited on the patio at Hank's Oyster Bar on DC's Southwest Waterfront. He sipped a Guinness Stout, and the froth tickled his lip as the velvety-thick liquid coated his throat. What was better than the first sip of a frosty Guinness?

A seventy-five-degree breeze warmed his body on one of those rare March days that previewed spring. For a business day, a surprising number of people strolled along The Wharf bordering the Potomac. Most looked like tourists, but some were probably locals playing hooky. A long, wooden pier curved into the river, and dozens of boats bobbed at their slips. Sailboat halyards clanked against masts like wind chimes.

Meili exited the dining room and scanned the patio. She spotted him, and the tension melted off her face. She weaved through diners, sidestepping a busboy to reach him.

Nathan set down his glass and stood to greet her, feeling guilty for starting without her. "Thanks for meeting me."

She ignored his extended hand and threw her arms around his neck. She pulled him into a hug. Her breasts pressed against him, and her body warmed his.

"Thank God you didn't get killed," she said.

"I, uh, I'm fine."

She maintained the embrace but looked up with soft, brown eyes. "I worried about you when the reports came in."

"It got a little hairy. We lost our CI."

"I know. I'm sorry." She stepped back, her eyes misty.

"I ordered a beer," he said. "I can't sit by the water without one. It's a character flaw."

"I'd be drinking nonstop, if I'd been in a shooting."

"Two shootings."

He slid back her chair—the first time he'd ever done that. The dynamic between them dictated it, but what had changed?

She sat and pushed her menu aside. "I just read your report. You took down half that ISIS team by yourself."

"We had three teams out there and SWAT and HRT standing by."

Her eyes gleamed. "You're modest. You shot three of those bastards and—oh, I'm sorry. This must be hard. How are you handling the aftermath?"

"Shooting those ISIS fucks didn't bother me. If they wanted to live, they could have surrendered. We took most of them into custody without deadly force."

"Still, it must be traumatic."

"We're trained to assume that by our softening culture, but the men I shot needed killing. Especially Ghulam. Another couple of seconds and he'd have blown an airliner out of the sky. That American Airlines flight coming in from LA was an Airbus A321neo, filled with 220 passengers. Ghulam wanted to annihilate them."

Meili looked down at her plate. "I've never fired my gun outside the range."

"It was my first time too."

She met his eyes. "And your second. You're not shaken up?"

"Not even a little. I'm proud I did what had to be done."

The waiter came and Meili ordered a sauvignon blanc, a fruity wine, but perfect for the first flash of spring. It was delicate, like her. Maybe *delicate* was the wrong word for Meili. *Feminine* worked better. She'd been as tough as the male recruits in their FBI class. Not as strong, of course, but mentally tough. And she could shoot too. All without losing what made her a woman.

She touched his hand across the table, and he realized he'd been staring.

"You still with me?" she asked.

"Sorry, my mind's hazy from lack of sleep. I was stuck at the airport for hours. We had multiple crime scenes, and a dozen suspects to process. My team did anyway. Eddie, Jimmy, and I were sidelined because of the shootings. They interviewed us for hours."

"Was OPR reasonable?" she asked, referring to the Office of Professional Responsibility.

"The shoot team responded, and I got lucky and pulled an old salt who wasn't looking to bust balls. He checked all the boxes, but we had plenty of civilian witnesses, and it was obvious what happened."

"How long till they issue a ruling?"

"Could be weeks, but Rahimya's pushing to get us back on duty. The prosecutor needs our help."

"Who's your AUSA?" she asked, referring to the United States assistant attorneys who prosecuted the FBI's federal criminal cases.

"Sam White."

"Lucky."

"Yeah, he's a pit bull. Smart as hell and aggressive. Rahimya sent a junior agent to accompany Sam to the defendants' first appearance this morning. We're holding them on a complaint, then we'll get a grand jury to indict on as many charges as possible. With the murder, they'll get life sentences."

Meili's wine came, and she sipped it. She licked the cool liquid from her lips, and Nathan stirred. Meili set her glass down but didn't release the stem. She stared at it.

"What?" he asked.

"I'm proud of you."

His cheeks warmed. "Thanks. Eddie and Jimmy eliminated a terrorist too. And the rest of the team did their jobs. That thing could have gone sideways fast."

"But it didn't."

"No." He leaned back, fatigued. "No, it didn't."

"Any plans for filling your days while you're waiting for clearance?"

"Havana Syndrome."

"I knew you'd say that." She agitated the wine, sniffed it, and took a tiny sip—every movement feminine.

"I thought you'd be pissed."

"Nothing I've said or done has dissuaded you from sticking your nose into our case. Besides, it's hard to be mad at a hero."

"Stop."

A forty-foot schooner motored past the pier with its sails down, and moored boats bobbed in its wake. Meili gazed after it then returned her attention to him. "What I'm about to share with you stays between us, agreed?"

His heart thumped in his chest. He nodded.

"I got an Interpol hit on that photo you gave me."

His senses came alive. "Who is he?"

"Ming Ho."

"Who's that?"

"He was ID'd during a counterintelligence operation. He's a broker between China's Ministry of State Security, which is their civilian intelligence service, and are you ready for this?"

"You're killing me."

"The Triads."

His mind raced. If Sergei Popov had turned over actual intelligence and not disinformation, that meant the Chinese government, or the Triads, or both, were involved with Havana Syndrome.

Nathan rubbed his neck. "Why would the Chinese risk a war by using a high energy weapon to attack low-level employees? Why target Reagan?"

"Maybe she was getting too close to something they wanted to stay hidden. Or maybe they were aiming at someone else and hit her."

Nathan straightened in his seat. "The ambassador's office was directly above her."

Meili nodded. "They could have been using local assets with minimal training. In my experience, when governments are involved, incompetence usually explains incomprehensible behavior."

"Maybe . . ."

"We may never know the answer."

"What's your plan?" Nathan asked.

"We find Ming Ho."

"*We?*"

Her mouth tightened. "I thought about not telling you I'd identified him, but you'd track him down yourself and interfere. And withholding this didn't feel right . . . on a personal level. You developed the lead."

"I appreciate it." Nathan's phone rang, and Eddie's personal number displayed on the screen. "I've got to take this." He got up, stepped over the rope designating the patio area, and crossed the sidewalk to the water's edge. He answered.

"Where are you?" Eddie asked.

"Having a beer with a friend. I'm following up on something."

"Yeah, right. Listen, I'm calling because Rahimya said we'll be back to work the day after tomorrow. She asked me to prepare warrants for the Golden Dragons who manufactured or distributed the fake documents."

"We can't charge them with terrorism because we can't prove they knew the documents would be used for attacking the airport. We can only charge forgery. And possibly aiding and abetting or conspiracy."

"I said that, but Rahimya reminded me we'd planned to take everyone down once ISIS forced our hand."

Nathan sighed. If the Chinese were somehow involved, and Ming Ho was linked to both Chinese intelligence and the Triads, Nathan needed to move tactically. If the FBI took down a bunch of Golden Dragons, Kei would be useless to them, and how would he get close to Ming Ho without Kei?

"Tell Rahimya we want to keep our source in place until we can develop more serious charges and—"

"I don't think she'll go for that," Eddie said. "The airport attack's dominating the news cycle. She wants every shred of evidence and no loose ends."

Eddie was right. The attack on Reagan National had reignited worry about Islamic terrorism. The prosecution of Ghulam's jihadists would be front page news for weeks, and that would center the FBI in the media spotlight. Rahimya's team looked like saviors, but one prosecutorial misstep, and they'd go from heroes to zeros.

"Tell her we'll speak with the AUSA about potential charges. That should buy us time."

"Time for what?" Eddie asked.

"I need our CI to find a man named Ming Ho."

"Who?"

"He's a conduit between Chinese intelligence and the Triad. If anyone can find him, it's our guy. Set up a meeting ASAP."

"How about we wait until we're back on duty?" Eddie asked.

No sense getting Eddie in trouble too. "Set the meeting and text me the details. You don't need to come."

"You can't meet a source alone."

"I'll have someone with me. Call him now." Nathan hung up and returned to the table.

"Problem?" Meili asked.

"That was Eddie. We'll be reinstated soon."

"Then we better find Ming Ho fast. Unless you're too busy drinking beer."

Nathan laughed. "Do you know where he is?"

"I have a couple of addresses and the names of his previous associates from that old counterintelligence case. Figured we'd start there."

"I may have a better idea," Nathan said.

Meili raised her eyebrows. "I'm all ears."

"It's time to introduce you to Kei."

66

Bashir hurried down a hallway after Trent Hamilton in the executive wing at Langley. Hamilton carried a stack of folders under his arm and held a briefing report in his free hand. He scanned the intelligence paper as he prepared to meet the deputy director.

"Did you hear me?" Bashir asked.

"What was that?"

"I said, it's possible the Russians aren't behind this."

"Psychogenic causes," Hamilton said. "I see no reason to doubt our report."

"There's a possibility the Chinese are involved."

"Humph. I don't need another wild theory. We presented the White House with our analysis, and we won't deviate."

"This is coming from Agent Burke."

Hamilton slowed and looked over his glasses at Bashir. "You told me Burke was off the investigation."

"That was before he met Sergei Popov in Kyiv."

Hamilton stopped. "I authorized twelve grand to reimburse your Ukraine expenses, and your report mentioned nothing significant other than Popov's denials."

Bashir waited for two young women and an Air Force colonel to pass them in the corridor. He shouldn't overreach in case his speculation turned out to be wrong. "I think Burke held something back, something Popov gave him."

"He passed the polygraph."

"Yeah, there's that. But those things can be beaten."

Hamilton continued walking, and Bashir hurried to catch up. For an older man, Hamilton moved with purpose.

"Meili Chan met with Nathan the other day, and she returned to the office full of energy."

Hamilton hesitated outside the Office of the Deputy Director. "What did she say Burke found? And why would Burke tell her and not you?"

"They've become close. They met each other at the academy. I think—"

"Maybe I should've hired her instead of you."

That barb stung. Bashir had sacrificed much to reach this point in his career. Failing this mission would damage his self-esteem more than he cared to admit.

"I asked Meili, and she said when she checked on Burke after the airport incident, he didn't talk about Ukraine."

"Get to the point. I'm thirty seconds late for meeting with one of the most powerful men in the free world. You have any idea what a deputy director of Operations can do?"

"There's a chance she told me the truth, but I checked her computer after she left the office and—"

"How'd you do that?"

"Better you don't hear the details," Bashir said. "Isn't that what you told me when you brought me on board? We're already operating in a legal gray area."

"You have ten seconds."

"Chan ran a number through the NSA database. It came up in a counterterrorism investigation involving Triads. Guy named Ming Ho acted as a cutout for Chinese intelligence."

"Chan could be working on anything."

"Her group's singularly focused. I ran my own checks and called in a couple of favors. Ming Ho lives in DC. The Chinese use him for black ops, and he has hooks into the Triads, which China uses for wet work when they want deniability."

Hamilton stared daggers at Bashir. "How's this related to the FBI's investigation of Havana Syndrome?"

"I was hoping you could tell me."

Two analysts Bashir recognized from the Russian counterintelligence group strolled by. After they passed, Hamilton leaned close. "I brought you into this to make problems go away, not create them."

"You told me to keep tabs on what the FBI is doing."

"Havana Syndrome is mass hysteria. Get the FBI in line, or I'll find someone else who can."

Hamilton disappeared into the director's suite, and Bashir stared at the closed door. Leaping to conclusions and fixating on evidence that supported them had led to many intelligence failures. What was Stalin's secret police chief's famous quote? *Show me the man and I'll show you the crime.*

This was no way to run an investigation.

67

Kei stared at the floorboard in Meili's Malibu and refused to make eye contact with Nathan or Meili. They'd parked on Constitution Avenue beside the National Mall. Tourists strolled across the brown grass, and sun glinted off the Washington Monument. Meetings like this were common near FBI Headquarters.

Kei shifted uncomfortably.

"What?" Nathan asked.

"I cannot find this man for you," Kei said.

"Why not?"

Kei's eyes hardened. "Why can I find him? You think I know all Chinese people?"

"Ming Ho is a Chinese national with connections to the Triads. Your reaction when I mentioned his name confirms you've heard of him."

Kei's eyes darted back to the floor.

"Stop fucking around," Nathan said. "Tell me why you don't want to help."

"I do not know this man."

"This is vitally important," Meili said. "We must find—"

Nathan touched Meili's leg to stop her. He had a relationship with Kei, and after a few weeks working together, Nathan knew appealing to Kei's morality or sense of duty wouldn't work. Kei had agreed to become an informant to reduce his pending charges.

"Lying violates your cooperation agreement," Nathan said.

Kei wrapped his arms around his stomach but didn't look up.

"We're on the same side," Nathan said. "You went undercover against the Triad and ISIS, yet Ming Ho scares you. Tell me why, and we'll work it out together."

"I can't find him. I—"

"Keep lying, and I won't ask the prosecutor to reduce your sentence. But tell the truth, and I'll fulfill my promise."

"But—"

"Jerk me around, and I'll shred our agreement. Want to take your chances in court?"

Kei looked up. His face rarely showed emotion, but his forehead had turned into a topographical map of worry lines.

"I can't help you if you don't come clean," Nathan said.

Kei stared at the headrest. "Ming Ho is very dangerous man." He spoke in a monotone, as if hypnotized.

Meili glanced at Nathan and grinned, but Nathan ignored her. Getting a source to reveal a guarded secret was a delicate dance. Kei was terrified, and Nathan needed to earn his trust and make him fear the FBI more than Ming Ho.

"This man . . ." Kei stopped then started again. "Ming Ho very powerful in Hong Kong. He know everyone."

"Do you—" Meili started.

Nathan touched her shoulder to silence her. He waited.

"Ming Ho speaks to Triad boss," Kei said. "He meets top party official. He has their personal numbers."

"Does he hold an official role in the government?" Meili asked. She didn't seem able to control her curiosity. Nathan let it go.

"He is not party official," Kei said, "but he as powerful as political committee. More dangerous to me. Understand?"

"Because of his connection to Triad leadership?" Nathan asked.

Kei nodded. "Working for FBI is dangerous, but betraying Ming Ho is suicide."

Time to shift tactics. Pushing Kei wouldn't work, and ignoring his fear would seem like Nathan didn't care. In the handler-source relationship, trust was everything. Kei wanted to avoid prison, but he wouldn't sacrifice his life.

"I understand," Nathan said.

Kei's shoulders sagged.

"See, that wasn't so hard," Nathan said. "I won't let you get hurt. I've got to sleep at night too, and to be honest, I like you. You helped us take down ISIS, and I won't get you murdered."

Kei exhaled, and his body deflated. He cleared his throat. "Thank you very much. I go now?"

"I need you," Nathan said. "Our friends . . . my wife . . . they've been hurt by whoever Ming Ho's assisting." Nathan loathed sharing personal information with a CI, but he needed Kei to abandon his comfort zone. Showing they shared an enemy would help. Source control relied more on emotion than intellect.

"Ming Ho did this?" Kei asked.

"I need you to find him," Nathan said. "I promise to keep your involvement between the three of us. We use a confidential informant number instead of your name in our official reports, but I won't even trust that. Help us locate this asshole, and no one will ever know who gave us the information. You have my word."

Kei clucked his tongue, struggling with the decision. What Nathan had left unsaid was if Kei didn't help, Nathan would send him to prison, and Kei would have risked his life infiltrating ISIS for no benefit.

"I do not know where he live," Kei said. "He has homes in Hong Kong and America."

"But you can find him," Nathan said.

"Yes."

"The clock's ticking."

"I do this for you, and you talk to judge?"

"I'll ask for no jail time," Nathan said. "Taking down those jihadists at the airport was a huge win. I'll have no problem getting my management to back you, and the prosecutor will listen to the FBI's recommendation. After that, it's up to the judge."

Kei nodded, his face placid like a winter lake.

"Kei?"

"I text you in two hours."

68

Nathan drove Meili in his silver Ford Mustang down the wooded street in Northwest Washington, DC. They passed towering brick residences, probably worth millions. The entire Washington, DC Metro area had become a real estate goldmine. The ever-growing federal government had created a permanent population of government employees earning six figures, even during times of economic hardship. Federal dollars were inflation proof.

"It's coming up," Nathan said.

"Which one?" Meili asked from the passenger seat of .

"Third on the right. This is a dead end, so don't stare. I'll make a U-turn at the end and head back to the main road. I just wanted to eyeball it."

"Not my first surveillance."

Nathan laughed. "You've been a supervisor for what, three years? That's long enough to get rusty. Stick with me, kid."

She swatted him on the arm. She'd been touching him a lot. He didn't hate it.

Nathan downshifted the Mustang, and its motor rumbled. He loved the throaty roar of the five-liter V8 engine. He'd taken his personal car because he was still on administrative leave. Meili had objected when he picked her up, but his Mustang fit into the affluent neighborhood better than his B-ride, and she agreed.

He rolled past another massive house, and Ming Ho's DC residence peeked out between rows of shrubbery. Kei had given him the address and assured him Ming Ho was in DC working on a project, at least for the time being.

"That's it," he said. "Behind those oak trees."

A three-story brick residence with portico's and three chimneys rose above a manicured lawn. Nathan observed it without moving his head, because a house like that would have a security system with video surveillance. A diligent security officer, bodyguard, or Chinese intelligence agent would notice people staring at the dwelling.

Meili raised her phone to her ear, as if she were talking to someone, and snapped photos as she examined the property. Nathan rolled past, keeping the mansion in his peripheral vision. It appeared as it had in Google Earth, but those images were long out of date, and nothing substituted seeing a subject's home with his own eyes. A red Mercedes 500 SL convertible was parked outside a closed three-car garage.

"Nothing came back under his name in DC, Virginia, or Maryland?" Meili asked.

"Not anywhere. I ran LEXIS-NEXIS and a credit check too. It's as if he doesn't exist."

Nathan passed the residence, and sun reflected off the Washington Reservoir behind it. Few homes had water views inside the District.

"Passport entry?"

"Nothing at the borders," Nathan said, "and Homeland Security never heard of him."

Meili drummed her fingers on her leg. "Does Kei have Ming Ho's aliases?"

"The Golden Dragons call him 'the Emperor.'"

Meili laughed. "Come on."

"I know. It's dramatic, but this guy has real influence. He's obviously using fake documents to slip in and out of the US."

At the end of the cul-de-sac, smaller residences lined the street. He swung around the circle and drove back out—faster this time. He ignored the residence as they drove past.

"Who lives there?" Meili asked.

"Kei thinks Ho's the only resident, but the Emperor's known for keeping frequent female company."

"Bodyguards?"

"Kei only saw him once, and that time, Ho had an entourage of six heavy hitters. That was a month ago. The Emperor asked, or I should say *told* the Golden Dragon leader to handle a problem."

"Problem?"

"That's all Kei said. The Golden Dragons trust Kei because of his financial contacts and smarts, but they haven't accepted him fully, at least not yet."

Meili smiled. "You want to keep Kei in place so he can rise through the ranks?"

"That's the long-term plan, if the ISIS case doesn't burn him."

"Then we'll make sure he survives this, but you understand the importance of my investigation, and I hope you're prepared to give up your long-term undercover, if necessary."

"Kei will testify, if needed. Once he signed on the dotted line to go after Mohammad, he became ours. He's dead if they find out he cooperated, and he needs us to protect him. His only other option is to flee and be hunted by the Triads, Chinese government, and US law enforcement. He's a smart cookie, so I'm sure he did the math and realized he made the right choice by trusting me."

Nathan turned onto a commercial street lined with businesses and parked outside a closed lawn equipment repair shop so they could talk in private. He needed Meili on the same page.

"Can Kei set a meeting with Ho?" Meili asked.

"He's got no legitimate reason to request a face-to-face with somebody like the Emperor, but I'll craft a scenario where he claims he found a new military weapons supplier. If we devise a sting with enough importance to the Chinese government, they may ask Ho to contact the Golden Dragons without Kei ever having to mention his name."

"You're a sneaky bastard."

"We have work to do first," Nathan said. "Let's get a current photo of this guy, then we can uncover his relationship with Chinese intelligence."

"If it exists."

"You read the intelligence report. Kei's not the first person to report on Ming Ho's connections."

Cars zoomed past, and their exhaust left contrails in the cool air. Clouds thickened, enhancing the gray March day. Winter hung around like an unwanted houseguest.

"Ho's house is a tough location to cover," Meili said. "What do you recommend?"

"Pole camera on the closest streetlight to monitor the front, then build a hide someplace out back. Like across the reservoir."

"I've been behind a desk for years," Meili said. "You mean a hide, like in hunting?"

"Exactly. Agents burrow into a bush and set up an observation post. I'd prefer to use a nearby house, but I ran checks on the neighbors, and I don't trust them to keep a secret. We switch agents every twelve hours and resupply the hide. Between the pole camera and mobile surveillance team, we'll have him blanketed."

"*We?* I'm using the Special Surveillance Group for this," Meili said.

"This shit's too advanced for the SSG. I'm talking about surveillance techniques utilized by the special operations community."

"You learn that in Afghanistan?" she asked.

"The Brits taught me. The SAS runs a special surveillance team, and I embedded with them for a couple of months. This is old-school surveillance. If we can show the connection to Chinese intelligence, we can ask NSA for a dirt box to record the cell phones coming from that location."

"Dirt box?"

"Digital Receiver Technology. It acts as a portable cell tower and identifies wireless signals in the area."

Meili nodded. "If we identify his numbers, I'll have my people get up on his phones. This is as close as I've been to finding an answer in years, and I don't want the Emperor slipping through our fingers. It's time to bring in the whole team. I'll put my toughest guys in the observation post."

"They aren't your best choice," Nathan said.

"Then who?"

He grinned.

"You're on ice until OPR clears you from the shoot. Besides, your supervisor needs you on ISIS."

"I'll be back on duty in a couple of days," Nathan said. "Eddie can assist the prosecution for now. I want to have eyes on Ming Ho myself. Can you talk to Rahimya for me?"

Meili exhaled. "That should be a fun phone call."

69

Nathan stepped onto Pennsylvania Avenue, across from the Hoover Building, and glanced at the US Capitol, nine blocks away—a sight he never took for granted. He strolled around the block and loitered outside the employee's garage entrance where Meili had instructed him to wait. She'd sounded excited, but she'd already assigned her team to help surveil Ming Ho, so what news did she want to share? And why had she insisted they not meet in her office?

He stood away from the building, where the sun could find him, and watched the ramp to the underground garage. A moment later, she climbed the ramp in high heels and made her way down the sidewalk. She wore a pencil skirt, silk blouse, and navy jacket. Dressed to kill.

"You didn't have to doll up for me," he said.

"Funny." She flashed him a side-eye. "Walk with me. I've got a meeting in the West Wing."

"The White House?"

"I told Bashir we found a connection to the Chinese government," Meili said, "and he insisted I brief the CIA. He asked me to give them everything we—"

"Don't trust them. Not after they blamed Havana Syndrome on victims."

"Bashir doubts that conclusion too," Meili said, "which is why he invited me to Langley, but I got the feeling he encountered resistance."

Meili strode down the sidewalk, westbound toward the White House, and Nathan scurried to catch up. How did she move that fast in high heels?

"Then how did—"

"Bashir requested a meeting with the national security advisor."

"Frederick Richardson?" Nathan asked. "I had no idea Bashir wielded that kind of clout."

"He got me got five minutes with Richardson after the morning brief. Bashir said he'd do most of the talking, but he wants me there."

"What did your boss say?"

Meili looked at him and smirked without breaking stride. "I may have forgotten to mention it."

"Is that smart? If you don't inform your chain of command, they'll be livid."

"How ironic coming from you. I'd tell them, but they'd stop me. Havana Syndrome has become a political third rail since the CIA report. I'm afraid they wouldn't allow me to pass information, and they know nothing about Ming Ho. I've kept him off the radar."

"You'll get in big trouble if—"

"I have a plan."

Nathan cocked his head and waited. Sweat beaded under his shirt from their pace, yet Meili showed no sign of discomfort. Impressive fitness.

"I'll call my ASAC when he's in his daily front-office meeting," she said, "and leave a message saying I received an urgent briefing request. Bashir said he'd back me up. I'll turn my phone off when we reach the White House. My ASAC will be angry, but he can't say I didn't inform him."

"Still . . ."

"I know I'll be in hot water."

Meili didn't wait for the light at Fourteenth Street, and she crossed against traffic. Nathan put himself between her and oncoming cars, more out of habit than necessity. Some would consider that misogynistic, but evolution had imbued in him the need to protect women. They were brilliant and empathetic, better at so many things, but men were physically stronger. It explained why one gender dominated law enforcement.

Fighting to protect women and children was ingrained in the male psyche.

Cognitive dissonance put him on edge, and he rubbed his neck. "I have to ask, why the change? You've been fighting me tooth and nail since this started."

"That isn't fair," she said. "I let you inside."

"But you resisted my help."

Meili bit her lower lip. "Let's just say things are different now—between you and me." She looked away. "And to be honest, you've achieved more in a week than my team has accomplished in years. You're a wrecking ball, but you make things happen."

Her praise filled him, and he couldn't suppress a grin. "I've always been proactive."

Meili giggled. "Now, I understand why your boss is constantly annoyed with you. That poor woman must have an ulcer."

"I get results, so she gives me rope, but if I fail, she'll hang me with it."

"Then don't fail."

"Not planning on it."

She slowed and squeezed his forearm. "You've always impressed me."

His face warmed, and he met her eyes. "Want me to go in with you?"

"Bashir's meeting me at the visitor's gate." She checked her watch. "Nuts, I better call my ASAC."

Meili took her phone out of her clutch and dialed. "Hi, Deanna, it's Meili. Is Tom in . . . oh, too bad. Will you connect me with his machine so I can leave a message?"

Nathan caught snippets of her message, telling her ASAC she was rushing into an urgent meeting in the West Wing with their CIA liaison, and she hoped he'd come.

Meili hurried, but she retained her elegance and moved like a supermodel on the streets of Soho. Fast-walking pleased him. Nothing frustrated him more than dragging along someone who lumbered as if they had all day.

They passed the Willard Hotel, then headed north on Fifteenth Street. Meili hung up and smiled. "That should do it."

"What if he calls back?" Nathan asked.

Meili powered off her phone. "I'm officially out of pocket. I'll deal with the firestorm later."

"You're sure?"

"You stuck your neck out and gave us our best lead, while I played by the rules and went nowhere. It's time I worry less about my career and more about the mission."

"I love it when you talk like that."

They crossed onto East Executive Avenue. The guard checked their identification, then Meili turned to him. She leaned in and kissed his cheek, and electricity crackled through him. She winked and hurried up the path toward the White House.

He watched her walk away. He turned to leave then looked back at her. Meili had stopped about thirty feet away. She stood alone on the path leading to the East Wing. What was she doing?

Meili's hands shook. She took a step and stumbled.

Something was wrong.

She bent at the waist and flailed her arms for balance.

Nathan lunged forward before he'd made the conscious decision to help. He raced down the path.

Meili spun in a tight circle and collapsed. She landed hard on her backside. Her hands went to her head. She rolled on the ground clutching her temples.

A high-pitched whine filled the air, and Nathan searched for a plane or whatever the hell caused it—but the sky was clear. A wave of nausea flowed through him.

The sound stopped as Nathan reached Meili. Her skirt had ridden up on her thighs, revealing ripped nylon. She thrashed on the pavement.

"Meili, what happened?"

Saliva drooled out the corner of her mouth, and she stared at him without comprehension.

Nathan looked up at the White House. "Someone help, please!"

A Secret Service police officer wearing a white and black uniform, leapt off his post at the Visitor's Center and raced down the path toward them.

Nathan returned his attention to Meili. "Hang in there. Help's coming."

She groaned and rolled onto her side.

Nathan took out his cell phone to call 911, but it had powered off.

"What the hell?"

He turned it back on, and it rebooted as the Secret Service officer reached them.

"Did she fall?" the officer asked.

"She's been attacked," Nathan said. "Call an ambulance and alert the White House that there's a high-energy weapon somewhere close."

70

Bashir raised on his tiptoes and peered over the shoulder of a Secret Service police officer in the East Wing's entrance hall. Being short had its disadvantages. The White House had been locked down as a precaution because of an unspecified occurrence outside the Visitor Center. Trent Hamilton had wandered away in search of information.

Bashir scanned the curious mixture of guests and called Meili for the fifth time. His call went straight to voicemail. Again.

"This is Bashir. We're still trapped inside. Nobody in or out. I assume you didn't make it through security before the incident. Not sure what's happening, but no chance Richardson will see us today. He had trouble squeezing us in even before this mess. I'll try to reschedule and get back to you if . . . hold on, Hamilton's back."

Bashir put his hand over the telephone. "I'm leaving a message for Meili Chan. Any chance we get her in here today?"

"Hang up," Hamilton said.

"Wha—"

"They took Agent Chan away in the ambulance."

Bashir gawked.

"Hang up."

Bashir ended the call. "What's wrong with her?"

"I spoke with the shift commander. Chan collapsed outside the Visitor Center and—"

"What the hell happened? She's in her thirties and healthier than me. What are they saying?"

"Calm down," Hamilton said. "It's a medical issue."

"That's your answer for everything," Bashir said. "If she's sick, why'd they seal the world's most important building?"

Hamilton scowled. "Someone told responding officers Chan was attacked."

"Attacked by who?"

Hamilton shifted in his Italian loafers. "A witness mentioned a high-energy weapon."

Adrenaline dumped into Bashir's system, and he flexed his hands. "We're under attack."

Two staffers standing nearby turned and looked at him.

"Keep your voice down," Hamilton said. "And don't jump to conclusions."

"Are you kidding me?" Bashir breathed through his nose to quell his growing anger. "I invited the FBI supervisor leading the Havana Syndrome investigation to brief the national security advisor about possible Chinese government involvement, and she's attacked outside the White House. You think that's coincidence?"

Hamilton grabbed Bashir's elbow and escorted him away from the staffers. "We don't have evidence this has anything to do with—"

"She wasn't punched by a vagrant. And who suggested a high-energy weapon? How would anyone know what that was? Chan was coming alone. Who would be—"

Nathan.

"What?" Hamilton asked.

"I have to make a call."

"Wait a minute. I don't want you charging off half-cocked. We don't understand what we're dealing with yet."

"That's what I need to determine. And I'm not half-cocked. I'm fully cocked and ready to fire."

Bashir found a quiet spot near the staircase and dialed Nathan.

"Burke."

"Nathan, it's Bashir. Where are you?"

"Talking to MPD and Secret Service outside the White House."

"You were with Meili when it happened?"

"It's a microwave attack."

"How do you know?"

"I walked Meili over from HQ, and she was fine. No problems. Then she went down hard."

"They're saying she has a medical condition."

"That's bullshit. She started shaking, then she grabbed her head and collapsed. I ran to her, and when I got close, I heard a high-pitched whine, and my phone shut down by itself. I felt something too. Meili's reaction was classic Havana Syndrome. And it's the second one I've seen."

"Dammit."

"That's all you can say?" Nathan shouted. "You invited her here, and she gets attacked by the weapon she's investigating. Who the hell knew she'd be in the White House today?"

Good question. "I don't know, but I'll find out. I—"

"How could the Chinese respond this fast? They must've been in the capital prepared for an operation. A high-energy weapon would be cumbersome and tough to move."

"Not necessarily."

"I saw marks on the apartment floor near the Tallinn attack, so it's heavy enough to gouge wood."

"What are the police doing?"

"Searching the area, but they could have concealed a weapon in a van or a dozen businesses facing the White House."

"We'll check them all," Bashir said.

"So will I."

"Trust me," Bashir said, "I want to sort this out as much as you."

"You want my trust? Show me results."

"I'll get back to you, okay? Hello?" Bashir checked his phone. Nathan had hung up.

71

Nathan rode in the cargo area of a white Nissan panel van as he pictured Meili lying on the sidewalk. His heart ached, but she was receiving the best care possible, and he needed to focus. The van slowed, and Nathan shifted into a crouch. He wore all black, with loose-fitting cargo pants, sweatshirt, and navy watch cap. He had turned in his government-issued handgun after the airport shooting, so he carried his personal back-up gun, a .40 Glock 27 with a three-and-a-half-inch barrel and nine-round magazine. Nathan wiggled his toes to get the blood flowing.

Insertion into an observation post for a close target reconnaissance was the most vulnerable part of the operation. All it took was one sleepless neighbor or dog walker to compromise the mission.

The FBI agent behind the wheel glanced at him in the rearview mirror.

"What?" Nathan asked.

"Aren't you the agent who smoked those terrorists at the airport?"

"We had an entire team out there."

"Nice fucking job."

"Thanks," Nathan said. Hopefully, the agent would not inquire further, because Nathan remained on administrative suspension. He had met the driver, a member of the Havana Syndrome team, earlier that night. Luckily, Meili had set up the surveillance before her attack.

Poor Meili.

After her attack at the White House, Nathan had been interviewed by Secret Service, FBI, and Metropolitan Police, then he'd stayed for hours in case law enforcement searching the area found anything—but they discovered nothing. He had tried to visit Meili at the hospital, but she was undergoing a battery of tests and could not have visitors. At least an MPD officer guarded her hospital room, which meant the FBI thought she'd been targeted. For now.

"Thirty seconds," the driver said.

Nathan lifted a black nylon backpack off the metal floor and slipped it on. The pack contained a powerful transmitter, extra batteries, flashlights, logbook, food, and water. He grabbed a plastic Gorilla box and slung the strap across his chest. Inside he carried a Canon EOS-1D DSLR camera with a Canon EF 600mm f/4L IS III USM Lens. Meili's team had not provided night vision goggles or a long-range listening device, but at least he possessed the minimum necessary gear.

"Ten seconds."

The van slowed, and Nathan opened the door. He'd disabled the interior light and greased the sliding door to minimize sound. The van halted, and he stepped onto the street, careful not to bang his cargo against the metal body. He slid the door closed until it clicked shut, and the van continued down the street.

Clouds hung low in the inky sky, which blotted the moonlight and cast the street into darkness. Residences along Chalfont Place remained dark at two o'clock in the morning. Nathan hurried down Chalfont Court, an intersecting street that led to a dead end. He walked along the sidewalk—not too fast and not too slow—and scanned windows for movement.

He paused at the first residence, a single-story brick colonial, and glanced around. The neighborhood remained silent as a graveyard. He continued between two houses and crossed soundlessly through a backyard and down a slope into thick brush.

He picked his way deeper into the undergrowth, feeling his way.

The Dalecarlia Reservoir contained fifty acres of water and transected the District of Columbia and Maryland. It supplied DC residents with most of their drinking water. Ming Ho's house was on the northern side, within the city limits of Bethesda. It lay a hundred yards to the east, along the shore.

An undeveloped wooded peninsula stretched out before him into the reservoir. The stark facade of a water processing facility was visible on the far bank. It was a federal facility, so it would have security cameras, but none should be pointed at the residential area on the northern shore where he crouched. He'd stay hidden—just in case.

Nathan proceeded with caution, tapping his toes before stepping to avoid cracking branches. Sweat rolled down his back as he pushed through fallen trees, thorny shrubs, and rotting vegetation. Trees soared twenty feet overhead, and fallen branches had never been cleared. Miserable terrain for hiking, but perfect for concealment.

Something scurried under the brush. A snake? A rodent? He had feared spiders since childhood, an irrational phobia, yet black widows inhabited woods like these. It didn't matter. The wildlife would acclimate to his presence. He was here to stay.

The peninsula spanned forty yards across and sixty deep. He stopped in the middle and headed east until he could see the shore. It took thirty minutes to reach the water and have an unobstructed view of the northern shore. He stopped and listened to the forest. Crickets chirped around him.

Three houses faced the water on the northern shore, with Ming Ho's in the middle, equally distant from the others. A rusted chain-link fence protected the reservoir, which fed fresh water into the purification plant. How easy for a terrorist to dump toxins into the reservoir to poison the city's water supply. Filters would screen out most pollutants, but they couldn't catch everything. He should research that to satisfy his curiosity.

Nathan's eyes had adjusted to the dark, and he searched for a place to create the hide. The ground sloped down to the water and would provide natural back support but also make him visible once darkness lifted. Retreating to flat terrain would provide better concealment. He backed away from the shore where a large shrub covered a depression in the earth.

Perfect.

Special forces had a saying that went something like, "this place sucks, let's live here." The more inhospitable the terrain, the better for concealment.

He glanced back at the house and confirmed his line of sight, then moved around the bush and knelt. Nathan unslung the Gorilla box, slipped out of the knapsack, and unsheathed a seven-inch KA-BAR knife. He pushed away branches and burrowed into the bush. A single branch cut across the middle and refused to move. He bent it and dug his blade into the soft wood. It gave way beneath the sharp steel. He swept the ground, leveling the area inside the bush, then pulled his gear in after him.

Nathan crawled forward and peered through dead leaves across the water to Ming Ho's residence. The bush provided natural concealment, but once the sun rose, he'd feel more exposed. He backed out of the bush and gathered twigs and leaves then reentered the hide and filled holes between the branches, like a bird making a nest.

A bird of prey.

He unpacked his radio and inserted an earpiece, then draped a black towel over his head. Satisfied no light or sound would escape, he turned on the radio, illuminating himself with the screen's glow. He switched to the prearranged local channel, which his cover team should be monitoring.

"Eagle Two, Eagle One in position."

"Good copy, Eagle One," an agent replied. Two agents waited in a van several blocks away in case Nathan needed emergency extraction. Another six surveillance cars were spread throughout the area, prepared to follow Ming Ho when he departed his residence.

Nathan wedged his radio against a root then emerged from under the towel. He kept his earpiece inserted in case the cover team tried to reach him, but protocol was for him to initiate contact from the hide.

Nathan removed the camera from the Gorilla box, attached a tripod, and screwed in the massive telephoto lens. He popped off the lens cap and aimed the lens at the house, keeping it six inches inside the bush. The vegetation covered him like a dome, and everything inside would appear dark and indistinguishable from the surrounding fauna.

Nathan settled behind the camera and used another towel to shield the light from the LED screen. He powered it on, and a fuzzy image appeared. He played with the dials until the northern bank of the reservoir came into focus, then he panned right and centered Ming Ho's residence in the viewfinder.

The two-story brick structure had a gabled roof with three dormer windows. Five windows on the second floor probably belonged to two bedrooms and a bathroom. Floor-to-ceiling windows extended across the first floor, with a kitchen on the left, dining room in the center, and living room on the right. A wooden deck ran the length of the house.

Five thousand square feet was spacious, but not ostentatious for a man who wielded the power and influence Ming Ho had in both China and Washington, DC. Had the Emperor chosen a modest home to stay under the radar? In the District, a house with a waterfront view cost millions, which made it a mansion in China. China may be a military power with a nuclear arsenal, but their average annual income was under five thousand dollars. That's what central planning did to economies.

The windows remained dark, with no sign of life. Nathan zoomed out. A flight of stairs led off the deck into the yard, which sloped down to the chain-link fence protecting the reservoir.

Nathan removed a rubber mat from his backpack, unrolled it, and lay on top. It provided comfort, but more importantly, it kept him dry. He flopped his hood over his head. It wasn't necessary, but the black fabric concealed him.

Surveillance, like baseball, was often a game of inches.

He tugged open the Velcro cover on his watch. The luminescent dial showed it was 3:30 a.m., the witching hour when people were deep in REM sleep. He fought natural biorhythms to stay awake. They needed to understand Ho—see where he went, whom he met, and what he was doing in the country. Ho may hold answers to Nathan's questions, unless his connection to Havana Syndrome was bullshit, and the Russians had spread disinformation to create a red herring.

Nathan lay prone and rested on his elbows to watch through the viewfinder, but even lying down became exhausting over time, and he adjusted his position, wiggled his toes, and stretched his muscles every few minutes.

At least it gave him something to do. Evading detection on surveillance could be terrifying when the stakes were high, but mostly, it was tedium smothered in boredom.

He zoomed in and scanned the residence. No change. He blinked and focused on the water. If he stared at one spot long enough, his mind played tricks on him. Moments like these made him reconsider his life's path.

Tomorrow, he'd report to his office and mollify Rahimya by convincing her he was pursuing the ISIS prosecution and preparing to indict the Golden Dragons, but the last thing he wanted was to arrest the Dragons for minor charges and blow Kei's cover. He'd call the AUSA in the morning to discuss their options. Hopefully, Nathan would determine Ho's connection to Havana Syndrome before he testified before a grand jury about the Golden Dragons.

He zoomed in again and scanned the living room. Slivers of clouds tickled the moon and gave him brief glimpses of the interior. He zoomed out and stopped.

Wait. What was that?

He zoomed back in. Had he seen movement? He stared hard at the three-inch color LCD and focused on the living room interior. A couch, chairs, and—

There.

Something moved through the hallway. A light came on, and a man entered the kitchen. He was about five-six and wore khakis, a blue Oxford shirt, and a dark blazer. He resembled the photo of Ming Ho.

Nathan's fingers rolled over the grooved lens, and he zoomed in tight on Ho's face. He clicked a series of photos. Ho could be fifty or sixty. Hard to tell. He had cropped brown hair and round wire-framed glasses, like a mid-twentieth-century Marxist. Commies shared the same fashion sense.

Nathan keyed his radio. "Eagle Two, Eagle One."

"Eagle Two, go."

"Got movement in the house. Subject Alpha. Asian male, five-six, one-fifty, dark jacket, and glasses. Looks like he's making coffee. He'll be on the move soon, so wake up the surveillance team."

"We're up and ready now. Call the ball, Eagle One." The guy didn't seem to appreciate Nathan's sense of humor.

Ho walked toward the front of the house and out of view.

"Standby. Subject's out of sight."

"Copy."

Nathan zoomed in. The LED screen flickered. Ho had turned on a foyer light. He moved down the walkway outside the living room window.

"All units, Alpha is on the move."

72

The surveillance team's radio chatter cackled in Nathan's earpiece as Ho drove his Mercedes out of the neighborhood and west into Glen Echo. The agents didn't sound like a well-oiled machine, which made sense, since the Havana Syndrome group had focused on witness interviews, liaison, and documenting incidents. Surveillance was a perishable skill, and poor execution could burn them.

Nathan waited for a break in the radio calls, then he transmitted. "Eagle Two, Eagle One. Switch to channel seven."

"Switching."

Nathan rotated the top dial on his radio through the preprogrammed channels to the secondary frequency dedicated to their surveillance.

"We're with you, Eagle One. Problem?"

"I need you to replace me," Nathan said. "The house looks empty, and I've got photos of our subject. I need to see where he goes with my own eyes."

A long silence. The two agents were probably arguing about which of them had to get dirty.

"Eagle One, Eagle Two. Tom's headed to you."

"I'm texting my exact GPS coordinates. I'll leave a glow stick facing west, out of sight of the residence. Tom should have no problem locating my hide."

"Copy."

"I'm headed back now. I'll text when I'm two minutes from the pickup location."

"Good copy. Switching back to channel three."

Nathan snapped the cap onto the lens, closed the box and knapsack, and backed out of the hide. He cracked the glow stick and shook it until it illuminated, then leaned it against the bush where it would only be visible to Tom.

The sun would not rise for another hour, but the sky glowed with predawn color and made it easier to retrace his steps across the peninsula. The sounds of the surveillance team continued in his ear, but their transmissions garbled as they moved south into Virginia. He'd pick up communications once he was back in his car with access to a stronger radio.

Surveillance could take weeks to fill in the missing pieces of the puzzle. The attack on Meili had been a bold and rash move. The Chinese were worried, which meant he must be getting closer to the truth. He was fortunate Ho had remained in the country. If the Chinese sensed the FBI was getting too close, they'd evacuate Ho. The fact that he remained in DC, meant the Chinese still needed him. If Ho was involved in these directed-energy attacks, his presence indicated more to come.

Finding the Chinese connection could be the difference between life and death.

73

Nathan sipped a Venti dark roast Ethiopian coffee from Starbucks as he reclined in his car and struggled to stay awake. Surveillance had followed Ming Ho to an office park off Avion Parkway in Chantilly, Virginia, about thirty miles west of DC. The Chinese asset had parked in a gated lot monitored by a security guard in a booth and surveillance cameras on the building's corners—not unusual for an area inhabited by dozens of government contractors. Private companies supporting the DOD, the DOJ, and other government entities dotted Washington's suburbs.

"Oh-Nine," an agent transmitted. "Target exiting building."

"Oh-Two, copy," the group's senior agent responded. "Six and Seven prepare for take away."

"Six in position."

"Seven ready."

Nathan parked in a lot across Route 50. He'd let surveillance follow Ho away, then he'd check that building and figure out what the Emperor had been doing in there.

After several minutes, the surveillance team announced Ho was through the security gate and onto Avion Parkway. Ho turned east on Route 50 toward the city. The surveillance team's calls slowed as they settled in behind the target. Ho could be returning home, meeting with an intelligence agent, or God knew what else, but Nathan's instincts told him to check this building. Someone was nervous, and Havana Syndrome had to be their top priority.

A quick Google search on his phone showed the building belonged to Silver General, a company that provided office space for various industries. Three companies inhabited the building. Aviation Solutions and TelCom Industries were both DOD contractors, but he'd never heard of the third, Three Gorges Technology. A Google search revealed a primitive webpage that mentioned high-tech solutions to low-tech problems.

He needed to investigate.

Nathan looked down at his soiled black clothing. He looked like a failed cat burglar. He popped his trunk and removed a bag containing a fresh shirt, slacks, tie, and an old sports jacket—attire he kept in the car for last-minute calls to court. Nathan changed and headed toward Silver General.

He stopped in the driveway and rolled down his window to speak with the security guard. The officer worked for DC Shield, a contractor that provided security all over the DC metro area.

"Nathan Burke. I'm here for a meeting with TelCom industries."

"May I see some ID?"

Nathan took his driver license out of his credential case, careful not to display his badge. He would use it if necessary, but if the guard mentioned the FBI to anyone, Ho could catch wind of it and disappear.

"Park anywhere, and check in with lobby security," the guard said. He handed Nathan a pass and raised the gate.

Nathan parked and entered the building.

In the lobby, a guard sat behind thick glass. On the wall beside the entrance was a digital sign with the building directory. Nathan skimmed the divisions and names under Aviation Solutions and TelCom Industries, then read the section for Three Gorges Technology. He read the names and stopped at the second listing. He stiffened.

Dr. Zhang Qaing, High-Energy Research.

74

Reagan gripped the phone and gazed through the windowpane at barren branches that ringed the backyard like prison walls. Self-pity bubbled into her chest, but she forced it back down, refusing to allow herself to feel like a victim.

"Say that again," she said into the phone.

"Judge McAvoy scuttled the lawsuit," Paul Johnson said.

Reagan had heard from Paul three or four times since her return to DC. He'd become the de facto spokesman for victims of Havana Syndrome who felt abandoned by the State Department. Adding her name to the list of plaintiffs suing the government for libel and defamation of character had been a tough decision for her, but fighting back bolstered her self-worth, and it had been her only option.

Now the lawsuit was dead.

"What happened?" she asked.

"I've only skimmed the ruling," Paul said, "but it appears the judge tossed it because the government couldn't admit certain classified intelligence into evidence. The threat to national security outweighed our interests."

"But can't our attorney refile if—"

"This isn't the end. We can narrow the suit's scope or go after individuals' public statements. This ruling won't stop us from seeking justice."

The bedroom door opened, and Vince leaned in. He'd arrived home the night before, and after they'd made love, he'd fallen sleep. They hadn't had time to catch up. He nodded at the phone and raised his eyebrows.

She held up her index finger. "Listen, Paul, I have to run. Keep me posted on developments."

"Don't lose faith. We'll get these bastards to acknowledge what happened to us."

"Talk soon." She hung up.

Vince frowned. "Paul again?"

"Update on the lawsuit."

"You need to stay away from that goat rope. Every plaintiff will be shunned in government circles."

"I agreed to have my name added to the suit, but—"

"Tell me you didn't do that." Vince expelled a long sigh and rubbed his face. "You're shooting yourself in the foot. You won't be able to—".

"Calm down. The judge threw it out."

Vince stopped, and tension seemed to lift off him. He looked . . . happy. "That's a relief. This thing would have hung around your neck forever. You—"

"How can you be pleased?" she asked. "The lawsuit was our chance to force State to admit what happened. It was our only hope to defend our sanity and find justice . . . unless Nathan discovers something."

Vince's face sunk at her mention of Nathan, and his frown returned. "Your ex won't heal your wounds."

"Not physical ones."

"What the hell does that mean?"

"This has devastated me. I'm a mess, and my pain compounds my brain fog, making everything harder to handle. It's a physiological superstorm. And the government's response makes everything worse. Their mass hysteria theory has destroyed my professional reputation and made it hard to recover . . . emotionally and physically."

"I understand, but—"

"Nathan's hunting the people who attacked me."

"He's only a GS-13, and he's not even assigned to the investigation."

Her eyes misted. "He never questions my story."

Vince paced at the foot of the bed and flexed his hands, as if he didn't know what to do with them. "One man can't solve a phenomenon the Feds have been investigating for years."

"He believes in me." Her tears came, and she choked back a sob.

Vince knelt beside her. "I have faith in you too."

"Do you? You don't seem convinced I was attacked."

He took her hands in his. "I'm sure about you."

"You think it's all in my head."

"I don't know what happened, but I know you're not crazy. I'll do everything in my power to help you."

"Nathan's risking everything to solve—"

Vince's face clouded, and a vein in his forehead bulged. "Nathan had his chance with you, and he blew it." He leaned close. "I won't take you for granted, and I won't ever leave you."

Her chest convulsed with a sob. Vince did care. "This hasn't scared you away?"

"I came home early to be with you."

"I don't know." She blinked away her tears. The shades were drawn, but the room seemed brighter.

He reached into his pocket and removed a velvet-covered jewelry box. "I came back to give you this."

She held her breath.

He opened it. A stunning, princess-cut diamond glinted in the lamplight.

"Vince, I . . . oh, my God."

"Will you marry me?"

She bit her lip, unable to speak. She nodded and caught her breath. "Yes, I'll marry you."

75

"Dad?" Amelia asked. "Will Mom get better?"

Nathan glanced at his daughter sitting beside him in their car. She clutched her Dora the Explorer lunch pail against her chest. She looked teensy, more fragile than before. He had been so focused on identifying the people responsible for Havana Syndrome, he had neglected the person he loved most. A wave of guilt turned his stomach.

"Your mother will be fine."

"When?"

"She's sick, baby. These things take time."

"When will she move back home?"

His nausea spread. "Your mom and I are taking a little break."

"Is that what you call Vince?" Pain glowed behind her eyes. She was growing up fast and understood more than he'd realized.

He drove down Massachusetts Avenue NE, between Union Station and the Capitol. After his surveillance in Chantilly, he'd picked up Amelia and Bruno from Vince's home to resume his parental duties. He missed his daughter. And his dog. The Rottweiler lay in the back seat, pouting because Nathan had refused to open the window. Winter held on, a frosty reminder that spring had not yet arrived.

"This is hard for all of us," he said, "but your mom and I love you, no matter what happens."

Amelia stared out the window. She stayed silent and wrapped her arms around her lunch pail.

He turned onto Eleventh then took Capitol Street along Lincoln Park. Teenage boys wearing knit caps and sweatshirts tossed a softball on the hard-packed ground. Everyone seemed desperate for warmer weather. A man walked his dog, a poodle mix, or doodle-something, or whatever they called those mixed breeds. They were smart, but Rottweilers were intelligent and tough.

Nathan parked across from the condo. He had a reserved spot in the garage, but it required a longer walk. Besides, he liked to look out the window and check on his car. He dealt in the business of evil.

Amelia cracked her door.

"Wait, honey," Nathan said. He got out, opened the rear door, and took firm hold of Bruno's leash. The Rottweiler leapt out and strained against the leather as he stared at the Doodle. Nathan took Amelia's hand, and they crossed the street.

Their neighbor, Betty Cook, breezed out of the main entrance. Bruno's ears perked up when he spotted her.

"Good afternoon, Mrs. Cook."

"Oh, hello, Nathan." She smiled. "Amelia, Bruno."

Bruno stretched toward her, wagging his tail.

"Let's go, boy," Nathan said.

Bruno whined and leaned his full weight against his collar, pulling toward Betty.

"Do you mind if Bruno says hello?"

Betty stopped and turned. "Of course not. I've missed my buddy. He acts tough, but he's a big softy... especially when I have Beggin' Strips in my pocket."

Bruno dragged Nathan and Amelia across the sidewalk, as if he pulled a dogsled. Betty knelt, and Bruno licked her hands, He leaned against her leg.

"He loves you," Nathan said.

"It's mutual. I'm back from my sister's, so if Bruno or Amelia need sitting this week, I'm available."

"Best neighbor ever. I'll reach out." Nathan tugged Bruno away and led him and Amelia up the steps.

"Oh, Nathan," Betty said.

He stopped. "Yes?"

"Did your brother ever find you?"

Nathan's blood ran cold. "What?"

"Your brother. He was here this morning with his friend, looking for you. He didn't remember your phone number, so I gave it to him. I take it you aren't close?"

"I don't have a brother."

Betty raised her hand to her mouth. "Oh, my. I—"

"What did he look like?"

"Short hair, like you, and big. Muscular. I just assumed..."

Nathan's eyes darted over the street. Parked cars were unoccupied, the man walking the poodle crossed the park, and the teenagers had gone. His condo windows remained dark.

"Mrs. Cook, may I ask a huge favor?"

"I'm so sorry about—"

"Will you watch Amelia and Bruno while I check our condo?"

"Of course. Amelia, come here, my dear." She reached out and Amelia took her hand, and Nathan handed her the leash. "I shouldn't have given him your number, I just thought he—"

"Don't give it another thought. It's a misunderstanding. I'll stop by to pick up Amelia and Bruno in a few minutes."

Betty headed toward the building's main entrance with Amelia and Bruno.

"Mrs. Cook?"

She glanced back.

"If I'm not back in ten minutes, call the police and report a burglary in progress. Tell them I'm there."

Betty's face turned ashen. She nodded then led Bruno and Amelia inside.

Nathan unbuttoned his jacket and laid his hand on his Glock. Searching a home alone was a tactical error, but calling the police could be an overreaction that would cause him further problems if word reached

Rahimya. He could call Meili, but she lay in a hospital bed, recovering. Nathan had involved Eddie in the Havana case more than he wanted, but maybe Eddie was available.

He moved against the wall beside the elevator and kept his eyes on the windows as he dialed.

"Hey, man," Eddie said. "I met the AUSA this morning and—"

"Later, partner. Someone was snooping around my house. I just got home with Amelia, and I need to search it. You free?"

"Heading home, but I can turn around."

"Where are you?"

"Bethesda."

"Don't bother," Nathan said. "It'll take you an hour in this traffic."

"Call for a patrol unit."

"Yeah, I wanted to avoid that, but I don't have a choice." Nathan disconnected and dialed the police.

"911. What's your emergency?"

"This is Nathan Burke. I'm a special agent with the FBI. I just arrived home and my neighbor said someone was trying to get into my condo. Can you ask a free unit to swing by?"

"You gotta suspect on scene?"

"Not sure."

"They break in?"

Nathan trapped the phone between his ear and shoulder so he could keep his right hand on his gun, then he checked the elevator door. Locked.

"My front door's secure, and the only other exit is the fire escape."

"I'll enter a call, but it'll take a minute. We're having a crazy night. Full moon bringing out the nuts. Know what I mean?"

"How long?"

"Twenty minutes, give or take."

Nathan thanked her and hung up.

The men who had spoken with Betty possessed bad intentions. Too much of a coincidence only one day after Meili's attack. Were they Russians or Chinese? Triad or ISIS? They could be OPR investigating his shooting, but why would legitimate investigators make up a story?

Those guys had come to hurt him.

If someone was inside and Nathan waited twenty minutes for the police, they could slip out the back, and he'd lose his chance to identify them. But if he rode up the elevator and they lay in wait, he'd be a sitting duck.

Don't be a victim.

He jogged around back, staying close to the wall and out of view of the upstairs windows. Nathan peeked around the corner at the rusted fire escape that zigzagged up to his tower windows. He hustled to the bottom gate and typed in his security code. The pad beeped, and he yanked open the wrought-iron gate. It creaked.

He froze and watched the windows. Nothing.

Nathan drew his Glock and aimed upward as he climbed. The metal groaned under his weight. He stayed slow and steady, his eyes on the windows.

He stopped on the first landing and crouched beside the window, listening. Only traffic noise. Was he being paranoid? He tucked his Glock in tight to avoid flagging his movement, then he peered into the window.

Two armed men waited in his living room.

76

Gooseflesh rose on Nathan's skin. The men bracketed his elevator door with their backs against the wall. They held Berettas with attached silencers.

They wanted to kill him.

He should shoot through the glass and extract his revenge for threatening his family. They wanted to murder him, and they deserved to die. But shooting from the fire escape was a legal gray area, because deadly force required an imminent threat, and Nathan could flee—unless they pointed their guns at him.

He wished they would.

He slipped back behind the brick wall and dialed his phone.

"911, what is your emergency."

"Special Agent Nathan Burke," he whispered. "Two armed men have broken into my home. I need backup, now." He gave his address.

"Sir, can you escape or hide?"

"I'm covering them from the fire escape. They're wearing black pants and jackets, and both have silenced Berettas."

"The call's dispatched, sir. You need to leave flee and take shelter."

Fuck that.

"I'm not going anywhere. Tell your officers to approach without sirens.

"Sir, you need to—"

Nathan ended the call and dropped his phone into his pocket. He wouldn't hide like a coward while men violated his inner sanctum and waited to do him harm.

He leaned around the brick and squinted through the glare on the glass. The shorter man moved to the front window and looked out at the park. Sunlight illuminated his Asian features. Was he Triad?

The man looked toward Nathan's car then shrugged his shoulders at his partner. The second man by the elevator was brawny, as Betty had described.

The Asian thug shifted on his feet, appearing antsy. They knew Nathan had arrived. Hell, they'd probably watched him park. Had they seen him speak to Betty? They must be wondering where Nathan and Amelia had gone.

How long would they wait?

A siren wailed somewhere to the east, then an emergency horn honked to the south. The police were coming—without stealth. When one of their own was in peril, cops didn't hesitate, and Nathan was part of the thin blue line.

The Asian man pressed his face against the window. He'd spotted an approaching squad car. He yelled something at the muscular man, and they bolted across the room toward the fire escape. Nathan started to withdraw, but too late.

They'd spotted him.

The Asian raised his Beretta and fired. Nathan jerked his head out of the window as glass shattered beneath a hail of bullets. Nathan clung to the brick as bullets ricocheted off the metal railing with high-pitched whines.

A car screeched to a halt somewhere out front. The cops would force the burglars to either barricade themselves inside or take the fire escape.

The shooting stopped.

Nathan glanced down. He'd never reach the bottom before they picked him off. But if he stayed put, they'd lean out and shoot him.

Move.

He grabbed the railing and exploded out of his crouch. He bounded up the fire escape as fast as his legs could propel him. Nathan had to reach the tower. He arrived at the next level and glanced down. The beefy crook stuck his head out the second-floor window and swept his gun over the fire escape below. Then he looked up—directly at Nathan.

No time to run.

Nathan jammed his Glock's barrel between the landing's metal grating between his feet.

The man swung his Beretta up.

Nathan fired five times, as fast as he could pull the trigger. The killer grunted and slumped against the railing. He didn't drop his gun.

Nathan leaned over the railing to get a better angle.

The Asian man poked his head and gun out the window and opened fire. Bullets cracked through the air.

Nathan fired back.

Bullets clanked against the iron inches from Nathan's face, and fragments of hot lead sliced through his check.

"Fuck this."

Time to go.

Nathan pushed off the fire escape and dove for the closed window. Gunfire filled the air. His elbow and shoulder smashed into the windowpane. Glass shattered, and pain sliced through his shoulder. He tumbled through the frame.

He closed his eyes, bracing himself as he crashed onto the hardwood floor. His momentum carried him forward, and he rolled over broken glass. Shards tore through his khakis into his skin.

He lay on his back, gritting his teeth. His legs and arms burned from a dozen cuts, and wetness seeped beneath his clothing. He opened his eyes as dust settled in the waning light.

A bullet thwacked off the windowsill, and then the shooting stopped.

Nathan rolled onto his knees, and glass dug into his kneecap. He staggered to his feet and backed away from the window. Would they come up the interior staircase to finish him or flee down the fire escape?

Nathan limped to the far side of the room and pressed against the brick. He swiveled his sights between the window and the stairs. He listened for footsteps, but his ears rang from the gunfight.

Nathan edged toward the stairs, checking the window as he moved. He quick-peeked over the top step. The stairwell curved left, with no sign of his pursuer.

Something clanked on the fire escape

Nathan knelt and aimed at the window.

More noise on the metal steps. They were making a run for it.

He hurried across the room to the window, and glass crackled beneath his shoes. Sirens filled the air. He looked over his gunsight and leaned out.

The men reached the parking lot. Nathan aimed, but they raced along the side of the building, and the fire escape obscured his shot. The muscular man staggered and held his ribs.

Nathan draped his leg through the window frame, and blood ran over hassock onto his shoe. He ran his fingers over his pant leg, and shards of glass pricked him. Blood dripped out of his sleeve too. He wasn't losing enough for it to be life-threatening, but he'd need stitches. He dialed as he pounded down the fire escape.

A police car screeched across the pavement below. Nathan stuffed the phone in his pocket and pulled out his credentials. He didn't want to holster with armed killers in the area. He held his badge high as he stepped off the fire escape.

Two police officers exited the car and drew their weapons.

"Police," Nathan yelled. "Federal agent." He aimed his Glock at the ground to minimize their perception of a threat.

"Drop the gun," the younger officer shouted.

Shit. No sense taking a chance. He laid his Glock on the pavement. He raised his badge up and showed them his empty hand.

The officers closed.

"Watch the corner," Nathan said. "They're both armed." He pointed toward where he had last seen the suspects.

"Get on the ground!" the younger officer said.

"I called in the burglary. Two suspects are running east. Asian male, about five-six, and white male, six-three and muscular. Both wearing black jackets."

"I said get down."

Nathan's shoulder and leg throbbed, and his shoe had filled with blood.

It squished under his sock. The thought of getting on the ground didn't thrill him.

"I'm hurt."

"I don't care. Lie down—"

The older cop clasped the younger officer's shoulder. "It's okay." He approached Nathan and took the credentials out of his hand. "You're the FBI agent who called?"

"Nathan Burke. We're losing them."

The older officer waved for the younger to lower his gun, then he broadcast the description of the suspects.

"Need EMS?" the young cop asked.

"I need stitches and antibiotics."

The older officer finished talking on his radio. "You shot?"

"Negative. The glass cut me when I dove through the window. They popped off a dozen rounds."

"Lucky."

"Can I pick up my gun?" With two killers running free in the neighborhood, being unarmed felt like being naked.

"Okay, why don't you—"

Both police radios cackled. "I've got a runner," another officer reported. "Asian male, black clothing. North on A Street."

Nathan retrieved his Glock and holstered it. The younger cop ran to the car.

"Hold on Speedster," the older officer said. "We're sticking here with our witness. Take a statement but keep your eyes open in case the other perp circles back. Marty and Jesse can clear the apartment."

Nathan's eyes drifted to the parking lot where the two men had fled. What was that on the ground? He limped toward the corner of the building and stopped. A trail of crimson splattered the black asphalt. The blood grew more voluminous closer to the corner. Nathan drew his gun and signaled for the older officer to follow him. He leaned around the corner.

The muscular burglar lay face down in a dark lake of arterial blood.

"You can stop looking for the second suspect. He's dead."

77

Bashir looked up as ASAC Mark Dalton entered the FBI office. Mark was Meili's boss and the man who oversaw the Havana Syndrome group.

"Whoever's here, gather around," Dalton said. "I have an announcement."

Bashir moved into the common area between cubicles but hung back as FBI agents and analysts formed a semicircle around Dalton.

"Listen up, people," Dalton said. "I received a call from the SAC. As of right now, your surveillance on Ming Ho is on hold."

"What's happening?" Jim Felix asked. Jim was Meili's unofficial backup, and with Meili incapacitated, he'd become the acting group supervisor.

"This is coming from above," Mark said. "With Meili hospitalized, they want an operational pause."

"We've only been on Ho for a day and a half," Jim said, "and we've already tied him to a high-energy research firm. Why stop now?"

"It's not up for debate," Dalton said. "The powers that be ordered us to stand down. I'll get more clarification later, but I want whoever's out there to return to the office now. We clear?"

Jim sighed. "On it, boss."

"Very good," Dalton said. "And I just got off the horn with the hospital.

The good news is Meili's conscious and alert. The docs are hopeful for a full recovery. I'll pass on more when I have it."

Agents and analysts smiled and exchanged glances. Meili was obviously a popular supervisor.

"She still under guard?" Jim asked.

"MPD will keep an officer outside her room until we can determine what happened. I'll keep you updated, but for now, return to work as normal."

Bashir shook his head. Nothing seemed normal.

Dalton left and the room degenerated into conversations about Meili and the surveillance termination. Bashir grabbed his encrypted cell phone and moved into the hallway. He needed privacy to call Hamilton.

"News?" Hamilton asked without preamble.

"The FBI canceled the team watching Ming Ho."

"That was my call."

Bashir gasped. "Yours?"

"They're bumping into areas where we have interests. They could uncover an asset."

"Ho's an agency asset?" Bashir asked.

"I'm not talking about this over the phone, and it's not your concern."

"If you keep me in the dark, I won't be able to understand what—"

"I've given you everything you need to do your job."

Yeah, right. Bashir's neck muscles knotted, and he flexed his neck. "Did you hear about Burke? Two shooters broke into his house."

"Of course, I heard."

That was fast. The details of the story hadn't been in the news. "Was it Russians?"

"That's for the FBI to determine."

"Maybe it was a psychogenic delusion."

Hamilton remained quiet for what seemed an eternity. Finally, he spoke. "Are you becoming a problem?"

The way he said it—quiet and devoid of emotion—sent chills through Bashir's chest. "I'm saying the stakes have increased. First, Agent Chan, and now, Burke. It may be time to rethink this."

"Not your J-O-B. You're there to report on the FBI and nudge them when we require course corrections. You still able to complete that mission?"

"Yes."

Hamilton hung up.

Bashir pocketed his phone. He sighed and leaned against the wall. What was happening? He'd better identify the players and figure things out before they destroyed his career.

Or worse.

78

Rahimya stood beside an MPD police car parked outside Nathan's condo, her body rigid and face pinched like a hawk. Nathan leaned against the cruiser's hood, craving a cigarette—a habit he'd dropped ten years before. His torn sleeve and trouser leg flapped in the wind, cut open by EMS when they bandaged his wounds. The bleeding had stopped, but he needed stitches.

"Those men were hired guns," Rahimya said. "Probably by ISIS."

"Radical Islamists wouldn't hire outsiders for this kind of work. Not to mention we wrapped up that crew."

"Then who? Triad thugs?"

"This is about Havana Syndrome."

Rahimya glared at him. "You mean the case you promised to stop investigating?"

"Technically, I didn't use those words."

"Knock it off, Nathan. You're still sticking your nose into one of the Bureau's highest profile cases?"

"I'm protecting my wife. This is about family."

"Your off-the-books investigation may be putting your family at risk. If Amelia had entered the apartment with you . . ." She left the last part unsaid, but Nathan's guts still twisted into a knot.

Curtains parted in Betty Cook's condo, and Amelia's pale face peeked out. Nathan waved, and she placed her palm flat against the window. She looked scared. Had she witnessed the violence?

"I need to warn everyone associated with this case," Nathan said.

"Assuming your theory's correct, who's at risk?"

"Dr. Camilla Reyes, for one." He pulled out his phone and scrolled through his address book.

Rahimya raised an eyebrow. "You have her on speed dial?"

"It's not like that. She thought someone was following her, and I told her to stay with family until we figured things out. She left her cell at home to avoid being tracked and gave me her sister's number."

"Hello?" a woman answered.

"My name's Nathan Burke. I'm calling to speak with Dr. Reyes."

"She's not here."

"I'm glad you're being careful," Nathan said, "but it's okay. I'm the FBI agent who sent her to stay with you."

"I'm not being cagey," the woman said. "Camilla only stayed one night. She had to return to the office."

Doom spread through Nathan like an ocean mist. "I'll try her cell."

He hung up and found Reyes's number. He dialed, and it went right to voicemail.

"Problem?" Rahimya asked.

"She returned to work, and she's not answering."

The coroner's wagon slowed in front of his condo. Nathan jerked his thumb toward the intersection, and the vehicle rolled around the block.

Nathan dialed the main number at Dr. Reyes's office building.

"Aura Research Associates," a receptionist answered.

"Nathan Burke calling for Dr. Reyes."

"One moment sir. I'll put you through."

The phone rang several times, and then Reyes's recorded message played. Nathan hung up and called the operator again.

"This is Burke again. Dr. Reyes's phone went to voicemail. I need to speak with her urgently. Is she in her office today?"

"I saw her this morning. She may be in the lab. I'd try later."

"Thanks." Nathan hung up. Later may be too late. He looked at Rahimya. "I told her to stay out of town and lie low."

"Guess she didn't listen."

"I should have taken her to her sister's house myself and made sure she understood the danger."

Rahimya frowned. "You can't force people to protect themselves."

"She only stayed away for one night."

"Witnesses think it's easy to disappear from their lives and go into hiding, but it's not. Dr. Reyes has a thriving academic career, and she probably decided the risk wasn't serious enough to endanger her position."

"She's wrong."

Rahimya nodded.

"Can you drive me downtown?" Nathan asked. "I need to warn her the stakes have increased."

"Shouldn't you see a doctor?"

"It can wait."

Rahimya scowled. "You know, you can be a real pain in the ass."

"You don't see the threat?"

"I'm not buying your Havana Syndrome theories, and your obsession takes you away from the most important case of your career."

"Let me see if my neighbor can keep watching my daughter, then I'll change clothes and meet you at your car. I promise I'll get convictions on the ISIS investigation, but first, I need to stop these assholes from hurting anyone else."

79

The receptionist at Aura Research Associates looked annoyed with Nathan. "Like I said on the phone, I saw Dr. Reyes this morning when she brought me a latte from Starbucks. She's my favorite scientist here. I mean, who else cares about my caffeine level?"

"Her phone's going to voicemail," Nathan said. "Any idea where she is?"

Rahimya sighed and looked at her watch.

"Aura Research occupies six floors," the receptionist said, "and the physics lab is in the basement. She could be anywhere."

"Do you have an intercom to page her?"

"No, but if you leave your number, I'll have her contact you as soon—"

Nathan held out his gold FBI shield, and light glistened off it. "This is an urgent federal matter." He hadn't wanted to associate the FBI with Dr. Reyes, but the tightness in his gut told him this was serious.

"You're welcome to wait here. You know . . . it's funny."

"What is?" Nathan asked.

"You're the second person looking for Dr. Reyes today."

Icy fingers climbed Nathan's spine. "Who else?"

"Some serious-looking guy in a suit, first thing this morning." Her eyes rolled over Nathan's body. "He was built like you."

"I need to find her. Now."

"I can take you to her office. It's—"

"I know the way."

Nathan jogged to the elevator with Rahimya in tow. Her heels clicked on the marble floor.

"Who do you think was asking for her?" Rahimya asked, puffing with exertion.

"Same people who came for me. She never should've returned."

"Witnesses can be stubborn."

They entered the elevator, and Nathan hit the button for the sixth floor. "This time, I'm not giving her a choice. Can we stash her in one of our safe houses?"

"Absolutely not. This isn't related to Islamic extremism, and I don't recommend you share your conspiracy theories with the Havana group. Not without more evidence."

"You realize two men just tried to assassinate me."

Rahimya shook her head. "I've taken two guns from you this week, so I'm aware of the situation, but we don't know this is related to what happened to your ex-wife."

"Not my ex."

The elevator doors opened, and Nathan hurried down the hall. Being a cop meant protecting the innocent, and an evolutionary drive propelled him. He stopped at Reyes's office.

The door was ajar. Dr. Reyes sat at her desk facing her computer with her back to him.

Nathan breathed a sigh of relief and flashed a thumbs-up to Rahimya, who struggled to catch up. She looked pissed. He probably shouldn't push her too hard.

Nathan wrapped his knuckles on the door. "Dr. Reyes?"

She didn't turn around. Had she been ghosting him? He'd need to deal with her anger, because the burning lacerations on his body proved the critical and imminent nature of the conflict.

He pushed the door open and rapped again. "Dr. Reyes, it's Nathan. We need to talk."

Nothing.

A chill spread through his bones, carried on the icy winds of death that followed him. Nathan moved into the room and edged around her desk. Her chest moved with inhalations, so she was breathing. Was his concern for nothing?

"Dr. Reyes?"

She stared at her computer screen, her eyes wide with horror. Drool ran down her chin and dripped onto her blouse.

"Oh no."

Nathan placed two fingers on her carotid artery. Her pulse was strong but slow, and her breathing seemed normal. He squeezed her shoulder.

"Can you hear me?"

No response.

He turned to Rahimya. "Call 911."

Rahimya ran to the desk and dialed. Reyes's pupils were dilated. Her body functioned, but her mind did not.

"We're too late. Too damned late."

80

Reagan opened her front door—she now thought of Vince's home as hers—and forced a smile for Amelia and Nathan, who waited on the stoop. Amelia grinned and wrapped her arms around Reagan's legs, warming her heart. Maybe leaving Santo Domingo had been a good move.

She kissed her daughter's head and moved aside to let her inside. Amelia's footfalls echoed through the foyer as she raced into the house, probably exploring. Who knew what went through her mind?

Bruno tugged at his leash, trying to follow some invisible scent, and Nathan held him back without enthusiasm. Nathan looked worn out. He wouldn't feel any better after she shared her news.

"You look awful," she said.

"Nice to see you too."

"Seriously, you okay?"

"Rough morning." His forehead wrinkled, as if he was contemplating telling her more, then he blew out a long breath. "I just put a scientist working on Havana Syndrome into an ambulance. I think she was attacked."

Reagan's heart skipped a beat, and her hand covered her mouth involuntarily. "In DC?"

"Dr. Camilla Reyes. She studies directed energy at Aura Research Associates."

"What happened?"

"My best guess is some sort of high-energy attack."

Tears formed in Reagan's eyes. Another attack. Was anyone safe? Nathan put his arm around her. He made her feel both safe ... and disloyal. Should she tell him her news now, with everything happening?

"Will she be okay?" Reagan asked.

"I don't have her prognosis yet. She was conscious, but unaware. Her brain seemed scrambled."

"Oh my God."

"Directed energy can do that."

Reagan scanned the street. She was vulnerable. They all were. She met Nathan's eyes—his exhausted, red-rimmed eyes. "You have to find who's doing this and stop them."

"I'm trying."

"You heard the lawsuit was thrown out?"

"Yes."

"The victims are counting on you. I'm counting on you."

"I'm making progress, but since they put me on administrative leave, I've had to operate outside the system."

"Be careful. If you lose your job, you'll be out of the investigation completely. You're our only hope."

Nathan nodded. "Thanks for taking Amelia."

"I wish I could take Bruno, but Vince is allergic. Think he'll be safe alone?"

"I doubt whoever sent those hitmen will make another attempt anytime soon, but I'll keep Bruno with me whenever I can."

"I can't believe this is real. The men at your house are related to what happened to me, aren't they?"

"I think so."

"What's going on?"

"That's what I'm trying to find out."

"Can you come inside for a minute?"

Nathan's eyes lit up.

"There's something I need to tell you, and you may not like it."

His face fell, and guilt weighed her down. Hadn't she hurt him enough? She should wait to tell him. He had a full emotional plate. "You know, this isn't a good time. Let's chat when you pick Amelia up."

"You can't do that to me," he said. "You obviously have bad news, and I'll imagine every horrible thing until you tell me."

She nodded, and dread darkened her as she led him into the living room. She settled on the edge of a sofa cushion, and Bruno plopped down beside her.

No judgment, Bruno.

Nathan remained standing, as if distance afforded him protection. There was no easy way to break the news.

"Vince proposed to me."

Nathan flinched. "Wha—"

"I said yes."

Nathan bit his lip and closed his eyes. Bruno must have sensed his distress, because he lumbered to his feet and padded across the floor. He leaned against Nathan's leg.

"We're still married," Nathan said. "Is that a detail you forgot?"

"We need to resolve that."

Nathan snorted. "Interesting way to describe the destruction of our marriage."

"This is difficult for me too. I never planned any of this."

"You've known this guy for a few months, and you're ready to throw away our life together?"

"We weren't working, not for a long time. You know that."

"Amelia needs a mother to—"

Reagan tensed. "That's not fair. I'll always be her mother, and between my chronic health issues and my involvement in the lawsuit, State probably won't deploy me again. Ever."

Nathan rubbed his forehead, and Bruno glared at her. Was she imagining that?

"It's a lot to process," Nathan said. "Your health's improving. You'll recover."

"I hope so."

"How can you give up on us so easily?" His eyes blazed. "We haven't tried to—"

"There's nothing easy about this. I didn't plan to meet Vince. It just happened, and I can't control my feelings."

"Dammit. Why—" Nathan's phoned vibrated with an incoming text. He read it. His hurt expression disappeared, and his features hardened. Professional. She'd seen that look before.

"What is it?"

"I've got to meet someone right away."

81

Nathan turned his Ford Mustang into the parking lot of a Holiday Inn on Eisenhower Avenue in Alexandria, Virginia. He headed to the far end where a dark blue Honda idled in the last spot.

"That him?" Eddie asked from the passenger seat.

"Has to be."

Bruno stuck his head between the front seats, as if he wanted to see the car too. Amelia was safe at Reagan's, but leaving Bruno alone at home seemed risky. Nathan used his personal car because he hadn't been cleared from the last shooting incident. Would he ever get his guns back? He carried a five-shot, .38 Smith & Wesson revolver in an ankle holster, his last personally owned firearm.

Nathan pulled in beside the CR-V and rolled down his window.

The tinted window lowered. Bashir looked at Nathan, then at Eddie. "He okay?"

"That's why I brought him. Bashir, meet Special Agent Eddie O'Shaughnessy. Eddie took out a terrorist outside the airport."

"Nice going, kid," Bashir said. "I've gotta be at Langley in an hour, so I'll get to it. I wanted to meet in person to warn you the CIA pulled strings to kill the Ming Ho surveillance. They—"

"Are you fucking with me?" Nathan asked. "Why would they do that?"

"They're claiming it's now an intelligence operation."

"The CIA has no mandate to run intelligence operations inside the US," Nathan said. "Playing the national security card won't work when the FBI has jurisdiction over domestic counterintelligence ops."

"Bells went off at Langley when you connected Ming Ho and Dr. Zhang Qaing at High-Energy Research. I don't know the details, but you touched on a high-level foreign counterintelligence operation. They can't take over the FBI investigation, but if it endangers a foreign operation with national security implications, they'll squash it. FBI management's playing ball and shutting it down."

"Why are you telling us this?" Eddie asked.

Bashir stared at him long and hard. "This stays between us, right?"

"You have my word," Nathan said.

"I don't like the way the OGA handled this," Bashir said, referring to "Other Government Agency," slang for the CIA. "I'm getting suspicious of their intentions, especially those of my boss."

"Trent Hamilton."

"Yeah."

Nathan nodded. "I appreciate the warning."

"Keep your head down," Bashir said. "When you can't see your enemy, you're likely to get taken off the board."

"I'm not feeling real secure as it is," Nathan said.

Bashir started to roll up his window then stopped. "Oh, and Nathan?"

"What?"

"Love your dog." Bashir motored out of the lot.

They watched him go. Bruno laid his head on Nathan's shoulder.

"What now?" Eddie asked.

"We need evidence, and if the FBI won't help, I'll get it myself."

"You heard him," Eddie said. "Meili's group is standing down. And Rahimya wants you on the ISIS case. We've gotta prepare indictments."

"I need to do this first."

"Do what?"

"Better you stay in the dark. What I'm planning is unsanctioned."

"You can trust me, partner."

Nathan stared into Eddie's blue eyes. Sharing his plan could make

Eddie susceptible to administrative or criminal actions, but Eddie could help if things went south.

Shit. No good options.

"I'll execute a CTR on Ho's residence."

"CTR?"

"Close Target Reconnaissance. I need to get inside that house, but we don't have enough for a search warrant."

Eddie scowled. "Maybe surveillance will give us PC."

"You mean the surveillance the government just suspended?"

"Yeah, okay," Eddie said. "But if you get in legally, you can use whatever you find."

"Chinese operatives have infiltrated our government, and too many people know we've identified the Emperor. If we wait much longer, he'll be in the wind."

"You can't solve this alone," Eddie said.

"I don't have a choice."

"Sure, you do." Eddie grinned. "I'm going with you."

Guilt tightened Nathan's chest, He'd be involving Eddie in an illegal act, but the connection between Ming Ho and High-Energy Research was the missing link they'd been seeking. The answer lay just out of his reach.

"I can't ask you to do that," Nathan said.

"You didn't ask. This is big, and I want to protect our country too."

"I'm committing a felony. If I get caught, my career's over, and I'll go to prison."

"There's no other way? I mean, Bashir said the CIA will look into it."

Nathan sighed. "I wish I could trust them, but these are the same people who claimed the anomalous incidents were psychogenic."

"FBI's still involved, and CIA needs us for jurisdiction."

"It's moved into the hands of politicians. The Chinese, or someone inside their government is behind Havana Syndrome and the attack on Meili. Why they orchestrated a directed-energy attack on domestic soil remains an open question, but Ming Ho is the key. Freezing out the FBI reeks of coverup."

"Why would CIA do that?" Eddie asked.

"That's the million-dollar question. I can't let this opportunity slip through my fingers."

Eddie punched him on the shoulder. "I already said I'm in. You don't need to convince me."

"You'll be risking your career . . . and your freedom."

"I trust your judgment."

Nathan rubbed his neck. Each course of action was fraught with risk. "I could use support on this CTR."

"Let's go. You're not getting any younger."

82

Bruno strained against his leash as he tracked an unfamiliar scent on the sidewalk along Chalfont Place. Nathan sauntered behind him and surveyed Ming Ho's residence. The sky glowed orange, and shadows darkened the neighborhood.

Nathan had concealed a high-resolution video camera in his satchel, and he casually aimed it at the residence. He needed a closer inspection before he tried to defeat the lock. Bruno pressed his nose to the ground as they crossed Ho's driveway, and Nathan tightened the leash to slow him. Behind the red Mercedes, the garage door stood open, and the first-floor lights were on.

Ho was inside.

Nathan ushered Bruno across the street and returned to the Mustang. Bruno jumped into the back seat, and Nathan climbed in beside Eddie.

"Well?" Eddie asked.

"He's home, and the garage is open. I'll enter there. Interior doors have simpler locking mechanisms."

"Why don't we wait until he goes out?"

"No idea when he's leaving, and time's short."

Eddie rubbed his face. "Bodyguards?"

"Surveillance didn't observe anyone else in the house before they stood down."

"Breaking into an occupied house is batshit crazy."

No kidding. "I've got no choice."

"He catches you, you'll get locked up."

"Unless he shoots me first."

Darkness blanketed the block. Nathan played the video he'd taken and zoomed in on the front door. Both the doorknob and deadbolt had keyholes. Primary entry locks were the most difficult to defeat, which made a secondary entry point preferable.

"Wait until he's asleep?" Eddie asked.

"He may set an alarm before bed," Nathan said. "He went up early last night, and if he follows the same pattern, he'll have a drink by the fire then head upstairs. I need to get inside before he sets that alarm."

Under normal circumstances, with a surreptitious search warrant in hand, a tech agent would accompany Nathan and deactivate the security system or cut power to the block. But Nathan was alone. Except for Eddie.

"How will you deactivate the alarm before you leave?" Eddie asked.

"He may not have one. I didn't see signs or stickers on the windows, and Rockville PD didn't have contact info. I'll take my chances and escape before he knows what happened."

"I don't like this."

That makes two of us. "Ready to get dirty? I need your eyes on the back windows. Tell me when he's moving and warn me if he's close."

"Last chance," Eddie said. "You sure it's worth the risk?"

Good question. Breaking into Ho's house was a violation of Nathan's ethics—and the law. But politics held the FBI back, and his country was under attack. The system had been corrupted. He sighed.

"If I wait, Ho could return to China. This is my last chance to get the evidence we need to stop the attacks."

Eddie nodded. He exited the car and headed toward the peninsula. Nathan opened a bag and transferred its contents to his jacket pockets. He waited fifteen minutes, then cracked a window and patted Bruno's head.

"You watch my car, buddy. If anything happens to me, Eddie will take you home."

Nathan slipped out and hid the key on the rear tire, where Eddie knew where to look. He inhaled to steady his nerves and then hurried down the street.

The downstairs lights glowed as he approached, and a shadow passed through the dining room. Ho headed into the living room, a good sign because the garage was on the opposite end.

This was crazy.

Illuminated homes around the cul-de-sac appeared to be occupied, but the chill kept people inside.

Now or never.

Nathan tugged a black balaclava over his face to conceal his identity from Ho's cameras, then he turned up the driveway. He kept his eyes glued to the windows. If Ho came out and spotted him, Nathan would remove the mask and claim he was searching for his missing dog. Then he would retreat to his car and scrap the mission.

Nathan passed the Mercedes, which Ho had left in the driveway the previous two nights. Nathan reached the house and continued into the garage.

A plastic tarp draped over a convertible and sagged in the middle. The garage was immaculate. Tools hung from corkboard and plastic containers had been stacked neatly against the far wall. Cleanliness revealed Ho's mind. This man paid attention to details and did things right.

Nathan slinked along the wall to an interior door above a concrete step. He placed his ear against the wood and listened. Classical music vibrated from inside, too muffled to identify the composer. That confirmed it—Ho was awake and probably by the fire.

The door's brass lock was a standard model that could be defeated with enough practice. Everything Nathan did violated FBI protocol. And the law. But Nathan didn't have time to build a case or the political support to investigate.

This should be interesting.

He inserted his earpiece and keyed the radio concealed inside his jacket. "You in position?" No need for call signs, since he and Eddie were the only ones there.

"Affirmative. Lights on downstairs. He was in the kitchen, adding ice to his drink. At least that's what it looked like through binos."

"Where's he now?"

"Back in the living room."

Nathan could wait for Ho to sleep and gamble he wouldn't set the security system . . . if it existed. Or Nathan could risk surreptitious entry now. The house had to be alarmed.

Magic time.

Nathan slipped on latex gloves. He removed a snap gun from his jacket pocket—an automatic lock-picking device for pin-tumbler-based locking mechanisms, which he'd procured from tech under the ISIS case number. He inserted the rod that protruded from the pistol-like instrument into the keyway.

He pulled the trigger.

The snap gun popped as the rod struck the internal pins and depressed them. He jiggled the handle, but the knob didn't move.

"Shit."

He removed the rod from the mechanism and replaced the gun in his pocket. That would have been too easy. He dug out an aerosol can of lubricant, attached a plastic straw to the nozzle, and sprayed oil inside the lock.

He opened a leather case with lock-picking tools and removed a pick, raking tool, and tension wrench. He inserted the wrench into the keyway and turned it as he applied light tension. He slid the pick over the wrench and tried to picture the interior mechanism as he probed. The pick bumped into a binding pin, and he added pressure with the wrench.

He fumbled with the lock, and sweat rolled down his forehead into his eyes. This looked easy in the movies, but it required years of practice, and Nathan had never mastered the technique. The FBI had sent him to a specialized entry class, where he'd struggled to pick the easiest locks. The class had taught him one thing.

Bring a locksmith on operations.

Nathan's eyes burned, and he wiped away perspiration with his sleeve. He reinserted the pick and flattened the pins until the springs disengaged. The last pin shifted into position, eliminating the need to use his rake. He increased pressure on the wrench, and the mechanism clicked. Nathan turned the knob.

The door cracked open.

Nathan held the knob and slid the tools back into his pocket. He keyed his radio.

"I'm in," he whispered. "Anything?"

"Subject's still in the living room. North side."

Click, click.

Nathan inched open the door. It creaked, and he stopped. He aimed the lubricant at the doorjamb and doused the hinges.

The door opened into a short vestibule, and light from inside illuminated him. Bach's *Brandenburg Concertos* filled the air. He slipped inside and closed the door. He stood in the hallway with his heart pounding.

Beside the door, an electronic keypad glowed. Ho had an alarm, which made Nathan's gamble worth the risk. No matter what happened.

Nathan peeked into the family room, a rectangular space with cozy furniture and a lamp beside the couch. The kitchen came next, with the foyer on the right, separating the dining and living rooms. An interior kitchen door probably led to the basement.

He crossed the family room on his toes, and a Persian rug absorbed the sound.

"Target's moving," Eddie's voice exploded in Nathan's ear.

Nathan froze.

"Headed your way."

83

Nathan glanced back at the garage door in a panic. He'd never make it. Footfalls echoed in the foyer. His heart thumped like a kettle drum.

"Hide," Eddie said.

Nathan moved forward, toward the kitchen. A shadow darkened the tile.

He leapt out of the entryway and flattened against the wall. His fingers tingled with fear. Ho's footsteps crossed the kitchen.

"He's at the sink, getting a glass of water," Eddie said.

Nathan wiggled his toes to burn off anxiety. Glass clinked in the kitchen. Was Ho preparing for bed?

"He's staring into the family room," Eddie's whispered through Nathan's earbud.

A jolt of adrenaline surged through Nathan's body. Had he left the door ajar?

"Headed toward you."

Nathan stood beside a couch, opposite the fireplace. The only other pieces of furniture were two leather chairs and a coffee table. Could he hide beneath the table?

Footfalls closed on him. Too late.

Nathan pressed against the wall and willed himself to be invisible.

Ho entered the room, four feet away. He stared straight ahead and continued into the vestibule leading to the garage.

Move. Nathan sidestepped into the kitchen and tiptoed across the tile. Thank God he'd worn rubber-soled boots. He watched Ho over his shoulder.

Ho stopped at the garage door and typed a code into the security pad. Its light flashed green.

Nathan ducked into the dining room and scurried around a long cherrywood table. Behind him, windows overlooked the driveway.

Footsteps clicked across the kitchen tile—coming his way.

Nathan crouched behind the table and rested his fingers on the ground in a modified sprinter's crouch. If Ho spotted him, he'd bolt for the front door.

Ho crossed the dining room, with only his calves visible from beneath the table. He entered the foyer, and his shoes clacked against the marble.

Ho trudged upstairs. He shut off the foyer light, drowning the downstairs in darkness. Nathan exhaled.

A door upstairs clicked shut. Ho creaked across the floor above. Nathan remained still, a statue in the darkness. He listened to the sounds of the house.

Another door opened, followed by the muffled sound of running water. Nathan's eyes adjusted to the dark, but he didn't move. His gamble to enter the house while Ho was awake had been the right call, and now that he'd made it inside, he had no need to hurry. He shifted on his feet and waited for Ho to go to bed.

"Bathroom light went out," Eddie said. "I can't see anything. There's still an upstairs light on in the southwest corner. Let me know you're okay."

Click, click.

"Phew," Eddie said. "I don't know how you escaped, but nice job."

Click, click.

Nathan rose and stretched his legs but did not move his feet, wanting to avoid a creaking floorboard and alerting Ho to his presence.

Ho's footsteps moved overhead. A television came on, followed by the squeak of bedsprings.

Ho was down for the night.

"Bedroom light's out."

Click, click.

Nathan waited another forty-five minutes, which felt like hours. He dug out a penlight and flicked it on, casting an eerie red glow. Nathan kept the light away from the windows in case anyone walked past. He scanned the room. Nothing there but china, silverware, and serving platters. The living room, dining room, family room, and kitchen were places visitors would access. If Ho kept anything of value, it would be upstairs.

Hopefully, not in his bedroom.

Nathan flexed his knees to circulate blood, then he took a tentative step toward the foyer. No sound. He moved again, more fluid this time.

He raked his light over the staircase then extinguished it. The steps were oak, with a worn, maroon runner rug covering the center. Walking on carpet would minimize sound, but the center of a steps were their weakest point and most likely to groan under his weight. Ho had ascended without sound, but Nathan outweighed him by fifty pounds.

Nathan placed a toe on the polished wood of the first step, an inch from the bedroom wall. He shifted his weight onto his foot. No noise. He exhaled.

He took another silent step then paused and listened. A television droned in Ho's bedroom. Was he watching something, or did he sleep with the sound on? Nathan used his television for company—anything to drown out bad memories that ran on a loop.

He climbed another step, careful not to brush against the wall. He ascended, pausing and listening after each step. The deliberate effort exacted a physical and psychological toll, but the staircase was a fatal funnel, and he needed to be careful.

Nathan stopped on the top step and leaned close to the bedroom door. An anchorman's muffled voice droned through the door.

Nathan moved down the second-floor hallway. He flicked on his penlight and held it in front so the light would not leak under the bedroom door. Two doors on each side of the hallway and one at the end. All closed.

He stopped at the first door and tried the knob. Unlocked. He twisted the brass handle and opened it. Hinges groaned. He stopped. He peeked into a luxurious bathroom. Empty.

He closed the door and crept forward.

Across the hall, he entered a bedroom, a rolling sea of blue and white fabrics and paint. The room was unoccupied, so Nathan shut the door and continued down the hall.

He opened the next door and glanced into another bedroom. He ducked back into the hall, and when he released the knob, the locking mechanism snapped shut with a clank.

Nathan stopped dead.

Something rustled in Ho's bedroom. Had Ho heard the sound? Was he coming to investigate? Nathan stood in the hallway, vulnerable.

Don't think—act.

Nathan slinked into the bedroom. He left the door open an inch and watched the master bedroom. He concentrated on the knob, waiting for movement. The low light and distance made everything fuzzy.

Ho's bedroom door opened.

Nathan yanked his head back and used his hand to guide the door silently shut. He kept the knob twisted, because releasing it would make noise.

He waited.

Thump. Wood squeaked.

Ho cleared his throat, somewhere near the end of the hall.

A drop of sweat ran beneath Nathan's balaclava. If Ho opened the door, Nathan would explode forward and drive him into the wall, then dash downstairs and out the front door.

Wood groaned. Closer.

Nathan held his breath and coiled his body—ready to attack. Another footstep, farther away. The door opened in the final room Nathan had yet to examine. He pressed his ear against the wood. Blood rushed past his eardrum. A door far away clicked shut. Was Ho inside that room or coming back?

Footsteps passed by Nathan's location and continued to the master bedroom. Ho opened and shut his bedroom door, and a few seconds later, the television turned off. Ho groaned, and the bedsprings sang out again.

Nathan rested his forehead against the doorjamb. Had Ho heard the click and gotten up to investigate? Nathan would wait until the Emperor had fallen asleep.

Nathan eased open the door, placed his palm over the latch, and slowly released the handle. The bolt clicked, but his skin absorbed the sound. He stayed in the bedroom with the door ajar, not wanting to risk closing it. He listened to the night and waited.

"Doing okay?" Eddie asked.

Click, click.

"My heart can't take much more of this. I'm five out if you need an extract."

Click, click.

After an eternity, snoring emanated from the master bedroom.

Nathan exited the bedroom and closed the door behind him. The bolt clicked, and he held his breath.

The snoring continued.

Nathan continued to the final room and swung open the door. Ho's office.

Bingo.

He slipped inside and shut the door. A desk faced the windows, bookshelves covered one wall, and file cabinets lined another.

Nathan tiptoed to the desk, which held a twenty-seven-inch MacBook. The computer screen was black. Nathan rubbed his latex glove on his pants leg to remove any oil or grime, then nudged the mouse with his knuckle. The screen came to life, and the cursor blinked in the password box. Luckily, Nathan had planned for that.

He reached into his back pocket and removed an electronic device he'd checked out of the Washington Division's technical division under the ISIS case. After the shootings, agents had conducted sensitive site exploitation of ISIS vehicles and personal property, and they'd executed search warrants at operatives' residences. They'd recovered numerous drop phones, laptops, and other evidence, and Eddie obtained search warrants for them. The device Nathan had checked out would defeat any laptop's password requirement and allow them to enter the data into searchable software for analysis.

At least that's what he'd told Rahimya.

He stuck the drive into the USB port on Ho's computer. Its light flickered, and it hummed as it downloaded the contents of Ho's hard drive. Nathan watched the door while the device copied everything.

It finished blinking, and Nathan slipped the device into his pocket. He moved to the file cabinets and skimmed through their contents. They contained legal documents from Ho's many limited liability companies. Nathan photographed a few documents that looked interesting.

Don't push your luck.

With the data from Ho's computer safe in his pocket, he needed to get out. Nathan opened the office door and peered down the hall into blackness. Ho's snoring continued. Nathan entered the corridor and closed the door. He tiptoed to the stairwell and crept downstairs.

He stopped at the front door. He could disengage the interior bolt, throw the door open, and race across the lawn, but that would activate the alarm, and when Ho spotted the unlocked door, he'd know an intruder had gained access. The goal of a CTR was to get in and out undetected. Of course, CTRs usually involved an entire support team.

Nathan moved through the dining room into the kitchen and checked the back windows. All locked with the security system's telltale electronic contacts attached to the sides.

No way around it—he had to set off the alarm.

It would take Ho time to wake up, assess the situation, and react. He'd probably focus on the stairs, thinking someone had broken in. If Nathan exited through the garage and stayed close to the house, he could flee through the backyard and be shielded from the bedroom windows. Better than no plan.

Nathan keyed his radio. "I have the package. I'm exfiltrating now. Be ready at the extraction point."

"Finally."

Nathan grasped the handle of the door leading to the garage. Maybe Ho would blame the alarm on an attempted burglary, or an animal, or a technical glitch. He'd have no evidence anyone breached the house. That was something.

Nathan flung open the door and klaxons blared.

He slipped into the garage and closed the door then raced around the house. He sprinted across the backyard. Dogs barked, and lights came on inside a neighbor's house. But Nathan was already two homes away.

Up ahead, Eddie waited on Chalfont Place.

Nathan flung open the passenger-side door and hopped in. The car lurched forward before he had time to shut the door.

Eddie drove out of the neighborhood.

Nathan leaned back in the seat, and Bruno licked his cheek. Adrenaline pumped through his veins.

He dug into his pocket and showed Eddie the device.

"How we gonna decrypt that?" Eddie asked.

"We're not," Nathan said.

"You giving it to tech under the ISIS case?"

"Everything's probably in Cantonese or Mandarin. It'd stick out like a sore thumb."

"Then what?"

"It's time to trust someone and ask for help."

84

Bashir strolled along the western edge of the Tidal Basin and stopped at the Franklin Delano Roosevelt Memorial. Two bicyclists in Spandex rode past, followed by a woman pushing a baby carriage that probably cost more than his first car. His eyes moved to a teenager on a skateboard when he noticed Nathan standing still against a hunk of granite. Watching him.

Bashir's cheeks warmed at being unaware of his surroundings and caught off guard by an FBI agent. Nathan's tradecraft was better than expected.

Bashir nodded and joined him.

"Guess we're even for me surprising you in Kyiv." Better to admit his shortcoming than try to hide it. Only insecure people did that.

"What did you find?" Nathan asked, apparently not in the mood for verbal sparring.

"You carrying your phone?" Bashir said.

"Yep."

"Give it to me."

Nathan scowled but handed it over.

Bashir removed a tiny metal box from his briefcase and placed both Nathan's and his cell phones inside. "I can't understand how we convinced our population to bug themselves."

"I thought the government wasn't listening."

"That's naïve. Phone manufacturers and the telecom industry glean data and analyze content. The government looks behind the curtain."

"That's illegal."

Bashir snorted. "If analysts peek at data, who's there to complain?"

Nearby, a young couple held hands as they read inscriptions carved into the stone.

"Who are you afraid is listening? The Chinese?"

Bashir pointed to the stone beside them. "Ever read these inscriptions? FDR was president for twelve years, but these are the quotes they chose. It's telling, don't you think?"

Bashir walked along the memorial and read portions of the quotes.

. . . social justice . . . throwing out of balance of the resources of nature throws out of balance also the lives of men . . . The test of our progress is not whether we add more to the abundance of those who have much; it is whether we provide enough for those who have too little . . . It is time to extend planning to a wider field . . . it must be a peace which rests on the cooperative effort of the whole world.

"And your point?" Nathan asked.

"He spouted collectivism, central planning, and global governance."

"He pulled the country out of the depression."

Bashir smirked. "Many economists believe government intervention in the market extended the depression by years."

"Did you ask to meet to give me an economics lesson?" Nathan asked.

"Remembering our history is important. The Soviets infiltrated all levels of our government with the goal of destroying it, and FDR's administration was riddled with Soviet agents. The deputy secretary of the Treasury Department was a card-carrying Russian spy, and many believe Harry Hopkins, FDR's advisor who lived in the White House, was a Soviet agent. Decoded KGB messages in the Venona Papers prove the almost unthinkable level of penetration into our government and cultural institutions."

"You're confirming Russians are behind Havana Syndrome?"

"No, but the Chinese adopted Soviet tactics. I brought you here to remind you of the past before I shared what I found on the hard drive."

Nathan's face hardened. "This can't be good."

"It's as bad as it gets. Ming Ho was in direct communication with an American official."

"I can't take it anymore. What'd you find?"

"Ho was careful. He used dozens of email accounts to communicate with eleven people secretly. Most draft folders had been deleted, but not this week's messages. Ho gave instructions to a high-ranking official."

Nathan stretched his back. The poor guy looked stressed. And rightly so. He stepped closer to Bashir and lowered his voice. "What kind of instructions?"

"When to expect calls and where to receive a dead drop. They spoke cryptically, but Ho claimed they were taking on water, and the official needed to take drastic action and plug the leaks. The dates correspond with the attack on Meili."

"Who's the official?"

"Ho used an alias, 'Emperor,' and the US official called himself 'Mohr.'"

"I don't get it."

"Karl Marx's nickname was 'Mohr.' Your Chinese agent is dealing with a proud Marxist, an ideological infiltrator."

"Who?" Nathan asked.

"It's not that easy," Bashir said, "but I checked the data on Ho's WhatsApp and other communication applications and identified ninety-eight internet telephone numbers he used. He's running at least fifteen illicit businesses. I ran his telephone numbers through high-side databases, and NSA returned hits on dozens of intelligence cases."

"Through the CDR program?"

Bashir nodded. "You never heard me say that."

After 9/11, the NSA collected metadata to include telephone records of American citizens in the Call Detail Records program. Congress reined in the scope of the collection in 2015, ordering American citizens' identities to be masked and their content deleted if they weren't involved in criminal activity. Whistleblowers claimed the NSA hadn't complied with the law.

"Did you identify Mohr?"

Bashir surveyed the grounds. They were alone. "I followed the data through two hops and found something disturbing."

Nathan grimaced as if he had an ulcer. No sense keeping him dangling any longer. "Ho routinely called a 202 number, which NSA tentatively identified as an American citizen. I called in a huge favor and had it unmasked."

"And?"

"It belongs to Bojing Sòng."

"Why's that name familiar?"

"He's a Chinese American with dual citizenship, and he runs the Chinese American Business Alliance. He's active in the Confucius Institute and a big donor to both Republicans and Democrats. Ho and Sòng communicating isn't unusual, but within minutes of their conversations, Sòng called someone else. The data includes two degrees of separation from our target number, so I uncovered Sóng's contacts, including (202) 456-1414."

Bashir waited for Nathan to react.

"Sorry," Nathan said. "Is that number supposed to mean something to me?"

"It's the White House switchboard."

An icy breeze chilled Nathan's core. "Who did he call inside the White House?"

"That's what we need to determine."

"How?" Nathan asked.

"Ho set up a meeting for tomorrow morning with someone named Wûshi. We need to witness it. Whatever they're doing, they're getting desperate. This thing is about to blow up."

85

Nathan stood beside Meili's hospital bed. She looked pale and gray, but she was lucid, and she'd insisted he update her. After what she'd gone through, he owed her the truth about everything . . . except his late-night burglary of Ming Ho's residence.

"Then it's confirmed," Meili said. "The Chinese are behind this."

"Chinese involvement worries me more than the Russians," Nathan said.

"Why?"

"We've been playing cat-and-mouse with the Russians for a hundred years, but the Chinese have infiltrated us too. They've poked the bear before, but this time it's different."

"Meaning?"

"The risk-reward equation bothers me. China had to know we'd retaliate if we pinned this on them. My guess is with the evidence we uncovered, we'll impose economic and diplomatic sanctions—at a minimum. We may ramp up our naval presence in the South China Sea. This is an overt act, and we can't rule out military action."

Meili closed her eyes and rubbed her temples. "I agree, but the same is true for Russia."

"The Russians have a track record of killing dissidents overseas, but a direct attack on our diplomatic staff would be a huge escalation. Knowing the ramifications, why did China take the chance, and how does injuring our employees benefit them?"

"Intimidating people could dissuade Americans from entering foreign service."

Nathan sat on the edge of her bed and lowered his voice. "I'm worried these incidents were tests in preparation for a massive Chinese attack against all our foreign spies and diplomats."

"Why?"

"That's what's making me nervous. This could be a prelude to a full-scale military offensive. China could be preparing to take Taiwan. Or Japan. What's their game?"

Meili winced and held her head, obviously in pain. She answered without opening her eyes. "Maybe it's something we're not seeing. Something smaller in scale."

She looked so vulnerable. He placed his hand over hers, and she smiled.

"There's a meeting this afternoon between Ho and someone named Wûshi," he said. "They're meeting in a couple hours. Eddie's at the location now, setting up to take pictures. I want your team to cover it."

Meili sat up and grimaced. She leaned back on the pillow.

"You okay?" he asked.

"Wûshi is not a person's name."

"It's not—"

"Wûshi means 'warrior' in Mandarin. Ho's meeting an agent from Chinese black ops. He's meeting an assassin."

Nathan's phone rang. Eddie.

"We missed something," Eddie said.

Nathan's stomach cooled. "What do you mean?"

"The meeting was pushed up. Ming Ho just walked past the parking garage near the Confucius Institute."

"Maybe he came early to scope out the location."

"I don't think so. He turned down Eighteenth Street, and he's standing in front of a parking garage under a residential building."

"I'm at the hospital with Meili now. I'll have her call Tom to get an arrest team over there. If Ho's meeting—"

"Arrest team?" Eddie asked. "I thought we were watching to identify his Chinese intelligence contact."

"Meili said *Wûshi* means *warrior*. Ho's meeting a black operator. The guy probably has blood on his hands, and we need to stop him before he kills again."

"I'll keep an eye on him and . . . hold on." Traffic sounds came over the line. "A Hyundai pulled into the garage, and the driver made eye contact with Ho. I think it's Wûshi."

"Standby," Nathan said. He covered the microphone. "Meili, get Tom on the phone and send whoever's available to the garage at Massachusetts and Eighteenth. Ho's meeting the assassin."

"Ho's heading inside," Eddie said.

"Eddie—"

"Yeah, he's walking down the ramp. This is it."

"Shit. I'll get the team over there."

"No time," Eddie said. "I'm going in."

"No, don't. Meili has Tom on the other line." Nathan looked at Meili. She nodded and raised four fingers. "He's got four agents headed to you."

"This thing will be over in five minutes."

"Maintain visual on the exit. You did a great job seeing the unspoken signal between them. Take Wûshi away when he leaves."

"But we want to observe the meeting and confirm he's working with Ho."

"And we will, if the team arrives in time."

"I can go down—"

"Absolutely not," Nathan said. "Ho's a professional, and he'll look for surveillance. You can't walk into a garage without drawing attention."

"I'll grab my car. It's right around the corner and—"

"Do not go in. Ho will spot you, and the other guy's a killer. It's too dangerous. Wait for the team outside and take down the make, model, and license plate number of Wûshi's vehicle. Follow him if you can, and I'll vector the team to you."

"Wûshi's driving a white Hyundai. We're gonna miss this. It's time I pull my own weight and—"

"Eddie, don't be stupid. You'll burn it."

"I'm following my instincts."

"It's not safe."

"Sorry, boss, I can't hear you. I think I'm losing the signal."

The line disconnected.

86

Nathan dialed Eddie again, but the call went to voicemail. Nathan's shoulders tightened, and a sour taste filled his mouth. He shouldn't have let Eddie go alone.

"Dammit," he said. "I'm going up there."

"Call 911 and ask MPD to back him up," Meili said.

"They'll scare our targets, and if we burn it, Wûshi and Ho could disappear. Maybe Eddie will smarten up and back out."

She leaned forward, looking miserable. "You told him to wait, and my team will cover him."

"Eddie's excited, and your guys are four miles away."

"You were emphatic, and he listens to you when—"

"He's just a kid," Nathan said. "He wants to impress me. I better get there before something bad happens."

Nathan hustled out of the room and jogged to his Mustang, which he'd parked with his blue light and police plaque displayed on the dashboard. He wasn't supposed to use those in his personal car, but he'd committed far worse violations in the past twenty-four hours. He jumped in, plugged in the light, and slapped the magnetic base onto his roof.

He raced around Washington Circle and headed north. Traffic sucked, as always. He weaved in and out of lanes, hitting the gas then slamming on brakes. The odor of burning rubber filled the compartment as his brake pads overheated.

He kept one hand on the wheel and punched Eddie's number into his phone. It rang once, twice, three times—*come on, Eddie, pick up*—then went to voicemail.

Nathan hit the number again. He shouldn't disrupt Eddie's surveillance, but instinct told him the kid wanted to be a hero. That was Nathan's fault for telling him to break rules. Nathan often put himself in danger—hell, he had done it last night—but he had a decade more experience than Eddie and could better assess risk.

This time, the call went directly to voicemail. Had Eddie hung up on him, or was the wireless signal unable to penetrate layers of concrete in the garage?

Nathan stopped at a red light three blocks away from the garage. He pulled down his blue light to avoid alerting their targets, but without it, he couldn't get around the traffic congestion.

"Fuck it."

He pulled to the curb in a no-parking zone and threw his placard on the dashboard. He locked the car and headed north on foot. He kept a brisk pace but didn't run, to avoid drawing attention.

He slowed as he neared the garage. Traffic was bumper to bumper. Nathan stopped two buildings from the garage and scanned the pedestrians. Eddie was nowhere to be seen—unless he'd suddenly become more adept at surveillance.

"Dammit."

Nathan dialed Tom's number to check on the team. "I'm at the location. No sign of Eddie."

"Traffic's a bear," Tom said. "We're still east of the White House. I'm guessing another fifteen minutes, maybe more."

"I'm worried," Nathan said. "I'm going in."

"I advise you to wait for us."

"I gave the same advice to Eddie, and he didn't listen, which is why I have to hurry."

"Eddie on foot or in a car?"

Nathan scanned the parked vehicles and didn't see Eddie's Subaru. "Not sure. The new target's an Asian male driving a white Hyundai."

"Copy. Be careful."

"Out." Nathan hung up and headed into the garage.

If Tom's crew arrived in time, they could follow Wûshi away from the garage and either get an MPD cruiser to make a pretext stop or they could lose the subterfuge and detain Wûshi themselves. They didn't have enough to charge him, and taking blatant action would blow their investigation, but all evidence indicated Wûshi was a killer. Sometimes, overt action was necessary to expose conspiracies and disrupt plans without prosecuting suspects.

Stopping these attacks was the priority.

The entrance ramp sloped down at a steep angle as he passed the automated gate. Nathan's footsteps echoed on the battleship-gray floor spotted with engine oil. He slowed to avoid slipping on the smooth surface. The garage offered a single point of entry, making it a poor clandestine meeting location, but the tiny space made countersurveillance easier, as did its proximity to the Confucius Institute. But still, it was an odd choice.

The ramp curved left past an office, where a dumpy, balding man lounged behind levered blinds reading a girlie magazine. Nathan hurried past without him taking notice. The garage smelled of exhaust and mildew, a toxic combination.

Tink, tink.

A metallic sound echoed from somewhere below. A door shutting?

Nathan rounded the corner onto the second subterranean level, passing a half dozen parked cars. He slowed his pace and scanned the rows with his peripheral vision.

No sign of Wûshi or the Emperor. If he spotted them, he'd show no recognition and continue to the next level.

Tink, tink . . . tink.

More clicking sounds. The sound distorted off the enclosed cement walls and triggered a memory—not a door shutting or an alarm engaging, but something familiar. He couldn't put his finger on it . . .

Suppressed gunshots.

Nathan swept aside his jacket and grabbed his belt where his holster should be attached, but he'd surrendered his duty gun. He tugged his backup .38 caliber revolver from his ankle holster.

A woman screamed.

A door slammed. Tires squealed. Nathan braced himself in a stable, three-point stance and aimed at the ramp below him.

A green Honda careened up the ramp and headed right at him. Nathan slipped his trigger finger onto the trigger and applied gentle pressure. He lowered his front sight on the windshield and centered it on the driver's head. Something was wrong.

Blonde hair.

Nathan lifted his finger off the trigger and leapt against the wall. The Toyota hurtled past, as a wide-eyed blonde woman clung to the steering wheel with white knuckles. She continued up the ramp and disappeared.

He pointed his gun forward and continued down to the lowest subterranean tier. He leaned around a wall and scanned the lot. The overhead lights were out, but the outline of eight parked cars was visible in the glow of an exit sign at the far end.

The smell of gunpowder hung in the air.

Nathan held his penlight in his support hand and pressed the knuckles of his gun hand against his wrist. He activated the light with his thumb. The beam cut across the space, glinting off windows. The air looked fuzzy near the end. Gunsmoke?

A white Hyundai was parked at the end. Nathan eased around the corner and stopped.

Eddie's anxiety toy lay broken on the floor.

Nathan's stomach turned to ice. He stepped over it, swinging the muzzle of his gun from side to side. He paused at the first car, a Toyota, and crouched behind the engine block. He peeked over it.

Where was Eddie?

Wûshi and the Emperor could be hiding and waiting for Nathan to move into the clear for an easy kill.

He stayed in a crouch and crept behind a Chevrolet. He surveyed the cars on the opposite side then aimed forward as he moved to the next car. He repeated the process again, moving closer to the Hyundai. The garage was silent as a tomb. Dread spread through him.

He popped up behind a Mercedes and had a clear view of the Hyundai. Someone sat in the passenger's seat, bathed in shadows.

He aimed at the man and slipped around the front of the Mercedes. He approached the Hyundai. The features of the person in the passenger seat came into focus.

The Emperor.

Where was Wûshi? Nathan's eyes flickered left and right, ready to shoot and move.

He passed an SUV and stopped. A body lay on the ground to his left.

"Eddie!"

Nathan aimed at the Hyundai as he sidestepped across the pavement to where Eddie lay prone, not moving. Nathan's foot splashed in something. A pool of blood leaked out from under Eddie.

Nathan squatted beside him. Eddie wasn't wearing his vest. Nathan felt for a pulse. Nothing. He was still warm. Nathan would perform CPR—after he'd handcuffed Ho and located Wûshi.

He strode toward the Hyundai, closing fast. He stopped fifteen feet away.

Ho sat in the passenger seat with his mouth open and a bullet hole in his forehead. Blood dripped over his lifeless eyes, painting his face like a death mask.

Nathan spun around, sweeping the garage with his barrel. Nothing. He moved to the Hyundai and visually cleared it. The lock had been punched on the driver's side of the Hyundai. A stolen car.

His eyes drifted to the exit door. Wûshi had killed the Emperor and escaped upstairs to the street.

He was gone.

Nathan raced back to Eddie. He rolled his partner onto his back. Eddie had been shot three times in the chest and neck.

He was dead.

87

Bashir turned his agency-issued Honda off the George Washington Parkway and parked in an overlook across from Georgetown. Twenty parking spaces faced a low stone wall, and at the bottom of a steep hill, the Potomac's green water flowed past. Behind him, a grassy median separated the parking lot from cars whizzing past on the parkway. His was the sole vehicle. He'd stopped on the way to Langley, because something didn't make sense about these attacks, and he needed to think before he told anyone at the CIA.

The information Nathan had stolen from Ming Ho's computer suggested the Emperor was involved with Havana Syndrome. Ho didn't admit it explicitly, but his emails about "operations" corresponded with the recent attacks. It wasn't enough to charge him in court, but it passed the accepted threshold in intelligence work. More troubling was Ho's contact with a governmental official, someone important enough to require clandestine communication. And the call to the White House switchboard was disconcerting.

Early evidence had pointed to Russia as the culprit, but even though that theory made sense, the CIA still claimed psychogenic causes were behind Havana Syndrome. Would Nathan's evidence implicating Chinese operatives get the CIA to retract their analysis? And why had the CIA taken such a strange stance when much of the scientific community disagreed?

The answers hovered outside his grasp.

Bashir dialed his encrypted cell and went through the Langley operator to reach Trent Hamilton's secretary.

"It's Bashir Gemayel," he said. "Mr. Hamilton in?"

"He told me not to disturb him," the secretary said, "and he's in a foul mood."

"This is urgent, and his disposition won't improve if he hears what I've discovered from the deputy director."

She sighed. "Standby, I'll put you through."

A moment later, Hamilton picked up. "What's the emergency?"

"I said it was urgent," Bashir said, "not an emergency."

"Don't fuck with me. Not today. What you got?"

"Nathan uncovered something, and it points in a new direction."

"Does it relate to the surveillance you told me about?"

"Yes, and it confirms his theory. His target orchestrated the recent attacks. His emails are damning, and more disturbing are the calls he's making. Someone in government has been covering his tracks."

The line hissed with silence.

"You there?" Bashir asked.

"Thinking. Where are you now?"

"An overlook on the GW. I can be there in twenty minutes if you—"

"You think someone in our shop is involved?"

"Could be someone in-house or elsewhere in the IC."

"You have the proof?"

"I have the emails and call logs in a folder on my laptop. Nathan's got a copy too. I had them translated."

"If we're talking about a mole," Hamilton said, "let's not have the conversation here. Stay where you are. I'll be there in forty minutes.

88

Nathan stood at the foot of Meili's hospital bed. Aches and pains from his exertions over the past few days radiated through his body. He and the entire FBI Washington Division had assisted the MPD in the search for Eddie's killer, but the dragnet had failed to locate Wûshi. He'd been grilled by Rahimya and then the OPR. They had questions about the investigation he'd conducted while on administrative leave, and another interview was scheduled for tomorrow.

He watched Meili as an array of equipment beeped and dinged. Why had he come? Maybe her anguish when he broke the news about Eddie had fed his need to see her.

Or maybe he needed comforting.

"I'm so sorry about Eddie," Meili said.

"It was my fault. I encouraged him to think outside the box and do what was right, even if it violated policy. But Eddie was too inexperienced to trust his instincts. He—"

"You told him not to go in. I heard you."

"He shouldn't have even been there. Now OPR's investigating, and Rahimya told me I won't be coming back to work anytime soon."

"You were trying to do the moral thing. It's just . . ."

"What?"

"I warned you about going off on your own."

Nathan's anger fired inside him like a hot kiln. "CIA pressured FBI to pull surveillance off Ming Ho."

"Bashir told me," she said. "CIA needed to deconflict our surveillance with a long-term intelligence collection operation. I got the feeling Ming Ho was either an asset or close to one embedded in Chinese intelligence."

"That's bullshit. Ho dealt with a highly placed US government official. We have a traitor working with the Chinese. Someone at CIA pulled strings to protect the mole."

Meili shifted uncomfortably. "That's quite an accusation."

"I have the emails between Ho and someone he called 'Mohr.' From the content and timing, it seems the Chinese worked with an American traitor to launch directed-energy attacks."

Meili pointed to the side table with her half-eaten breakfast. "Bring me my phone."

He snatched it off a plastic tray and handed it to her. "What are you thinking?"

"I'm not saying I believe your theory, but if someone at CIA is covering for a mole, we can't trust anyone there."

"And?"

"Bashir Gemayel came to us right before this massive escalation in attacks."

Nathan's stomach hollowed. "Bashir has been assisting me. Off the books."

"Has he?"

"You think he's working for the other side?"

Meili dialed. "It's your theory, but after the attacks against Eddie and me, I'm not dismissing any possibilities."

"What—"

"Hey, Dave, it's Meili," she said into the phone. "I'm recovering, thanks. Listen, I need a big favor ... uh-huh, yeah, I know."

Nathan wanted her to put the call on speaker, but she was asking for a personal favor, so he didn't push.

"What do you know about Bashir Gemayel?" Meili asked. "He's our OGA liaison, and he's been with my group for a couple of weeks."

Nathan paced while Meili passed Bashir's information to her contact. Could Bashir really be involved? If the Chinese employed him, why would he help Nathan analyze Ho's hard drive? Unless Bashir had created the emails and phone contacts.

"Yeah, I'm still here," Meili said. "Uh-huh . . . uh-huh . . . Wait, say that again." She sat up in bed and pain flashed across her face.

"What?" Nathan asked.

"You're kidding me."

Nathan moved closer.

"You're damn right I'll report this. How could this happen? Yes, I will. Thanks, Dave."

Meili hung up and gawked.

"Tell me," Nathan said.

"Bashir Gemayel was never officially assigned to my team. According to headquarters, no CIA liaison was attached to the Havana group."

"But then how did—"

"Word came down from someone at headquarters to our SAC, then Bashir showed up. I never saw the documentation."

Nathan cocked his head. "You mean Bashir just attached himself to your group without authorization?"

"Someone greased the wheels. I'll call my ASAC and get to the bottom of it."

"You do that," Nathan said, "but I'm tired of being one step behind these assholes. I'll confront Bashir myself."

"I want to be there when you do."

"You're not ready to be discharged."

"The doctor told me I could go home tomorrow or the next day."

"That's not today, is it? I know you want to question him, but I can't wait."

Meili swung her legs off the bed. "Get my clothes out of that drawer and help me sneak out of here."

89

Bashir set his laptop on the center console of his vehicle. He opened it and plugged in a portable hard drive that contained translations of the data from Ming Ho's computer. He wanted to review everything before he briefed Hamilton.

His phone rang, and he answered.

"Where are you?" Nathan asked.

"Arlington, reading the translations."

"We need to meet you."

"*We?*"

"Meili and me. It's important."

What was Meili doing out of the hospital? "I hadn't heard they released her."

Nathan snorted. "It was more her decision than her doctor's."

"Not surprising."

Hamilton would arrive at any moment, and Bashir would summarize what he'd found before their analysts dug into the files. The hard drive showed a connection between Chinese intelligence and organized crime and would be a goldmine of intelligence. It'd take weeks to decipher everything.

"I'm briefing my boss shortly," Bashir said. "Shouldn't take long. How about meeting in an hour?"

"Where?"

"The GW Parkway overlook in Arlington. Look for my CR-V."

"We'll be there."

Bashir hung up and returned to reading off his computer.

A young female driver with raven hair parked two spaces away from him. She didn't look in his direction as she fiddled with her phone then placed it in the holder on her dashboard. She could be taking in the view, or more likely, stopping to return phone calls. A scenic overlook outside DC rarely saw much activity, especially during work hours on a weekday. If she didn't leave soon, he'd ask Hamilton to change locations, though that wasn't really necessary. Despite Hamilton wielding significant power inside the CIA, his face was unknown to the public. Even if the woman saw them together, she wouldn't take notice.

Bashir created a new folder and filled it with Ho's emails that likely involved Havana Syndrome, because they correlated with dates of attacks. He downloaded the suspicious calls to the White House operator and moved them into a new folder. These two folders contained the most damning evidence, but the Emperor's private drive would not just contain leads on Chinese intelligence operations, but also on dozens of transnational crimes. When his chief analyst received the data, he'd smile like it was Christmas morning.

Something outside the car flickered in Bashir's peripheral vision, and he looked up. The twentysomething woman had her door open. She climbed out of the driver's seat and stood in the doorway. She wore pink sneakers, black running tights that hugged her body like a second skin, and a pink spandex top—revealing and sexy, but hardly a defense against the chill.

He studied her, enjoying her beauty. She faced away and held the roof for balance as she reached back and grabbed her foot. She stretched her quad then switched legs, giving Bashir a guilt-free opportunity to ogle.

"I've got to start dating."

Being a CIA case officer meant abandoning a normal life. Traveling around the world made it difficult to meet people, and on those rare occasions when he did, the CIA's constant demands made it impossible to sustain relationships. Not to mention the impact stress, brutal hours, and the vital importance of his work had on relationships. His love was his adopted country and protecting her would always be his first priority.

Bashir created a third folder and imported the intelligence he'd collected on the Emperor. This man would be the key to unraveling the Havana Syndrome conspiracy and exposing the mole's traitorous infection inside the American government.

He checked his watch. Hamilton should've been there by now. He adjusted the rearview mirror and looked back at the parkway. What the hell was taking him so long? His boss knew the importance of the information Bashir had to share.

He stole another glimpse at the girl. His body jolted with adrenaline. She stood beside his passenger door, staring at him.

Bashir smiled to cover his shock and started to roll down the window. Her right hand came into view. She held a semi-automatic pistol with a suppressor screwed onto the barrel.

He reacted without thinking. He slammed his car into reverse, knocking his laptop onto the seat as his foot moved to the accelerator.

But too late.

The first bullet struck him in the jaw, tearing bone and muscle from his face. The pain came in an instant.

His car rolled back, and he stomped on the gas pedal. The engine roared, and he exploded backward toward the Parkway.

He choked on blood and broken teeth as he twisted to locate her. She took a three-point stance and fired with both hands.

Bashir tried to dive below the dashboard as glass fragments filled the air. Two bullets struck him high in the chest. A third shattered his larynx. His body went numb, devoid of feeling beneath his neck.

He collapsed onto the passenger seat and shook with convulsions as he drowned in his own blood. He stared at the floor, unable to move. The car bounced and careened over grassy earth then crashed against a tree.

He couldn't breathe, but at least the pain had vanished. He felt nothing at all. His vision blurred, replaced by a gray void.

And then there was nothing.

90

Nathan tapped his brakes as traffic backed up on the GW Parkway. DC's congestion was horrific, probably because people constantly smashed their vehicles into each other. Maybe the mixture of driving cultures was to blame, but whatever the reason, everyone seemed in a constant hurry, and daily accidents proved it.

He glanced at Meili in the passenger seat. She had dark circles under her eyes and beads of sweat on her forehead, but escaping the hospital seemed to have buoyed her spirit. She must have sensed him looking, because she locked him with her deep brown eyes.

He refocused on the road as the traffic slowed to a crawl.

"The scenic overlook's up ahead," he said. "Hopefully, we'll reach it before the accident or whatever's causing the backup."

"How will Bashir react when we confront him?"

"Not well. The question is how did he get assigned to your team—and what was he doing there?"

"If this is an official CIA op, things will get ugly fast. Targeting the FBI is forbidden. They'd need serious approvals to run an op against us."

The Camry in front of them stopped, and so did Nathan. Traffic moved again, but he gave a three-car-lengths buffer before following. Being rear-ended would trigger an onslaught of bureaucratic accident forms.

"It's possible he's acting on his own and there's a criminal element in play," Nathan said, "but the Havana Syndrome connection is too coincidental. My biggest concern is he's working for someone else or—"

"China?"

"We'll find out soon."

The driver in front of them craned his neck to view something up ahead. The overlook was close.

A feeling of dread seeped into Nathan's bones. "This can't be good."

"What?"

The line of cars continued forward, and the overlook appeared on his right. A car had crashed into the only tree on the median. A foot to the left or right, and it would have entered the road. Nathan exited the parkway and slowed. The car was a Honda CR-V.

Bashir's car.

The Honda's backup lights glowed, and its engine smoked. The accident had just happened. Nathan screeched to a stop and slammed his car into park to block the entrance to the overlook. He drew his .38 revolver and cracked his door.

"Hey," Meili said. "You're not supposed to carry a gun."

"That's Bashir's vehicle. Call it in."

Nathan climbed out and aimed at the Honda as he approached. The parking lot was vacant. He scanned the wall and the woods beyond. Nothing.

The Honda's engine growled as it revved in gear, and its windshield was spider-webbed. He closed on it.

Bullet holes peppered the glass.

He approached the passenger side. He lifted on his toes and peeked over the dashboard. The vehicle looked empty. He surveyed the woods. No shooter in sight.

He squinted through the passenger window.

Bashir lay crumpled in a pool of blood.

Nathan yanked open the door and shoved the car into park. He pressed his fingers against Bashir's carotid artery.

Bashir had a weak pulse.

"Call an ambulance," Nathan yelled over his shoulder. "Bashir's been shot!"

He rolled Bashir onto his back to evaluate him. Half of Bashir's throat had been torn away by a bullet and frothy blood bubbled out. Nathan holstered his gun. He took off his jacket and pressed it against Bashir's neck to stem the bleeding and create a seal so Bashir could breathe.

Blood gurgled through Bashir's bloody shirt. More bullet wounds. Bashir's face grayed.

"Bashir? Hey buddy, it's Nathan. Can you hear me?"

Bashir blinked.

"Hang in there. Help's coming." Bashir's wounds were catastrophic, and he wasn't breathing properly, but patients needed hope.

Bashir's eyes rolled back, and he shook his head as if trying to stay conscious. His features softened, and his muscles lost their rigidity. His entire body slackened.

"Stay with me, pal," Nathan said.

Bashir's mouth opened and closed, as if trying to speak.

"Save your strength," Nathan said.

"Hmm-un," Bashir mumbled.

"What's that?"

"Hmm-il-un."

Nathan lowered his ear close to Bashir's mouth.

"Hamilton."

91

Bashir died.

EMTs had worked on him on the way to the hospital, but by then, the life had long left his body.

Red and blue emergency lights from State Police cars lit the parking lot like a seventies disco. The sun dipped below the trees as Nathan and Meili finished answering questions from homicide detectives. Nathan led Meili back to his car.

"I still think I should have told them about Bashir monitoring my group," Meili said. "If that's what he was doing."

"We may never know, but if you tell your chain of command, this thing will blow up, and we'll never solve it."

They'd be grilled again by FBI and CIA investigators. And once they exposed Bashir's unofficial attachment to the FBI's Havana Syndrome group, the OPR and the Office of the Inspector General would get involved.

"I'm not comfortable with this," she said.

Nathan slung his arm over her shoulder. "I appreciate your waiting a couple of days to tell anyone. I need time to figure this out before any internal investigation."

"If only we'd reached him sooner."

"Guess Bashir was innocent," Nathan said.

"Not necessarily," Meili said. "Even if the Chinese killed him, it doesn't mean Bashir wasn't involved. Maybe he became a liability."

"My gut tells me Bashir was a straight shooter. He connected me with Popov and provided evidence linking Ming Ho to both the attacks and a government mole."

"Hmm. Whether or not he was complicit, it's clear someone felt threatened by him. Probably Chinese intelligence."

"Or whoever's orchestrating this at CIA."

Meili looked confused. "Why would CIA help China launch attacks against our own people?"

"They got him attached to your group. The operation could be sanctioned by their director. CIA's been playing politics since their inception. FBI too. We let politicians use us to target their opponents, and we turn a blind eye when crimes involve politicians who support us. They use us to get elected, and we use them to consolidate our power. Corruption supports corruption."

"I guess..."

Nathan sighed. "Or a Chinese agent inside CIA could be running an unauthorized operation."

"It'll be impossible for us to unravel the inner workings at CIA. It'll require congressional hearings."

"That'll take years," Nathan said, "but I have a shortcut."

Meili cocked her head. "Why does that scare me?"

"Bashir introduced me to his boss at the agency. If anyone knows how Bashir got assigned to your group, it's Trent Hamilton. Bashir said his name with his last breath."

"You don't know Bashir meant Hamilton was involved," Meili said. "He didn't say enough to make it an admissible deathbed utterance. Maybe he wanted you to tell his boss what happened... or warn him."

"Bashir knew he was dying." Nathan choked back his emotion and covered it by clearing his throat. "He named his killer. If Hamilton didn't do it himself, he had it done."

"You can't know that."

"I'll confirm it when I confront him," Nathan said.

"What'll you say?"

"I'll make him tell me what's going on. I need to identify the mole, and then I need to find Mohr."

"And do what? From how you described those emails, we don't have enough to prosecute him. And since you acquired that evidence without a search warrant, it's inadmissible."

"Three of my colleagues have been murdered. I'm not going to prosecute him."

"Then what—"

"I'm going to kill him."

92

Reagan startled awake in bed, her earbuds still connected to her laptop and a sitcom streaming. The clock read 2:28 a.m. She reached for Vince, but he was in Santo Domingo again. She listened to some new show she had never seen. The plot and dialog were inane. Either modern shows had been dumbed down or she had become more discriminating. It didn't matter. She just needed the sound to distract her from her memories of the incident that ran on a loop in her mind.

The disorientation and terror of stumbling across her cubicle floor rushed back to her. Reagan's stomach turned, and she sat up.

Amelia stood in the doorway watching her.

Reagan flinched and yanked out her earbuds. "You scared me."

"Sorry, Mommy."

"What are you doing up?"

"Someone's here."

"Honey, you're having another nightmare. Go back to bed."

"Someone's in the house." Amelia pointed out the open door into the dark hallway. "Downstairs."

Reagan's hair rose on her neck. Was Amelia having difficulty discerning nightmare from reality, or was an intruder in the house?

"Baby, did you have a dream?"

"No, Mommy." Her eyes widened, and her lower lip quivered. She ran across the room and jumped onto the bed, clinging to Reagan.

"Don't be afraid. Everything will be fine."

Hopefully.

Reagan slipped off the bed and breathed deeply to counter her dizziness and nausea. When would her symptoms end? She stepped into her slippers and moved toward the door. Amelia hung off her waist like a panda cub.

"Baby, you have to let go."

Amelia shook her head.

"It's okay." She gently pried Amelia off her then walked to the door and poked her head into the hallway. The staircase was cloaked in darkness. The doors to the bathroom and guest bedroom were closed, as she'd left them, but Amelia's bedroom door stood ajar.

The house had quieted like a cemetery at midnight. She leaned closer to the staircase and strained to hear anything beyond the pounding of her own heart.

Something creaked on the floor below.

Reagan's body chilled as if the cold March wind blew through her. She held the wall for support.

Was her mind playing tricks? Houses settled as wood contracted in the cold. How foolish to let childhood fears become phobias. She was the adult now, and she needed to be strong. For Amelia.

Another groan of wood. The sounds came from Vince's office downstairs. Had he left the window unlocked? She canted her ear toward the stairwell, her feet riveted to the floor, frozen by fear.

Thump, thump, thump.

Footsteps moved into the foyer. She opened her mouth to scream, but fear snatched her voice away. She covered her mouth.

Thump, creak.

Someone stepped onto the stairs. Reagan scurried back into the bedroom. She shut the door and twisted the lock, a useless deterrent since one swift kick would shatter the hollow door.

She raced across the room on her toes with her arms out for balance. Amelia had her fingers in her mouth, and tears spilled out of her eyes.

Reagan snatched her around the waist and carried her to Vince's side of the bed. Vince owned a revolver for target shooting. Had he taken it to Santo Domingo or left it?

Footsteps padded up the staircase.

She opened the nightstand drawer and dug her hands into a pile of papers, office supplies, and other junk. She swirled her hands through the jumble, searching for the cold steel of Vince's revolver. It wasn't there.

Thump, thump.

Whoever was sneaking up the staircase was close.

Reagan spun around. The walk-in closet brimmed with clothes, shoes, and the clutter of life. No time to search for the gun in there, but they could hide.

She trudged across the floor, hugging Amelia close to her body. Dizziness washed over, and she blinked to orient herself. The moment passed. She stopped with her hand on the closet door handle.

What was she thinking? Squirreling away in the closet might fool a burglar, but what if someone had come for her? Or Amelia? Fear stabbed her heart.

Thump.

The prowler reached the second floor. Reagan dashed into the master bathroom and gently locked the door behind them. She moved to the window and attempted to open it with one arm.

Stuck.

She laid Amelia down on the floor then fought with the window. It probably hadn't been opened in years, and the wood frame had swelled from the bathroom's humid atmosphere. She strained with all her strength, and it ground open.

A door creaked open down the hall. Someone was searching for them.

Reagan stuck her head out the window. Vince's two-car attached garage lay to her left, and the shingled roof stretched out below her.

Amelia whimpered.

Reagan knelt beside her and grabbed her daughter's face in her hands. "Baby, there's no time for this. I need you to be strong. We're climbing onto the roof. I'll call the police and—" She'd left her phone on the nightstand.

"Stupid, stupid, stupid." If she lived through this, she could beat herself up later, but now, she needed to save her daughter.

She grabbed Amelia under the arms and lifted her onto the sill. *God, she's getting heavy.* Reagan lowered her headfirst through the window.

"Mommy—"

"I've got you. When your hands hit the roof, I'll feed your legs through, then lie flat and don't move."

Amelia wheezed.

"Are you having an asthma attack?"

"My chest is tight."

"Your inhaler's in your room. Hang in there, baby."

Reagan dropped Amelia onto the roof, grabbing her nightgown for purchase and holding on as her daughter's weight shifted onto the rough shingles.

Behind her, the master bedroom doorknob rattled.

93

After answering questions from investigators from what seemed like every federal agency from the CIA to the National Park Police, Nathan had driven Meili to FBI headquarters. He had parked on D Street and waited in his car while she briefed her ASAC and SAC, both of whom had returned to the office to get a handle on what had happened. It was well after midnight when he returned to the Hoover Building to collect her.

She climbed into the passenger seat, with drooping shoulders, dark circles under his eyes, and her face blanched like a corpse.

"I should take you back to the hospital," he said.

"Drive me home."

He waited for her to change her mind, but she stared forward, obviously in no mood to debate. He threw the car in gear and headed to her apartment in Arlington.

"Want to tell me what happened?"

"My bosses weren't thrilled about your presence, but I told them Bashir asked both of us to come."

"Did you explain the situation?"

She closed her eyes and sighed. "I rehashed the evidence we have pointing to China and explained the roles we believe Ming Ho and Wûshi had in the attack."

"Are you in trouble?"

Meili shook her head without opening her eyes. "We have a dead FBI agent, and that changes the equation."

The reference to Eddie hit Nathan like a kick to the chest. He stared at the road as they crossed into Virginia. Things had been moving so fast he hadn't had time to mourn. He couldn't afford the distraction. He'd deal with his emotions later.

He glanced over, and she looked at him with misty eyes.

"I'm sorry," she said. "That sounded insensitive."

He nodded. "I know what you meant."

"This must be hard for you."

He shifted in his seat. Talking about feelings was not in his wheelhouse, especially when focusing on them could unleash a torrent of emotion. "Did you tell your bosses about Bashir's role?"

She didn't answer and stared a hole in him, but he returned his eyes to the road and maneuvered through Arlington.

"I guess we're done talking about Eddie?" she asked.

"I'm concerned about your boss—"

"I didn't tell them I discovered Bashir's unofficial attachment to my team. It was hard to dodge the real reason we planned to meet Bashir, but I said we wanted to discuss Ming Ho."

She leaned back and closed her eyes.

He drove through the Courthouse and Clarendon neighborhoods and stopped outside her building. Restaurants and retail stores surrounded the luxury apartment building, which was only seven Metro stops from FBI headquarters.

He activated his flashers and escorted her inside, past a doorman and up the elevator to the fourth floor. The high-end residential building looked new and retained the odor of fresh paint but lacked the charm of historic structures that populated the District. He stopped outside her apartment and held her while she searched in her purse for her keys.

"I'm worried about you," he said.

"I'm not myself. I still have migraine headaches, and I feel like a guest in my own body. The doctors said it'll get better with time."

She opened the door, and he held her. "Let me check first."

"But—"

Nathan stepped into the vestibule and drew his gun. He flicked on lights as he made his way through the kitchen and living room, then to the bedroom. He stood in the doorway, debating whether to enter the intimate space then crossed the room and cleared the closet. The apartment was clean, contemporary, and feminine.

And free of hit men.

He walked out and met Meili in the kitchen.

"You thought someone was waiting to hurt me?"

He looked into her eyes. "You were attacked once before. Dr. Mandel, Eddie, and Bashir are dead, and someone turned Dr. Reyes's brain to mush. That could have been you. I won't let that happen."

Her eyes glistened. She leaned in and kissed him on the lips. He froze with surprise then melted into her soft lips. He held their passionate kiss until she pulled away.

She grinned. "I've wanted to do that since the academy."

"I, uh, yeah. Me too." He sounded like a babbling idiot.

"I'd ask you to stay, but I can't keep my eyes open. You understand, right?"

Nathan nodded. "Call me if you're feeling sick, or if you hear anything, or—"

She placed a finger on his lips. "I'll be fine. I promise."

He left and waited in the hallway until he heard her set the bolt, then he headed to his car.

Meili had seemed amused at his fear someone could have been waiting for her, but the threat was real. Everyone attached to this investigation—everyone who fought the psychogenic theory—was in danger.

Reagan.

It was after two o'clock in the morning, but he dialed her number as he raced across the sidewalk to his car.

No answer.

He called again, and it rang seven times before going to voicemail. Why the hell wasn't she answering? Was this another power play? He'd asked Reagan to watch Amelia, which probably wasn't fair considering Reagan's own health issues, but Betty seemed to be out of town, so what choice did he have?

Unless someone had made his babysitter disappear.

No, that was crazy. He was seeing conspiracy theories everywhere, but sometimes, conspiracies were real, and if he hadn't yet identified any of them, he was probably missing something.

Was Reagan a target?

He jumped in his car and drove down Washington Boulevard. At this hour, the streets were empty, and he sped through red lights. His vehicle hurtled down the street as terror took hold inside him.

Was he paranoid? Spinning out of control?

Trust your instincts.

He jumped onto I-66, and a few minutes later, his tires squealed on the ramp as he exited into Falls Church. Nathan roared down North Washington Street.

He headed for Vince's house.

94

Reagan flung her upper body through the bathroom window, and the windowsill dug into her stomach. She foundered with her feet in the air, wobbling above Amelia, who lay flat on the sharply sloped roof. Amelia gawked with wide eyes.

The bedroom door crashed open behind Reagan. Footsteps moved across the floor. She'd be discovered any moment.

Reagan reached for Amelia, but her fingers grazed sandpaper-rough shingles. The girl was too far away.

Something clunked in the bedroom. She had seconds left.

Reagan flexed her abs, tightening her core, and swung her legs. The momentum carried her forward. She dragged her body over the sill and onto the roof. Her stomach stung where the metal frame tore her skin. She landed on her elbows and dragged her legs through the window.

Something banged against the bathroom door.

Reagan tucked her knees beneath her, careful to keep her weight away from the roof's edge. She crawled toward Amelia. Her daughter sniffled, and tears ran down her cheeks. Reagan hugged her close and leaned back against the roof.

Vertigo threatened to take control.

Wood shattered from inside the bathroom. The intruder had kicked down the locked door and had to know she'd been inside.

She should have shut the window.

She lumbered to her feet, keeping one hand in contact with the roof, and lifted Amelia. She leaned away from the house and looked down. The driveway lay fifteen feet below, so the fall wouldn't kill them, but breaking a leg would only delay the inevitable.

Shower curtain rings clanked against the rod as somebody ripped the fabric back. He was coming for her.

Reagan shifted onto her toes and climbed higher, putting the dormer between her and the bathroom window. She continued up the roof then straddled the dormer.

The window creaked.

Reagan peeked over the edge at the crest of the man's head, three feet below. He strained out the bathroom window and scanned the street.

She held her breath.

"Mommy?" Amelia wheezed.

The man twisted in the window and stared directly at her.

95

Nathan spun the wheel hard right, and his tires screeched as the weight of the car shifted onto North Maple Avenue. His headlights illuminated Vince's house.

He tapped the brake to cut his speed. His desperate need to protect his family was probably paranoia, and he didn't want to scare them for no reason.

The house grew closer. The lights were off. Nathan exhaled. He was acting crazy and—

"What the hell?"

A man climbed out of the second-story window—the Asian assassin who had tried to kill him. The man stepped onto the shingles and balanced outside the open window. He turned, and he stared at Nathan's car.

Above the killer, Reagan balanced on the dormer, clutching Amelia.

Nathan jammed the gas pedal to the floor and cut the wheel. His tires bounced over the curb, and he hurtled across the lawn. He slammed on his brakes, and the car slid sideways, tearing up the dirt and grass.

He slammed the car into park and drew his weapon as he leapt from the vehicle. The man dove back through the window and disappeared from view. Nathan raked his barrel over the second-floor windows, searching for a target.

The man didn't reappear.

Nathan approached the house in a modified crouch.

Glass shattered from somewhere behind the residence. The man was fleeing.

Nathan sprinted across the lawn. *Dammit.* He was always one step behind these assholes. He slowed as he approached the backyard, because ignoring tactics would hasten his own death. He stopped and leaned around the siding, only exposing his head and gun barrel.

The backyard was empty.

He looked back at the house. The rear door was ajar.

Nathan scanned the fence and the neighbors' homes. He couldn't abandon Reagan and Amelia to search the neighborhood. He crept to the door, alternately covering the windows and the fence. The intruder could pop up at any time. The broken door could also be a ruse, and the killer waited inside to ambush him.

Searching alone sucked.

Nathan sidled against the house and quick-peeked through the open door. Darkness shrouded the interior. He spun into the kitchen, muzzle first, and pivoted right along the wall toward the living room. He swept the darkness with his handgun. Nobody there.

Something drummed down the stairs.

Nathan aimed at the foyer, ready. Reagan bounded onto the tile with Amelia in her arms, and he depressed the muzzle.

"Reagan!"

Her face softened with relief. He breezed across the room and grabbed her. "Let's go. The house isn't safe."

He dragged them out the front door and onto the walkway as he scanned the neighborhood. No sign of the intruder.

"Get behind my car."

Nathan shielded them with his body and covered the front windows. Just in case. The girls cowered behind his car's engine block while Reagan helped Amelia use an inhaler. Nathan squatted beside them and scanned the neighborhood as he dialed the police.

"911, what's your emergency?"

"I just interrupted a burglary in progress." He gave the operator their address and a description of the suspect. He hung up.

"How'd you know we were in trouble?" Reagan asked.

"Instinct." How could he explain the need to protect them? Defending his family was a sixth sense.

"That man . . . he wanted to hurt us, Nathan."

"It's okay. I got here in time." He pulled Reagan and Amelia into a bearhug. A siren wailed in the distance.

"This won't happen again," he said.

"How can you say that?"

"The Chinese killed Dr. Mandel, Eddie, and Bashir, and they destroyed Dr. Reyes's brain. They probably attacked Meili too."

"Meili?"

"The FBI agent whose been helping me. The Chinese used a cutout, but he's dead too. Unfortunately, I just allowed their assassin to escape."

"The man in my house?"

"Same guy who tried to murder me."

Reagan gasped. "What will you do?"

"Bashir's boss at CIA may be involved, but I don't have enough for an arrest warrant. Even if I did, CIA has blocked lawsuits and spewed disinformation about Havana Syndrome. They won't have trouble distancing themselves from these murders."

"Then we're out of options."

"Someone's covering up Chinese involvement in attacks against our personnel. Our enemies have attacked hundreds of patriots and led us to the brink of war, but coming after you and Amelia is too much. I'll handle this myself."

"You're going rogue."

"I'm protecting my country and my family."

"How will you hold them responsible without evidence?"

"I'll confront Bashir's boss, but first, there's something I have to steal."

"Steal? Nathan, I don't think this—"

Two police cars with flashing emergency lights turned onto the block.

"The police, Mommy."

"Go to them," Nathan said. "I'll be back."

Reagan took Amelia's hand and led her down the driveway. "The good guys are here, baby. We're going to be okay." Reagan waved at the officers.

Nathan waited to make sure they were safe, then he slipped around the house and disappeared into the night.

96

Nathan sat in Dr. Mandel's idling car, which he'd taken from the deceased man's residence after breaking into the house and finding the keys. Nathan held his cell phone to his ear and waited for the CIA operator to connect him. He glanced into the back seat at the item he'd stolen. How many felonies would he commit before this was over?

And would his plan work?

Bruno raised his head from the passenger seat, as if reading Nathan's thoughts.

"It's okay, boy. Sorry to drag you with me, but after this, home won't be safe for a while."

The phone clicked then rang twice.

"This is Trent Hamilton."

"You're a difficult man to reach," Nathan said.

"It's the middle of the night. This is a difficult time after the loss of our colleague."

Liar. Nathan gritted his teeth. "The Bureau lost people too, which is why I'm calling. Bashir was murdered because he had evidence linking the Chinese to Havana Syndrome—"

"There's not a shred of evidence implicating the Chinese."

"I've seen it."

"You told me Russians were responsible. Isn't that why you took an illegal excursion to Ukraine?"

Nathan ignored him. "Chinese intelligence used Ming Ho as an intermediary with the Triads. The Chinese produced a portable directed-energy weapon, and they've used it inside the United States."

"I see you've bought into Russia's disinformation."

"Why would Sergei Popov point the finger at China if Havana Syndrome is a psychogenic phenomenon?"

The line hissed, and Hamilton stayed silent. He couldn't argue contradictory positions. "A foreign power wouldn't assassinate Americans on our soil."

"It's happened before," Nathan said. "We've disrupted the Iranians from kidnapping American citizens here and from trying to assassinate members of a former administration. But it's worse than that."

"I'm waiting."

"Ming Ho's hard drive proves we have a mole."

"Where?"

"Inside the intelligence community."

"That narrows it down to about 850,000 thousand people." Hamilton sounded skeptical, but his voice rose an octave. Stress caused that.

Time to set the trap. "That's for the Bureau to investigate," Nathan said. "But it won't be as hard as you think."

"Oh?"

"I have evidence from Ho's computer."

"You have a copy of the data from his portable hard drive?" Hamilton asked.

How did he know about the drive? And why call it a copy unless he knew Bashir had the original? "I didn't realize you'd heard about it."

"Bashir briefed me, but from what the police told me, whoever killed him took his laptop. I need that intelligence to unravel all this. You have the only copy."

"Meet me."

"I'll send someone to bring you in."

"I'm not coming to the agency. I don't know who to trust." *You traitorous snake.*

"I'd say you're being dramatic, but not after what happened to Bashir. How do you want to handle this?"

"I know you. Come alone. I'll give you the drive if you promise to protect it. But if I see anyone else, I'll disappear."

"Where and when?"

Nathan smiled. "Glen Echo Park in one hour."

"I'm on my way."

97

Glen Echo Park nestled between MacArthur Boulevard and Clara Barton Parkway in Glen Echo, Maryland, three miles northwest of Washington, DC. On the other side of the parkway and the C&O Canal, Cabin John Island protruded into the Potomac River. Last fall, Nathan and Amelia had spent a lazy Saturday at the park, a perfect location for a meeting with Hamilton because of its proximity to Langley.

And its isolation.

Nathan finished unloading then parked in the empty lot opposite a sign hanging over the entrance. The main building combined architecture from three centuries, from its stone tower to its art déco building.

Nathan sent a text.

I'm here.

Five seconds later, the reply came in.

All set.

Bruno whined in the back seat. Nathan stopped. Bruno would be an easy target if left alone.

"What do I do with you, boy?"

He got out and opened the back door. Bruno leapt onto the pavement. He looked at Nathan and wagged his tail.

"Explore," Nathan said, "but stay close."

Bruno raced through the entrance onto the park grounds. The sun wouldn't rise until seven o'clock, which meant astronomical twilight would begin around five thirty. That gave him three and a half hours of darkness. And privacy.

Nathan followed Bruno under the roof and into the tiny park. Founded in 1891, the park offered theater, dance, and artist residencies, while retaining its late-nineteenth-century amusement-park charm. The Dentzel Carousel dominated the space opposite the entrance and had been the park's centerpiece since 1921. A dozen other buildings stood empty, and dark neon lights gave the park an eerie stillness.

Windows circling the antique merry-go-round were dark too. The front door stood open where Nathan had broken into it with a crowbar. Bruno ran past with his nose to the ground, exploring an invisible world of scents. He disappeared behind a building. Nathan backed into the shadow of the carousel and watched the entrance.

What am I doing?

He took out his badge and stared at it. More than a gold-plated hunk of metal, it stood for something. Something real, beyond philosophy, identity, or power. It represented an oath, like the one he'd taken to defend the constitution. That badge was a promise he made to stand between criminals and citizens, between good and evil. It was a sacred shield that announced he would risk his life for what he believed in. And he'd done so. Everyday.

I have no choice.

Twenty minutes later, after the night chill had settled deep inside his bones, headlights flashed across the parking lot. A metallic-blue BMW parked beside his car. A door slammed. Hamilton passed under the sign wearing a black turtleneck sweater with a charcoal field jacket and dark khakis. He looked like a burglar. He walked with a faltering gait, almost hesitant, as if unsure what Nathan intended. He should be worried.

Hamilton stopped beside the popcorn stand.

Nathan stepped out of the carousel's umbra. "Were you followed?"

Hamilton startled. "How would I know?"

"There's a mole in your house."

Hamilton sneered. "So you said."

A bitter wind blew through the park, carrying the sickly-sweet smell of cotton candy, a ghost of childhood memories.

"I spoke to Bashir before he died," Nathan said.

Alarm flashed in Hamilton's eyes—like heat lightning—all the confirmation Nathan needed.

Nathan drew his gun.

"What are you doing?" Hamilton asked in a measured tone, seemingly both concerned and curious.

"You're the traitor. You had Bashir killed."

Hamilton flashed a cruel smile, as frigid as the night air. "I'm many things, Agent Burke, but a traitor isn't one of them."

"You covered up the Chinese attacks. Why?"

"What's your plan here?"

Nathan's chest tightened. "Answer my question."

"You misread the board. You've got it wrong. Everything I've done has been to protect my country, not betray it."

Nathan raised his gun and pointed it at Hamilton's face. "I want the truth."

Hamilton stared down the barrel. "You're treading into deep water here. You don't understand what you're doing."

"Explain it to me."

"Get that fucking thing out of my face."

Nathan lunged and struck Hamilton on the bridge of his nose.

"Ugh," Hamilton groaned. He stumbled back, holding his face. Blood leaked between his fingers.

Nathan charged and clasped Hamilton around the neck. He pivoted, slipped behind him, and pulled Hamilton off balance. Hamilton wiggled his feet like a marionette.

Nathan squeezed Hamilton's neck in the crook of his arm, slowing the blood flow through the man's carotid arteries into his brain.

Hamilton thrashed and kicked. Nathan bore down.

Hamilton went limp.

Nathan lowered him to the ground and released his hold. Hamilton's eyelids flickered. He'd regain consciousness in seconds. Nathan tucked his revolver into his waistband and handcuffed Hamilton behind his back.

Bruno raced across the park, his toenails clicking on the pavement, He bumped into Nathan, almost knocking him to the ground. Bruno bared his teeth and growled at Hamilton, ready to bite.

"Take it easy, boy. I've got this."

"Ohhh," Hamilton groaned. He shook his head, then his eyes widened in apparent fear and confusion.

Nathan reached under his arms and hoisted him to his feet. Hamilton staggered, unsteady. Nathan grabbed his elbow and wrist and applied a police-escort hold.

"Inside the carousel. Let's go."

"You'll go to prison for this."

"I'm willing to die for my country. And for my values." Nathan torqued his wrist

Hamilton grimaced and rose on his toes. "Okay, okay."

Nathan led him into the carousel. Brass poles impaled fifty painted animals around a Wurlitzer organ. The statues stared back as if ready to come to life. Nathan dragged Hamilton onto the platform and shoved him down at the feet of a painted lion. He yanked a bungee cord from his pocket and affixed the handcuffs to the lion's paw. Hamilton wasn't going anywhere.

"You're an FBI agent, for chrissakes. You can't do this."

"This isn't law enforcement," Nathan said, "You committed an act of war. Civilian police procedure doesn't apply."

"But you can't—"

"I won't let Chinese operatives escape because I'm following DOJ use-of-force policies designed to deal with bank robbers.

"Chinese? What are you babbling about?"

Nathan snorted and moved to a tarp covering an object the size of a dishwasher. "You're gonna tell me everything."

"Or what?"

"Or I'll scramble your brain, and you can spend your remaining years on earth drooling like an idiot in a psych ward."

Nathan tore the tarp off the directed-energy weapon he'd stolen from Jakob Mandel's residence.

Hamilton's eyes widened.

"It's what you think it is," Nathan said.

"Where'd you get that fucking thing?"

"You can thank Dr. Mandel for keeping a souvenir. Oh, right. You can't because you killed him."

Hamilton's eyes darted around the space, desperate. He seemed to finally understand his peril. "It had to be done. You don't understand."

"Help me."

Hamilton licked the blood off his lips. "We did what was necessary to protect our country from infiltrators and internal enemies."

"At first, I thought Russians were behind this, but evidence points to the Chinese."

"Russian or Chinese," Hamilton spat blood onto the floor, "it's a false dichotomy. They represent the same ideology—collectivist societies run by elites. Russia transformed from communism to oligarchy, but the application of power remains the same. And China never changed. Both are totalitarian regimes, and I've been fighting them my entire career."

Rage fired through Nathan's body. "Fighting them? You've been covering for them by positing anomalous health incidents. Blaming victims. I have evidence to prove it."

"You're wrong."

"Then who's responsible?" Nathan asked.

Hamilton shifted uncomfortably on the floor. He looked disgusted. He shook his head.

"I asked you a question," Nathan said. "Not going to talk?" He flicked a switch, and the high-energy weapon hummed to life.

Hamilton spit blood again. "Okay, okay. Turn that fucking thing off."

Nathan didn't move. "Tell me who did it."

Hamilton sighed. "We did."

Hamilton's confession hit Nathan like a sledgehammer. The carousel room chilled as he stared at the CIA official chained to the merry-go-round. What did Hamilton mean? Nathan's mind whirled. He tried to regain his composure.

"By *we* you mean the US government?"

"Not officially, but a handful of us. Patriots. Some anomalous events may have been mass hysteria, but—"

"Chinese intelligence orchestrated the attacks."

"Maybe. But the incidents on US soil and several overseas were our doing. We've been plugging leaks—"

"CIA's behind Havana Syndrome?"

"We're not sanctioned. I directed a tiny cabal of black operators to target the people making us weak, political people who prohibited us from doing what's necessary."

What was he saying? A rogue group in the CIA used Chinese high-energy attacks as cover to target their domestic political enemies? They killed Americans for politics?

"What about American citizens like Dr. Camilla Reyes?" Nathan asked. "She was apolitical. She only sought the truth."

"Reyes would have exposed us, eventually."

"You mean she would have proven the incidents were attacks or revealed your complicity?"

"Both."

"And my wife?"

"A mistake. We were aiming at the ambassador a floor above her."

Nathan clenched his fists. "How many attacks were yours?"

Hamilton looked at the floor. He seemed tired but not defeated. "My team executed three attacks overseas and two domestically."

"How? We abandoned that technology decades ago."

"You think we'd sit back and watch the Russians and Chinese develop directed-energy weapons? If they outpaced us, we'd be vulnerable. I won't allow a few weak-kneed pacifists prevent us from defending our country."

"You're a traitor."

"Bullshit. I acted on orders, directives from the highest level."

"I have proof the Chinese planned these directed-energy attacks. Were you were working for them?"

"I told you the truth. Let me go."

Nathan paced. It didn't make sense. Ming Ho had connected Chinese intelligence with the Triads and facilitating recent attacks. The Chinese must be responsible for assaults on American embassy personnel too. But Hamilton claimed his team had executed some of them. It didn't mesh, unless...

"Who gave the order?"

Hamilton shook his head. "You'll get us both killed."

Nathan patted the directed-energy weapon. "Tell me or spend the rest of your life being spoon-fed applesauce."

"You're a dead man already. I guess it doesn't matter what I tell you." Hamilton sighed. "Frederick Richardson directed everything. He's been using my office to activate special assets within the CIA. He identified State employees who pushed back against this administration's policies. They had to be stopped."

"And the DEA and FBI agents in Estonia?"

"They would have cleared the Russians. They came too close to our black project."

A sickness turned Nathan's stomach. "But that family... the children."

"Collateral damage. I didn't endorse that. I'm a patriot."

"You're a murderer," Nathan said. "And you—"

Nathan paused and straightened. Suddenly, everything made sense. This stupid, stupid man. He had attacked Americans and killed innocents—all for the wrong reason.

He strode across the room and stood inches from Hamilton. "You still don't get it, do you?"

"Get what?"

"You're a pawn. Richardson manipulated you. You thought you were fighting for our country, but you took out targets *for the Chinese*."

"That's absurd. I'd never betray my country."

"It was a false flag operation."

"What? How?" Hamilton stared at the ceiling, then his eyes flared with understanding. "Oh my God."

"The mole in the White House, it's Richardson. He tricked you. He works for the Chinese."

Hamilton looked uncertain. Scared.

Nathan dug through Hamilton's jacket pocket and grabbed his cell phone. "What's the code?"

"Fuck you. You're out of control."

"You don't know what out of control looks like," Nathan said. "Give me your code."

"Forty-two, forty-three, forty-four."

"If that code sends an emergency distress alert, the only thing your friends will find here is their former deputy director babbling incoherently in a pool of his own urine."

Hamilton frowned. "Type in eleven, nineteen eighty-nine. The month the Berlin Wall came down."

Nathan plugged in the number and unlocked the phone. He scrolled through the addresses until he found the one he wanted.

He held the phone close to Hamilton's face so he could read the name. "Have him meet you here. Make sure he comes alone."

"You're making a mistake."

"It won't be the first time."

Nathan pressed send. The phone rang three times, then Frederick Richardson picked up. "Why are you calling on this line?"

"We've got trouble," Hamilton said.

"You've always got trouble. What have you fucked up this time?"

"It's Agent Burke. He knows we're involved. He—"

"I knew you couldn't be trusted with this," Richardson said. "You were supposed to take care of that problem days ago."

"We tried."

"What's he got on us?"

"Evidence from Ming Ho. He's blackmailing us. I have a copy."

Richardson laughed. "Blackmail. See, I told you there aren't any more heroes. Pay him off and be done with it."

"It's more complicated than that. He claims the Chinese are behind the attacks I planned. You told me we were eliminating internal threats, not working with our enemies."

"Right now," Richardson said, "the only common enemy we have is Nathan Burke. Pay him off."

"I need to show you what he has, and I need to do it now."

"If you think I'm dragging myself out of bed at three o'clock in the morning, I'll—"

"Meet me at the National Zoo in an hour, same place as last time. If you don't show, I'm giving everything to the FBI. I don't appreciate being used."

The line was silent, but the call remained connected.

"You're playing a dangerous game," Richardson said.

"So are you. Meet me in an hour, or we'll finish this conversation in federal prison."

Nathan hung up the phone. "The National Zoo?"

"I've met Richardson at the Big Cats Exhibit three times when we needed privacy. When we had other... emergencies."

"You mean when he needed you to betray your country."

"I didn't know he was working for the Chinese. I've told you everything I know, and I did what you asked. Now what? You plan on killing me?"

"I'd love to watch the life ebb out of your body."

Hamilton set his jaw. "Then make it fast."

"Nothing would make me happier, but I'm not you. I believe in the sanctity of life. And the rule of law. Well... mostly."

Hamilton opened his eyes. "Then what?"

Nathan stepped back and peered between the animals on the merry-go-round. "Did you get all that?"

Meili emerged from the shadows carrying a digital video camera. "Every last bit."

"You can't use any of that," Hamilton said. "You coerced my confession."

"I didn't coerce anything," Meili said. "I received a call from Nathan and found you tied here with this video camera recording. We may not be able to use what you said in court, but we have the story now, and there's plenty of evidence tying you to these crimes—from Bashir's dying declaration to your phone records linking you to Richardson."

"If you prefer, I can always flip the switch on Dr. Mandel's weapon," Nathan said.

Hamilton shook his head.

Nathan turned to leave.

"Where are you going?" Meili asked.

"To finish this."

99

Nathan held Bruno's leash as two maintenance workers passed by carrying coffees and speaking in groggy, early-morning tones. The men continued through the staff entrance at the Smithsonian's National Zoo and Conservation Biology Institute in Northwest Washington. The zoo wouldn't open for hours, but already a dozen employees had arrived to bring the place to life.

Nathan waited for the men's voices to fade then led Bruno through the gate. He acted as if they belonged. The gate had no guards at the early hour, though Hamilton had told him the buildings inside would be secured. Hamilton claimed he had the zoo's chief of security in his pocket, Nathan's ace in the hole if things went wrong.

The CIA had its tentacles everywhere.

Nathan followed signs to the enclosure holding lions and tigers, but he could have followed the growls as animals entered their habitats. Nathan strolled down Olmstead Walk along byzantine pathways bordered by lush vegetation. The odor of straw and manure wafted on a light breeze.

Bruno sniffed the air and pranced with excitement. He should have stayed in Dr. Mandel's car, but it may have been reported as stolen and leaving Bruni alone was dangerous. After he handled Richardson, Nathan would take an Uber back to his car at Reagan's, but who knew how this meeting would end? Better to have Bruno with him if he had to make a hasty exit or lie low for a while.

The sky glowed twilight gray as the path opened up in front of the Great Cats Exhibit. Fifteen feet below, a dark moat separated the pathway from a four-tiered rise known as Lion-Tiger Hill. Dirt, bushes, and leafless trees covered the habitat, and two gorgeous Sumatran tigers watched him from the middle level, motionless, like statues of the Sphinx.

Had Hamilton and Richardson chosen this spot to plan their deception because they considered themselves predators?

Bruno stared at the cats with his tail up and muscles rigid.

"Easy, boy."

Wooden posts supported a single crossbar along the perimeter to remind tourists not to topple into the moat. As if tigers weren't warning enough. Nathan looped Bruno's leash around the crossbar but didn't tie it. He scratched the dog behind his ears, and Bruno leaned against his leg.

Footsteps echoed off the path, and a diminutive, middle-aged man came into view. He wore a tweed coat and a Trilby hat to ward off the cool morning. Nathan had never met Richardson, but his beach-ball body and beady eyes matched his online photographs.

Richardson spotted Nathan and stopped. He scanned the area then continued down the walkway to Nathan in front of the exhibit.

Bruno's body tensed.

"It's okay," Nathan said in his most reassuring tone. "I think."

Richardson scowled. "You're Special Agent Nathan Burke."

"Richardson."

"I was expecting someone else."

"Hamilton couldn't make it."

Richardson looked down his nose. "If you expect to get money from me, you're sadly mistaken."

"I don't want your filthy money."

Richardson's features hardened. "I won't play a guessing game. What do you want?"

"To meet you, Mr. Richardson, or should I call you Mohr?"

Richardson's mouth dropped open, confirming Nathan's theory. "I don't know who that is."

"Mohr. The name you used when Ming Ho passed communications from the Chinese government to you."

Richardson's eyes turned to slate. "I've no idea what you're talking about, and I won't play games. Get to the point. They've let the animals into their enclosures, which means they'll be open soon."

"You ordered attacks on our people. You saw the opportunity to wipe out the administration's political enemies and blame Russia."

"You're clever, Special Agent Burke. Too clever by half."

"You attacked the embassy in Santo Domingo and disabled our agents in Tallinn."

Richardson glanced around then reached into his coat. Nathan swiped back his jacket and rested his hand on his revolver.

"Easy, Agent Burke. I'm having a cigarette." Richardson removed a pack of Camels and showed it to Nathan.

Nathan let his jacket fall back into place.

"I should walk away and have you taken care of, but I don't think you're stupid enough not to have made copies of the evidence. I also don't think you'll go away until you get what you want, so I'll play ball."

"You ordered the murder of an innocent Estonian family."

"I told them that was counterproductive. Drawing blood from Americans would require a reaction. It was too much, too fast."

"Who's *them?*" Nathan asked.

"We live in a new world," Richardson said. "A global economy. The Cold War's over, as is the era of two superpowers vying for dominance. International corporations dictate policy now. Half our government's initiatives are decided in back rooms in Davos. And social media giants are owned by the same billionaires who set policy and offer the products the public clamors to possess. People buy their services and gadgets while their media overlords cancel and censor opponents and reinforce political cronies. The idea of a democratic republic is antiquated. We all work for some master, but I'm smart enough to choose my own."

"You can justify treason any way you want," Nathan said, "but there are fundamental differences between America and communist regimes like China."

"Maybe, but the application of power isn't different. If ideologically driven nation states end up ruling the world, I'm picking the most ascendant. We're soft and on the decline. You can't disagree with that."

"The Chinese population's stuck under the boot of totalitarianism. They're mired in poverty. Central planning under the communist regime you're helping has resulted in millions of deaths and a population barely living above subsistence. Those who object to authoritarianism are thrown into work camps. Is that the dystopian world you want to bring here?"

Richardson flipped his wrist in the air. "God, you're dramatic. Your old-world patriotism has no place in the modern world. At least when I leave the administration, I'll have a hundred million in offshore accounts."

Nathan laughed. "Despite your desire for a new world order, your treachery comes from the oldest motivation. You want to make a buck."

"I made a fortune."

"You betrayed your country."

"This is tiresome," Richardson said. "I'm leaving."

"No, you're not." Nathan reached inside his jacket.

Richardson stepped back, but his face showed no fear. He flashed a thumbs-up over his head.

The hair rose on Nathan's neck. He glanced over his shoulder as a man stepped out of the shadows with an MP-5 submachine gun tucked into his shoulder. He looked through an EOTech holographic sight and aimed at Nathan's chest.

Stupid to let someone get behind him. Obviously, Richardson had brought protection.

The man stepped into the open—Wûshi.

"You told me you came alone."

Richardson shrugged. "Obviously, my suspicion of Hamilton was justified."

"Or did you bring Wûshi to kill him, like you murdered Bashir?"

Wûshi stood thirty feet away. An easy shot for a trained assassin. He had Nathan dead to rights, making it suicidal to attempt to fight or flee. But after Richardson's admission, how could they let Nathan live? These men had killed for far less.

Nathan moved imperceptibly until his hand touched the edge of his jacket. He would have to be quick. Impossibly fast. He had no choice.

"Put your hands in air," Wûshi said in a heavy Mandarin accent.

Nathan coiled like a spring. "Okay. Don't shoot." Would his deflated tone make Wûshi relax? Nathan only needed a second.

Fuck it.

Nathan brushed his jacket back and drew his revolver from his waistband as he dove to the pavement. He swung his barrel toward Wûshi and squeezed the trigger.

Flames shot out of Wûshi's MP-5.

Hot lead seared through Nathan's shoulder. Bright crimson clouds colored his vision. Time faltered, as if he were simultaneously alive and dead.

Then he lay on his back.

Nathan's handgun clattered to the ground halfway between him and Richardson. Nathan looked at Wûshi.

The assassin lowered the submachine gun's muzzle. Wûshi sneered, then pain flashed across his face. He winced, and his mouth opened. His M-5 dangled from his hand. Wûshi lowered his gaze to his chest, where a red stain expanded over his shirt. Crimson droplets spattered the pavement at his feet.

Wûshi looked at Nathan and tried to raise the barrel again, but the submachine gun wobbled in his grip. He dropped it. He staggered forward then spun in a circle and collapsed.

Nathan's only shot had found its mark.

Bruno barked and tugged at the leash looped around the crossbar.

Nathan rolled onto his side and sat up. Blood oozed from his shoulder and his left arm had gone numb. He pressed his palm against the wound to stem the bleeding. He battled hyperventilation as his body compensated from the trauma.

Richardson appeared horrified. Ordering a murder or sending troops into combat felt nothing like experiencing death firsthand. Seeing it, smelling it.

Richardson snapped out of shock and stared at Nathan's gun laying on the pavement. His eyes drifted up and met Nathan's.

Richardson lunged for the gun.

Nathan rolled onto his hands and pushed himself to his knees. His shoulder screamed in protest.

Richardson snatched the revolver off the path. He pointed it awkwardly at Nathan. "You lose, Agent Burke."

Nathan drew a leg beneath him and shifted weight onto his toes, ready to attack.

Bruno flashed across his vision, his paws barely touching the ground, and leapt into the air. Bruno struck Richardson in the chest with 120 pounds of pure muscle.

"Aaah!" Richardson screamed. He flew backward, and the crossbar caught him behind his knees. His feet rotated over his head, and he went over the side.

Bruno landed near the edge, and Richardson grabbed his collar like a lifeline. Bruno's paws skidded toward the edge as Richardson dangled over the moat.

Nathan dove and wrapped his arm around Bruno's waist. Bruno yelped and strained, but Richardson weighed too much.

Bruno ducked his head, and his collar slipped off.

Richardson tumbled into the abyss, splashing into the moat's rank water.

Bruno scampered away, spooked. Nathan crawled forward and looked over the edge. The water rippled from the impact then went still.

Richardson broke the surface, flailing and sputtering. "My back!" He looked up at Nathan, His face contorted in torment. "Help me. I'm hurt."

"I'll call for help," Nathan said, "but I'd keep your voice down."

Richardson squinted with confusion. Then his eyes went wide with terror. He whirled around, splashing in the water as a tiger descended to the lower tier. It crept along the concrete edge of the moat with its bulging muscles and gleaming teeth. It stared at Richardson.

"Get me out of here," Richardson screamed.

"Stop yelling."

The tiger coiled into a hunch then vaulted into the air. It splashed onto the water within feet of Richardson.

"Save me."

"Call the Chinese."

Nathan clambered to his feet. He stumbled away from the wall as the tiger roared. Richardson's screams filled the air.

Then silence.

Nathan walked to Bruno, whose ears were raised in alert mode. Nathan patted him on the head.

"Good boy."

100

Reagan snuggled beside Amelia on the living room couch and skimmed a front-page article in the *Washington Sentinel*, which read, "President Imposes Economic Sanctions on China for Havana Syndrome." She flipped to page three to read about the ongoing congressional hearings searching for co-conspirators in the CIA.

The agency claimed Hamilton had worked alone, but many congressmen didn't believe them, considering Hamilton had admitted on tape that he'd used agency assets to target Americans. Hamilton's claims that Nathan had threatened him with a directed-energy machine seemed fantastical, and since investigators found nothing at Glen Echo Park, it remained an open question. Both the press and Congress bared their fangs as they went after the CIA and pushed the White House to hold China accountable. Reagan set the paper down and smiled.

Closure.

Someone knocked on the door.

"Will you get that, honey?" Vince called from the other room.

Reagan ran her fingers through Amelia's hair, but the girl was too engrossed in a book to notice. Reagan rose and walked to the front door, careful not to move too fast. Dizziness lingered at the edges and threatened to upset her equilibrium. But she'd improved.

She peeked through the peephole.

"Nathan."

Reagan swung the door open, filling with lightness and warmth. She threw her arms around him and pulled him into a bear hug.

"Ouch," he said. "Watch the arm."

She released him and stepped back to look at him. His left arm hung in a sling. "Sorry. I'm relieved to see you. I didn't know you were discharged."

"Doc said I'll get the cast off in a few weeks. They expect me to regain full function."

"Thank God. Please come in." She led Nathan inside.

"Daddy," Amelia screamed and ran to him. She slammed into him like a linebacker.

"Wow, you're getting big," he said. "Did you grow over the last two weeks?"

Amelia blushed. "When are we going home, Daddy?"

Nathan met Reagan's eyes and raised his eyebrows.

"Whenever your dad's well enough to take care of you," Reagan said. "But remember, I'm working in DC now, and you'll stay here on weekends."

Once news of the Chinese conspiracy behind Havana Syndrome had been revealed, the State Department quickly changed their tune and offered to send Reagan back to the Dominican Republic. She'd refused because any agency so quick to dismiss her claims could never be trusted. Instead, she accepted a job as an international relations commentator at a national television network. Her experience with Havana Syndrome and her connection to Nathan, the man of the hour, had elevated her reputation. Vince would return to DC once his Dominican assignment ended next year, and she'd deal with his future deployments as they arose.

Nathan knelt beside his daughter. "I've got a big meeting at the FBI today, but then I'll convalesce at home for a few weeks. They gave me medicine to control the pain, so we can manage alone. How about I pick you up tomorrow morning?"

"I missed you," Amelia said.

Nathan hugged her. "Me too, baby, and don't worry, I'll bring you back to spend time with your mom every weekend." He looked at Reagan with moist eyes. "Tomorrow okay with you?"

"I'll have her packed and ready. You can eat lunch with us . . . if you want."

Nathan beamed. "I've got to head to that meeting, but I appreciate the offer. You seem more energetic. How's your recuperation?"

"Occasional migraines and dizziness, but most days are tolerable. I'm trending up."

"Good to hear." Nathan stood. "I've been worried—"

"Agent Burke," Vince said as he walked in drying his hands with a dish towel. "Good to see you up and around. You've had an interesting couple of weeks."

"Congratulations on your engagement," Nathan said.

That took her breath away. Had Nathan come to terms with their situation? Had he forgiven her?

Vince cleared his throat. "I, uh, I'm sure this is awkward for you, but I . . ."

Nathan laughed. "To be honest, I didn't take the news well at first, but—"

"Reagan told me you were upset."

"A lot has changed," Nathan said. "I'm happy for you. Really."

"Come out back with me," Reagan said. She grabbed his hand. "I haven't had a chance to talk to you since everything happened."

She led him outside, while Vince took Amelia into the living room.

Reagan shut the patio door and turned to him. "Did you say that to Vince to be polite or do you mean it?"

A sad smile flickered across his face. "Maybe it took a bullet wound to wake me up. I realized I can't blame you for leaving me. I—"

"No, I shouldn't have—"

"Please, let me finish," he said. "Things hadn't been good between us for ages, and that was my fault. You were right when you said I prioritized my job over you, and the DR was your turn to shine. I told myself family came first, but my job always took precedence. Seeing the betrayal, the infiltration by the Chinese . . . all of it. It changed me."

"We're both responsible for—"

"Fault doesn't matter," Nathan said. "Let's move on, for Amelia's sake. She needs a father and a mother."

Reagan squeezed his hand. "You said you'd find the people who hurt me." She choked back her emotion. Her eyes welled. "You promised to protect me, and you did."

"I'll never stop protecting you . . . and Amelia. When I was lying in that hospital bed, I realized the only people who cared about me, I mean really cared, were you and Amelia, and . . ."

A flutter of jealousy passed through her chest. "And?"

"Well, there's someone else now."

"Agent Chan?"

His eyes lit with surprise. "How'd you know?"

"Women see these things. Is it serious?"

"It's just beginning. But I'm optimistic."

101

Nathan sat across from Meili on the outdoor patio at the Elephant and Castle on Pennsylvania Avenue. Flowering plants dangled out of iron flower boxes beside their table, and the scent of lavender hung in the air. The harsh winter's bitter wind had disappeared, and April ushered perfect weather into the District. He sipped his coffee and let the sun warm his face.

The J. Edgar Hoover Building loomed over the street three blocks away. They had a meeting with their entire chain of command in about an hour.

"Do you think the deputy director will press us about Hamilton's interrogation?" Meili asked.

"It's Hamilton's word against mine. You arrived afterward, remember?"

She nodded. "We still have legal issues over Hamilton's allegations of torture."

"I'll take the heat, but I don't think it'll go anywhere. Not with his recorded confession."

"The confession his attorney claims you coerced?" she asked.

"There's no evidence of that on the video, thanks to your selective recording. Hamilton claimed many things, but it won't matter. He'll be in prison forever."

"You think Richardson really duped him?" Meili asked.

"We'll never know for sure, but when I called it a false flag operation, his surprise looked genuine. Either way, he knew he violated the law and abused his position. He arranged the murders of Americans because he wanted to suppress their ideas. Two doctors are dead, as well as an FBI agent and a patriotic CIA officer. Not to mention all the damaged lives overseas."

"How much was caused by China, and how many incidents can we blame on Hamilton's rogue CIA group?"

"We won't know unless he cooperates, but we proved one thing—these were not psychogenic health incidents. The Chinese wanted to disrupt our personnel as part of their hegemonic strategy. It's a thousand-year plan to rule the world."

Meili's phone vibrated, and she picked up. "Uh-huh . . . okay." She hung up. "That was my ASAC. They're ready for us."

Nathan paid the bill, and they walked down Pennsylvania Avenue to FBI headquarters. The hurried through security and up to the executive level.

Nathan scanned the executive conference room as they entered. A dozen of the FBI's top brass crowded around the table, and the director of the National Counterterrorism Center sat beside an empty chair at the head of the table.

"What's NCTC doing here?" Nathan whispered to Meili.

"Shh."

"This may not be what we anticipated."

Nathan waved at Rahimya, who sat against the far wall with a handful of other group supervisors and program managers. She pointed to empty seats at the table. Nathan held a chair out for Meili then settled in beside her.

A moment later, FBI Director Donald Haverhill entered the room, and everyone stood.

"Sit, sit," Haverhill said. "I won't waste our time, but it's important for me to get us all in one room and set a few things straight. First, thanks to Group Supervisor Meili Chan and Special Agent Nathan Burke for solving Havana Syndrome for us. Those incidents put our national security at risk and incapacitated many brave employees. The work of these two fine agents has done our country proud. They—"

"Don't forget Eddie O'Shaughnessy," Nathan interrupted, "And Bashir Gemayel, Dr. Mandel, and Dr. Reyes. They gave their lives protecting our country."

Haverhill's face reddened, and he stared at Nathan. The tension in the room became palpable. His cheek twitched, then he took a breath. "The sacrifices of Agent O'Shaughnessy and all those injured in service to this country will never be forgotten. They'll be publicly honored."

Nathan nodded. "Thank you."

"I asked our OPR chief to attend," Haverhill said and nodded to a beefy man across the table, "because I want the internal investigations wrapped up quickly."

"Sir, if I may," the OPR chief said. "I—"

"Don't worry, Stan," Haverhill said. "I won't interfere with your process, but wrap it up soon. The Chinese are coming for us. All of us. And I don't want bureaucratic self-sabotage to undermine our ability to fight back. China probably obtained directed-energy research from Russia—"

"Or they stole it from us," Nathan said.

Meili swatted his leg under the table.

"Exactly, Agent Burke," Haverhill said. "Communists have a long history of cooperation, and Russia and China collaborate against their common enemies. Thanks to Supervisor Chan, it's clear the Chinese used high-energy weapons to eliminate a handful of diplomats, intelligence officers, and agents who tried to uncover Chinese aggression around the world.

"Frederick Richardson was their mole in the White House, and he manipulated the CIA through a false flag operation. Trent Hamilton thought he was eliminating political targets interfering with the administration's priorities, when, in fact, he had become an unwitting dupe for the Chinese. Dr. Mandel was going to expose the CIA's involvement in microwave weapons research and Dr. Reyes discredited the CIA's psychogenic thesis. Both were killed for their intellectual honesty.

"It'll take months to determine the extent of the damage Trent Richardson caused and to identify Chinese infiltrators he helped to rise in power. It'll also take time for the administration to respond to China, which is why we can't get bogged down in internal investigations. I've spoken to the attorney general, and he agrees. Our country needs the FBI to get aggressive now more than ever."

Haverhill spoke for a few more minutes, summarizing the FBI's strategy and underlining the importance of their investigation, then he dismissed everyone.

In the hallway, Nathan shook hands with upper management and assured Rahimya he'd return to the office when his doctor medically cleared him. They still had Triad members to arrest and a terrorism trial to prepare.

Meili took Nathan by the arm and led him away from the crowd to the window. Nathan gazed through the thick glass at the facade of the Department of Justice across the street.

"How's Kei?" Meili asked.

"I think we can get the evidence in without putting him on the stand, so we won't burn him. The AUSA agreed to ask the judge for no jail time. Kei will walk free, just like I promised."

"I'm glad it's over," Meili said.

"Over?"

"The director made it clear he won't support an internal case against you. He wants this in his review mirror, which means nobody will prosecute you."

"There's work left to do."

"You exposed the Chinese conspiracy. Richardson and Ming Ho are dead. And Hamilton will go to federal prison."

"The Chinese won't stop."

"You killed Wûshi, and the other members of the Emperor's crew fled to China," Meili said.

"Probably, but they were other infiltrators and officials behind these attacks."

"Meaning?"

"I won't stop hunting until I've captured or killed the enemies of our country. This is only the beginning."

THE KHORASAN RETRIBUTION
Nathan Burke Thrillers #2

When the lines between duty and revenge blur, FBI Special Agent Nathan Burke faces a race against time to stop a deadly plot.

In the midst of intercepting a massive shipment of Chinese fentanyl in Arlington, Virginia, FBI Special Agent Nathan Burke and his new partner, Bridget Quinn, find themselves in a fierce shootout outside a mosque known for its radical ties. The operation results in the seizure of one hundred kilos of opioids, but it's only the beginning.

As Nathan investigates the fentanyl's origins, the nation is rocked by a series of horrific terror attacks utilizing opioids. The death toll rises, and Nathan races the clock to identify the terrorists and stop the attacks. His investigation uncovers shocking truths that challenge everything he thought he knew.

But what Nathan doesn't know is that a shadowy figure, leading the elite terror cell known as the Phantoms of Khorasan, has a dark agenda for America. And he is driven by a single, lethal objective—revenge.

Bestselling author Jeffrey James Higgins takes readers on a gripping journey from the intense streets of Washington, D.C., to the heart of a terrorist's vendetta. In this pulse-pounding thriller, Nathan Burke faces his most dangerous adversary yet in a battle where the stakes couldn't be higher. Perfect for fans of Jack Carr and Vince Flynn.

Get your copy today at
severnriverbooks.com

ACKNOWLEDGMENTS

My wife, Cynthia Farahat Higgins, has supported my writing at every step. Thanks, my love. Without you by my side, it would be hard for me to write.

Thanks to my parents, Nadya and James Higgins, and my friend, Stephen Cone, who read early drafts of *The Havana Syndrome*. Their notes and support make me a better author.

Writing in isolation would be difficult, but my literary community keeps me going. Thanks to International Thriller Writers, Sisters in Crime Chessie and New England chapters, The Virginia Writers Club, and The Royal Writers Secret Society.

I'm forever grateful to Andrew Watts, Amber Hudock, Julia Hastings, Mo Metlen and the entire team at Severn River Publishing. Last but not least, thanks to my editors, Randall Klein and Janet Fix for improving my work.

ABOUT THE AUTHOR

Jeffrey James Higgins, author of the Nathan Burke Thrillers, is a retired supervisory special agent who writes thrillers, short stories, scripts, creative nonfiction, and essays. He has wrestled a suicide bomber, fought the Taliban in combat, and chased terrorists across five continents. He received the Attorney General's Award for Exceptional Heroism and the DEA Award of Valor. Jeffrey has been interviewed by CNN, National Geographic, and The New York Times. He's a #1 Amazon bestselling author and has won numerous literary awards, including the Claymore Award, PenCraft's Best Fiction Book of 2022, and a Reader's Favorite Gold Medal. Jeffrey is an active member of the Authors Guild, The Virginia Writers Club, International Thriller Writers, Sisters in Crime, and the Royal Writers Secret Society. His first three thrillers are *Furious, Unseen,* and *The Forever Game.*

Sign up for Jeffrey James Higgins's newsletter at
severnriverbooks.com